"For ~~~~

Enjoy!

Fallen

Angel

K. C. Berg

To the unbidden angel who held my feet to the fire from which this book was born . . . thank you.

Part One: 'Beth'
Chapter One

Whump, thump, whump, thump, whump, thump . . . the windshield wipers faithfully swiped at the falling snow in a relentless attempt to clear the glass, but the road—and the world beyond—remained concealed in a blanket of darkness and swirling snow. Beth took a deep breath and consciously loosened her 'ten and two o'clock' death grip on the steering wheel. She was three hours into a commute that should have taken less than an hour and a half, and she just wanted to be home. She'd seen the forecast and had been aware of the approaching snow, but as usual the forecasters had been way off in their reports, and the two inches of a dry, powdery snow they'd predicted was now buried beneath an additional four inches, with no end in sight. To make matters worse, she hadn't seen a snowplow in more than an hour; even they had given up and gone home to wait out the storm.

Her cell phone, an antique compared to the smart phones that every teenager now carried in their pocket, was resting on the passenger seat, its cord plugged into the car-charger and 'at the ready'. The soft glow from its screen illuminated the truck's interior without being a distraction. The time in its display read 10:43; Beth squeezed her eyes shut for a brief second before forcing them to focus on the white curtain that swirled beyond her headlights and the laboring wiper blades. It was hopeless; even traveling at twenty-eight miles per hour, she couldn't make out where the pavement ended and the shoulder of the road began. With a heavy sigh, she pushed in the clutch and guided her 1995 Bronco to the white-on-white area where she believed the blacktop gave way to gravel. She took the vehicle out of gear, set the parking brake, turned on her flashers, and pried the curled fingers of her left hand from the steering wheel. Her butt ached from too many hours in the well-worn seat, and her shoulders felt like they were on fire. With yet another sigh, she closed her eyes, rolled her head from side to side to sooth her aching muscles, and began an honest assessment of her situation. It wasn't good.

Beth was a seasoned driver; she'd lived in northeastern Wisconsin her entire life and had been driving its roads, in every season, for more than thirty years. She didn't particularly like winter roads, but they were a fact of life if you lived in this state year-round. Still, she could not recall a snowfall like this before. Visibility had rapidly dropped from a mile, to a half mile, to one hundred feet, to twenty feet, to 'guess where the end of your vehicle's hood is' in less than thirty minutes. Now, as she stared out into the darkness and watched the swirling flakes that were momentarily captured in the Bronco's headlights, she was disoriented and overcome with a feeling of 'wrongness'.

Something about the snow didn't fit. Sure, it was late December, and Wisconsin was known for its howling nor'easters—storms where winds drove the snow perpendicularly from the northeast for hours on end. Four and five foot drifts were not uncommon, making travel all but impossible. Adolescent males, confident that they were invincible in their four-wheel drive Dodge Rams, hit the roads in such storms as a rite of passage into some aspect of manhood. Later, with their trucks buried in drifts that exceeded the height of the vehicles' doors—let alone the axles—they somehow made their way home on foot, wiser if not older.

But this storm was not the standard nor'easter. For one thing, the wind was wrong. It was directly out of the south, not the northeast. Still, snowstorms with prevailing southerly winds were not unheard of. No, Beth decided, it was more than the wind that was wrong. It sounded crazy, she knew, but it was Stephen King snow. It belonged in one of the author's far-fetched novels that Beth so enjoyed; a novel where a car, or a dead cat, or a dead child, somehow came to life for the grisly purpose of terrorizing some small town.

Whump thump, whump thump, whump thump, the swiping blades managed to clear two symmetrical half-circles of glass on the windshield, but the side windows were quickly growing opaque under layer upon layer of relentless snowflakes. Beth took a deep breath and continued her assessment.

In addition to the storm feeling 'wrong', she had no idea where she was. Oh sure, she was headed north on Highway 32, but that was all she could be sure of. Was she safely parked on the shoulder of the road, sitting in her own lane, or parked in the middle of the blacktopped area strictly reserved for oncoming traffic? Worse, if she stayed where she was, would the county plow that eventually happened along even see her, or would the driver's first indication of the parked vehicle be when the two-ton blade impacted with her truck and sent the Bronco flying?

Searching for a distraction, she glanced down at the fuel gauge. With a sense of relief, she noted that she still had three-quarters of a tank. Stopping to gas up at the last filling station she'd passed had been a good idea; however, the large cup of coffee she'd bought to help her stay awake had not been. Her straining bladder was protesting the 16 ounces of caffeinated liquid and the unending stretch of road. She threw her head back hard against the headrest. Once again, as she had many times in her life, she questioned the advantage of being a member of the 'softer' sex. If she were a man, this wouldn't be any problem. She'd simply step out of the vehicle, turn her back to the wind, and relieve herself without a second thought. Hell, she'd probably write 'I was here' just to kill time as she completed the task. But no, as a woman the process was slightly more complicated. She'd have to hunker down on the leeward side of the Bronco and hope that no wayward car, or snowmobile, or snow-blind owl, happened along while she was frozen in place with her nether-regions exposed to the biting wind and snow. Why again, exactly, had she chosen to live in Wisconsin her entire life? Peeing in the dark on the side of a county highway in the middle of a nor'easter was certainly not on the list.

She reached across and opened the glove box. Too many trips through the Burger King drive-through assured that there were plenty of napkins for just such an emergency. With a loud, almost theatrical, sigh—and the realization that she was sighing far too often as of late—she grabbed a handful of napkins and gathered her courage. She began to open the door, then paused. As a quick afterthought, she reached in and switched the headlights off and the dome light on. The dome light was more subtle than the glaring headlights, and it would help assure that she didn't become disoriented and wander too far from the safety of the truck. Hell, who was she kidding? If anyone *did* happen along, she was hoping the softly-lit vehicle interior would serve as a distraction; she hoped they'd focused on it and not on her, especially if her nether-regions were not yet safely tucked away.

Satisfied she'd thought of everything for this current— and pressing—challenge, she cleared her mind, braced herself for the cold, and pulled up on the well-worn handle. Groaning in protest, the Bronco's door opened into the wind and she had to lean against it to keep it in place as she stepped out. The driven snow, brutally cold, took her breath away and she began to reconsider the prospect of relieving herself, but her bladder would have nothing to do with turning back.

With her back to the wind, she stumbled around the back end of the Bronco and then around to the passenger side. There, in relative shelter from the driven snow, she took care of what needed to be done, refastened her jeans with cold and trembling fingers, and made her way back to the driver's side door. Her upper thighs and buttocks tingled from their brief exposure to the elements, and she was looking forward to climbing back into the Bronco's heated interior.

Through the snow-covered side window, the dome light glowed softly, bathing the vehicle's interior with a soft, yellow light. Relief washing through her, she reached for the door handle and depressed the button with a numb thumb. Nothing. The door did not budge. Refusing to believe the obvious, she pushed in on the button again; it stopped part way, and she knew what that meant. The door was locked. But, it couldn't be. She hadn't pushed down the lock button when she got out, and the vehicle did not have electronic locks (which were known to be temperamental and arbitrarily lock themselves); the only way to lock this door— or the passenger door—was to physically push down on the button from inside. Fighting back terror, she brushed the snow from the glass and glanced at the lock button which rested on the top back edge of the door. The mushroom-shaped knob was definitely depressed; its neck hidden within the door. Her gaze crossed the softly-lit distance to the passenger side, daring to hope. As she'd feared, that button was also in the down position. Somehow, both doors had locked themselves. To make matters even worse, her phone was resting right where she'd left it, on the passenger seat, and the keys were dangling from the ignition—warm, and safe, and dry—and totally inaccessible.

This couldn't be happening. Doors don't lock themselves. For one door to suddenly be locked was more than unlikely; for both to be locked was utterly impossible. She never locked the doors; it was a god damn 1995 Bronco, who would want it? With 208,000 miles on the original engine and drivetrain, she couldn't give it away—and the fact that it was all she could afford at this stage in her life was downright embarrassing. But, embarrassing or not, it was the truth; and right now she wanted nothing more than to be inside her aging vehicle with the heat cranked up and the blower on high.

Her heart began to race and panic threatened. It was physically impossible for her to have locked herself out of the Bronco; the doors had to have what—locked themselves? This was crazy! She pushed hard with her thumb against the button and tugged on the door again, wrenching on it with all her might. She swallowed hard, struggling to remain calm, to just think. The savage wind bit into her exposed skin and her eyes watered from the cold. She had to get back inside, but how? Could she find a stone somewhere and break the window? It would be an easy enough task—in July, when the surrounding countryside lay exposed to the warm, summer sun. Now, any suitable rock was concealed under two months' worth of snow and solidly frozen to the ground. Could she break the windows with her bare hands; would the safety glass yield to a pummeling from her exposed fists? She doubted that very much. Perhaps she could climb onto the hood and kick out the glass. Bad idea; she could hear the news anchorman now—"48-year-old woman found frozen to death with both feet stuck in shattered windshield . . . details at 10."

"Damn it!" The curse surprised even her, though she was the one who had uttered it. The words travelled through the darkness with an uncanny and surreal volume. They faded away, and she became aware of the silence that enveloped her. The wind had stopped; the snow had stopped . . . the only thing that persisted was the pounding of her own heart; it reverberated in her ears—a rhythmic, savage tempo that bordered on panic. As though she were a puppet controlled by an unseen master, she turned her head slowly and gazed to her left. Twenty feet beyond where she stood, a fierce wind drove the snow horizontally through the illuminated circle of space created by the Bronco's headlight beams. The wind was still there, not more than twenty feet away, but she could not hear it.

She released the door handle and slowly turned around. The night air had lost its bite, or perhaps it only seemed warmer without the wind. Her temples began to pound, and she realized that she'd been holding her breath. She exhaled and froze. She drew another deep breath, exhaling more slowly this time. Her breath was not visible; it didn't form a cloud that quickly dissipated in the cold, night air. How could that be? It couldn't have been more than fifteen degrees when she'd stepped out of the truck to answer nature's call. What was happening; what was going on? Whatever it was, it went far beyond self-locking Bronco doors . . .

She gathered her courage and took one hesitant step, then another. Slowly, tentatively, she crossed the twenty odd feet to where the storm still raged, captured in the headlights' glow. Afraid but curious, she held out a trembling hand and reached through the unseen barrier, and into the dark and snow beyond. The air was much colder there, and the wind-driven snow bit at her exposed skin like a swarm of angry insects. She instinctively pulled her hand back and brushed the snow away. Could she be dreaming? Could there have been some kind of exhaust leak and she had fallen asleep inside the Bronco without warning? That type of thing happened in older vehicles that were stranded in snowstorms. Also, a dream state would explain both the locked doors *and* the pocket of warm, snowless air that now seemed to surround her. She had a thought; she pinched herself, softly at first then with more determination. The pain *seemed* real enough; she wasn't sleeping as far as she could tell.

A small shadow appeared in her peripheral vision and floated slowly toward her. It was a butterfly—no, a moth; butterflies don't come out at night. But then, moths don't fly around in Wisconsin nor'easters, either. Still, that's what it was—or at least what it appeared to be. As she watched it fly, her thoughts were of a monarch—the effortless, flitting strokes of paper-thin wings. The flight of a moth is much more labored, as if the insect were hell-bent on reaching its destination before it ran out of strength or time, often crashing onto its landing spot and fluttering about, dazed and confused. This 'moth' did not labor in its flight, but floated with the effortless strokes of its sun-drenched cousin. Its wings were black, yet iridescent—changing hues as the insect approached the headlight beams. It was, in short, beautiful—and Beth questioned again if she was dreaming. The moth flew in front of the Bronco and disappeared from view. She took a few hesitant steps and peered over the fender. The moth had not disappeared, as Beth had suspected. It rested on the snow a few feet in front of the parked vehicle, slowly fanning its wings.

"Personally, I like the snow."

She gasped and whirled toward the voice. The vague silhouette of a man stood in the road not more than twenty feet away. She hadn't heard an approaching vehicle, and had no idea where he could have come from. She was terrified, yet not completely surprised. The Bronco's locked doors and the appearance of the moth had already set the stage for a solid dose of the "strange and unusual". Events were unfolding that she could neither predict nor understand. She retreated—one, quick step—until her back pressed against the idling truck. She could try to maintain her distance from this stranger, but it would be pointless to flee. Where could she run to? Beyond this small pocket of space, the storm continued to rage in the darkness. If she chose to stay, it might take hours for help to arrive. On the other hand, if she fled into the darkness, it might be days before anyone would find her. Stay or leave? Hours or days? It didn't seem to matter. She sensed that time was unimportant now; was it midnight yet—midnight in the twilight zone? Yes, it was, for she had somehow been transported to a world where a storm could be cordoned off by an invisible wall, and iridescent moths came from nowhere to rest on the virgin snow.

She swallowed hard and found her voice. "Who are you?"

"I've startled you; I'm sorry, but I suppose it couldn't be helped." His voice was deep, but gentle. He turned aside and began to walk. His slow, measured steps hugged the edge of the unseen barrier that was magically holding the storm at bay. She turned her head, then finally angled her entire body to follow him. He stopped when he reached the area illuminated by the headlight beams and turned to face her, bathed by the light. "Is that better?"

Beth studied him for a long moment, unsure what to say. He was of slight built and average height, maybe 5' 11". He wore no coat on this mid-winter night, only a Wisconsin Badgers sweatshirt and faded jeans. The clothing seemed too large, giving him the appearance of a one-time orphan that had somehow been spared the fate of growing up. His brown hair was shoulder-length, but well kept, and his face was clean-shaven with a hint of a growth that belied the late hour. His nose was straight and narrow, and rested easily between slightly hollow cheeks. On him, lean looked good, and spoke more of self-discipline than self-denial. Overall, she would later recall, he was unremarkable. Except for his eyes. Pierced by the headlight beams, they were sapphire-blue, porcelain pools without bottoms, and Beth had to brace herself against falling into their depths. "What . . . what did you say about the snow?"

"I said I like it. I find it peaceful, don't you?"

She ignored the question. "Where did you come from? I didn't hear a car, and you couldn't have walked here—not in this storm."

He smiled and his voice remained soft. "I believe a man can do anything if he sets his mind to it." His smile faded a little and Beth thought she saw a touch of sorrow in his eyes.

"The problem is, that's true whether it's a good thing or a bad thing he has in mind."

Beth tensed, wondering if he was talking about himself—about something he was contemplating doing—and she involuntarily side-stepped along the Bronco's fender. The words tumbled out before she could stop them. "What do you want?"

"Are you cold . . . would you prefer talking inside the vehicle?"

"I'm not getting in any vehicle with you," Beth replied, no longer concerned with—or even conscious of—the Bronco's locked doors.

"You misunderstand," the stranger reassured her with the same even tone. "I was only thinking of your comfort."

"I'll bet."

"It's sad, the lack of trust among people. It makes it so much harder."

"What—it makes *what* so much harder?"

"The journey, our lives—even something as simple as this."

"This?" Her voice went up a notch, laced with fear.

"A simple conversation," he reassured her.

"I asked you what you wanted." What had been simple fear in her voice was giving way to anger. She'd never liked being toyed with—not as a child and not later as an adult; this was no different.

"If I offer you a good faith gesture, will that make this easier?" he asked.

She shook her head without even considering the question. "No."

"Well, let's try it anyway, shall we? Hold out your hand."

"Are you, nuts? I'm not doing *anything* you tell me to do—you got that?!"

He took a deep breath and dropped his gaze; he appeared to be collecting himself. When he looked up again and his eyes met hers, there was no anger or impatience in his gaze. He seemed, what? *Amused,* she thought, *he finds this amusing!* Yes, there was definitely amusement there, and something else . . . a sadness, an urgency?

"What harm can come from holding out your hand?" He said. "I'm certainly not close enough to grab it, and see," he held his own hands out before him, palms up, "I don't have anything that I can throw at you, or harm you with. Now," he said softly, "hold out your hand."

Beth hesitated; what he said made sense. He *was* too far away to snatch her outstretched hand, and she could think of no other way she could be harmed by giving in to his request. But, it was the principle of the matter, wasn't it? If she gave in to this request, what would come next—was this simply the first step down a very slippery slope? She considered the events of the last few minutes—the Bronco's locked doors, the storm being held at bay by some unseen force, and now this stranger. If she refused to hold out her hand under the guise that she was not willing to give up whatever level of control she still maintained, she was fooling herself. There was no control to be had over the present situation; or, if there was, it certainly wasn't hers to claim. She had no choice in the matter; not really, so she held out her hand.

The stranger smiled. It was not an evil smile, or even a victorious one. It was a simple smile, warm and unrehearsed. He turned to look at the area in front of the Bronco and made a simple gesture with his left hand, just a slight flex of the wrist. As Beth watched, the moth fluttered up through the headlight beams. Impervious to the light, it left the lit area and hovered for a few brief seconds in front of the stranger before making its way to her and landing, soft as a whisper, on her outstretched hand.

Beth gasped. The insect was even more beautiful up close than it had been at a distance. The iridescent black wings were adorned with speckles of various colors, and its antennae were covered with fine gold hairs that shimmered even in the darkness. It stroked its antennae first with one forward leg, then the other, preening for her. Beth smiled in spite of herself. Whatever this insect was, it wasn't evil. Beth wasn't sure how she knew that, but she did. By extension, the man who had sent it to her could not be evil either. The doubting Thomas inside her head warned her that this was a massive oversimplification of the situation. She told it to shut up.

"Is this yours?" She heard herself ask without taking her eyes off of the wonder that rested in her open palm.

"No," he replied. "One creature cannot own another, despite what some men think." There was a short pause, then he asked, "Do you like it?"

"It's beautiful. I've lived in these parts my entire life, and I've never seen anything like it. It's not from around here, is it?"

"No, it's not."

"Did you bring it with you?"

A hesitation this time, then, "You might say that. It's complicated."

"It's so small, so fragile—how can it survive in this cold?" She wondered out loud.

"It doesn't feel the cold like you and I do. Temperature means nothing to it. I, on the other hand, am not as lucky." He looked toward the idling vehicle, then back at Beth. "Can we sit inside and talk?"

She stared in fascination at the moth, and only half-heard his question. "What?"

"Can we sit inside the vehicle and warm up?"

She forced her gaze away from the black bejeweled insect to the stranger, then to the Bronco. "Oh, no. I . . . I can't get in; it's locked."

"Are you sure?"

"Yes," she replied, but she found herself studying the moth again, as though the locked vehicle existed only in memory and held no real value in the moment.

The stranger approached the idling Bronco and grasped the driver's side door handle. He looked at Beth. "Do you mind?"

"I said it's locked," she replied, but she didn't look up and her response held no agitation or emotion of any kind.

"My name is Peter," the stranger said, studying her. Then he opened the door.

Chapter Two

Beth turned to look as Peter swung the door open and smiled at her. She started to protest, to tell him that what he had just done was impossible, but at that moment the invisible dome—or whatever had held the storm at bay—disintegrated. The frigid wind, enraged at having been diverted for even a moment, snatched at her and took her breath away. She reflexively turned her face away from the driven snow. When she chanced a look only seconds later, the snow had returned in all its fury, but the moth was gone. Her heart sank and she spun around, searching for the fragile insect, but all she could make out were tendrils of swirling snow disappearing in the darkness.

"Get inside," Peter raised his voice to be heard above the driving wind. Beth glanced his way, but hesitated, still searching for the missing moth. "Get inside before you freeze; we can talk."

With a final look into the frozen night, Beth crossed to the Bronco, stumbling through the several inches of snow that now covered the road. Peter held the door open for her, and closed it softly once she'd climbed inside. Moving gracefully, he circled around the vehicle, and was momentarily illuminated as he passed through the headlight beams. His head was bowed slightly against the wind-blown snow, but there was no urgency in his stride; he seemed at peace—or at least unaffected—by the onslaught. When he reached the passenger door, he opened it and climbed in. Beth pondered this, too, as she had not thought to reach across and unlock it, but pondering anything that was happening that night seemed futile.

Beth had a million questions; they jostled through her mind, fighting for position to be the first one asked. No winner was forthcoming, so she sat in silence and watched as the snow streaked across the Bronco's hood and continued off into the darkness. The words escaped her lips, soft and tentative. "What's happening—what's going on?"

She turned, angling her body to look at the stranger. He didn't answer right away, but simply sat in the passenger seat, his hands resting in his lap and his gaze resting on her. There was nothing threatening about him. She pondered that; a strange man appears from nowhere in the middle of a snowstorm only seconds after she realized that she had locked herself out of her vehicle. But, had she? She had not pushed down the lock button on either door; in fact, she hadn't locked the doors anytime in recent memory. Yet, they *had* been locked. So, how had he opened them? And what about the moth? She pulled her gaze away from the stranger and peered through the windshield at the falling snow. She half-expected to see the insect resting on the hood, fanning its wings gracefully in the driving wind. It wasn't there.

As though reading her thoughts, he reassured her. "You needn't worry; it's quite safe."

"But, where did it go?"

"Back to where it came from, I suppose."

"Will . . . will it be back—will I see it again?"

"Yes, I believe you will, but there are other things— more important things—that we need to discuss right now."

"Such as?" she asked, for she couldn't guess what was happening, or why she was sharing the front seat of her vehicle with a total stranger.

"Several things come to mind," he replied, "but let's start with you."

"Me?" Her voice rose, laced with uncertainty. "What about me?"

"I . . . Beth, I need your help."

"You need—", she stiffened and drew back, her mind conjuring up a multitude of different—and terrifying—things that statement could mean. Suddenly, her eyes grew wide and she turned to face him. "I never told you my name; you never asked. How did you know . . ."

"I need your help," he continued, ignoring her question. "I know you're frightened; that's understandable. But believe me when I say that you're not in any immediate danger. I'm not some psycho stalker, and I promise you that I came alone; there's no one else lurking out there in the storm, waiting to make his or her move."

"But," Beth interrupted, but Peter forged on.

"Let me finish. I promise there'll be time for whatever questions you may have, but allow me to lay the foundation, okay?" He looked at her for conformation. When she nodded, he continued. "I know you're wondering about our little winged friend, and the way the snow was contained— so to speak—and where I came from. Those are good questions and, like all good questions, they're hard to answer in a way that's easily understood." He chuckled softly before continuing. "Dr. Phil probably said it best. 'There is no reality, only perception.'"

Beth looked at him, confused. "Seriously—you appear out of nowhere, open locked doors with a mere touch, and the best you can do is quote Dr. Phil?"

"I take it you're not a fan?"

"I have a feeling that my daytime television-viewing habits have little to do with what's going on here."

"True enough," he agreed. "But you have to bear with me; there's no easy place to start."

"My mother always said that the best place to start was at the beginning."

"I suppose it is," Peter agreed. He stared through the windshield at the falling snow for a moment before turning back to meet Beth's gaze. "The problem is, the beginning was a very long time ago, and not apparently relevant to what's happening tonight."

"Would you please just cut through the bullshit?" Beth exploded. "I don't know who the hell you are, or where you came from, so why don't you just start there, okay?" Beth took a quick breath and attempted to rein in her anger as she waited for his reply.

"Fair enough. I'm—"

"Peter. Yes, I got that part. I just don't get why you're here."

"To find you."

"Well I, for one, didn't know I was lost, so if you'll just get the hell out of my vehicle, I can try to find the road again and get home." She was terrible at hiding her anger; she always had been. Her entire life had been a series of mishaps that she could trace back to some stupid incident that resulted from her wearing her emotions on her sleeve.

Peter smiled at her, a subtle understanding softening the lines on his face. "All of us want to get home, Beth, but some of us have a hard time finding the way."

Beth hardened her gaze and her eyes flashed. "Oh, I get it. Christ, you're some kind of religious freak come to save my soul." She leaned toward him, her shoulders squared and her body stiff with indignation. "Well, I don't need you to save me, got that? I don't need anyone to save me, and I sure as hell am not going to become your recruit and go out saving anyone else, either! Is that clear?

"Yes," he said, before adding, more slowly. "I understand that you don't trust me, and I don't blame you."

Beth choked back a laugh. "Trust you? Why would I trust you? You're not even smart enough to put on a coat before going out in a storm like this!"

"True enough," he nodded. "But, being smart really doesn't have anything to do with being trustworthy, does it? Besides, when you meet someone, shouldn't 'trust' be the default state, at least until that someone has done something that isn't trustworthy?"

"Sure," Beth agreed, the sarcasm evident in her voice, "unless, of course, you prove to be an ax murderer, in which case I guess I'm just screwed."

"It would be impossible to conceal an ax in such close quarters—and without a coat," he countered, a touch of humor in his voice.

"So you strangle me with your shoelace; let's not wrangle over details—dead is dead."

"I might be wrong," he stated, matter-of-factly, "but, if I were going to kill you, I probably could have done it by now. True?"

Their exchange felt like a Ping-Pong match, and she had to concede that point. She felt the tension easing out of her, and she fought to maintain it. She had to stay sharp; she couldn't let her guard down. "So . . . what now?"

"How about I take you home and we talk on the way?" he offered.

"I'm not telling you where I live," she objected, her voice edging up a notch again.

"3498 Windfall Lane," he stated. Without waiting for a response, he opened the passenger door and climbed out of the Bronco. In a matter of seconds, he'd strode past the front of the vehicle once again and opened the driver's door. "Slide over," he said as he began to climb in. Beth slipped from the driver's seat into the passenger seat, thinking—too late—that she should have offered more resistance. She should have thrown the vehicle into gear after he'd stepped out and driven to—where? She couldn't even *see* six inches in front of the Bronco, let alone drive off. Still, she could have done something, anything. She could have locked the door! Sure, like that would have done any good. "Buckle up," he said, oblivious to—or choosing to ignore—her 'flight or fight' state of mind. "The roads aren't very good tonight; it's best to be safe."

Chapter Three

For several long moments, neither spoke. Peter drove, his right hand relaxed on the wheel and his left hand resting on his thigh. He leaned back in the seat, apparently comfortable with both the ensuing silence and the task of guiding the Bronco through whiteout conditions at a steady forty-five miles per hour. Beth sat pushed back in the passenger seat, her right hand in a white-knuckle grip on the door's armrest and her left hand pressed hard into the seat between her and Peter. She was braced for impact with whatever object might suddenly materialize in the snow that was still obliterating the world six inches beyond the vehicle's hood. Awe and terror jostled for control in Beth's mind. How could Peter guide the vehicle so casually when neither of them could see the road, the ditch, or any sign of the forests, homes, and fields that no doubt lay on either side of them? Once again the question whispered through her; who the hell was this man?

"So, are they prevalent in this area?" Peter asked. He turned to look at her when he spoke, unconcerned with the inherent danger of taking his eyes from the road while driving.

"Are *what* prevalent in this area?" Beth asked, confused.

"Religious freaks. From your earlier reaction, I thought maybe you'd had one or two bad experiences with one."

"I . . . ah, no. I don't believe I've ever met one."

"Really? Then why the hatred?"

"I don't *hate* them," Beth replied, the anger creeping back in her voice.

The corner of Peter's mouth curved into a grin and he returned his gaze to the road. There was no sarcastic tone to his voice when he spoke, but the intent was clear. "Yes, of course. I could almost feel the love."

Beth was at a loss for an appropriate response, so she offered none. She didn't dislike religion, or religious people. Not really. She'd been raised Catholic; some people would say that pretty much explained everything about her life. Her stance was 'been there, done that', and she didn't want to go back.

"So, which part is the one that troubles you—being religious or being a freak?" Peter asked.

"Both," Beth's answer slipped out before she'd even considered it. Justification seemed in order. "Look, it's the principle of the whole thing. I don't go door-to-door telling people how much I love Delmonte Ketchup; I simply find it offensive when people go door-to-door telling others how much they love God. It seems like they're looking for brownie points or something. It's pathetic."

Peter looked at her, one eyebrow raised. "Pathetic? That's a little harsh."

"Whatever," she said, rolling her eyes.

"And I'm not sure that the ketchup analogy works."

She glared at him, her eyes flashing. "Can we please cut through the bullshit? You're freaking me out; this whole night is freaking me out." She took a long, deep breath, dropped her gaze and shook her head. When she looked up again, there was only confusion left on her face, and she spoke with quiet determination. "Will you please tell me what you want?"

There was a long moment of silence before Peter replied. He seemed lost in thought, searching for the right words. He finally countered her question with one of his own. "Do you know why you're here?"

"Here . . . in this truck with you?"

"No," he said, "here, on this earth."

"I haven't a clue," she said, "but I have the feeling you're going to tell me."

Another hint of a smile, then he said, "You were raised Catholic; most of what I'm about to tell you isn't going to make a lot of sense."

"I suppose I'd be wasting my time in asking how you know that—the part about me being raised Catholic."

"I know a lot about you, but that's not important. What's important is what *you* know—about yourself, and about this world, this life you're living."

"Mind if I turn on the radio?" she said. "I'd like to find the theme song from "The Twilight Zone" while we talk; I'm sure it's playing out there somewhere."

"Not all conversations require sarcasm, you know. I just thought I'd put that out there for you."

"Well, maybe mine do. This is my life, my truck, and— for all intents and purposes—my god damn nightmare. I can be sarcastic if I want to."

"You've already done the pinch test. You know you're awake, so this can't be a nightmare."

"And your point is?"

"My point is that this conversation is going to be a whole lot harder—and longer—if you're going to be sarcastic every time you speak."

"How about every other time, would that work?" Beth had looked away before asking the question, but she could feel Peter's gaze from across the Bronco's interior. "Alright, I get it. I'll try, but I'm not promising anything."

"Fair enough," Peter said. They travelled in silence for a long moment, then he began again. "Heaven isn't exactly what you've been taught. And before you start placing blame on Catholicism—or religion as a whole—understand that the reality of Heaven is a hard concept to explain."

"Why is that?" Beth's question was sincere.

"It's a matter of dimensions."

"Dimensions? Such as a flat, two-dimensional picture versus a three-dimensional object?"

"Something like that," Peter agreed. "You see, in this world people tend to believe things because they can see them."

"And touch them."

"Yes—and taste, and smell, and—well, you get the picture. For the most part, if we can't *see* something, it doesn't exist. Sound waves, viruses, atomic particles—many people balked at believing these things existed simply because they couldn't see them."

"I get that, but what does it have to do with religion or Heaven? People have believed in Heaven for centuries, and no one has come back from the dead and claimed to have seen it. We simply understand that it exists somewhere else—somewhere we can't see—at least, not while we're alive."

"Yes, and that's a very logical—and understandable— approach to grasping something that you have no proof even exists. You believe it simply because of what you were told."

"Well," Beth countered, "it's not like anyone has ever come back to verify it."

"With one exception."

"Yes," she agreed. She'd been raised in an awareness that Jesus had lived, and died, for mankind. Somehow, though, there had been guilt worked into those childhood lessons as well. The CCD, religious education, classes of her youth came back to her; the recitation of bible verses, the workbooks, the guilt of realizing that she'd rather have been somewhere—anywhere—else at the time.

"Confraternity of Christian Doctrine."

Beth returned to the moment. "What?"

"You were wondering what 'CCD' stood for."

"Do you know everything I'm thinking?" The concern in Beth's voice was genuine.

"Yes, pretty much." He smiled at her, offering her an open, warm, nonjudgmental look.

"Damn," she said, "that's not good."

"You're a good person, Beth, I wouldn't be too concerned."

"But—*everything*? I mean—"

"You're human. Whether or not you believe it, I can relate."

"Can you? I mean—are *you* human?"

He didn't answer as quickly this time, but there was no deception in his voice when he finally spoke. "I was, once. Let's leave it at that for now, okay?" She nodded and he continued. "Let's get back to the dimension theory, shall we?"

Outside, the wind-driven snow continued its horizontal race through the headlight beams and into the darkness beyond. Peter continued to drive at a steady 45 mph, apparently unaffected by the lack of visibility or the depth of the snow that now covered the road. Beth began to realize that she was safe with this man, and she relaxed slightly in the passenger seat. Slowly, her mind turned away from the nor'easter that was doing its best to swallow them whole and back to the conversation at hand.

"So," she asked, "Why is this dimensional theory so important?"

"Because you have to understand it before you'll be able to fully grasp why you're here—and why specific other people are very important to you. You need to understand about Heaven before you can do what needs to be done."

"Which is?"

She expected a pause before he answered, but the words came quickly and without hesitation. "There's someone I need you to save."

"Me? Save someone?" The idea was so absurd that she didn't even know how to argue against it. She wasn't exactly martyr material. She didn't attend church; didn't even belong to one, and she'd given up on praying years ago.

Praying was a lot like her childhood, she supposed; what was the use in talking if no one seemed to be listening? Yet, even when she *had* prayed, it wasn't for herself. She'd always thought it was selfish to ask God for things for herself. After all, she had all of the basic necessities: a home, a vehicle, good health—to ask for anything beyond that, when so many people in the world were without, just didn't seem right. No, when she'd prayed, it had been for someone else; when she'd prayed, it had been for—

Her heart gave a lurch. The instantaneous pain surprised her; she'd thought her heart had died a long time ago . . . had hoped it had. Hearts were good for nothing *but* pain, and she'd had enough of that for one lifetime.

Peter had not spoken, and she was suddenly aware of him reading her thoughts—knowing, without being told, exactly what she'd been thinking. She felt violated and ashamed, and all she'd been doing was thinking of—

"Life can be complicated, can't it?" Peter asked.

"Yeah, whatever the hell that means." Beth said nonchalantly. She stared out the side window, refusing to meet his gaze.

"I heard somewhere that it's better to have loved and lost than to never have loved at all," he remarked.

She turned to glare at him, her face reddened by anger. "That's a crock of shit. Whoever said that never lost at love, or they had a damn good divorce attorney."

"What would you know about divorce attorneys?" Peter asked, that quickly-becoming-familiar grin tugging the corners of his mouth upward. "You've never even been married."

"Just so I have this straight," she said, struggling to keep her voice level, "I'm not allowed to be sarcastic, but it's alright for you to be a smart ass and have all the answers?"

"I'm sorry." The grin vanished and he grew solemn. "It's been a few years since you've seen him; I didn't know it was still that raw."

"Bullshit," Beth exploded. "You're inside my head right now! Don't tell me you didn't know!" She took a deep breath and looked away. "Damn it." She shook her head, forcing back the tears. Who was she kidding? Even she hadn't known it was still that raw.

"It wasn't a bad thing—loving him. You know that, right?" Peter said.

She thought about it for a long moment, pondering what answer would be the right one. Whether she considered it to be a good thing or a bad thing changed without warning, sometimes from one day to the next, sometimes from hour to hour. Good or bad, the only thing that was certain was that she *had* loved him; she had never stopped loving him. It was a bridge she had simply lacked the desire or power to burn.

"We all make mistakes, right—isn't that what being human is all about?" There was a forced flippancy in her voice.

"Love is never a mistake, Beth, even when it doesn't work out the way you had hoped. Remember, there are three things that last," he said. "Faith, hope, and love, and the greatest of these is love."

"1st Corinthians, 13:13," she said, cutting him off, surprised she'd even remembered the source. "But," she continued, "thirteen is an unlucky number, isn't it? Convince me that the number thirteen appearing twice in that source is a coincidence."

"I can't," he replied. "How about you convince me that the verse is untrue?"

She thought for a moment before conceding. "I can't." A silence filled the vehicle; the laboring tires and the growl of the engine seemed to be light-years away. "What does it matter," she wondered out loud, "can you tell me that?"

Peter didn't answer. He drove on in silence, giving her some time to reconsider her own question. When he glanced at her again, the confusion on her face had faded and was being replaced by a growing realization that gave way to absolute panic.

"No," she said, softly. She shook her head, each side to side motion becoming more intense than the one before. "No—it can't be. It can't be him—you can't want me to save him!"

"Is he not worth saving?" Peter asked, but the question was undeniably rhetorical.

"I never said that! I just . . . I can't do it! You can't possibly ask me to do it!"

"Who better for the job than you, Beth?"

"I . . . I don't know; I don't care. Someone, anyone . . . you! You do it!"

"I can't; it wouldn't work."

"Why not? You can open locked doors without a key, why can't you do this?"

"Beth, be logical. What chance do you think I'd have of convincing a man I've never met that love is still a possibility; that life is not without meaning or value?"

"You . . . you want *me* to do *that*? How?" There was undeniable panic in her voice. *"How?"*

"I don't know the answer to that; honestly, I don't. I wish I did. It just doesn't work that way."

"What doesn't work that way," she had slid in closer to confront him, and she met his gaze full on.

"Doing His bidding," Peter said, a solemn tone adding credence to his words.

"You mean . . ." Beth's voice trailed off, and Peter nodded. Beth shook her head again. "No, this has got to be some kind of joke. I can't convince Sam of anything—I never could. He believes what he wants to believe. And if God thinks I can do it, He's got the wrong person. You've got to tell Him that; you've got to make Him understand!"

Peter simply studied the blowing snow that raced through the headlight beams. He switched hands on the steering wheel before shaking his head slowly. "I can't do that. God knows what He's doing; trust me on that one. It would be senseless to question Him."

"But I—" Beth began again.

"Look," Peter interrupted, "you're home."

Beth turned to gaze out the windshield and was shocked to see her garage door illuminated by the Bronco's headlights. They hadn't turned any corners; Peter had never even stepped on the brake, yet here they were, safe and sound. He reached up and punched the garage door opener that was clipped to the sun-visor, and together they watched as the door lumbered upward. When it was fully open, Peter eased the Bronco inside, put the vehicle in park, and switched off the engine. Reaching for the button a final time, he closed the garage door, sealing the storm outside.

The ensuing silence was as heavy as a wet woolen blanket, and equally stifling.

"I can't do this," Beth whispered. "I can't . . ."

Peter drew another deep breath. When he looked at her, there was a sad, but gentle smile on his face. "You can do this, Beth. You're stronger, and wiser, and more brave than you think. But, more importantly, you love him."

She shook her head again, fighting back the tears. "But . . . but, what if I fail—what happens then?"

"You won't fail, Beth. You can do this."

Beth hesitated. "Are you going to help me? Are you going to bring that moth and make Sam understand that there are things that exist that we can't explain? Are you going to be there?" There was genuine panic in her voice.

"No," he answered gently. "I can't help you with this. It's something you've got to do on your own."

"Alone—you want me to do this *alone*? You don't know what you're asking! I can't do this alone!"

Peter folded his hands on his lap and appeared to study them. Slowly, he raised them, palms together and fingers pointing toward Heaven—or where Beth imagined Heaven to be. He closed his eyes, and a look of serenity washed over his face. Quietly, he said, "Be gentle with this one, Lord. His heart is good, but broken. There is an emptiness in him that You can fill; a persistent pain that You can ease. Please hold his heart in the palm of Your hand, and grant him peace."

Beth's mouth fell open, but no sound came out. She closed it and swallowed hard. "That's . . . How do you know that? That's the prayer I wrote for . . . How do you know those words? I never told anyone. I . . ."

Peter smiled at her, his eyes brimming with compassion. "What made you think that no one was listening, Beth? He's always listening. Sometimes, He chooses to not answer—at least, not in the way we expected, but that doesn't mean that He's not listening." Then, the conversation came to an abrupt end; Peter was simply gone.

Beth sat staring at the empty driver's seat. The engine clicked and creaked as the cooling metal contracted in the confines of the small garage. There was no other sound. A single tear spilled down her cheek, followed by another, and another. She swallowed and sniffed loudly. "Where is Heaven, Peter, and what am I supposed to do? I . . . I can't see Sam again, I just can't—don't you understand? What am I supposed to do?" From outside the garage, the wind racing over the shingled roof moaned and whistled, but offered no answers.

Chapter Four

Beth knew, without even opening her eyes and looking at the clock, that it didn't pay to go back to sleep. It was not yet 5 A.M., and her apartment was already stifling hot. She'd turned off the air conditioner upon retiring, hoping to save some money on her August utility bill, a decision she now regretted. But, in all fairness, it wasn't the heat that had awakened her. It was the dream.

Over the course of the last seven months, Beth was certain that she could have forgotten all about that snowy and surreal ride home with the stranger. She could have convinced herself that it had never happened—that she'd imagined the whole thing; it would have been so easy to do—if it weren't for the dream.

Beth had been plagued by recurring dreams her entire life, so this really wasn't something new. As a young child, she'd enjoyed the recurring dream that she could fly. She simply flapped her arms and she could soar like a bird. It was dumb, she knew, but she'd liked that dream; however, she would eventually discover that the things she enjoyed in life were never destined to last. Later, the dreams changed; they morphed into restless journeys with a recurring theme. In those dreams, she was always trying to find her way to— where? That was never quite clear, but she spent what seemed like hours on end searching for the way. It always started the same; she was driving and the road would end in a tangle of buildings. From there, she proceeded on foot through a maze of corridors and strange rooms. Ultimately, she ended up somewhere high—the top of a stairway, or on a balcony—that led nowhere. Terrified by heights, she stood frozen in place, heart racing, not daring to move. In another version of the dream, the road did not end—at least, not in a tangle of buildings. Instead, it angled upward, a section of a cloverleaf in same strange city. But the ribbon of blacktop did not circle around and level back off. It ended—just ended—several hundred feet above the ground. And she always saw the jagged end of the blacktop when it was too late to stop.

She supposed she had Peter to thank for those dreams ending. Peter, the stranger who could drive unaffected through a ruthless winter storm—the man who could open locked doors, and recite a private prayer that she had never shared with anyone. Peter, whose unexplained presence was preceded by the arrival of a winged luminescent creature that resembled a moth but wasn't a moth at all. Who needed dreams when reality was so unexplainable?

But, had it been reality or had she imagined it all? It had felt real—undeniably real, but the inevitable passage of time had caused her to question the events of that night. Even if he *had* been there, and even if he *had* driven her home, how could he have simply disappeared before her very eyes? It didn't make sense; there was no logical explanation for what had happened that night. Therefore, by default, it couldn't have happened.

So, as close as she could figure, the dream had started at about the time she decided that Peter didn't exist. She didn't make the connection at first, because the dream didn't contain snow, or luminescent winged creatures, or a person who disappeared without a trace. That would have been too easy. No, it was a dream about Sam . . . dear Sam.

She crawled out of bed, her hair matted to her head and her T-shirt clinging to her body like a second skin. Two blocks away from her second floor apartment, the owner of a small bakery had already begun his day's work, and the smell of fresh bread wafted in through her open patio door. The sun, like her, was up and adding even more heat to the early morning air. In the block behind her, Mr. Adam's Shih

Tzu was terrorizing a squirrel, and somewhere further off an infant was crying. Screw the utility bill. Beth slid the patio door shut, switched on the wall-mounted air conditioner, and headed for the bathroom.

Sam. She turned on the shower, cranked up the hot water, and stepped under the spray. The water pressure was good, but the scalding deluge did little to derail her train of thought. In the dream, she was back at the Copperhead, a popular supper club in downtown Evansville. It was where she had first met Sam. That was ten years ago. She'd been thirty-eight; Sam, the owner, was thirty-two. The Copperhead was exactly as she remembered it. If you were lucky enough to find a parking spot directly out front—as she always was in the dream—you simply crossed the sidewalk, climbed four concrete steps, pulled open one of the double oak doors, and stepped inside. As the club's name implied, it was decorated in a southwestern flair, complete with spurs mounted on the wall to serve as coat hooks, and cactus-shaped lanterns illuminating the booths in the bar area. The walls were painted in a subtle yellow, and the seats were covered in a flame upholstery pattern in golds, rusts, and browns. Done incorrectly, it could have been tacky, but somehow the Copperhead made it work—or maybe it was Sam who made it work.

Sam was . . . well, Sam. He was one of those rare individuals who could talk to anyone and make them feel like they were the only person in the room. He listened, nodded at the exact right moments, and was not afraid to touch the other person—a gentle resting of his hand on your arm, a quick embrace—in a way that never seemed intrusive or threatening. Beth had imagined that angels would communicate with humans in that very way if they'd been allowed to walk the earth.

Beth could still remember the first time she had seen him. She'd gone to the Copperhead as a bartender in

response to a 'help wanted' ad. The place was relatively
deserted, and Sam had been seated on the customer-side of
the bar. He was a solid man, rugged yet attractive in a free-
spirit sort of way. The years of being a lanky youth were
well behind him, but he was aging well. There was no gray
yet in his short brown hair, and his face held a boyish charm.
Beth had long-ago noticed that, for some unfair reason, men
would tend to become foxier with age. A touch of gray, a
few wrinkles around the eyes, often made a man more
appealing, as though his life experience magically made him
more desirable. Women simply got older.

Beth had been unaware that Sam owned the
establishment, and the bartender on duty—a redhead, fifty-
six year old woman named Miriam who was dressed in a
fringed leather jacket and skin-tight black leather pants—had
tested her abilities by having her mix a variety of drinks for
him. Several highballs later, Beth had acquired both the job
and two new friends. Four years after that, Miriam would
lock up the Copperhead and head out at the end of her shift
on a relatively uneventful night. People could only speculate
on what happened next. Most felt it was a drunk driver,
intent on spending what little money he had left in his wallet
at a 24-hour casino located eight miles down the road, who
hit her head-on when she was a mile from her home.
Speculation was all they had because, incredibly, no one ever
learned who the other driver was. The individual had been
behind the wheel of a stolen vehicle, and the owner had been
cleared of any wrong-doing. The guilty party had simply
fled the scene; he hadn't turned up in any emergency room
or hospital for treatment, and no one remembered picking up
a stranger—or anyone, for that matter—on that lonely stretch
of highway that night. In short, the driver who'd killed their
dear friend was never found. Sam had been devastated, and
Beth had cradled his head to her bosom as he'd cried
uncontrollably for the better part of a night. He never
seemed to recover from the loss, and Beth would soon view
Miriam's death as the beginning of the end for the

relationship that she and Sam shared, and for her role at the Copperhead as well. In the dream, though, Miriam was happy and well. She greeted Beth as the younger woman stepped behind the bar, ready to begin her shift.

"Got a bunch of wild ones here," Miriam would say, nodding toward the crowd, and Beth would smile in acknowledgment. "Maybe your Mr. Right is in this bunch. Do you feel lucky?" Miriam added, her blue Irish eyes twinkling merrily.

"As if I'd marry a loser who hung out here," was Beth's consistent answer, dream after dream.

Sam would appear then, weaving his way through the crowd to stand at the bar. "Seven & Seven," he said, half shouting to be heard over the juke box. "Lonesome Loser" by the Little River Band was blasting through the speakers. When it faded away, Meat Loaf's "Two Out of Three Ain't Bad" would begin playing. Cigarette smoke hung heavy in the air, and everywhere Beth looked she saw people jostling to be close to one another. No one wanted to be alone.

Moving in slow motion, as was often the case in dreams, Beth handed Sam his drink. His eyes, always his most striking and memorable feature—the brown eyes of a common deer, somehow wise beyond measure—locked on hers, and for a moment she couldn't breathe. Since time began, poets have written that 'love at first sight' overpowers all. Beth knew they had it all wrong. Love that arises— explodes—from the depths of an established friendship will conquer 'love at first' sight every time.

In the dream, Beth would hand him his drink and their hands would brush against one another just as a woman stepped up on Sam's right. She was graceful, slight of build, and beautiful—everything Beth had never been. She wore a form-fitting, strapless black dress. With the bar between them, Beth should not have been able to see the stranger from the waist down, yet she could. Dreams worked that way, disregarding reality yet seeming none the less real for it. Accentuated by black, fishnet stockings, her long legs carried her with a fluid grace. She stopped when she reached Sam and stepped in close to him, poised on one leg, the other raised and bent coyly at the knee. She kissed him lightly on the cheek. Sam turned to look and surprise registered on his face. He smiled, leaned toward her, and whispered something; her jet-black hair slipped to one side when she shook her head and laughed at his remark. Then she was leaning into him, pressing her firm breasts against his arm. She whispered something in return, and Sam laughed aloud—laughed as Beth, and the Copperhead, and everything else in the world disappeared from his view. In the blink of an eye, Beth was left standing alone at the bar, a whiskey sour in her hand, condensation from the class gently slipping over her fingers and onto the polished surface below.

The hot shower had grown tepid. Beth turned the water off and grabbed the towel from the rack. She dried off briskly, rubbing her skin until the towel felt like sandpaper and her skin burned from the friction . . . still, the pain did little to drive the dream from her mind. Even the memory of it was upsetting, though she couldn't say why. Luckily, she didn't have it every night, but each time she did the details became clearer and the dream became longer. It was only within the last two weeks that it had grown to include the woman, and her and Sam's disappearance into thin air. Beth rubbed harder until her skin was raw. "Damn it," she cursed, whispering even though she was quite alone and there was no one else to hear. "Damn it, damn it, damn it!"

She threw the towel aside and strode toward the bedroom to get dressed just as the phone rang. Though most people thought it archaic, Beth had gone ahead and activated the phone line in the apartment when she'd moved in.

Cellphone reception had been spotty in the area at that time, and she'd gotten a good price on the phone service when she'd purchased her internet package. That had been seven years ago and, truth be told, although she was online almost every day, she seldom used the telephone portion of the package deal. On occasion—when she'd misplaced her cellphone, or forgot to put it on the charger—she would use the wall-mounted, museum-bound phone to order a pizza, or to check what movie was playing at a local theater. Aside from those rare occasions, it sat idle; it had probably rung less than a dozen times in all those years. Perhaps that was why the sound of it now sent chills down her spine and spread goose bumps across her damp, exposed flesh. She remained frozen in her bedroom doorway, her arms crossed defensively beneath her exposed breasts, hugging herself. She stared at the ringing phone, unable to move. After a dozen or so rings, it fell silent.

Suddenly aware that she'd been holding her breath, Beth exhaled loudly through her nose, not unlike the way a horse snorts when it has been held in one place for too long. Shaking her head, she took two steps into the bedroom before she stopped and turned around. She didn't want to go into the kitchen; she didn't want to cross to the phone, but she had an undeniable urge to pick it up and listen. It had stopped ringing; whoever had been trying to call had hung up. It had been a wrong number; she was certain of that. It was 5:13 A.M. No one she knew would be calling at that hour—bearing either good or bad news. She'd grown up being jostled from one foster home to another, she had no siblings or parents. Sue and Rebecca were the only two people in the area that she socialized with, but she was not even sure they would qualify as friends. They were also her co-workers who waited tables at the Eagle Crest Resort, a posh supper club in Baraboo Wisconsin where Beth still made her living mixing drinks. Neither of them would be up at this hour, nor would they have been calling her if they were.

Still, the urge was there. She started toward the now-silent phone, moving with short, uncertain steps. She felt like that stupid, overly-apparent victim in a B-rated horror movie, the one everyone in the audience is screaming at, "Don't open that door!" or "Don't go back in that house!" Yet, the character always does, and the crowd predictably changes its mantra to, "If you're that stupid, you deserve whatever it is you're about to get," and a giant cleaver promptly splits him or her in two. Beth did not believe for a minute that a cleaver would suddenly burst through the wall, nor did she believe that Freddy Krueger would be waiting on the other end of the telephone line when she picked it up. Not *if* she picked it up, but *when*. She could not stop herself.

The telephone was mounted on the wall next to the refrigerator, which rested at the far side of the kitchen. Fingers of sunlight stole into the kitchen from an adjacent window; they cut a swath through the room and illuminated swirling dust particles that hung in the air. Beth stepped through them, her flesh momentarily bathed in the early-morning, mid-summer sunlight. The exposed skin welcomed the warmth, but it did nothing to lessen the chill that had settled bone-deep within her. Moving with sudden and unforeseen conviction, she quickly covered the last few yards that separated her from her destination, her damp feet sticking to the worn linoleum as she moved. She snatched the phone off the receiver before she could change her mind and raised it to her ear, certain that the familiar dial tone was all she would hear. But Miriam's voice reached out to her from somewhere inside the hard-molded plastic and collection of wires that had been, up until a few moments ago, an ordinary telephone.

"Good morning, Beth. I've missed you."

Chapter Five

Beth's mouth went dry and her heart fluttered within its ribcage prison. It couldn't be Miriam; she'd been dead for six years. Dead people don't use telephones, nor do they walk up behind you and tap you on the shoulder in a grocery store, or do any other random act of being undead. That's not the way the world works.

"Don't be scared, Beth, it's okay,"

Miriam's voice reached out to her, enveloping her in a blanket of familiarity. Beth had missed this woman terribly. For months after the funeral, Beth had still expected the matriarch of the Copperhead to walk into work and assume her rightful place behind the bar—as if the accident and all the sorrow that followed had been some terrible mistake. Miriam, like Beth, had been pretty much alone in the world. She'd never missed work to entertain visiting family members, and never talked about siblings or relatives of any age, shape or size. In truth, the woman had taken Sam and Beth under her wing, loving and guiding them like the children she never had. Lord knows they both needed it. After the accident, Beth had helped Sam make the funeral arrangements. They had both been completely overwhelmed; there had been so many final choices to make, so many heart-wrenching tasks that needed to be done. Beth remembered little of it; she supposed she'd operated in a state of shock and simply muddled through.

Both she and Sam survived the initial days without Miriam there, although Beth could not say how . . . and those days turned into weeks, and the weeks into months. In time, Beth could think of her departed friend without being buried in a renewed and raw sense of loss. But, what wouldn't Beth have given to erase that tragic loss and return to the early days at the Copperhead? It had been the only time in her entire life when—what? When her heart had been light and anything had been possible. It was, she realized long after the fact, the only time she'd truly been alive. Now, leaning against the wall in her kitchen, with the phone cord twisted around her index finger, Beth felt the loss anew.

"Beth?" Miriam's voice sounded so close, so real.

"I'm . . ." What was she—terrified, confused, certifiably insane? "I'm," she began again, "I'm here."

"I know you are, Sweetie. So am I."

Beth glanced around the kitchen, suddenly aware that she had not yet bothered to get dressed. She felt both physically and emotionally exposed. She supposed that talking to a dead person on the telephone might do that to you. A dull pain caused Beth to glance down at her hand. The exposed tip of the finger that was wrapped in the phone cord was turning purple. She quickly unwrapped the digit and searched her mind for something to say. Nothing came.

"I've missed you, Beth."

"Yeah, me too." Beth blinked back the tears; where could they have come from so quickly? "Why . . . why did you have to go, Miriam? It wasn't the same without you. Sam never got over your . . ." Beth couldn't bring herself to say the word.

"I always hated cop outs, Beth. You know that. So now, saying 'It was my time' sounds like exactly that—a cop out. But, there's really no better way to put it."

"Well, it sucked. You can't know how hard it was."

"Sure I can, Beth. I was there."

"No—no you weren't. There was only Sam and—"

"Are you happy, Beth?"

"What?" Beth winced involuntarily. Leave it to Miriam to cut to the heart of the matter. But then, she had never bothered with small talk when she was alive, why should being dead make any difference? "What the hell does that have to do with what we were discussing?"

Miriam laughed, and the familiar, melodic sound felt like a balm for Beth's soul. When the laughter faded, Miriam said, "It's about time you got tough; maybe my dying did some good after all." Beth closed her eyes and bit her tongue. Miriam waited for a beat before adding, "You're so much like me, Beth. Did I ever tell you that? That's what I loved best about you, I guess, the fact that I could see so much of myself in you."

"And Sam, what did you see in him?" Beth asked, not sure where the question had come from. It was Miriam's turn to be silent. Beth began to wonder if she had left. A lump rose in her throat and new tears threatened. She didn't want Miriam to leave, not ever—and yet . . . People who were passionate about the paranormal would argue with her, but Beth was pretty sure that this was a very shitty way to begin the day. When she was certain Miriam had gone, Beth turned to hang up the phone, but before she could Miriam asked,

"The question is, what did *you* see in him?"

Beth froze, uncertain how to respond. After what seemed an eternity she sighed deeply and began to wrap the phone cord around her finger once again. The silence taunted her, dared her to speak. "You know the answer to that, Miriam—you better than anyone."

"It's been six years since I died, Sweetie, and five years since you left the Copperhead and ended up here. All that time gone, all those miles travelled—and what do you have to show for it? You love him as much today as the day you left."

Beth swallowed hard. "What difference does it make? At some point, a person has to accept the facts and cut their losses."

"But at what cost, Beth, and how long can you afford to keep paying?" A short pause ensued, then Miriam added, "I know you're hurting, Sweetie. If I were there, I would hug you. I would hold you in my arms and tell you how much you mean to me, how special you are—"

"Well, you're dead, Miriam." Defensiveness crept into Beth's voice. She didn't intend to be mean; hurting Miriam was the last thing she wanted. Besides, was it even possible to hurt a dead person? Beth had nothing to base that opinion on, but somehow she felt it was. This made what she'd said even worse. But this wasn't about sparing Miriam's feelings; it was about survival, about getting through yet another day, and another. It was about somehow keeping all of the pain tentatively locked away in that deep pit that had once been her heart. This was the only way she knew to keep going on.

"Go to him, Beth. He needs you," Miriam's voice was gentle.

"Sam doesn't need anyone," Beth replied.

"You're wrong."

"Wouldn't be the first time, probably won't be the last, but I won't go back there."

"Why, Beth?" Miriam pleaded.

"Because I can't." Beth knew how pathetic that sounded, but how could she explain something that even she didn't understand? Her breathing quickened, and her heart hammered. Yes, she still loved him—would always love him. How she wished that weren't true. But it was her reality, and she'd learned to live with it the best she could. The wound would never heal; she accepted that. On some days, his face only crossed her mind once or twice; on other days, he was a subtle, continuous ache that she endured even as she fought to keep it from tainting or erasing even the smallest pleasures life might toss her way; on the worst days, she stayed inside her apartment and drank to numb the emptiness that threatened to swallow her whole. True, this was no way to live. But to see him again would be like fileting open a poorly-healed scar with a rusted razor blade. It made no sense, and there was no way it would turn out well.

"Jinx is failing; Sam is thinking about putting him down." There was pain in Miriam's voice, a subtle affirmation that emotions existed even in the spirit realm.

"Jesus," Beth whispered. She closed her eyes and leaned against the wall.

"He's listening. Jesus is listening, always, you know that, Beth, don't you?"

Though she hadn't intended the remark as a prayer, she caught Miriam's meaning. "No, I don't," Beth whispered without opening her eyes. Guilt buried deep in her Catholic upbringing forced her to justify her answer. "It doesn't even make sense. Why would He be? With all the wars, and famine, and cruelty on this earth, why would He care about a sick horse—"

"Or one broken heart?" Miriam cut her off. "Because He wants you to be happy."

"Really," Beth scoffed and was instantly sorry. "Well, I'm not getting that message, and there's nothing I can do for Jinx. I'm not a veterinarian. He's got to be—what, sixteen years old now? That's old for a horse; none of us live forever."

"You could say 'Goodbye'", Miriam said softly.

Jinx appeared in her mind's eye and Beth embraced the image. Miriam astride the bay gelding, cantering across the north pasture at Thunder Ridge, the horse's ebony mane and tail flowing in the wind and the rhythmic sound of hoof beats echoing through the late-afternoon stillness. Horse and rider moved as one, Miriam bent low over the animal's neck as his long strides covered the meadow with a fluid grace. Although there had always been a few dozen horses on the ranch at any given time, Jinx had been Miriam's favorite, and the wall of the tack room had been covered with ribbons and photographs of the winning duo that spanned a decade of competitions.

Beth tried to imagine what Jinx looked like now, in failing health and well along in years. Even healthy, the image of Jinx without Miriam always seemed to be wrong on some level. Beth had found herself avoiding the gelding during her last visits to Thunder Ridge following Miriam's death. It had been awkward seeing the animal. Batman without Robin, the Lone Ranger sans Tonto—the missing piece was painfully obvious and it broke her heart.

"Go to him, Beth," was all Miriam said.

Beth turned and carefully placed the phone back in its cradle. The conversation was over. Miriam was gone. It was something Beth *felt* more than *knew*. The room was suddenly more empty, and there was a renewed sense that Beth was once again facing the world alone. She thought about Miriam's request. *Go to him.* By *him*, had Miriam meant Jinx or Sam? Did it even matter? Something built within her and exploded without warning.

Bullshit—this was bullshit, plain and simple! Beth was furious. First Peter, now Miriam—who the hell were they to bring up Sam? Where did they get the right to pry into that part of her past? Oh sure, she could see where Miriam might have been curious—might have wondered about what had happened after she died. But damn it, she *had* died, so what business was it of hers now? If she had cared that much, she should have never gotten behind the wheel of her car that night. She should have walked home; she should have . . . should have . . . should have never left them—should have never died. Beth ran to the bedroom and threw herself on the bed, sobbing. She cried for what seemed an eternity; cried until there were no tears left and she drifted into a mercifully dreamless sleep. When she woke several hours later, the apartment's air-conditioner had brought the temperature down to a frigid 68 degrees. Beth hadn't been troubled by the chilled air; someone had folded the loose half of the covers over her as she slept.

Chapter Six

Beth rose at 4 P.M., showered for the second time that day, and got dressed for work. It was Friday; the Eagle Crest Resort would be hopping that night. A menu that featured several variations on the traditional Wisconsin Friday-night fish fry and all the trimmings, as well as a full-menu of steaks and burgers, always assured a large crowd eager to end the workweek and unwind. With wait times of an hour or more to get seated for their meals, people sat at the bar— or milled around close to it if they hadn't arrived in time to claim a stool—and drank as they waited. Many of them would be regulars, but enough strangers found their way in each week to keep Beth's job interesting. That was good. Tonight Beth would embrace any challenge bartending might throw at her. She needed the distraction.

She dried and brushed out her page boy hair, spritzed on just enough hairspray to keep several renegade strands from curling upward, and applied foundation, eyeliner and mascara. The whole process took less than five minutes. She stole a quick glance in the mirror before heading out. At 5'3" wearing 1" heels, dressed in faded jeans and a loose-fitting red knit top that didn't hug her 138 pound frame too tightly, she had no misconceptions about her ability to catch a man's eye—or the lack thereof. At 48, the lines were starting to appear around the corners of her eyes and mouth. Also, her dishwater blond hair was going gray too soon, and she was too damn stubborn, or worn out, to do anything about it. The silver strands framed her face with a subtle accent that she'd grown accustomed to. Besides, the last thing she wanted was to have to buy a box of hair-color every month—or worse, make an appointment at a salon and waste good money fighting the aging process when she knew full well which one of them would win in the end. No, she'd earned the gray hair—each and every strand. And the fine lines and wrinkles? She'd earned them, too, she supposed. Too many smiles, or too many frowns, or too many tears. Either way, she'd paid the purchasing price.

She left her apartment and hurried into the garage. The air was hot and stifling in the familiar enclosure, and it smelled of motor oil, gasoline and old wood. She fired up the Bronco, switched on the air conditioner (which amazed her by working yet one more time), backed out, and closed the garage door. The commute to work took her eighteen minutes; she filled the time by avoiding certain thoughts—or at least trying to. Sam, Miriam, Peter and Jinx all shared the 'do not think about' list, but every quarter of a mile she caught herself evicting one or another of them from her mind. When it became apparent that she wasn't going to win this battle either, she decided a compromise was in order. Peter seemed the least threatening—or the most distant— figure on the list, so she finally allowed her mind to settle on him. Truth be told, she had often caught herself wondering about him in the months that had passed—the way he had just appeared and later disappeared, their strange conversation, and the dimensional theory that he had mentioned but failed to explain. There were so many questions and no answers to be found.

At the age of 48, she prided herself on her ability to formulate questions that couldn't be answered for all aspects of life. In fact, to Beth it seemed that her entire life was the unanswered question of 'why?' In a high school English composition class, she developed a fondness for analogies. She had used them from that point forward to explain everything in her life that didn't work out the way she wanted it to. She'd finally decided that she was a sparrow in a world full of swans, or a traveler who arrived at the boarding gate only minutes after the flight had departed. In her opinion, she had always been a step out of time in a dance that she hadn't even desired to join. And death? Death would be a one-time plummet from the high dive board when no one had ever bothered to teach her how to swim.

The most common analogy for her life, though, involved the 'Tilt 'o Whirl'—her favorite ride at a carnival that she'd visited with one of her foster families. The ride featured circular enclosures that spun around on a track that rose and fell beneath them. If you leaned hard to either the right or the left, depending on which position the car was in at the top of the rise, it would proceed down the hill spinning so rapidly that you were forced back against the metal grate so hard you couldn't breathe. The best part was, once you got it going, the ride seemed to gain momentum—spinning in either direction so forcefully that you had to close your eyes and fight to keep your head from scraping against the metal back plate. On the flipside, though, there were times when, no matter how hard you leaned—in either direction—the car would not spin at all. It seemed to balance itself on the crest of every hill, favoring a stationary position to a position of twirling momentum. That was, Beth thought, her life. She knew what was required of her, and she did her best to complete each task, but the results were the same. Her life was stationary, and she just wasn't enjoying the ride.

That was, Beth had long ago decided, the initial thing that had attracted her to Sam. He was always in control of the ride. In his life, the car spun to the right if he wanted to go right, and to the left if he wanted to go left. If it didn't, he'd shut down the entire carnival until the damn thing was fixed. It was just that simple. He was the same way with people. There were no gray areas for him. He let everyone know what was expected of them. If they delivered, all was well. If they didn't, he cut them loose and moved on without so much as a backward glance. He didn't waste time on things that didn't work. In his world, there was no such thing as 'might have been' or 'could be'. There was only what 'is'. Period. His decisiveness was so rare among humans—and sometimes so cruel—but it never failed to work in his favor. He simply was who he was.

Damn it, damn it, damn it! He'd done it again; he'd snuck into her thoughts, forcing her wandering mind even further off track and pushing himself to the forefront yet again. That was how it had been for five long years. If she hadn't exiled him from her mind by now, if she hadn't yet forgotten him, what hope did she have of ever doing so? Had Miriam been right in suggesting she go back—was that the only way to find the closure she truly needed? She didn't want to even consider it. What was the smart thing to do; what would Sam have done in a similar situation? Damn it again! She pulled into the rear parking lot of the Eagle Crest Resort, exited the Bronco, and headed for the employee entrance, grateful for the bustling kitchen noises and raised voices that drifted through the open door. She hoped they'd be busy as hell tonight; there was no room for Sam in her head when patrons were hollering for drinks and slamming money down on the bar.

Someone once said, 'Be careful what you wish for', the implication being that getting what you wish for might be a bad thing. The kitchen at the Eagle Crest Resort stopped serving at 10 P.M. At midnight, the bar still featured 'standing room only' and Beth was beginning to think how nice it would be if everyone would just drink up and go home.

On the busier nights, the resort's owner Jake would step behind the bar and help out. He had assumed the 'serving' position around 9:30 that night and was still there. Beth knew the resort had turned a good profit, not just because she could no longer feel her feet, but because Jake had been smiling from ear to ear every time she glanced his way. The fifty gallon metal refuse bin that served as a container for empty glass bottles sported a heap that threatened to start cascading down the sides. The matching container for empty cans had already been emptied twice. The front pockets of her jeans bulged from tips, and the jar at the end of the bar was also full. If every night were this busy, she could afford to move out of her small apartment and buy something nice, real nice—some place as nice as the Thunder Ridge Ranch.

Her stomach dropped and the smile that she'd managed to keep plastered on her face all night slipped away. It was always like this though, wasn't it? Every time she managed to put the past behind her, it was only temporary. She couldn't function like a chicken with its head cut off indefinitely, and as soon as she slowed down—as soon as she turned off the automatic pilot and started navigating her own way again—her mental wheels slipped back into the worn, familiar rut that was Sam, and the ranch, and everything she only thought she'd left behind. *Nice analogy*, she told herself, *but it's getting a little old.*

By 12:45, the crowd had thinned to a paying body on every other stool. Beth knew that there was a good chance that Jake would cut her loose at 1 P.M. and close the bar by himself. He often did that on nights when she'd run herself ragged and the intake had been good. She was tired; it would be good to go home.

"Someone down there wants to talk to you," Jake said a few minutes later, nodding toward a stranger seated at the far end of the bar as he drew yet another glass of beer from the tap.

"And I want to win the lottery," Beth replied. She was washing glasses in the sink beneath the bar, rinsing them and tipping them upside-down on the stainless steel shelf to drain.

"Be nice; you'll get better tips," Jake said.

"I'm here to work, not visit," Beth countered. "Besides, I won't get any tips if I'm standing around talking to one customer. Generally, that's just not the way it works."

"Go be nice and see what the guy wants. When you're done 'visiting' as you put it, you can punch out and go home."

"Gee thanks, Jake, you're all heart," Beth snorted. "I'll bet you were going to cut me loose at one o'clock anyway."

"That's a possibility, but you'll never know, will you?" He winked at her and turned away to refill yet another glass. "Take him a drink seeing you're heading down there. A longneck Bud; tell him it's on the house."

"Yes, master. Right away, master," Beth replied. There were too many people left in the Eagle Crest for her to do her Quasimodo imitation and get away with it, so she simply grabbed two bottles of beer and headed for the far end of the bar. The lighting down there was every bit as good as the lighting in the rest of the bar, which meant it sucked. Still, she could tell the man was no one she knew long before she set the bottle down in front of him.

"On the house," she said. Two stools were stashed behind the bar for those rare periods when business was slack and a bartender actually got the chance to sit. Beth grabbed one of them, positioned it in front of the stranger, and sat down. "Jake said you wanted to talk to me." Beth's voice was casual, relaxed. She looked the stranger in the eye and took a long draw on her beer while she waited for his reply. She'd worked in taverns most of her life and knew the cardinal rule well. If you're a woman, you never show weakness. Uncertainty and weakness earmark potential victims. Look every man in the eye and hold his gaze, from the moment he arrives until he drains his last drink and staggers out. No exception. The eyes she held now were a striking gray, and equally confident; they met her gaze and held it. There was a short period of silence, then the stranger extended his hand across the bar. She accepted it without hesitation; show no weakness.

"I'm Mark, Mark Guard."

"Nice to meet you, Mark. I'm Beth."

"Yes, I know." A short silence ensued.

"What's this about, Mark," Beth asked, grabbing the proverbial bull by the horns.

"I'm not taking you away from your work, am I? I wouldn't want to get you in trouble with the boss."

Beth studied him. He was in his upper fifties, fit, and good-looking in a rough sort of way. The actor Sam Elliott in the movie "Roadhouse" came to mind. Mark sported the same style mustache, but his hair was shorter and the rest of his face was clean-shaven with no trace of a 5 o'clock shadow. He wore a black turtleneck sweater and, she assumed, jeans, though she did not possess x-ray vision to see through the bar to confirm that assumption. The sweater in August seemed odd, but the bar was air-conditioned and perhaps, like Elliott, he'd ridden in on a motorcycle and suspected the ride home would be a cool one.

"No, it's okay. I'm almost ready to punch out for the night," she regretted the words as soon as she spoke them. It sounded like some kind of invitation, announcing that her shift was over. If Mark had taken it that way, he gave no outward indication. He took a long drink and set the bottle back down on the coaster.

"Have you called Wisconsin home for long?"

Beth hesitated for a second or two. Hesitation could be mistaken for weakness, but she really didn't want to play 'twenty questions' at this hour. She decided to go along with it long enough to see where he was heading.

"All my life," she answered.

"But not here in Baraboo?"

"No," her reply was quicker, but there was an edge to her voice.

Mark smiled, and his eyes shone in an understanding way. "You don't like small talk, do you." It was a statement, not a question, but she answered anyway.

"Nope. Do you?"

"Can't say that I do. I'm a firm believer that life is just too damn short to waste it beating around the bush."

"I couldn't have said it better myself," Beth concurred. "So, what is it you wanted to talk to me about?" Mark hesitated and dropped his eyes for just a second. When he looked up again, the merriment that had been there had been replaced by concern. Beth's stomach knotted. "Don't tell me," she said, her voice lowered to almost a whisper, "you're here about Sam."

"Not entirely," Mark said, holding her gaze. "What I have to say has more to do with you than it has to do with Sam."

"Listen, Mister," the edge in Beth's voice had hardened considerably and she slid off the stool as she spoke. "I don't know who you are or where you came from, but let's get one thing perfectly clear. I'm getting a little sick and tired of all this 'cloak and dagger' shit. So just get the hell out of here and don't come back, okay?" At that she spun and walked away. "I'm clocked out," she told Jake seconds later as she pushed past him and rounded the end of the bar, heading for the door. "Don't expect me tomorrow until you see me," she threw back over her shoulder, slipped through the exit, and was gone.

She drove home in silence with the radio off and both front windows rolled all the way down. The fragrant night air swirled through the vehicle's interior. The earthy smell of a freshly-plowed field told her that a farmer was readying his soil for a crop of winter wheat. A few miles farther on, windrows of drying hay filled the night air with a perfume that Beth never tired of smelling. It was a tiny piece of heaven right here on earth.

Heaven . . . what did she know of heaven? As a child she'd been taught that heaven was somewhere high above her, somewhere in the clouds. It was a place where people went when they died, but only if they'd been very, very good. On the other hand, if they'd been bad, they'd end up somewhere beneath her, in a place called hell. You *ascended* or *descended*; that was what she'd been taught. But, if you weren't good enough to go to heaven, or bad enough to go to hell, you ended up in a place called purgatory, where supposedly you waited while your sins were erased—how that happened she wasn't quite sure—and you would finally be admitted into heaven. So, the question begged to be asked, where was purgatory? If heaven was 'up', and hell was 'down', then all that was left was a lateral move—to one side or the other. Which meant what, that purgatory was right here? That sounded about right. Her life certainly felt like a purgatory—an existence meant to purge everything from her that wasn't good. Except on nights when the scent of freshly-mown hay was in the air, then this *was* heaven, without a doubt.

She approached her driveway shortly before 1:30 and began to pull in. "Shit," she cursed under her breath and slammed on the brakes. The Bronco screeched to a halt, its front end dipping wildly as the vehicle stopped dead. The engine, unaccustomed to such abuse, sputtered in protest and died away. Beth sat in the resulting silence, cursing beneath her breath. Framed in the headlights of the Bronco, a motorcycle rested to one side of the driveway, and Mark was sitting on the front steps of her apartment, patiently waiting.

Chapter Seven

Beth stormed out of the vehicle, abandoning it in the middle of the road with its headlights still blazing. She slammed the driver's side door and circled around the front of the Bronco, taking the shortest route she could to the impending confrontation.

"You are one persistent son-of-a-bitch, I'll give you that," she growled at him, her fists clenched at her sides. "I'm not even going to ask how you knew where I lived; I can only imagine. But I want you out of here—now!"

"Beth, we really need to talk," Mark began.

"*You* need to talk; I need to sleep. And that's exactly what I'm going to do. Now plant your ass back on that bike and get the hell out of here, understand?" Her voice had gone up several notches and a light came on in a first-floor window.

"Beth, there's really no need for this; you're causing a scene—"

"Don't you dare tell me what 'there's a need for'. If you don't leave this instant, I'm calling the police!" Too late, Beth realized she'd left her handbag in the truck, but it wouldn't have done any good anyway. Her phone wasn't in her handbag; it was locked inside her apartment, plugged into the charger, exactly where she'd put it almost twenty-four hours earlier.

"Beth, if you'll just listen—"

"What's going on out there?" an angry voice bellowed. The window with the light on had been raised and a red-faced, elderly man was studying them, his eyes squinting to see into the dark yard.

"It's okay, Sir, we're fine," Mark said, his voice even and nonthreatening.

"Beth, is that you?"

She fumbled to remember his name and it came to her. "Yes, Mr. Burke."

"Is this man pestering you? Do you want me to call the police?"

Beth thought about it. It sounded like a good idea, but even if the police *were* called, Mark would probably be long gone by the time they arrived. And then what, she'd discover him seated on the edge of her bed when she'd finished answering all of the policeman's questions and had finally been allowed to go inside? No, she decided. This had to be dealt with now, and she was the one who had to deal with it.

"No," she finally said. "It's okay; I'm sorry we disturbed you."

Mr. Burke looked skeptical. He studied Mark for a long moment before addressing Beth a final time. "Well, I'm not going to bed until this joker leaves, so if you need anything, just holler, okay?"

"Thanks, Mr. Burke, but I'll be fine . . . really."

The elderly man took a long last look, as though he were memorizing Mark's face so that he could pick him out of a lineup, before he closed the window and allowed the drapes to fall back in place. True to his word, the light remained on and Beth knew he would be listening for the motorcycle to start up and drive away.

"He's a good man," Mark remarked. "He's got a good soul."

"He's also got a 12-gauge shotgun loaded with rock salt that he keeps in case of intruders, so I'd be going now if I were you."

To Beth's surprise, Mark laughed. It was a genuine sound, and Beth relaxed a little in spite of herself. When he finished, he looked at her. Even in the darkness, Beth discerned a twinkle in his eyes. He was a difficult person to stay mad at for any length of time.

"Can I offer a suggestion?" He asked.

"Please, I don't need any more advice on my past, or what choices I need to be making."

His smile broadened and he nodded toward the Bronco. "I was simply going to suggest that you get your vehicle off the road and into the garage before someone comes along and sideswipes it, that's all."

"Yes," Beth agreed, though there was no sense of urgency in her voice. "I suppose that would be a good idea." She studied the stranger for a brief moment, then she retraced her steps to the Bronco, climbed in, and started the engine. When the vehicle was safely parked in the garage, she returned to the front step. Mark was exactly where she had left him.

"There's room for two if you'd like to sit," he said, waving his hand over the cement slab. "You've been on your feet all night; I'm sure you could use the break." He slid over, creating even more space. Knowing that Mr. Burke would still be keeping an eye on the situation, Beth hesitated for only a second or two before sitting down on the concrete step next to him. After she'd settled into place, he continued. "I'm sure you're wondering who I am."

"Nope, got it all figured out," she replied without even looking at him. "You'd be the ghost of Christmas to come."

"What?" he asked, eyebrows raised.

"You're number three. First is the ghost of Christmas past, then the ghost of Christmas Present, then you. Although you talk way too much to fit the part."

Genuinely confused, or feigning it very well, Mark asked, "You've been visited by two ghosts?"

"Well, only the second one was a ghost for certain. I'm not exactly sure what the first one was, but he definitely wasn't human. And now there's you."

Mark smiled. "Well, I hate to burst your bubble, but you've got it all wrong. For one thing, it's not Christmas. For another thing, you're not Ebenezer Scrooge, and finally, I'm not a ghost."

"No, I didn't think so," Beth agreed. "But then, stranger things have happened lately." She raised both hands and combed her fingers through her hair, front to back. It was something she did when she was overly stressed or overly tired. At the moment, she happened to be both. She followed that by giving her head a quick shake before turning to look at him. "I've gotta ask, how'd you know where I lived?"

"Your friends are a little too trusting. I told Sue I was your uncle and she practically drew me a map. You really ought to set her straight about that sort of thing."

"I'll be sure to do that, right after I beat the crap out of her," Beth said.

"That sounds a little harsh; perhaps you should try a simple lecture first and see how that goes."

Beth drew a heavy breath. "Listen, Mark. It's been a long day and I'm really tired. Why don't you just say whatever it is that you came all the way out here to say so I can go to bed and get some sleep, deal?"

"Okay, if that's what you want. Do you know what an old soul is, Beth?"

"Not really," she shrugged. "I've heard the phrase before, but I've never really thought about it. You know, like sometimes a baby is born and someone will look at it and say, 'It's got an old soul.' I'd look at the same baby and all I'd see were wrinkles and a whole lot of work."

Mark smiled again; he seemed to do that a lot, and Beth felt herself warming to him. "They are that," he said.

"They are *what*—wrinkled or a whole lot of work?"

The smile morphed into a chuckle. "Both," he replied.

"But," Beth said, "the question remains—are they old souls?"

"Some are, most aren't," Mark said.

"And how is a person to tell which are and which aren't?"

"You don't; it's not important." Mark looked up and pointed to the night sky above them. The front of the apartment faced north, and the Big Dipper spread across the heavens, surrounded by countless twinkling dots of light. "Which of those are stars?" he asked Beth.

She squinted in the direction he was pointing. The specks of light all seemed to be stationary; there were no apparent airplanes, asteroids, or satellites among them, so she answered, "All of them."

"Nope," he politely disagreed. "Some of them are actually distant planets."

"They're heavenly bodies that twinkle in the night sky; that makes them stars."

"By your definition. But even if I allow that interpretation, you're still wrong. Some of them are not heavenly bodies at all. Did you know that a star can die, and we would still be able to see it? Depending on how far away the star is, it can take years for its light to reach us—or to stop reaching us, as the case may be."

"Years?" Beth asked.

"Yes, years. For example, one star—Proxima Centauri, in the constellation of Centaurus—is slightly more than four light years away from us. That means, if it died tonight, four years from now there's a good chance that you would still be able to see it."

"Really?" Beth was overly tired and therefore easily stunned.

"So, which of those twinkling lights are stars," he asked, "and which are simply streams of light from where a star used to be?"

For the life of her, Beth couldn't think of a single smart ass remark, so she kept her mouth shut.

"The answer is, it doesn't matter. If you perceive them to be stars, they're stars. There is no such thing as reality; there's only—"

"Perception," Beth finished for him. Then, with an edge to her voice, "You've talked to Peter, too, haven't you?"

"Actually, that quote has been attributed to a life-strategist—"

"But you heard it from Peter," Beth interrupted; her brow furrowed and a frown momentarily covered her face. "Did he send you here?" Mark's silence was confirmation enough for Beth. "Damn it." She rose from the step and strode a short distance toward the road, swearing softly under her breath. When she stopped, she stuffed her hands deep in her pockets and looked up at the stars, both the faux and the authentic. This was too much to wrap her mind around. The fight was going out of her, and that scared her more than anything. Obviously, Peter—and whatever other powers conspired to alter her destiny—were not about to leave her be. She had been fooling herself. There was no choice to be made; Peter and Miriam weren't out there somewhere, waiting for her to decide on a course of action. The gears were already in motion, and they would remain in motion, with or without her consent.

No! The protest rose from deep within her. This was her life, damn it, and no one was going to force her to do anything she didn't want to do. She'd fought too hard, suffered too much, to get to where she was at; turning the reins over to someone else—human or otherwise—was not acceptable. Her mind was made up; she would continue to resist whatever it was they had planned. But, if she followed that course of action, how many more Marks would end up in her driveway, or be waiting to speak to her from across the bar? And how many days, or months, or years, would have to go by before she wouldn't hesitate to answer her own phone, afraid that Miriam was waiting to scold her from the other end of the line? Her head pounded and she wanted nothing more than to go up to her apartment and climb into bed. *There you go*, she scolded herself, *some fighter you're proving to be!*

The truth she needed to accept was this; even if she went down fighting, the end result would be the same—she would go down. But, if she gave in—if she embraced whatever it was that was happening, as unbelievable as it might be—what then? Instantly, her thoughts turned to Sam; after all, it all centered on him, didn't it? Her chest tightened and a deep, familiar ache filled her. She knew this pain well; she thought of it as her phantom broken heart. She'd often heard stories of people who had lost entire limbs only to report that they still felt them—an itch, an ache—even though the limb was no longer there. Her heart was no longer there, of that she was certain. She'd lost it long ago and had long since tired of waiting for its return. Still, in rare moments such as this, the resonating pain would remind her of what she had lost, forcing her breath to catch in her throat and her eyes to tear.

She swiped the heels of her hands across her moist eyes even as she whispered, "What is it you guys want from me?" She was certain that she had spoken too softly for Mark to hear, but he had left the step and come up behind her without her knowing that he had even moved.

"To believe," he said.

"Believe what?" her voice broke and fresh tears spilled down her cheeks.

Mark smiled and gently placed his arm around her shoulders. "How 'bout we discuss this over coffee." Turning her around to face him, he raised an eyebrow and asked, "You *do* know how to make coffee, right?"

She nodded and wiped away the new tears with one hand even as she pulled the apartment keys from her pocket with the other. In another life, letting a stranger into her apartment at 2 A.M. would have been a very bad idea. In that life, she would have wisely called the cops the moment she saw the motorcycle parked alongside of her driveway. Mark posed no threat; she was certain of that even though she couldn't say *why* she thought him to be so safe. Still, as she climbed the apartment steps with Mark in tow, she was struck by the feeling that the other life—with all its very-real dangers—had somehow been safer than what she was now facing. Perhaps the old saying was true; people preferred the devil they knew to the one they didn't.

Part Two: 'Sam'

Chapter Eight

Seated at a desk in a small back office, Sam sipped his coffee, finished checking the appropriate boxes on the beer distributor's order forms, and signed his name at the bottom. He was dressed in faded blue jeans and a white polo shirt that was no longer new, but new enough to wear while ordering Miller Lite. He was clean-shaven, and his brown hair—showing a hint of gray at the temples—was close-cut and neatly combed. He wore glasses, something that had become a requirement for reading and completing paperwork two years prior. With the signature completed, he slid them to the top of his head and looked around.

The office was small, but cozy. A pair of grey filing cabinets, which contained most of the business records for the last seven years, stood in the right-hand corner. In the opposite corner was an open, waist-high, imitation oak cabinet that held a wireless HP computer printer; two packages of unopened paper were neatly stacked on a shelf farther down. The floor was gray tile, well-worn but clean, and the walls were white and bare, with the exception of displayed copies of the Copperhead's framed tax ID form and business seller's license. The desk, which had probably been a rescue item from the Green Bay Saint Vincent DePaul store decades earlier, was solid metal and heavier than Fort Knox. Sam supposed that its weight was the main reason why it hadn't been replaced with something more modern; it would take four men and a forklift to remove it. On its worn, army-green top rested an equally old desk blotter, partially covered with a desk calendar (thankfully displaying the current year), a coffee cup inscribed with *I Don't Do Mornings* that served as a pencil holder, and a Dell laptop. As he looked around, Sam tried to find one item that hadn't been exactly where it was when he'd first set foot in this room twenty years earlier. Aside from the calendar, laptop, and printer, nothing had changed.

Business had been darn good at the Copperhead the last three months; good enough that he almost regretted selling the place to Dan Mosch. That had been what—almost five years ago? Sounded about right; he had signed the closing papers almost a year after Miriam's death, and one month to the day from when Beth had left. There was no sense dwelling on it; he knew that. What was done was done, and he had no regrets . . . at least not about selling the Copperhead.

He rose and stretched, wincing as his back cracked loudly. That was a good thing, he reassured himself. When he managed to crack it this early in the day, he knew he wouldn't have to deal with the annoying twinge that had become part of his life right around the time he turned forty. It didn't seem fair that, when a man finally reached an age when he seemed to have his head on straight, his body started falling apart. Hell, it was stupid to waste time thinking about it. He drained the last of his coffee, secured the signed forms to a clipboard, and hung the lot on a hook next to the office door. It was only 7:46 A.M.; when the beer truck pulled in at 2 P.M., the forms would be waiting.

Sam loved mornings and always had his duties at the Copperhead completed long before the first staff began straggling in at noon. Even though he no longer owned the supper club, at the time of the sale he had been offered a healthy salary to stay on as manager and he'd accepted the offer. He saw it as a 'win-win' situation; he still had keys to the place, and could come and go as he pleased. He still managed the staff—most of whom were good friends—and he still mingled with the patrons and kept his finger on the pulse of the surrounding communities. What he didn't have was the worry and stress that was routinely associated with the mortgage payment and maintaining the balance sheets for the business. In addition to these perks, the financial proceeds from the sale of the Copperhead, and the increased measure of free time that came from no longer owning the supper club, had made it possible for Sam to pay down the mortgage on the Thunder Ridge Ranch and keep Miriam's dream alive.

With the order forms completed, Sam was free to head back to the ranch until mid-afternoon. He did his customary quick walk-through before leaving. The bar had been wiped down; its heavily-varnished surface shone in the sunlight that angled in from an eastern window. The floors had been swept, the carpet in the dining area had been vacuumed, and the two ice machines behind the bar had finished making their mounds of glistening cubes and were silently waiting for the arrival of the impending crowd. Everything seemed to be in order, yet Sam felt uneasy. It wasn't anything he could immediately put his finger on. The sun was shining, there were no earthquake warnings—either pending or expired—posted for northeast Wisconsin, and none of the employees had scheduled the day off. As far as he could tell, there was no reason for the vague knot that rested in the pit of his stomach. He shrugged it off, pulled his keys out of his pocket and headed for the staff parking lot at the rear entrance.

The back door of the Copperhead was situated at the end of a long hallway. The door was a designated fire exit, and the hallway also accommodated doors to both the men's and the women's restrooms. The walls of the hallway, originally paneled in dark oak, had been painted white by the new owner. The resulting starkness had been quickly deemed too 'sterile' for a supper club, and Sam had brought in some paintings from the ranch house to remedy the problem and add color to the empty space. The painting that hung directly between the two restroom doors had been one of

Miriam's favorites. Sam had walked past it countless times without so much as a glance, but it caught his eye today.

The painting, hanging slightly askew, portrayed a typical pastoral setting. The autumn scene featured an old barn that rested, now slightly cock-eyed, at the far right side of the canvas. A dirt path led from the barn, passed through a gate that adorned a split-rail fence, and disappeared into a woods that—to give the impression of distance—rested higher up, and thereby farther back, on the canvas. Behind the woods, and even farther away, a rustic mountain range covered a large section of the sky. It had been the mountains that had intrigued Miriam. She had said that she wanted to visit them some day. When Sam had pointed out that it was just an artist's impression of a mountain, and thereby impossible to visit, she had smiled at him in a patient and somewhat condescending way—the way a mother might smile at her son when he announces that he ate fourteen million, gazillion jelly beans at his friend's house. The mother doesn't want to upset the child—or accuse him of lying—but there's no way in hell she believes the statement either. Miriam had seen something real in those mountains, and Sam had never bothered, or taken the time, to figure out what it was. What was most sad, he now realized, was that he'd never even asked her about it. *Well*, he thought as he straightened the picture, *it was too late to fix that now. What's done is done.*

Outside, the sun shone brightly. Sam squinted as he locked the back door of the Copperhead and headed for his truck. The key fob, complete with keys for the supper club, numerous locks at the Thunder Ridge Ranch, and the vehicle that was parked in the mid-August sunlight, rested in his hand, but he didn't bother to depress the button that would unlock the doors. The truck, a black 2010 Toyota Tundra equipped with a regular cab and chrome trim, wasn't locked. Sam, like most everyone else in a hundred-mile radius, didn't bother to lock his vehicle. Hell, most times the doors to his house weren't locked. Although crime rates were climbing here—as they were everywhere—this wasn't Milwaukee or Chicago where any item not tied down was likely to be carried off, and every door that wasn't locked was likely to be passed through. Besides, locking the truck doors simply didn't make sense when the windows were open to let in the cool morning air. More importantly, Sam was relatively sure that no one would want to steal his assortment of Brooks and Dunn, or Tim McGraw CDs and there was nothing else of value stored in the vehicle.

The blacktopped parking lot absorbed the August sunlight and radiated the warmth into the morning air. On one side, the lot was flanked by the Copperhead supper club; to the left of the building, Highway 70 bordered the lot. On the two remaining adjacent sides, forests of white pine blocked any hope of a breeze. Even though it was not yet 9 A.M., Sam's shirt was clinging to his back by the time he'd started the Tundra, rolled up the windows and switched on the a/c. Driving the speed limit, Thunder Ridge Ranch was only ten minutes away. Sam had long since stopped pondering the irony in that; when she'd left work that fateful night, Miriam had been only two minutes from home when a Dodge Ram had crossed the centerline and ended her life. Two minutes. She'd been a good friend, and a better mother to him than the woman who had brought him into this world; Sam would have sold his soul for the chance to alter those two minutes.

The accessory panel on the dash of his truck displayed the outside temperature as 83 degrees when Sam pulled into the driveway at the Thunder Ridge Ranch a short seven minutes later. Screw the speed limit. The roads were good, his brakes and tires were well-maintained, and the majority of the people who used this road for their morning commute were already at work. Besides, Sam knew all of the cops in a fifty-mile radius by their first name; more than a few of their kids took riding lessons at the ranch. If they wanted to pull him over for speeding, that was their choice. Until they did, Sam would get from 'Point A' to 'Point B' as quickly as was possible without endangering himself or anyone else; it was that simple.

Thunder Ridge Ranch was situated on the west side of Highway 70, so the faces of the buildings were bathed in brilliant morning sunlight when Sam pulled into the gravel driveway. The ranch-style house and attached garage, both adorned with stone veneer siding, rested to the left of the wide driveway. To the right of the drive, a handful of horses grazed in a two-hundred by four-hundred foot paddock surrounded by a freshly-painted, white board fence. At the west end of the enclosure, the original two-story, wooden stable—also freshly painted—shone like a jewel in the August sunlight. The stable, built in the traditional style of barns of that era, was oblong with a shingled gambrel roof. The short end faced the house; it contained a set of large double-doors with a window at each side. Eight Dutch doors graced the long wall of the building that faced the paddock, their top halves open wide to the morning air.

While the sections of the stable that faced the house and the road appeared much the same as when the structure was first built, the west side of the building had been extended a full two-hundred feet. The added area housed additional horse stalls, a tack room, a feed room, and a small indoor riding arena. West of the house, on the opposite side of the driveway from the stable, a white, thirty by fifty foot pole building served as a machine shed and an additional place to pile hay in the winter. Farther down the driveway were an outdoor riding ring and more pasture areas that extended for another two hundred and forty acres, and ended where the alfalfa and corn fields began.

When it was built in the late 1800's, the owners had never envisioned the showcase the ranch would someday become. It had been built to be functional, not beautiful.

Miriam had changed all that when she'd purchased the property in 1988. In addition to giving the ranch a facelift by simply completing all of the maintenance that had been neglected for so many years—replacing rotted boards, painting the structures, and re-roofing the barn—Miriam had designed and added a unique water garden on the east side of the house, in full view of any motorists who passed by. She'd started by constructing a four-foot deep pond, a full twenty by thirty feet. A stone walkway encircled the pond, and a collection of perennial and annual flowers adorned beds along the path. Three large koi—Adam, Fritz and Bub—lived in the pond and readily accepted food pellets from anyone who offered. A bench at the north end of the pond, equipped with a frequently replenished, moisture-proof container of koi food, enticed people to sit and feed the pond's inhabitants. In essence, the entire garden served as a small piece of heaven for those who visited or worked at the ranch.

The most eye-catching fixture in the water garden, though, was not the flowers that changed with each season, or the large koi. It was the unique pairing of a windmill and waterwheel. Miriam had found and purchased an antique metal windmill that had been rusting in a local farmer's field. She'd dismantled the fifty-foot structure and restored it to a fully operational state, then erected it between the house and the road. When the wind wheel, a flattened-circle comprised of fifteen metal fins fastened to the top of the structure, caught the wind, a series of gears and a pumping rod drew water from the pond. The water traveled up a pipe and exited a spout located twelve feet up. The spout directed the flow of water into the top of a water wheel—not unlike the kind that used water from streams or rivers of early America to power the massive wheels that ground corn in the gristmills. At the Thunder Ridge Ranch, its task was simpler; the waterwheel caught the water, turned beneath the weight of the load, and re-deposited the sparkling liquid—now rich with oxygen—back into the pond. The windmill had been restored with such precision that even the slightest breeze set the wheel into motion, and passing motorists on the highway often stopped to admire and photograph the cascading water.

The air was dead calm and the windmill motionless when Sam pulled in the drive. He parked the Toyota in front of the garage, but he didn't enter the house. Instead, he turned and crossed the gravel strip to the stable. He grabbed the handle and the right-hand door swung outward on well-oiled hinges. Sam stepped inside and pulled the door closed behind him.

The inside of the stable smelled of timothy hay, horses and sweet molasses. The stagnant air was warm, but not uncomfortably so. The heat would build throughout the day, though, and Sam made a mental note to come out and prop the double doors open once the sun went down. The stable was equipped with sixteen stalls, eight on the right whose Dutch doors opened onto the padlock that faced the road, and eight on the left that did not have immediate access to the outdoors. Horses held in these stalls had to be led out to the pasture by hand, and released once there. On this particular morning, all of the stalls were empty except one. Jinx stood in the last stall on the left, his head draped over the side. He saw Sam enter and nickered softly.

Sam crossed to the old horse and rubbed him gently behind one ear. "How you doing this morning?" he asked. The horse leaned into Sam's touch, his eyes half-closed. Sam allowed his eyes to wander over the animal's frame. The gelding had lost considerable weight over the last several months. Examinations by two local veterinarians had proved inconclusive. They'd checked his molars to make sure he was able to chew his feed properly. They'd listened to his stomach for unusual digestive sounds, checked his heart and lungs, dewormed him as a precautionary measure, and checked his feet and legs for founder. Neither had been able to suggest a treatment plan because neither had been able to pinpoint the problem. Sam had taken to keeping the animal indoors to limit his activity, and he was giving him an extra measure of feed laced with additional oats and molasses. Despite three weeks of this 'treatment', there had been no improvement, and Sam feared what neither vet had wanted to say out loud. The horse was failing due to simple old age or cancer, neither of which was treatable—both of which were fatal.

Sam's stomach knotted as he stroked the animal's neck. He hated this, not only because he never liked to see an animal suffer, but because he seemed helpless to do anything about it. When life gave him a problem, he dealt with it. If it was fixable, he fixed it. If it wasn't, he simply let it go and moved on. He'd outgrown that segment of his life when he struggled to control everything and everyone that came his way. Gratefully, he had learned that control over external factors in his life was impossible. That did not mean that he simply tossed his hands in the air whenever a problem presented itself, and it certainly didn't mean that he just walked away. Far from it. He was the first to roll up his sleeves and work at finding a solution. The difference was, he'd gotten better at identifying what could—and by extension, what couldn't—be fixed. The problem before him now, Jinx's failing health, was rapidly slipping into the 'could not be fixed' category, and that caused the knot in his stomach to tighten. He needed to decide exactly how long he would wait to see improvement before he gave up hope, and how long he would put off doing what would then need to be done. He patted the horse's neck a final time and headed for the house. The day was just beginning and the ranch would not run itself.

Chapter Nine

"It's good to see the sun for another day; they should get that eighty acres of hay off this afternoon."

Sam was seated at the island. A stack of bills were spread out before him and he paused with a pen poised over the checkbook at the sound of Bud's voice. The hired man stood in the doorway between the mudroom and the kitchen. He was dressed in faded jeans, cowboy boots, and a worn white cotton shirt. He'd removed his cowboy hat upon entering, and he now held it at waist-level in front of him, curling its rim as he spoke.

"If we get a decent third crop, the mow will be full."

"That's good," Sam replied and turned his attention back to the waiting bills. "Then we'll start piling it in the shed. If we have another winter like the last one, we're going to need every bale we can get." He signed a check, tore it from the checkbook and laid it with the corresponding bill.

Bud, a tall, weathered man, took one step into the room. His hair was long, gray, and neatly drawn back in its customary ponytail. His narrow face and high cheekbones were covered with deeply-etched lines, and his eyes were a charcoal brown that seemed to change to black when the man was angered, drunk, or both. Luckily for everyone around him, that didn't happen very often. The man was sixty-eight years old—or seventy-eight—no one knew for sure and Bud wasn't saying. He didn't have a social security number, or at least none that Sam was aware of. Sam had paid the man in cash for as long as he could remember. The hired hand had come with the ranch when Miriam purchased it, and she had kept him on. He was a good worker, didn't cause any trouble, and had a special way with the horses. Rumor had it that he was a descendant of the Potawatomi tribe that had called northern Wisconsin home for centuries before the white man arrived. Bud neither confirmed nor denied the rumor. He stayed in a small furnished room above the stable, minded his own business, did his work, and was more than capable of taking over the ranch if Sam had to be away for any length of time. Still, the man had never asked for a raise, larger living quarters, or even a title to go along with his position. Sam had once asked him why, and the old man had replied that he had enough money to live on, liked being close to the horses, and thought titles were horse shit, plain and simple. Sam remembered chuckling at the reply, and then giving Bud a raise anyway.

"There are only two weeks left in the new trainer's trial period," Bud stated.

"Sounds about right," Sam agreed and retrieved the next bill from the top of the pile.

"She is good with the horses." Bud's voice held no inflection, but Sam looked up at the man, sensing something that wasn't being said.

"But?" Sam prompted.

"I do not like her."

"I see," Sam said. He laid down the bill and the pen he'd been holding and gave Bud his undivided attention. "Anything you care to share?"

Bud shrugged. "I do not like the woman."

"But she's good with the horses," Sam countered.

"Yes."

Sam looked away and ran his hand through his short hair. Turning his gaze back to Bud, he said, "What is it about Cassandra that you don't like?"

Bud shrugged again. "Sometimes, in the summer, the sky is very blue and the air is calm; still, you can sense that a bad storm is coming."

Sam tried to make the connection, but the pieces of the conversation refused to fit together. "Agreed," Sam said, "but what does that have to do with our new trainer?"

"That is how I feel when she is around."

Sam was speechless. This made no sense at all. Sam had always prided himself on being logical. He believed that, if a person thought about a problem or situation long enough and carefully enough, they could usually figure it out. He had also long ago discovered, though, that women were an exception to this rule. He'd spent countless hours thinking about Cindy and Beth, and he was no closer to understanding them now than he was years ago. And, Cassandra *was* a woman. But, if she had been hired to train horses, and if the horses were getting trained, what was all of this crap about storms?

"I knew you would not understand," Bud said, "so I did not want to mention it."

"But you have mentioned it."

"Yes."

"Why?" Sam asked.

"I am hoping you do not offer her the fulltime position you promised."

Sam stood up and walked away from the island. He crossed to the frig and took out a beer. He held it at arm's length, offering it to the hired hand, who shook his head. Formalities completed, Sam twisted the top off and took a long drink, all the while studying Bud. He swallowed and said, "And what reason would you suggest I give her for going back on my word?"

"What reason does the storm cloud give for blocking the sun? It needs no reason; it simply is."

"Well, I'm sure she'll understand completely if I tell her that," Sam said. He took another quick drink and returned to the stack of bills. He sat back down at the island, set the beer to one side, and picked up the pen. With that done, he said, "I appreciate your candor, Bud, I really do. But, if we hired her to do a job—and if the job is being done—I don't see what the problem is."

"It is your call, Boss. I only wanted you to know."

"Yes," Sam agreed. "Well, now I know." There was a moment of silence during which Bud made no attempt to leave. "Is there anything else?" Sam asked, once again looking up from his paperwork.

"Jinx is no better," Bud stated, his voice devoid of emotion.

"No," Sam agreed. "He doesn't seem to be any better."

"Miriam would not want to see him this way."

"Well, Miriam isn't here anymore." This wasn't going at all well. There was an edge to Sam's voice that he immediately regretted. He and Bud had always hit it off, and Sam was surprised at his level of irritation with the man. He laid down the pen, picked up the beer and took another drink.

"Is the coffee still hot?" Bud asked, pointing to where the coffee-maker rested on the counter.

"Should be," Sam replied.

When Bud did not leave his spot at the doorway, Sam got up, fetched a mug from the mug tree that sat next to the coffee-maker, and filled it. He walked it over to the hired hand. Bud accepted it with a steady hand, took a drink, and scowled. "You make this?" he asked.

"You see anyone else around here?"

"There are directions on the back of the package," Bud stated. "Perhaps you should try reading them."

"Complete waste of time," Sam replied. "They involve measuring, and it's a whole lot quicker and easier to just pour some in."

Bud took another sip and his scowl deepened. Sam shook his head. "Relax old man—if it hasn't killed you yet, it's not going to. Besides, at your age I should think you've survived a lot worse."

"Had typhoid once."

"See? I told you; you're tough."

Bud took another sip of coffee before crossing to the sink and dumping it out. "Sorry boss, I'd prefer the typhoid."

"Well, if you're through insulting my coffee," Sam said returning to his task of paying bills, "perhaps you could get back to supervising that haying crew." Bud crossed back to the door, facing out, but he didn't leave. When a full minute had passed and the man's back was still framed in the doorway, Sam looked up. "Is there anything else?"

Bud rolled the brim of his hat into a tight coil, but didn't answer at first. He stood gazing into the mudroom as though something in the entryway demanded the old man's undivided attention, but there was nothing there. When he finally spoke, his voice was low, almost indiscernible, but Sam made out the words and a chill traveled up his spine. Bud turned back into the room, but he stood with his gaze lowered; he wouldn't meet Sam's eyes. "I saw Miriam last night," the old man whispered.

"You what?" Sam's voice remained low, but was cold as steel. He almost asked what the old man had been drinking at the time, but thought better of it. Bud had been on the wagon for eight years and counting; he didn't deserve a remark like that. "What are you talking about, Bud?" Sam demanded.

"She was in the stable when I came down to check on Jinx."

"Bud, Miriam is dead. You were there when we buried her."

"Yes, Boss, I was there."

"Then what are you saying? Do you think it was someone else driving her car when the accident happened, and Miriam . . . Miriam has been—what, hiding all these years and came back to check on a sick horse?"

"No, Boss. I know it was Miriam in that casket. I felt her spirit beside me when we lowered it into the ground."

The chill swelled into goose bumps and a trickle of sweat crept down Sam's spine. He'd known Bud for a good many years. The man was as level-headed as any man Sam had ever known. He never exaggerated, never lied, and never allowed his imagination to run away from him.

Having this unshakable impression of the hired hand made what Bud was saying all the more unbelievable.

"Bud," Sam began, but the old man cut him off.

"I know what you're thinking, Boss. I didn't believe it either. Not at first. I thought I must have been seeing things. I thought maybe I only *wanted* to see her standing by Jinx's stall."

"But?" Sam coaxed the old man.

At last, Bud looked up. The color had drained from the old man's face, and the lines in his skin appeared deeper, harder than they'd been earlier. "But then I saw Jinx. He was looking right at her, Boss. She reached out to him and he stretched his neck over the stall door until her hand was resting on his muzzle." The old man paused and swallowed hard. "There was nothing else outside that stall, Boss, no reason for the horse to do what he did." After a short pause, he added, "She was there, Boss. I know it as sure as we're standing here."

"For the sake of argument, let's say you did see something—"

"Not 'something', Boss; it was Miriam."

Sam took a deep breath and let it out. "Okay, let's say you saw Miriam, what does it mean?"

Bud shrugged. "I've been thinking about that all day. I finally decided to tell you so you could figure it out."

"Me?" Sam said, surprise evident in his voice. "Spirits and ghosts aren't my cup of tea, Bud. Dead is dead. There's no way Miriam was in the stable last night. I don't know what you saw; you might have been sleep-walking for all I know. I'd buy that a hell of a lot quicker than believing Miriam paid that horse a visit."

"Maybe," Bud began, hesitated, and began again, "maybe she knows Jinx is dying."

"And what, she came back to comfort him? Save him? Escort him over to the other side?" Sam ran both hands through his hair and shook his head firmly. He looked over at Bud, his face set. "Jinx is a horse, Bud, a dumb animal. I'm as fond of him as you are, but the fact remains that he's an old horse that we're probably going to have to put down in the next few weeks. We'll do it, and we'll bring out the backhoe and bury him—just like we've done with countless horses before him, and that will be that."

Bud's eyes narrowed as he studied Sam, and an anger flickered in their depths. When the hired hand spoke again, though, his voice was even and controlled. "You are wrong, Boss. You are wrong about the new trainer, and you are wrong about this. There is more to this life than what you see, my friend. Miriam was in the stable last night; I saw her and Jinx saw her. There is a spirit in every living creature. You can believe that I only saw Miriam because I wanted to see her—maybe even *hoped* to see her—but Jinx could not have wished to see her, or hoped she'd appear. You are right; he is just an old horse. So tell me, Sam, how did he imagine Miriam's outstretched hand—and how did he see something that wasn't there?"

The old man did not wait for any reply Sam might have made. He turned and walked out, leaving a silence that filled the room like an unseen and untouchable presence that waited for Sam to exhale so that it could steal his breath away.

Chapter Ten

The weather remained fair that day; in fact, no showers made their way to the Thunder Ridge Ranch for a full six days, but it seemed to Sam that Bud had been right—a storm was building none the less. Bud's claim to have seen Miriam, although not shared with anyone other than Sam, felt like a heavy, invisible cloud that covered the entire ranch. Colors appeared faded, sounds were muted, and the hands of the clock crept along their path—as though they were hesitant to advance for fear of what the next minute might bring. Sam did his best to shrug it off, but the feeling persisted.

On the bright side, over the next few days Cassandra made remarkable progress with the mustang gelding one of their clients had adopted through the Bureau of Land Management. Following his conversation with Bud, Sam had made a mental note to talk to the trainer at length, but he kept putting it off. In addition to the good news concerning the mustang, Jinx also rallied. His appetite improved and he showed a genuine interest in what was happening around him. Bud started taking the gelding for extended walks, and turning him loose in the paddock for an hour each afternoon. The old horse would circle the enclosure repeatedly, as though searching for something or someone, before he'd finally stand at the northeast corner, drape his head over the fence, and watch the water wheel rotate in the sunlight.

With second crop hay baled and safely stowed away in the stable's loft, no other chores were pressing. Taking advantage of the down time, Sam began putting in more hours at the Copperhead. The fall wedding schedule was already kicking in, and there was food to order and staff to schedule to cover the extra demands. He was grateful for the distraction of the increased paperwork that needed to be completed, but his world remained a little off plumb.

The feeling was not entirely foreign. There had been two other times in his life that Sam had felt this way; neither one, however, had involved anyone seeing a departed spirit return to visit a horse. No, the initial two were more traditional in the fact that they involved a relationship with a woman. No one needed to remind him that neither one had turned out well. The first time he'd felt the disconnect was when his ten-year marriage to Cindy was falling apart; the second was more recent—it was when Beth had simply taken off, without a word, for parts unknown. Sam had analyzed both events at length, trying to figure out if there had been warning signs he should have heeded, or something different he should have done to prevent either one from happening. His conclusions were muddled at best.

Aside from the pain they had caused—and the fact that a woman had played a part in each of them—the two experiences had little in common. He'd obsessed over the first event, his failed marriage, until he'd rationalized it to death. It was a common tale. He and Cindy had met in high school and fell madly in love. But then, what do teenagers really know about love? In his case, it hadn't been nearly enough. When Cindy announced that she was pregnant—big surprise—there'd been a hurried version of the infamous shotgun wedding. Three months later, she'd miscarried and they'd never conceived again. The sense of loss for the child he'd never met was real enough, but over time it morphed into a longing for the life he'd lost when, as mere children themselves, he and Cindy had committed themselves to trying to make it in a grownup world. They'd never had a chance. Adding to the extent of the tragedy was the fact that they spent ten years trying to prove the world wrong. One day, Sam came home from his job at a local lumber company to find the house empty. There was no warning, no note, and no Cindy. It felt as though ten years of his life had been ripped away, leaving him with nothing to show for any of it.

A million emotions had raced through him as he stood in that silent house—shock, frustration, disbelief—but the strongest had been anger in its purest form. The realization that Cindy had simply tossed away a decade of life—*their* life—together infuriated him. Who did she think she was? How could she simply walk out without a word, without giving them a chance to work it out? Who the hell gave her the right to say that it was over?

For months—some would say an eternity—after that, Sam took everything in life head-on and with teeth bared. He hated the world and everything in it. He closed down the local tavern five nights a week, but that was only because it wasn't open on Sunday or Monday. He started fights with his friends or total strangers over random comments, or a sideways glance he mistook as being aimed at him. Sober, drunk, right, wrong—it didn't matter to him. If the other man was willing—and even if he wasn't—Sam would be on him in an instant, fists cocked, his eyes sparking hatred. Eventually, Mr. Jackson at the lumber yard had to let him go; on most mornings, Sam punched in with a cap pulled low over his eyes and whiskey on his breath. No one in the yard felt safe working with him, and Mr. Jackson was not comfortable sending him out to any of the construction sites. Sam's life as he had known it was over, and—as he saw it— it was all Cindy's fault.

At some point, Sam came to his senses enough to pull up stakes, sell the house, pack up his belongings, and move from southern to northern Wisconsin. It wasn't a drastic move; most parts of the state were pretty much the same. It was still cold for too many months out of the year, there were still far too many bugs when it finally did warm up, and most people would have still given Sam the shirt off of their back if he'd asked for it. In fact, if he hadn't had to memorize a different zip code, and remembered to use it, Sam wouldn't have really known that his past was now three-hundred miles behind him. He stopped drinking, answered a 'Help Wanted' ad at the Copperhead, and the rest—as they say—is history.

For a while, no one knew about Sam's past except him. He worked hard as a bartender (or a bouncer when one was needed), kept his nose clean, and established a rapport with Ken Sikes, the owner. A short two years later, Sam was overseeing most aspects of the supper club. When Sikes saw how competently Sam managed the place, he decided that twenty-five years running the joint was long enough for his old bones; it was time to retire. Sam, who recognized a golden opportunity when one presented itself, used the proceeds from the sale of his house as a down payment and purchased the supper club on a land contract. The angry, bitter years were officially behind him; he had moved on.

Miriam came to work at the Copperhead six months after Sam purchased it. Her twinkling blue eyes and Irish smile won Sam over the instant she walked in, but he'd tried his best to hide it. Experience would soon assure him that no one—male or female—hid anything from this woman. She read people the way psychics read tarot cards, only with a mind-boggling level of accuracy.

She'd walked in wearing skin-tight faded jeans and a slightly less-faded denim cowboy shirt over a white, lace-trimmed top. Her red hair, obviously colored but looking good on her, was drawn back into a bun that was held in place by a wooden skewer driven through two holes in a tooled piece of leather. Sam tried to calculate her age, but the needle on his mental 'age scale' vacillated between forty and sixty, swaying back and forth with an absolute certain uncertainty. She tossed a folded newspaper onto the bar and smiled at Sam. It was a lop-sided smile that started on the left side of her face and gradually, almost seductively, spread over to the right. "The ad says you're looking for a bartender."

"You applying?" Sam asked, his poker face securely in place.

Miriam's smile intensified and she winked at him. "Maybe I should talk to your father; you can't possibly be old enough to be running this joint."

Sam's steadfast poker face crumbled and he smiled in spite of himself. He extended his hand and she accepted it without any hesitation. "I'm Sam," he said.

"Miriam," was her reply, and so the friendship began.

"Can you mix drinks from memory?" Sam began the interview.

She released his hand but held his eyes for a wee bit longer, then she moved around to join him on the proprietor side of the bar. "What's your pleasure?"

Sam hadn't touched a drop of alcohol since he'd arrived in Eagle River, but he made an exception that night . . . several exceptions in fact. He started out having her make a brandy old fashioned sweet, then he took her through concocting a Tom Collins and a few other standard drinks that people had a tendency to order at the wedding receptions that were commonplace at the Copperhead. Eventually he had her mixing Long Island Ice Teas for both of them. By that time, the interview had been over for the better part of an hour and the job was hers. Over the months to come, Sam would discover that what he had suspected that night was true; Miriam was level-headed, mischievous, and young at heart. She also had an excellent memory, was capable of shooting the shit with the best of them, and never took anything to heart that wasn't constructive and good. In short, she was the perfect employee, and an even better friend.

"You ready to talk about it yet?"

It was early on a Sunday afternoon. The Copperhead had been the venue for a wedding reception the previous day, but for the most part the mess had been cleaned up. The carpet was vacuumed, the toilet paper spools were refilled, and the liqueur shelves were restocked. Miriam was wiping down the bar for the third time, watching Sam as he rifled through a stack of order forms at the far end of the bar when she voiced the question.

"Talk about what?" he asked in return without looking up.

"That woman who broke your heart," she said, moving the rag back and forth across the bar, working her way to Sam.

"I don't know what you're talking about, Miriam," he replied. The silence grew awkward, so he asked, "Was that Cheryl that left early last night?"

"Yup, claimed she had the flu."

"She's on the schedule for today, too, isn't she?"

"Yup," Miriam made two more swipes across the bar.

"Maybe you should call Trish—"

"Already taken care of, boss. She'll be here at three to fill in."

Sam shook his head. "I don't know why I even bother to worry about the staff schedule; you've always got it covered."

"I had a few minutes to kill, that's all. It's no big deal. Besides, I get downright dangerous when I'm bored, so I made a few calls."

"Thanks, I appreciate it," Sam said, switching his attention to the next page down in the stack.

"Now, about that woman." Miriam had wiped the entire length of the bar and was now directly in front of Sam. She rested her elbows on the clean surface, laced her fingers together and rested her chin on her knuckles. "Who was she, your childhood sweetheart?"

Sam winced. The old wound, although completely healed over, had left a scar that was painful when probed. Miriam's remark was a sharp fingernail pressing into the memory. Sam spoke without looking up, "I assure you, Miriam, my heart is completely intact."

"Then look at me and say that," Miriam challenged him.

Sam ignored the remark and continued to enter figures on the form before him, but Miriam's gaze was a relentless magnet drawing his eyes up and toward her. When the discomfort became more than he could bear, he laid the pencil down and lifted his head. Her sapphire-blue eyes bore through him and held him in place; there was no hope of turning away. When he finally spoke, his voice was subdued and low.

"Let it go, Miriam. It's none of your concern."

Her gaze softened, by the tiniest degree, and she nodded so slightly that it was almost imperceptible. "She from around here?"

"No, she's not. And, before you ask, I don't know where she is now, and it doesn't matter."

"Well, that explains it," Miriam stated matter-of-factly.

"That explains *what*?"

"You . . . this place."

"And what, exactly, is that supposed to mean?"

Miriam smirked and straightened up. She shook out the damp bar rag and draped it over the faucet beneath the bar to dry. "You're here seven days a week—alone, I've never known you to go out on a date, you don't talk about your past, you don't discuss any plans for the future—"

"Maybe I'm just private; I like to keep things to myself," Sam countered, cutting her off.

"You're a virile, thirty-two year old man who doesn't appear to be dating anyone. In fact, no one who works here has ever even *seen* you with a woman."

"What do you gals do, stand around on break and discuss my love life?" Sam's voice edged up a notch.

"We'd sure like to, but we're short on material," Miriam's tone edged up an equal measure. She suddenly snapped her mouth shut and studied him, searching for a tell. "You're not gay, are you?"

"No," Sam exploded, rising off of his stool, "I'm not gay. I can't believe you even asked me that!"

"Then what?" Miriam persisted. "Why no dates, why no woman? This place," she said, stretching her arms out to either side, "is your whole life. But you can't live that way; no man can live that way."

"I can live any way I choose," Sam said, the anger ebbing out of his voice. "This discussion is over, and I'd thank you to never bring it up again."

"She's not worth it; no woman is worth it," Miriam said. "You've got to let her go."

"I have. That's why I'm here. Discussion over."

Sam had picked up his stack of papers and gone to the back office then, closing the door securely behind him. Miriam had watched him go, shaking her head slowly. She had grabbed the damp rag and a few stray bar towels that had been left behind the bar and carried them to the laundry room at the back of the supper club. She'd passed the closed office door and paused. When she spoke, it had been slightly more than a whisper. "If'n you let her go, my friend, then why are you still so sad?"

Chapter Eleven

Several months later, the Copperhead was enjoying yet another growth spurt. The economy was good; people were dining out more often, and an increasing number of couples were tying the knot. By then, Miriam had assumed the position of head bartender, but Sam still slipped behind the bar and pitched in from time to time. He liked to keep the workload manageable for Miriam and her staff, but he also enjoyed bantering with the guests who came in to eat on a busy Friday night, or were attending a Saturday wedding. Although his views on marriage had not improved with time, he bit his tongue with the wedding parties and kept his skeptical remarks to himself. In short, he'd buy the bride and groom a drink and toast them, but refrained from giving them the contact info of a local divorce attorney—just in case.

It was about this time that a woman entered the bar on a Saturday morning with a copy of the Copperhead's 'Help Wanted' ad in her hand. Her name was Beth Simons. She was a 5'3", thirty-eight year old, dishwater blond with compassionate, blue eyes and a nonjudgmental smile. Sam had to be honest; he had been hoping to find someone younger to fill the opening—someone with real sex-appeal to serve as a draw for his male clientele—but he'd warmed to Beth during the interview, and had left the decision to hire her (or not) to Miriam. As the bar clock passed noon and quickly travelled on to 2 P.M., it was evident that the trio at the bar—Sam, Miriam, and Beth—were developing a rapport. Although each heralded from different parts of the state—or country, as was Miriam's case—there was a level of comfort between them that belied their being strangers. They laughed, and exchanged superficial historical details, and became friends. No, it was not an in-depth pouring out of the heart and soul—that level of comfort and trust was still several months down the road—but it was a genuine connection that felt too deep to be only two hours old.

"You ever been married?" Miriam asked the younger woman.

Beth had been chuckling over a previous comment when the question was posed. She'd stopped laughing and the sparkle in her eyes slipped away. "No," was all she'd said, then, "You?"

"Yes, Ma'am. For thirty-two years, and to the most wonderful man in the world, thank you very much." Miriam caught the look of skepticism on Sam and Beth's faces. "What, you think I couldn't keep a man for that long?"

Sam shook his head with conviction, "No, that's not what we were thinking." Later, he would ponder the fact that he had answered for both Beth and himself, but at the moment it seemed perfectly natural.

"Then what?" Miriam had pressed him. By then, it was almost 3 P.M. They had stopped drinking the sample highballs that Beth had been making to prove her bartending abilities and had switched to drinking coffee forty-five minutes earlier, but their brains had not yet fully embraced the switch. Miriam had looked from Sam to Beth and back again, an exaggerated pout plastered on her face.

"It's just that," Beth had said as she winked at Sam for no good reason that would come to mind, either now or later, "where is he?" She'd spread her arms wide to accentuate the empty bar, and Sam had dropped his gaze to hide his smile.

"In Beaufort, South Carolina, if you must know," Miriam scolded, but her eyes did not share her words' sharp edge.

"What in the world is he doing in Beaufort, South Carolina?" Beth asked, trying not to giggle and thinking that this was the strangest job interview she'd ever participated in.

"He's filling a plot in the Beaufort National Cemetery, next to his mama, if you must know."

Both Sam and Beth froze, their smiles instantly gone. They exchanged a quick glance and Sam cleared his throat.

"Why didn't you ever tell me this; why wait till now?"

"You never asked; she did," Miriam said with a quick nod toward Beth. "I'd have told you if'n you'd asked."

"I'm so sorry—" Beth began, but Miriam cut her off.

"For what? You didn't kill him; the cancer did that all on its own. And the two of you can just wipe those pitiful looks right off of your faces," she scolded with more conviction. "That's why I don't generally tell people about Bobby; I hate those looks of pity I get. We had thirty-two years. Do you know how long that is?"

Beth and Sam exchanged another quick look, but neither answered her.

"It's an entire lifetime, that's how long it is. Bobby and I shared more love than either of you will ever know, and I ain't gonna be sorry about that. After all this time, he still makes me smile—and that about says it all, I reckon."

"I'm sorry," Beth said softly. "We didn't know."

"Of course you didn't. And if'n I'd wanted you to know, I'd have told you earlier, but I knew that these two sour-pusses," she said, pointing at both of them, "was exactly what I'd get. I made the most of it; didn't have much choice. A few months after he died, I was paging through a real estate brochure and saw the most beautiful horse ranch to ever grace God's good earth. So, I took the insurance money from Bobby's employer's plan, packed up a few things, drove a U-Haul truck to Wisconsin, and signed the papers on the Thunder Ridge Ranch. I've been here ever since. Now," Miriam turned to Sam and deftly changed the subject. "Are we hiring this here lady or not?"

Sam shrugged, but the hint of a smile returned to his face. "You're in charge of the hiring—"

"And the firing, don't forget that part," Miriam interjected, winking at Beth. "That's sometimes the funnest part."

"Funnest?" Sam asked.

"You making fun of me again, Sam?"

"You're in Wisconsin now, Miriam, we don't say 'funnest'. For Christ's sake—"

The smile was instantly gone from Miriam's face. "Don't you ever use the Lord's name in vain around me, young man. Everything in this sometimes rotten world is for His sake, but not in the way you meant it."

"I . . . I," Sam stuttered.

Miriam, having never seen her friend at a loss for words before, softened. "It's alright; I know you meant it in fun. But a little respect is not too much to ask, is it?" When Sam failed to answer, she remarked softly. "Alright then." Miriam turned to Beth, and the older woman's radiant smile was back in full. "Let's give you the nickel tour and introduce you to some of the other staff. You'll like them; I guarantee it. Either Sam or I hand-picked them all, and you'll never meet a finer bunch of people."

Beth, still struggling to wrap her mind around the sudden change their conversation had taken, forced a smile and nodded, "Sounds like fun."

The two women exited from behind the bar and made their way toward the kitchen. The Copperhead would not start serving for another ninety minutes, but some of the staff came in early and would have already begun prepping the food. Sam had no doubt that Miriam would acquaint Beth with whomever was present, and would introduce the others as they arrived. He watched them leave, his emotions roiling. The pleasure of the conversation they'd shared over the course of two and a half hours had ground to a halt at the news of Miriam's loss. Then, just as quickly, the compassion he'd felt for Miriam had been stopped cold when she'd chastised him for swearing. Sam did not stand for that type of rebuke from anyone. The fact that Miriam was a woman—and a friend—did not make it any easier. When had she become so religious? Was this something new, or had he simply overlooked it? But then, what was he expecting . . . did he think that people with a strong faith walked around wearing crucifixes around their necks—or got crosses tattooed on their foreheads? Did they interject "Hey, I've found God" into every conversation? No, he doubted it.

He rose from his spot at the bar and circled around to where the women had been mixing drinks. He washed his glass and set it on the shelf to drip-dry. The caffeine was rapidly getting the upper hand on the drinks he'd consumed earlier and he decided to retreat to the back office to file some paperwork before the evening rush began. As he stepped out from behind the bar, he glanced toward the kitchen and shook his head. Women, just when you think you have them all figured out, they change on a dime and leave you wondering what the hell just happened. He hesitated; was it alright to say 'hell'? He imagined it was. Why wouldn't it be? Perhaps he should ask Miriam when he got the chance. Suddenly annoyed, he stomped off toward the office. To hell with that! He'd say whatever he damn-well pleased, whenever he damn-well pleased—and if Miriam didn't like it that was just too bad. Of course, he had another option; he could just do it whenever she wasn't around.

Chapter Twelve

Life carried the next four years away without a trace. Miriam and Beth became inseparable in the first week, and remained that way till the end. On their days off, Miriam took Beth out to the Thunder Ridge Ranch. There, they saddled up two of the fastest horses on the spread and raced the hours away. Miriam rode Jinx, a chestnut gelding with a flaxen mane and tale, and Beth would ride whatever horse still needed a workout on that particular day. At the Copperhead, at least once every other week, Miriam would point out yet another unwed man to Beth and urge the younger woman to make her move. Beth would refuse on the grounds that, even though she was still young enough to fantasize about it, she was old enough to know better. Miriam always bought that excuse, and Beth gave her no reason to believe that she hadn't been completely honest. Besides, it was true enough—in the beginning. But time has a way of changing everything it touches, and the trio of friends at the Copperhead was no exception.

As the months passed, Beth began to feel herself being drawn to Sam on a level that had nothing to do with work, or even being friends. Her heart would begin to beat faster whenever he crossed her mind, and when she occupied the same room as he did, all was right with the world. It was never a relationship, not really, because relationships take two people and Sam was—well—the same old Sam. If he noticed that she spent far too much time gazing at him, or that she smiled too readily at his every remark, he didn't let it show. Beth found that odd in a sad sort of way. Sam could read the moods of the Copperhead's clientele without fail, and knew what they were feeling without being told. But when it came to Beth—or any woman for that matter— Sam did not seem to have a clue. It occurred to Beth that the man moved through life with emotional blinders on, and they kept him from seeing anything that might impact his heart.

"So," Miriam asked, quickly brushing past Beth to set a Whiskey Old-Fashioned sweet on the bar, snatch up several dollars, and rush off toward the till, "when did it happen?"

The June wedding had topped off at three-hundred and fifty guests and, as far as Miriam and Beth could tell, every single one of them preferred a mixed drink to the free beer that had been bought and paid for by the bride's family. The two women stationed behind the bar had been serving the clamoring crowd that remained bellied-up to the fixture for nearly four hours in perfect synchronization. The music from the band in the large hall swelled each time the door would open, then faded away as the door swung closed. Each time it happened, Beth and Miriam knew that another thirsty guest was worming his or her way up to the bar, a tumbler with the remnants of melted ice in hand, anxious to be served. Beth slapped the change she'd made for a fifty dollar bill on the bar by its rightful owner and snatched up the next empty glass. As she reached the mixing station, she replied, "When did *what* happen? Did I miss something?"

Miriam finished counting change at the till and slammed the drawer closed. She brushed past Beth and winked conspiratorially. "When did he get to you?"

Still focusing on the crowd and the empty glass waiting in her hand, Beth's brow furrowed in genuine confusion, but not for long. The realization that Miriam had figured it out stunned Beth. She'd been so careful to keep her feelings safely locked away; how had the woman known? Too late, Beth realized that her lack of a quick response was tantamount to a confession. She looked over at Miriam, who was giving her that endearing lop-sided grin. Before Beth could think of a reply, Miriam shook her head, mouthed, 'Later,' and turned back to serve another member of the waiting crowd. Dazed, Beth stared at the glass in her hand, wondering what Miriam thought about the matter.

"Can I have my drink sometime this century?" a voice called, slightly annoyed but trying hard to sound clever.

Snapping out of her reverie, Beth brought herself back to the task at hand and reached for the brandy. The bar wouldn't close for another two hours; for Beth, it would seem like the longest two hours of her life.

At 12:14 A.M., Sam joined them behind the bar and assisted in mixing and serving the wide assortment of drinks. The crowd grew louder and increasingly more demanding as the night wore on, but at 2:03 A.M. the staff finally herded the last of the wedding guests out and locked the Copperhead's doors. When the place was empty, Sam drained the water from the sink behind the bar, draped his bar rag over the faucet, rolled his shoulders to relieve the fatigue that was settling in, and told Miriam and Beth to go home. He'd have the cleaning crew come in early to tidy up the mess; they'd done enough work for the day. Miriam kissed him on the cheek in gratitude, drew two glasses of Seven-up from the soda gun, and led Beth over to a small side table. Both women slipped off their shoes and sat with an audible sigh.

"My feet are killing me," Beth said, massaging the right one gingerly.

"Mine were, but they went numb right around midnight. That's why I dragged us over here to sit for a spell; I had to check and make sure they were still attached to my ankles before I tried driving home."

"And are they still there?" Beth teased.

"Yup, and they're going to hurt like the dickens when the feeling returns. God willing, I'll be asleep by then."

"One can always hope," Beth agreed.

Sam approached them, car keys in hand. "Haven't you two had enough of this place for one night?"

"We'll be outta here in a few minutes," Miriam assured him. "I got my keys; I'll make sure the door is locked when we go."

"You girls had a heck of a night; were the tips good?"

"I'm going to order my custom Mercedes tomorrow," Miriam said, her smile just as fresh as it had been six hours earlier.

"And you?" Sam asked Beth. "What are you going to spend yours on?"

"A much wiser investment," she replied. "I booked the Chippendale Dancers for my next birthday bash."

"Is it here?" Sam tried, but failed, to suppress a grin as he asked.

"Where else?" Beth was also grinning. "And you're tending bar that night, remember?"

"Just as long as you don't ask me to dance, you've got a deal."

"Nope, I think I've got the whole 'dance thing' covered for that night, but I can pencil you in for the staff Christmas party if you want."

Sam shook his head. "I'm outta here. You two drive home safely, got it?"

"Don't worry; we'll be fine," Miriam assured him.

"Who's worried? I just don't want to have to find two new bartenders before the Carson wedding next weekend. There's four hundred guests invited to that one."

"Anyone ever tell you that you're a real peach, Boss?" Miriam asked.

"Not that I can remember." Sam gave them a lazy, two-finger salute and headed for the door. When he was gone, Miriam turned her gaze on Beth and raised her eyebrows questioningly.

"So, you gonna tell me about it?"

"About what?" Beth countered.

"About these feelings you have for our boss," Miriam stated matter-of-factly.

"I don't know what you're talking about. Sam and I are just friends. He's friends with all the staff, you know that."

"Uh huh."

"Uh huh what?" Beth was trying to be nonchalant, but the sweating glass of Seven-up refused to sit still in her hands. She spun it between her palms as it rested on the table, and the ice clinked softly.

"Have you been out with him?" Miriam asked.

"No!" Beth exploded, a little too quickly and a little too loud.

"Why not?"

Beth shrugged. "He's never asked."

"That's the dumbest reason I've ever heard of." It sounded like Miriam was scolding, albeit gently. "You know, it's the twenty-first century; you could ask him."

"Oh no, I couldn't," Beth shook her head a little too adamantly.

"Why, what are you afraid of? Are you afraid he'll say 'no', or are you afraid he'll say 'yes'?

"I'm not afraid of anything; I'm just old-fashioned and I don't think it's the girl's place to ask, that's all."

"That's a bunch of malarkey. You're just afraid he'll say 'no'."

"And what if I am? Do you think if I was any good at this dating business I'd still be single?"

"Has it ever occurred to you that he may be having the same thoughts?"

"Sam—afraid? Never."

"Careful there, Beth. If you put someone up too high on a pedestal, it's a pretty long fall." Miriam studied Beth for a moment before continuing. "Listen, Sweetie, there's something you should know, but I don't want you to take it the wrong way. I'm not trying to discourage you, I just think—if you're going to go into this—you should do it with both eyes open. Sam is damaged goods."

"What are you talking about?" There was an equal measure of disbelief and concern in Beth's voice.

"I know what you're thinking; he doesn't look damaged. Here, in this place," she glanced around the deserted bar and a knowing smile spread over her face, "he's safe."

Beth rallied. "At our age, Miriam, I think we're all a little damaged. That doesn't mean we can't be repaired."

"I see that in you," Miriam replied.

"See what?"

"You're a 'fixer'. You see what's broken in people and you want to set it right."

"And that's a bad thing?" Beth asked.

"It can be; it all depends on two things—'why' you're trying to fix the person, and whether or not they're 'fixable'." At the look of confusion on Beth's face, Miriam pressed on. "If you want to fix the person because their 'being broke' annoys you, that's not good. For one thing, it's not up to you to fix the world; that's way too big a job for one woman."

"And the other thing?" Beth pressed her.

"Some people aren't fixable—at least, not in this lifetime."

"And you think that Sam is broken, and that he's not fixable." Beth phrased her remark as a comment, not a question, but Miriam still replied.

"I know that Sam is broken—or at least a part of him is. That doesn't mean he's a bad person; not counting Bobby, Sam is probably the most kind and loving person I've ever known. That's what makes him so endearing, and also so sad."

"I don't understand," Beth spoke softly with a childlike disbelief, as though Miriam were explaining that Santa Claus was just a myth.

"I know you don't, and I'm not saying it's hopeless. I love Sam with all my heart, although I have a hunch that it's a little different kind of love than what you're feeling for the man. Still," she took a drink of her soda and bit down on a piece of ice that slipped in with the sip. "Still, getting back to the original topic, if you're hoping he'll ask you out that may never happen."

"How can you be so sure?" Beth said, frowning. Miriam reached across the small table and grasped Beth's hands.

"I worked with Sam for eight months before you came along," the older woman explained. "In all that time, he never went on a date that I know of. He never bought a woman a drink, he never exchanged phone numbers, he never brought a woman in here, and he certainly never left with one."

"Maybe he was just too busy trying to get this place better established. It's a lot for one person to take on."

"Yes it is," Miriam agreed. "It's also a great way to hide from whatever it is that's haunting you—whatever you can't face; you just keep too busy to allow it to find you." With Beth looking on, Miriam took another drink of her soda, wishing—too late—that she'd added a hefty shot of brandy before carrying the drinks to the table. "There's someone in his past, Beth."

"We all have someone in our past, don't we?"

"Do you?"

"No but—"

Miriam waved her hand to dismiss the question. "That's not the point. Sure, we all have a past; that's what makes us who we are. We carry our scars with us, and we choose how we view them; they're either ugly battle-marks of past struggles, or they're solid proof that we survived—that the struggle didn't kill us. The key thing in either scenario, though, is that they are *scars*. Scars imply a level of healing, a progression from 'injured' to 'whole'. In Sam's case," Miriam paused and took a deep breath. "In Sam's case, the wound never closed over."

"So you're saying that there's someone in Sam's past that he hasn't gotten over."

"Yes, something like that."

"Who?" Beth asked, still disbelieving.

"I don't know. I did ask him about it once, though."

"And?" Beth prompted.

"He almost bit my head off and thanked me for 'kindly not mentioning it ever again'. Those may have even been his exact words."

"So—what? You believe that, because Sam's been hurt, he's never going to give another woman a chance?"

"It's not that simple, Beth." Miriam caught the younger woman's eyes and held them. "You can't fall in love if there's nothing inside of you to give; you know that. Until— or unless—he puts whoever she is behind him, he can't move on."

"But, if you're right, how would I get him to do that?"

"You can't. It's something he's got to do on his own."

"And if he never does, then what?"

"Then you'll have to settle for being the best friend you can be for Sam. You'll simply be there for him, if or when he needs to talk, and you'll keep your distance when he doesn't." A note of sympathy made its way into Miriam's voice and Beth resented it.

"That's it . . . that's all I can do?"

"It's more than you know, Beth, believe me. It's more than you know." Miriam released Beth's hands and sat back. She turned sideways, draped her right arm over the back of the chair and crossed her legs. She studied the younger woman for several seconds, as though she wanted to say more but was trying to decide whether or not she should. She finally looked down at her glass, gave it a half turn, and asked, "Have you ever heard of old souls?"

"Old souls? No," Beth was still mulling over Miriam's comments and was genuinely uninterested in the sudden change of topic, but she didn't want to be rude.

"Some people believe that death is not an end, that we come back again—and again—if necessary."

"You mean reincarnation; yes, I've heard about that. Who hasn't?" Beth said, half-heartedly, her mind still somewhere else.

Miriam shook her head. "No, it's more than that. Reincarnation is a pretty broad—and somewhat controversial—topic. Some people go as far as to believe that people were once animals. I saw a talk show once where they hypnotized some man and he recalled his past life as a draft horse. It was pretty questionable stuff. Even people who don't believe that we were once animals still believe that we are forced to live multiple lives over and over again until we finally 'get it right'."

"And that's not what your theory of 'old souls' is about?" Beth's interest was growing, but she remained reserved.

"Yes and no," Miriam replied. "Yes, we do have things that we must learn in our lifetime. It might be compassion that we need to appreciate, or selflessness. The journey is different for everyone."

"And the 'no' part?" Beth said.

"The concept of reincarnation focuses on an *individual's* journey; it is an "I", "me" and "my" view of life. The old soul theory is about "us"."

"Us?"

Miriam smiled, uncrossed her legs and turned to rest her arms on the table. "Do you remember the day you walked in here?"

"Of course; it wasn't *that* long ago."

"Were you scared?"

"Sure, when I first came in. It was a job interview. Everyone is scared during a job interview."

"I remember when I first walked in here, too. I was a lot like you were that day. I was in a strange place, hoping to land the job but not knowing who I'd be working for or what they'd be like."

"And?"

"And then I saw Sam and everything was alright. I wasn't afraid anymore. It felt like . . . like coming home. Do you know what I mean?" Miriam glanced at Beth for a response, but none was offered. She pressed on. "Have you ever met someone and wondered where you'd seen them before—even if you're sure you never had? Or, have you instantly befriended a stranger because it just felt so right?" Miriam waited a beat, then added, "Do you believe in love at first sight?"

"What if I did—what if I said 'yes' to all of those things—what of it?" Beth's patience was wearing thin.

"Old souls don't travel alone; they travel together."

"What are you talking about?" Beth's irritation edged up a notch.

"We don't make the journey alone; we make it with others. We are bound to them by love, and they are never far away."

Beth rolled her eyes and pushed away from the table.

Miriam pressed on. "You and I are old souls. We've travelled together before; you just don't remember."

"And I suppose you do?"

"No, not in the way you mean. It's not the type of memory we're used to. I can't tell you where we lived, or when. I can't even tell you *who* we were, or how we died."

"So," Beth interrupted, "How do you know—"

"My heart knows," Miriam stated softly. "Doesn't yours?"

Beth stared at her friend, confused. Miriam had never talked like this before. She was the level-headed matriarch of the Copperhead. She was the one everyone went to when they needed advice. She didn't deal in bullshit, or lead people on. But this . . .

"This is crazy . . . you've got to know how crazy this sounds." Beth was shaking her head almost imperceptibly.

"I thought so, too, at first, but that was a good many years ago." The older woman smiled, and Beth saw a peace on her face that had never been there before. "Bobby was an old soul, too. Finding him again in this lifetime was the greatest thing that could have happened to me. I missed him so." Miriam dabbed at the corner of her eye with the ring finger of her right hand. "I only wish he could have stayed a little longer."

"You're telling me that you and Bobby were married in a previous life, so in this life you missed him until you married him again?"

Miriam laughed and the sound soothed Beth's freshly-frayed nerves. "No, it doesn't work quite like that. The only consistent element is the love. Oh, Bobby and I may have been husband and wife back then, or we may have been sisters, or cousins, or just friends. I may have been his father, or he may have been my wife. It doesn't matter; the only thing that matters is that we made the journey together."

"So, you're telling me that we simply live over and over again, falling in love with the same people—"

"Souls," Miriam corrected.

"Falling in love with the same souls, and the cycle never ends. Is that it?"

"I didn't say that the cycle never ends—"

"And what about heaven and hell? How do they tie into all of this, or shouldn't we even worry about sin or eternal damnation?"

The smile slipped from Miriam's face. "Hell is being mortal forever, Beth. It's the suffering, the sickness, the self-doubt, the dying. Hell is being separated from the true, unconditional love that is meant for each of us, and knowing that we were the ones that screwed it up. Hell is finally realizing that our true home exists, but never being allowed to go there. Hell is being separated from our companion old souls, and knowing that they've journeyed on without us. Hell is craving their love, but never being allowed to experience it again."

Beth stared at the table for a full twenty seconds before meeting Miriam's gaze. "Even if what you say is true, what does it have to do with Sam and me?"

Miriam tilted her head to one side and her gaze softened. "Do you love him?" she asked.

Beth swallowed hard. Did she? Was it love or obsession? Her thoughts on that changed from one day to the next. It wasn't that she *needed* him; she'd never needed anyone in her life. Yet, when he was close by, she felt as if the missing piece in her life had been set in place. She felt complete in a way that she had never known before. It was stupid, pathetic even. Why should the presence of one person make such a difference—especially if they didn't even know it? Miriam had been right; Beth *had* wanted to ask Sam out, but she was too afraid—afraid he'd say 'yes' *and* afraid he'd say 'no'. If he wasn't interested, she didn't want to offend him, or make herself a fool and him uneasy. On the other hand, she longed to feel his arms around her, pulling her close. Even now her heart quickened at the thought of it. But, if she didn't ask, and he hadn't yet said 'no', that hope could remain alive—a dream uncrushed that might someday be realized. As it stood, Sam was the only element of insanity in Beth's life, and she didn't know what to do with him.

"Define 'love'", Beth finally said.

Miriam smiled and thought for a moment before asking. "If you and Sam were standing in the middle of a busy street, and a truck was bearing down on you, would you jump clear of the truck's path or shove Sam to safety?"

Beth considered the scenario and her heart hammered within her. She closed her eyes and swallowed hard. She answered her friend without looking at her. "Yes, Miriam, I love him."

"Then you have to be there for him," Miriam said in earnest. "You've got to promise me; you've got to help him through whatever comes up the pike. Will you do that?"

"If he asks—" Beth began.

"No," Miriam said firmly. "There are no conditions; either you'll be there for him or you won't. He's not going to ask; he won't know how."

"This is crazy," Beth exclaimed. "Nothing's going to happen."

"Promise me," Miriam insisted.

"What makes you think I'll know how to help if he doesn't even know how to ask?" Beth said, confused.

"You'll figure it out if you love him. You'll figure it out and you'll pull him through. That's what old souls do for one another; that's the reason why we've made it this far."

"I'm sorry, Miriam, I just don't see it," Beth shook her head. "This whole 'old soul' theory, I just don't see it."

"Give it time, Beth. Think about it. You may feel differently tomorrow—or next week."

"And if I don't, then what?" Beth asked.

A sad smile played over Miriam's lips. "Then none of this will really matter, will it?"

With that, Miriam ended the conversation. She circled around the bar and dumped out the remaining ice from her glass. Following suit, Beth retrieved her purse from where she'd stashed it behind the ice machine and left the Copperhead. She walked to her car in silence. Neither friend had bothered to say good night. It was not that they were angry, they'd simply said all that they'd needed to say for the moment. Beth felt a touch of disappointment as she got behind the wheel of her Bronco and started the engine. What she had thought would be a 'woman to woman' conversation about her feelings for Sam had morphed into a discussion about philosophy and old souls. Perhaps she was just too tired to grasp what Miriam had been trying to explain. Beth would sleep on it and hope that it made more sense in the morning. For the moment, the thought of living countless lives—both before and after this one—was just too much to consider. *Besides*, she thought with a smile, *if she had shared a past life with Sam, that wasn't the sort of thing she'd have forgotten.*

Chapter Thirteen

Four months passed. The autumn weddings, not as popular as the June nuptials but still a main element of the Copperhead's business success, were in full swing. Miriam did not bring up the topic of old souls again, and Beth had still not made her move. She hadn't asked Sam out to dinner, or even for a drink. She decided that she could live with not knowing what Sam's answer would be, so she simply never asked. Sam continued to run the Copperhead with the utmost efficiency, and avoid any life changes or commitments outside of its walls. By then, the northern Wisconsin air had taken on a familiar chill, and the waning sunlight warned of the bitter cold that awaited anyone who was foolish enough to not head south for the winter.

On October 24th, one week before Halloween, Beth was sleeping soundly and dreaming she was riding a bay horse through fallen autumn leaves. In the distance, several men on horseback were preparing for a fox hunt. They reined their spirited mounts in and Beth's horse tossed its head and whinnied, longing to join its brethren. One of the riders drew a small, round silver object from his pocket and held it out toward her. He pressed a button at the center of the sphere and a bell sounded. Again and again he pressed it, and each time the crystal sound of the bell filled the air. Beth woke to the ringing of her phone. Drunken with sleep, she reached out to pick up the receiver and nearly dropped it back onto its cradle. It was 5:47 A.M. She awkwardly brought the phone to her ear.

"Hello?"

"Is this Beth Simons?" a voice asked.

"Yes," Beth answered, struggling to sit up in her bed. She glanced at the clock on the nightstand and her stomach dropped. No one would call at this hour with good news. "What is it?"

"Can you come down to the County Memorial Hospital? There's been an accident."

Beth was instantly awake. "Who is it—who's hurt?"

"If you could just come down to the hospital, Ma'am. Someone will fill you in when you get here."

For as long as she would live, Beth would never remember driving to County Memorial early that October morning. She couldn't recall if the sun crept over the horizon in a splendor of red and orange, or if rain clouds covered a then ominous sky. She would only remember racing down the tiled floor past the emergency entrance and seeing Sam standing there, alive and well. She'd thrown herself into his arms, thanking God and all the powers that be for keeping him safe.

She'd gripped him tightly, clinging to him with all her might, but he'd pulled free from her at some point and held her at arms' length. His eyes were red and swollen, and the pain Beth saw on his face broke her heart in two.

"It's Miriam," he finally choked out. "She's dead."

"How?" Beth asked, too stunned to feel the full impact of his words. Sam had tried to answer, but he couldn't form the words. He finally drew her in again and held onto her with a fierceness that threatened to snap her in two. A short time later, the doctors told them to go home; there was nothing there for them to do. Beth had walked Sam out to his truck and, after prying directions from him, had driven him to his apartment, leaving her own vehicle in the hospital's parking lot. She'd guided him up the walk, unlocked his front door, and helped him inside. The apartment was not what she'd imagined it would be. It was small and sparsely furnished, as though the soul that lived there was prepared to take flight at a moment's notice. Sam had slumped onto the nearest kitchen chair, and sat there with his hands clenched and his head hung low. Beth had taken him by the elbow and helped him up. She guided him to the bedroom, where he had collapsed in a fetal position on top of the covers. Beth had laid down beside him. She'd held him as the sobs wracked his body, seemingly without end. When he'd finally drifted off to sleep a little after 10 A.M., Beth had let herself out and walked the two miles back to the hospital. There, she'd retrieved her car and driven home, unable to comprehend the extent to which her entire world had changed in a few short hours.

Sam did not return to work at the Copperhead until after the funeral. By then, he had paid for Miriam's final arrangements, had picked out the casket, and had ordered an ornate headstone that was to be engraved, "Miriam Draskil: Loved and Cherished Friend. Godspeed on Your Journey Home". When the time came for the funeral, Beth had picked Sam up and driven him to the church. Beyond her own pain, her heart ached for Sam. He was silent, and distant, and his face was drawn and pale. Beth had tried to talk to him during the ride, but her questions had gone unanswered. After the funeral, Beth had driven him back home and led him up the now familiar walk and into the four-room apartment. As though sleepwalking, he had drifted over to the table and sank into a chair.

At a loss, Beth had followed and stood beside him. When he'd reached for her, she'd moved to stand beside him and cradled his head against her bosom, holding him close. At some point, he pulled away and raised his face to gaze at her, his eyes red and swollen from his tears. He wrapped his arms around her as though he were drowning and releasing her would have meant certain death. He had stood then, and embraced her again.

"She's really gone," he'd whispered, his chest rising and falling rapidly, as though he were struggling to breathe.

"Yes," Beth had replied softly, not knowing what else to say.

"Dear God, it hurts," Sam said, so Beth held him more tightly and whispered that everything was going to be alright.

Comforted by their closeness, the thought of being alone was suddenly unbearable. He had gently pulled free from her embrace and stepped back to gaze into her eyes. Before she knew what was happening, he had kissed her—softly at first, then with a growing passion. From there, he had drawn her to his bed and she'd gone with him, silencing the voices in her head that screamed that this wasn't how she had wanted it to be. In the end, though, she had loved him and wanted him too much to say no. Sometime later, he'd pulled away from her, muttering that he was sorry.

Sorry—for what? For what they had just done, for Miriam's death? Beth hadn't asked; she couldn't bear to know. She'd simply curled up next to him, his arm draped over her, and had clung to that arm as though she were now the one who was drowning and he was her savior. A short time later, when sleep had carried him away, Beth had slipped from his bed and gone home. The trip had been surreal, and—unlike the drive to the hospital on the fateful morning of Miriam's death—had remained etched in Beth's memory forever. The fading notes of the choir's rendition of "Amazing Grace", the faces of the mourners gathered at the graveside, the smell of Sam's skin as she'd lain in his arms, all accompanied her as the miles slipped past. Not only was her dear friend dead, but she'd crossed some invisible line with Sam that could not be uncrossed. Days later, when Sam finally reported for work and would not look her in the eye, the pain that had been slowly ebbing raised its ugly head with renewed fury and Beth knew that she had just suffered the second greatest loss of her life.

Chapter Fourteen

Although Miriam died in late October, it was close enough to the holidays that, for years to come, Beth would not be able to look at twinkling lights or hear a Christmas carol without feeling the loss of her friend anew. By default, in Miriam's absence Beth was moved into the head bartender position. Acting by rote, she interviewed and hired two new part-time servers and bumbled her way through assigning the task of making sure the Copperhead appeared festive for the upcoming holiday season. Every day Beth arrived at work and went about her tasks, and every day she expected to see Miriam walk through the door as though everything—the fatal accident, the preparations, the funeral—had been nothing more than a huge misunderstanding. And every day, new tears filled her eyes. Beth wiped them away with the heels of her hands and tried to pretend that everything was going to be okay.

Miriam was gone. Beth missed her friend dearly and struggled to accept that. She avoided the ranch; the thought of the familiar paddocks, the horses, the island in the kitchen where they had sat for countless hours drinking coffee and discussing life, were all unbearable without Miriam in each and every scene. But even harder than the loss of her friend was the impact Miriam's death had on Sam. Had Miriam been right—had Sam been damaged even before she'd died? If so, then that unseen fissure had deepened and spread. The Copperhead was no longer a 'safe haven' where Sam could pretend that nothing bothered him and all was right with the world. It was now a haunted site; a place where memories collided with reality and nothing was quite what it seemed. Wedding parties and their guests still celebrated there, couples still came in for the Friday fish fries and stayed until closing, but the gaiety and charm were only superficial.

Beneath that cover was the incredible abyss left behind by Miriam's death, and it threatened to swallow them whole.

Sam spent a great deal of time away from the Copperhead. He moved out of his apartment and took up residence at the ranch. Surprisingly, Miriam had been insightful enough to make out a will prior to her death. Even more surprising was the fact that she'd left the entire Thunder Ridge Ranch to Sam. With the property, Sam also assumed the mortgage on the place and all of the expenses and income that came from the boarding operation the ranch was based on. Even on those occasions when Sam *was* at the supper club, he was distant . . . withdrawn. Every one deals with a loss in their own way; Beth understood that, and she gave Sam the space he now seemed to need. The distance and emptiness magnified her own sorrow. Only one of her friends had been in that vehicle when the accident occurred, but Beth felt as though she'd lost both Miriam and Sam that fateful night.

Previously fulfilled by the challenge of playing mentor to the Copperhead's staff, Sam was now distant and generally unapproachable. Beth stepped up and did her best to fill the void Sam's disconnect created, but she lacked his charm and confident insight into the day-to-day challenges of running a supper club. Some of the staff submitted their resignations and left to wait on tables or fry food at a restaurant where managers still smiled when customers weren't present. Beth hated to see them go, but the loss of several employees paled in comparison to what she'd been dealing with since October. It wasn't that the Copperhead was now a bad place to work; it was probably still better than any other supper club in a hundred mile radius. The work was manageable, and the staff was respected and fairly compensated. But it was so far from what it had been prior to Miriam's death that the veteran employees could not tolerate the difference. They preferred to take a chance at being miserable at a new job than semi-happy working someplace where they had once been so content.

Beth knocked lightly on the back office door. It was Tuesday and Sam was busy reviewing the Copperhead's upcoming bookings and filling out the necessary food and liquor orders. At the sound, he stopped writing and looked up. Their eyes met and Beth managed a smile. Sam's expression was ambiguous—neither happy nor sad. It was— what? *Sterile*, Beth thought, *it held nothing at all.* Sam remained frozen, pen still poised. Beth wondered at that. Was he purposely trying to give the impression that he was truly too busy to spare more than a moment, or was she reading too much into it?

"I stacked the back bar and used the last bottle of lime vodka. I thought you might want to add that to the order," Beth said, still leaning against the doorframe.

"Thanks, I'll do that. How are we sitting with our Bacardi? There was a note on my desk that we were running low."

"No, we're fine on that," Beth said. "I found a case buried in the stockroom; that should get us past New Year's Eve."

"Speaking of which," Sam flipped over a few pages on his desk calendar, "Thompson Manufacturing booked Saturday, January 4th for their company holiday bash. You might want to have an extra bartender scheduled that night."

"But, Miriam's," Beth checked herself and started again. "But the memo that went out in September gave that as a tentative date for our holiday party."

"We can change that, can't we?" Sam asked. "Christ," he flinched, caught in the memory of the chastising Miriam had once given him. When he continued, his voice had an audible softness to it. "Half the people here are new employees anyway; they haven't even seen that memo." *Or met Miriam*, Beth thought, but she kept it to herself.

"Saying 'hell' isn't swearing; not really," she said. "It was using the Lord's name in vain that she hated so."

Sam nodded and lowered his gaze back to the waiting paperwork. Beth chewed on her bottom lip, searching for something—the right thing—to say. Nothing came.

After several seconds, Sam looked up. "Was there something else?"

"No. I . . ." Beth stammered. "Are you okay?"

Sam began to answer. He opened his mouth but closed it again, apparently changing his mind. After a beat, he said, "I'm fine. And you?"

Beth hated this game, but she hated herself even more for playing it. Neither of them was fine, but both of them were too damn stubborn to admit it, let alone turn to the other for help. Wasn't it bad enough that they'd lost Miriam—did they have to lose each other, too? She crammed her hands in her pockets to steady them and swallowed hard. "Sam, can we do lunch sometime and just—talk?" She curled her concealed hands into fists, but her voice was strangely steady when she spoke.

"What did you want to discuss?" Sam asked. The question was not meant to be sarcastic, and there was no sarcasm in Sam's voice, but it took Beth by surprise.

"Nothing in particular," she said. "I just thought it would be nice to—"

"Beth," Sam's tone was gentle, but firm. "How will talking about it change anything?"

Beth swallowed again, not sure what to say. "I just thought . . ." She stopped talking and returned his gaze. Finally she looked away. Quietly, she said. "You're right. I don't know what I was thinking. I'm sorry." Before he could respond, she turned and was gone.

Sam did not call out to her; he did not ask her to come back. He simply got up and softly closed the office door. Back at the desk, he sat down and buried his face in his hands. He didn't cry. He couldn't have even if he had wanted to. He had no tears left. He was just tired, so very tired. After a minute that could have been an eternity, he dragged his hands down his face and sighed. The hardest part of all of this was the helplessness. There was nothing he could do to fix this, to make it right. And with the helplessness came the anger. He was angry at Miriam for dying, angry at Cindy for leaving and not giving the two of them the chance to work it out, and he was angry at himself for not having the balls to tell Beth the truth about himself and how he'd failed everyone who had ever loved him. He was not going to put himself in that position again, not ever.

He felt far too old to be only thirty-six. But then, what did he expect? He'd been on the lam for the better part of his life—not from the law, but from the truth. His mother had run off when he was only three years old, and his father's resulting 'screw them before they screw you' attitude toward women had been the prevailing motto of their household. As the years progressed, women came and went, and Sam soon learned that getting attached to any one of them ended in heartache—for him if not for his father. His resulting view of women as transient beings warped his view of all females, young and old. Classmates, teachers, strangers in the grocery store—if they were of the fairer sex, Sam would study them with unbridled interest, as though they were but mythical unicorns that would vanish before his very eyes. To get to know them was pointless; to trust them was even more ridiculous. The analogy offered by his father fit perfectly. Women were like the traveling circus. You don't fall in love with a traveling circus. You look forward to its arrival, you enjoy the rides while you can, and you get on with your everyday life when it pulls up stakes and moves on. It was that simple.

But, Sam pondered now as he had been doing for years, if that was what he'd been raised to believe, how had Cindy gotten to him? How had she worked her way past his convictions and into his heart? He'd been foolish and let his guard down; it was as simple as that. The first time she had told him that she loved him, he'd believed it. In hindsight, he supposed it had been true. She'd loved him as much as any woman could love a man. But that never endured, did it? It hadn't endured for his mother; it hadn't endured for the parade of women who had come forward to take her place. And, ultimately, it hadn't endured for Cindy either.

But oh, how he had loved her. At least, he was certain it was love at the time. The passing years had given him a lot of time to analyze their relationship. Had it been Cindy that he needed, or had he been searching for the mother he had never known? Perhaps he had been, but still it had been far more than that. Cindy had verified him; he was finally a whole man when he was with her. He scoffed at that idea now. He'd been seventeen years old; what does a seventeen-year-old kid know about being a man? Still, they had made a commitment—to each other and to an entire life together, and those commitments had felt so very right. When she'd told him that she was pregnant, he'd been terrified. Was he ready to be a father? And even if he was, could he handle it if Cindy took off—as his mother had done? Could he raise a child alone; was he destined to be saddled with the same life his father had lived?

It has been said that over 90% of the things a person worries about never come to pass. That had certainly been true in the case of his self-doubt about raising a child—his child. When Cindy miscarried, she'd been devastated. It was early evening. She'd been feeling out of sorts that day, and started to panic when the cramping and the spotting began. Sam had rushed her to the emergency room, but there was nothing anyone could do. These things just happen, the doctor on staff had explained. It was nature's way of eliminating fetuses that were defective in one way or another—ones that might never have survived had they been carried full term. Although Sam had been troubled by the doctor's words, the thought that the child—his child—could have been flawed or malformed in some way, the explanation did make sense. And while he had experienced the loss on some level, Cindy was nothing short of devastated. It was, Sam later decided, the beginning of the end.

For the next ten years, they remained married—legally bound to one another and presenting themselves as husband and wife. But calling someone a wife or a husband doesn't make them one any more than calling someone a doctor gives that person the right to cut another human being open to remove his or her spleen. Sam had tried to be a husband. He'd found work and stuck with it; he'd performed maintenance on their vehicles and later on their small house. He'd seen to it that they had what they needed. True, most days that was only the bare necessities, but they managed to get by. When Cindy became restless and talked about getting a job—just something part-time to get her out of the house—Sam had tried to be supportive. He had rationalized what she must be going through, spending day after day alone in the house. It would be good for her to get out, to keep busy. If she also brought home a small paycheck, all the better. Maybe she could have some of the things Sam had always wanted to give her but couldn't afford. What she'd brought home was another man.

Sam blamed himself for her infidelity. He should have seen it coming, although for the love of him he couldn't imagine what signs he had missed, or what he should have been looking for. True, she'd been distant, but so had he and he hadn't been screwing around. In the end, ten years of marriage had led to a divorce, which had resulted in another ten years of analysis of the whole mess. Ultimately, he supposed, he was none the wiser . . . and he was still very much alone.

Miriam's entrance into his life had been a godsend. She was like no other woman he had ever known. It was her confidence, her no-nonsense view of the world that Sam had found so refreshing. Without his even knowing it, she had become a constant element of support for him. She'd laughed at his jokes, worked at his side, and gently rebuked him when he'd stepped out of line. She had also been there if he would have wanted to talk. She'd said as much, on several occasions, though he had never taken her up on the offer. Somehow, she had seen into him and recognized the pain he had walled off and hid from the world. He wished now that he'd have taken her up on the offer and told her what his life had been like, what it was still like. What good would have come of it, though? She couldn't have changed the past, and no one can change what still lies ahead, so it would have been a waste of time. But somehow, now that she was gone and it was far too late, he couldn't help but feel that he'd done the wrong thing by shutting her out. Perhaps that had been a mistake. Her death had sent him reeling, crashing back into the cruel reality that was his life. Fate seemed to be obsessed with beating the same message into him, time and time again. Loving someone, caring for someone, was a prelude to pain, to devastation, to caving inward where no one dare look for you. He'd had it with caring; it wasn't worth the price he ultimately paid.

Which brought him to Beth. She was still here, still vested in him as a friend. Although younger, she had many of the same qualities Miriam had. She was smart, compassionate, and level-headed. She was also pretty in a

down-home, country sort of way. Like Miriam, there was no
pretense with Beth. She was what she was; take her or leave
her. Sam found that refreshing; Cindy had made him leery
of games and people who played them. But still, what the
hell had he been thinking? He did not play it loose with
women. His father's constant 'changing of the guard', the
endless parade of the older man's latest and greatest
conquests, had disgusted Sam. He had vowed to never be
what his father had been.

For Sam, it was simple. There were two distinct types
of sexual contact with a woman. The first was sex for its
own sake—the physical contact and release that had nothing
to do with love—and yes, there were plenty of places to find
it if you knew where to look. The second type, and the only
type he really struggled with, was what the more
sophisticated members of the human race referred to as
making love. In Sam's mind, it was reserved for someone
you truly cared about, someone who had touched your heart
and kept a piece of it for their very own. That was it; black
and white. There was sex for simple enjoyment, and sex to
signify a deeper union, a commitment—spoken or
unspoken—to a woman who trusted a man enough to share
that closeness and surrender to him in the most intimate way.
Since his divorce, Sam had indulged in the first type
whenever the opportunity presented itself, and had avoided
the second type at all costs. That was simply where his life
had taken him.

So, what the hell had he been thinking when he'd taken
Beth into his bed? She wasn't some stranger who'd agreed
to please him. She was his employee and his friend; it had
been a bad move on either level. Yes, he'd been devastated
that day; they both had. Was that an excuse—any excuse at
all—for doing what he'd done? Still, she'd been willing
enough; it wasn't like he'd forced himself on her. Did that
make it alright, or just a little less terrible? He'd struggled,
time and again, to come to terms with it. When that failed,

when the memory refused to be neatly bundled and tucked away in some dark corner of his conscience, never to be revisited, he had tried to simply and completely banish it from his mind. The problem was, he saw Beth nearly every day, and the memory was her shadow. Hell, it was his own shadow; it was wherever he went.

So, the question now was, what was he going to do about it? Like all bells, it couldn't be unrung. Beth, like Miriam before her, wanted to talk to Sam. The difference was, Miriam had wanted to discuss the elements of Sam's past that refused to let him go. Beth probably wanted to discuss something much more recent, like what had happened between them on the day of Miriam's funeral—and every day since. Sam now regretted not talking to Miriam when he'd had the chance. Would the outcome be the same if he avoided the discussion with Beth? She deserved an explanation; he knew that. The problem was, Sam didn't have one.

He rubbed his forehead and sighed. This was getting him nowhere. He needed to complete the order that waited on the desk before him and work on the spreadsheet from the previous month. It had been over a month since it had happened, and although the current disconnect between them had not yet worked itself out, he was still holding out hope that it would. Just because he couldn't figure it out, that didn't mean that Beth wouldn't come to terms with it and simply move on.

Eventually, Sam realized, Beth did just that. She moved on. Oh, she'd probably stayed as long as she could. She'd poured her heart and soul into the Copperhead, and the supper club—also damaged by Miriam's untimely death—slowly began to turn itself around. But things were never the same between Sam and Beth, and he knew that he was to blame.

In hindsight, Sam realized that Beth had done it the same way it was done in cheap paperback novels and low-budget films. She'd left in the dead of night, saying nothing to anyone and taking only what she needed to get by. What Sam would probably never know were the details of that departure. Heading south, the headlights of Beth's Bronco had cut through the darkness. Mile after mile, she'd wiped away her tears and kept her foot pressed hard on the gas pedal. Ultimately, she'd left because she realized that it was entirely possible to miss someone when they are working right beside you. She loved Sam; she had long since accepted that, and she always would. She'd also accepted that what had happened between them had been a fluke; it had been two people drowning in a pain so real and so crushing that they'd clung to one another to simply get through that dreadful day. She could have lived with that, too. What she couldn't live with was standing four feet away from him and feeling a distance between them so immense that no voyager on the fastest sailing ship could have crossed it. She couldn't stand it that he was there—right there—and yet he wasn't. She couldn't torture herself by allowing her eyes to embrace something her hands could not. So it was that, in the end, she'd left behind no note, and no forwarding address to which her last paycheck could be sent. It was a clean break, or as clean as it could be, considering that she'd had left her heart behind.

Part Three: Reunion

Chapter Fifteen

"You want a leave of absence for *how* long?" Jake asked Beth, waving the form in front of her face as though she had never seen it, let alone filled it out and handed it in.

"I'm not exactly sure," she said. "Three or four weeks, I'm guessing."

"You're guessing? And who's going to take your place while you're gone?"

"Tim's doing a pretty good job; he's been here for over a month now. He knows the standard drinks and people like him. I'm sure he could cover for a while."

"For 'a while', yes—for three or four weeks, I'm not so sure."

"You won't know if you don't give him the chance," she persisted.

Jake studied her for a long moment and said nothing. She was a good bartender and he liked her; more importantly, the patrons liked her. He didn't want to see her gone for an extended period, but she'd never asked for any time off before and he owed it to her. "When you thinking about leaving?" he finally said.

"Tomorrow."

Jake's eyes widened, then narrowed. "That soon, huh? I don't suppose there's any talking you out of this," he grumbled.

"No. There's something . . . there's something I have to do. I'm sorry to spring this on you at the last minute, but it couldn't be helped."

Jake's gaze slid down the bar to the stranger who was seated there, the one who had brought Beth in on the back of a motorcycle a half hour earlier. The stranger didn't look like bad news, but then—if rapists, stalkers, and murderers walked around with neon signs plastered on their backs, there'd be a lot fewer victims and a lot less crime in the world. Jake glanced at the request form again and scowled. "You'll be back before the Smith wedding in October, right?"

"Absolutely," Beth said, though in reality she didn't have a clue.

Jake glanced at the stranger again. "I'd appreciate you giving me a number I can reach you at while you're gone. Just in case."

Beth snatched a dry coaster off of the bar and wrote the information from memory. She handed the coaster to Jake and watched him as he read it.

"The Copperhead? Isn't that the supper club in Eagle River where you worked before you came here?"

"Yes," Beth admitted.

"You thinkin' about getting your old job back?" Jake asked bluntly.

"No, this isn't about work. It's . . . it's personal."

"Hmph," Jake grunted. "If you're not back behind this bar one week before the Smith wedding, I'm going to road-trip up there and get you. Understood?"

"Clearly," Beth said. "I'll be back. Thanks, Jake. I really appreciate it."

Jake nodded at her, took a final glance at the stranger, then turned and left. Beth joined Mark at the far end of the bar, but she didn't sit. She remained standing, gazing at the door that opened onto the parking lot.

"Trouble?" Mark asked.

"No, we're good. Jake gave me his blessing."

"Then why the long face?"

Beth shrugged. "Nerves, I guess. I'm just not convinced I'm doing the right thing."

"It's not like we're on some clandestine mission, Beth. You're taking a few weeks off to visit an old friend. Where's the harm in that?"

It sounded so simple when Mark put it that way, so why didn't it feel simple? Dumb question. It wasn't simple because it involved Sam. For her, at least, nothing about Sam was simple. Would he be glad to see her, or pissed at the way she'd left? It had been five years; she couldn't imagine Sam holding onto anger for that long, but she had no way of knowing for sure. What would he say when she walked into the Copperhead? Hell, what would *she* say? *Hi, Sam. Miriam and two gentlemen—Peter and Mark—wanted me to come and see you, so here I am!* God, she didn't want to do this. After five years, it still hurt. The thought of him still caused her breath to catch and her heart to race. What she needed was therapy, not the opportunity to look into those eyes again and see—what? The emptiness, that's what—the emptiness that broke her heart right up until the day she left, and everyday thereafter. But maybe, maybe he was better now. Maybe it would be the old Sam who would be serving customers at the Copperhead, or tending to an ailing Jinx at the ranch. Right, Miriam spoke to her from the other side, and two complete strangers—only questionably human—were all interceding on behalf of a man who was doing just fine. No, this was not going to be any fun.

"So," Mark's voice brought Beth back to the moment. "What's the plan?"

"The plan?"

"When were you thinking of leaving?"

"In the morning," Beth said.

"Around seven?"

"That's as good a time as any," Beth replied. She slipped her hands in her pocket and exhaled slowly.

"Should I follow you on the bike, or would you like someone riding shotgun?"

Beth had accepted the fact that Mark was also going to make the trip to Eagle River, but she still wasn't sure why. What role was he playing in this—a mentor, a supervisor, a support group of one? It seemed wrong on some level, but then her nerves were so frayed that she couldn't trust anything her gut was trying to tell her. "You should probably take the bike; either one of us may decide to leave before the other is ready," she said.

"I don't think that will happen, but you're right. It would be best to keep our options open," Mark agreed. "Come on. I'll take you home. I'm sure you've got some packing to do, and you'll want to get a good night's sleep."

Beth didn't answer. She simply followed Mark out of the bar. Once he had the bike started, she slipped into place behind him and they headed out of the parking lot. Mark was right; Beth had some packing to do, but as for getting a good night's sleep, there was no way that was going to happen.

Chapter Sixteen

On a warm and humid August morning, the duo pulled out of Baraboo at precisely 7 A.M. In spite of the sleepless night, Beth had limited her morning coffee intake to one cup. She didn't want to have to pull into gas stations at every small town they passed through just to use the restroom—not with Mark behind her on the bike. Of course, as nervous as she was, that was still a very real possibility, but she preferred to stack the odds in her favor and limit her liquid intake. She'd stifled a yawn (fatigue or nerves?) and popped a couple of NoDoz tablets with the last swig of coffee. She had packed a few bags and stowed them in the Bronco the night before. There had been too many knots in her stomach to leave room for breakfast, so she simply grabbed her remaining suitcase and her purse, and had headed out to the Bronco. There was no turning back.

They would follow US51 north to US8 past Muskellunge Lake, then take US8 into Rhinelander. With a planned stop at Wausau for breakfast, they figured the trip would still only take about three and a half hours. That would put them at Eagle River at 10:30 A.M. It would be too early for the Copperhead to be open, so they would go directly to the ranch. After that, Beth had no clue what her next step would be.

It was a Thursday, so traffic was light. Beth maintained a steady speed of two or three miles per hour over the posted speed limit. The day was already warm, but she drove with her windows down instead of switching on the air conditioner. The changing countryside sped past her open windows. The forests were still a vibrant summer-shade of green. Before long, they would get that tired look that too many hot days and too little rain could give deciduous trees. The corn, lined up in tidy rows and reaching for the sky, was fully tasseled and making the most of the long hours of sunlight. Here and there, a hayfield rolled past, its alfalfa cut and resting in neat windrows that stretched like green ribbons across the brown face of the cut field. The smell of drying hay, rich and heady, swept through the Bronco and Beth inhaled deeply. She was trying hard to deny it, but this felt so much like going home.

After having to make only one unplanned rest stop, the Bronco and its motorcycle shadow pulled into Wausau right on schedule. She found a small diner, turned on her directional and pulled into the parking lot. Mark pulled up alongside, dropped the kickstand and switched off the bike's engine. They took a moment to stretch their legs, then Mark held the diner's door open for her and they stepped inside.

The restaurant was a quaint 'Mom & Pop' establishment with red and white gingham curtains and matching tablecloths. The floors, freshly waxed, gleamed in the midmorning sunlight, and a wall-mounted air conditioning unit was holding the temperature at a comfortable seventy-two degrees.

"Booth or counter?" Beth asked.

"Let's grab a booth," Mark said before sliding into one that offered a view of the parking lot and their vehicles.

A waitress in her mid-fifties brought them two menus and two glasses of ice-water. The badge on her shirt read "Madge". "Can I get you something to drink while you're deciding?" she offered.

"Coffee for me," Mark said.

"Nothing, thank you. The water is fine."

Madge made a quick note on her order pad and turned her smile back to Mark. If she was going to receive the customary 15% tip, it was obvious where the bull's share of the money spent at this booth would be coming from. "If you're good and hungry, our special is the lumberjack breakfast for $8.99."

"And what," Mark prompted, "is the lumberjack special?"

"Two eggs over-easy, toast, hash-browns, four sausage links, an order of bacon, and two flapjacks."

"You're kidding," Mark said.

"If you'd like, you can add an order of biscuits and gravy on the side for a buck."

"People don't really eat all of that, do they?" Mark asked, his brow furrowed with disbelief.

Madge's smile faded a little but she persevered. "Sure, and there's home-made pie for dessert."

"Dessert, with breakfast? Is that kosher?"

"You Jewish?

"No," Mark replied.

"Then what's the difference? You can have two slices," Madge offered.

"Alamode," Beth piped in.

"Now you're talking," Madge agreed and left to get Mark's coffee.

"If I ate all of that, I'd have to stretch out in the back of your Bronco for the rest of the trip and leave my bike here."

"I'm sure Madge would watch it for you," Beth said, smiling.

"You should do that more often," Mark said.

"Be sarcastic?" she asked.

"No," Mark replied, "smile." Beth responded by picking up her menu and trying to decide what she should order.

Twenty minutes later, with the majority of their food eaten and the check resting face-down on the table, Beth became aware that Mark was studying her. She rested her elbows on the gingham tablecloth and gazed out at the parking lot. The day was getting hot and the blacktop was beginning to shimmer in the merciless summer sunlight.

"What are you going to say to him?" Mark asked quietly.

"I haven't the slightest idea," Beth confessed.

"You're running out of time to decide, wouldn't you say?"

Beth turned her gaze to Mark; it was a determined gaze without even the hint of a smile. Her blue eyes appeared darker than usual, stormy. "You seem to forget, if it weren't for you and Peter, I wouldn't even be making this trip. This was *your* idea, yours and Miriam's."

"Miriam?" Mark asked, confused.

Beth had assumed that Mark knew about both Peter *and* Miriam, though he had never said as much. She considered that assumption, wondering how much to say. In the end, discretion won out and she said nothing at all.

"Who's Miriam?" Mark repeated.

Beth answered the question with one of her own. "So, you are no longer denying that you know Peter?" They faced each other for a long moment during which neither spoke. They were little more than strangers sharing a journey—but to what end—Beth wondered, and not for the first time. "What is your interest in Sam?" she finally asked.

"I'm not sure I know what you mean."

Beth continued to study his face. Was he being truthful? Would she even be able to tell if he wasn't? "Peter was concerned about Sam. He went as far as to say that I needed to save him. Pretty funny, isn't it—me saving someone? Peter said that I needed to prove to Sam that life is not without meaning or value." Beth hesitated, still studying the stranger who was seated across from her. "But you, you've never said what your interest in Sam is."

"Does it matter?"

"Yes, I think it does; very much so."

Mark dropped his gaze and shook his head. When he looked up again, his customary smile had returned. "We all want the same thing, Beth. We want things to be put right." He glanced out the window at nothing in particular before returning his gaze to her and continuing. "I'll be the first to admit that I am not nearly as elegant with words as Peter is. He's had a lot more practice, for one thing. For another, he's simply better with people. We can't all be the charmer that Peter is."

Beth considered that. She recalled Peter's self-confidence—the ease with which he handled both himself and their conversation. What Mark was saying rang true. She would let it go for now; to press Mark for a more direct answer seemed senseless. The outcome of what lay ahead had more to do with Sam's reaction to her return than it did with anything Mark might do or say. Her heart gave a flutter and her stomach knotted anew. She was less than two hours from seeing Sam. Not that long ago, she had sworn that she would never go back. Despite the fact that she was now making a pit-stop in Wausau on her way back to Eagle River, she remained confident that she would have never broken that promise. She had Peter, and Miriam, and— yes—Mark to thank for that. They'd convinced her that she needed to go back. She only wished that they would have convinced Sam of the same thing.

Mark left a generous tip, paid the check, and walked Beth back out to the Bronco. He waited as she fired up the engine, rolled up the windows, turned on the air conditioner, and pulled back out onto the highway. He fired up his bike and fell in behind her. Although the day was getting increasingly warmer, the air was soon flowing past him at sixty miles per hour. There was no finer feeling in this world. He studied the back end of the Bronco as they wound their way north. They would be at Eagle River soon. Everything was going according to plan. Except for one small detail . . . who the hell was Miriam?

Chapter Seventeen

At Rhinelander, the pair of vehicles turned off on WI17 and began the final leg of their journey. Eagle River was now less than twenty miles ahead. A short distance up the road, the Bronco began acting as its namesake implied. It started to buck, then slowed, and finally stalled. Beth guided it over to the side of the road and switched on her four-ways. She popped the hood latch, and as she opened the driver's door and stepped out, Mark pulled up alongside her.

"Trouble?" he asked.

"It died," Beth said.

"I'll take a look." He parked the bike, switched off the engine, and propped the bike on its kickstand. He moved to the Bronco and opened the hood. The examination lasted for only a minute or two, but to Beth it seemed like an eternity. Mark wiggled wires, checked connections, and removed the air filter for a closer look. "Turn it over once," he instructed. Beth climbed back inside and turned the ignition. The engine cranked over quickly enough, but refused to catch and fire. Mark raised his hand and she released the key. He circled around the front fender and came to the window. His hands were covered with grease, so Beth retrieved some napkins from the stash in her glove box and handed them to him.

"You got gas?" he asked, wiping the grease from his hands.

"Three-quarters of a tank."

"Then I haven't a clue," he said. "Could be almost anything. When's the last time you changed the timing belt?"

"The *what* belt? Beth asked.

"Well, then it could be that. Most manufacturers recommend you have them replaced every sixty thousand miles," Mark said, still rubbing at the grease with the rapidly shredding napkins.

Beth glanced down at her odometer. Every sixty thousand miles? She should have probably replaced it two or three times by now. Why hadn't anyone told her? She was making a mental note to find a new mechanic when a Dodge Ram, candy-apple red and sporting a serious lift-kit approached them from the north. It slowed, did a loud and hasty U-turn just past them, and pulled up to park behind the disabled vehicle. A young man with sandy-colored hair, wearing boot-cut blue jeans and a t-shirt with the arms cut off at the shoulder seams dropped out of the truck and sprinted to the Bronco's driver's door.

"Beth? Well, I'll be damned. I thought that was you! I'd recognize this old heap anywhere. It's been ages—how ya been?"

Beth smiled. "Hey, Rusty. I am *so* glad to see you. The Bronco seems to have died and—"

"For real?" Rusty said. "Well now, don't you fret. I can have Steve out here with the tow truck in less than thirty minutes."

Beth noticed Mark watching, a look of amusement on his face. She got out of the Bronco and handled the introductions. Rusty, this is Mark. Mark, Rusty. His uncle—"

Rusty took over the introduction. "Steve—Steve Hanson—he owns the repair shop on 3rd street. I can have this lady back on the road in nothing flat." Rusty turned back to Beth. "It sure is good to see you; I was afraid you'd left for good. The Copperhead just ain't been the same since you left—you and Miriam, that is."

Beth rested her hand on the young man's arm. "Thank you." A part of her wanted to tell the young man that he was just as sweet as she remembered, but she hesitated. It felt awkward and forward; perhaps she'd been away too long. In a blink, the opportunity had passed.

Perhaps sensing what she hadn't put into words, Rusty smiled and kicked at a loose piece of blacktop that was resting in the gravel. When he looked up again, he said, "Why don't you give me your keys, Beth. You and Mark here can head on out to Thunder Ridge on the bike. I'll call my uncle and we'll get this thing back to the shop. We can call you just as soon as we know what the problem is."

"That would be great," Beth agreed and handed him the keys. She reached into the vehicle to the passenger's seat and grabbed her purse. Taking a small notebook from the side pocket, she wrote down her cell number and handed it to Rusty.

"You got an old phone or a new one?" Rusty asked.

"Old. Why?" Beth asked, confused.

"You remember what it's like up here, Beth? If your phone ain't got 3G or 4G, it can be a hit and a miss getting a signal. In case we can't get through, is there a landline we can reach you on? Maybe at Thunder Ridge?"

"I . . . I'm not sure where we'll be staying," Beth said. At that remark, Rusty gave Mark a solid 'once over' and the younger man's smile faded a bit.

"Well, things haven't changed up here much, Beth. Everyone still knows everyone. If nothing else, I can call the

Copperhead and leave a message there. I'm sure someone will know how to get word to you."

Beth thanked Rusty again, said goodbye, and turned to where Mark was now seated on his bike, waiting for her. "What about my bags?" she asked. Mark gave an exaggerated shrug.

"Maybe someone at the ranch can give you a lift back for them once you're settled in."

Beth frowned, but there were no other options at this point. As a quick after-thought, she returned to the Bronco and transferred as many personal items—toothbrush, deodorant, and basic makeup—as she could into her purse. Satisfied that she'd grabbed all she could carry, she returned to the bike, situated herself on the seat behind Mark, and they were off.

Fifteen minutes later, Mark slowed down as the Thunder Ridge Ranch came into view. Not bothering to signal, he turned the bike into the drive and pulled up to the house. Before he could switch the engine off, Beth tapped him on the shoulder and pointed toward the stable, indicating that he should park there. Mark revved the engine before walking it backwards back onto the drive, then he put it back in gear and drove it the short distance to the stable. Before he could switch off the key, Beth had climbed off and was walking through the large double-door and into the murky shadows beyond. He switched off the bike and dismounted, swinging his leg over the bike's frame and straightened up. Just as he removed his sunglasses and positioned them on the top of his head, he sensed someone behind him.

"Can I help you?" The voice was deep, but not necessarily threatening. It was the type of voice that made you sit up and take notice—a preacher or a Supreme Court judge kind of voice. It was the type of voice that could go from velvet smooth to a thunderous pitch without warning; it was a voice that did not take kindly to being ignored.

Mark casually turned and studied Sam for the first time. He didn't need an introduction; he'd have known the man anywhere. Sam, however, was at a loss as to who stood before him. Mark extended his hand.

"I'm Mark."

"You got a last name—or a reason for driving that noisy bike up to a building that could well have some high-spirited horses inside?"

Mark grinned in spite of himself, which caused Sam's frown to deepen. "I'm sorry about the bike. To be honest, I was only following orders."

At that moment, Beth reappeared in the stable doorway. The summer sun highlighted her hair, and her face—flushed from the ride in on the back of the bike—glowed with a natural warmth. At the sight of Sam, she froze, and the color in her cheeks intensified.

Sam nodded, almost imperceptibly, and growled, "I should have known."

Chapter Eighteen

Sam was . . . beautiful. That was all Beth could think. He was, far and away, the best thing she'd laid eyes on in five years. Her heart skipped a beat, then fluttered uncontrollably as though trying to compensate for the pause. She wanted to reach for him, to pull him close to her and forget that the rest of the world even existed, but that would have been wrong somehow. It would have also been impossible. Her arms remained frozen at her side, and her feet were riveted to the gravel beneath her. The silence became an entity; a being of strength and mass that separated them, but try as she might Beth could not think of a single, 'unstupid' thing to say. As was often the case in the past, Sam came to her rescue.

"What are you doing here, Beth?"

"I . . . I heard that Jinx was ill and I wanted to see him."

Sam's eyes narrowed and his face clouded over like a summer sky when storm clouds roll in. "And how exactly did you hear about Jinx?"

"Bud told me," she stammered after the briefest hesitation. "I called to see how things were going and he told me about Jinx." Beth watched closely as Sam weighed the statement, but she couldn't tell how far into the "Bullshit Zone" his mental needle was leaning. That was, she decided, a good thing. When Sam did not respond, she pressed on. "I didn't see Jinx in his stall; he isn't—" Beth couldn't bring herself to finish the question.

"He's in the west paddock," Sam replied, still studying her.

As though released from some sort of spell by Sam's words, she turned away from where the men stood, set her purse on a wooden bench that was next to the open door, and sprinted around to the west side of the stable. She opened the gate, stepped through, and secured it again behind her. Jinx was standing at the far northern edge of the enclosure, his head and neck draped over the wooden rail. At the sound of the gate closing, his head turned and he whinnied in recognition of the unexpected visitor. He trotted over to Beth, crossing the distance with so much more effort than it would have taken the younger Jinx that still lived in Beth's memory. When he finally reached her, she cradled his head between her hands and kissed him lightly on his graying forehead.

"How you doing, old man?" she whispered to him, her face mere inches from his. "I came as soon as I could."

Jinx snorted and gently bobbed his head, as though he understood what Beth was saying. Beth stepped back to better study her old friend. He was much thinner than she'd remembered, and his coat lacked the sheen and consistency of a younger horse. The temple area above his eyes appeared sunken, and the eyes themselves had an opaque quality to them, as though the spirit that had always shone through was no longer entirely there.

"I'm so sorry," Beth said, still whispering. "I wish there was something I could do."

Jinx snorted again, more softly, and stepped up to press his head against her. Her heart sank as she stroked his slender neck. Why couldn't time stand still? Why couldn't Miriam and she still be riding the hills of the Thunder Ridge Ranch without a care in the world, Jinx tossing his head against the reins and the wind? Why had time contrived to bring her to this place, at this time, with an empty void where her dear friend had once dwelled? Because time was unfair; that was why, and she hated it for that.

"Did you see what you came to see?"

Beth heard the question clearly, but she didn't turn to face Sam and she didn't respond. She remained with Jinx, stroking him gently. Even with her back to Sam, she was painfully aware that he was standing there, watching her. "What did the vet say?" she finally asked.

"Which one?" Sam replied.

"Any of them." Beth's emotions were running close to the surface, but she was careful not to snap at him.

"There's no cure for old age, Beth. You should know that."

Beth waited for nearly a minute—an eternity in any conversation—before she said, "So what are you going to do?"

It was Sam's turn to hesitate, to allow the silence to stretch on. "When the time comes, I'll do what needs to be done."

"And when will that be? How will you know the time is right?" Beth rubbed Jinx's ears and pressed Sam for an answer.

Sam's voice softened and lost some of its defensiveness. "I'll know."

Beth gave no outward indication that she'd even heard. She remained with Jinx in the paddock, gently stroking the old horse and talking softly to him. Mark glanced from Beth, to Sam, and back to Beth again.

"Why don't we go into town and find a place to stay?" Mark asked Beth. "We can head over to the Copperhead when it opens and the two of you can catch up there. I'm sure Sam has work to do."

"No," Beth said, her back still toward the men. "I'm going to stay here with Jinx for a bit."

There was another long moment of awkwardness before Sam spoke. "You don't need to find a place in town. There's plenty of room in the ranch house. Beth knows where the spare bedroom is, and the linen."

"Are you sure we wouldn't be putting anyone out?" Mark asked.

"There's no one to put out; you're welcome to stay."

Mark looked to where Sam was standing at the paddock fence, his arms resting on the top board, gazing out at Beth and Jinx. Mark noted how Beth remained with the old horse, refusing to even turn around or look at Sam. He cleared his throat loudly. "Well, *I'm* going to head into Eagle River then and have a look around. Hate to come all the way up here and not even see it." When neither Beth nor Sam offered a comment, he returned to his bike and settled on the seat. Taking care not to upset Jinx—or Sam—he walked his bike a good distance back into the driveway before firing up the engine. A few seconds later, he was heading down the road, shifting gears in the hot morning sunlight. Too late, Beth thought of the Bronco and her bags. She could have asked Mark to check on them. Oh well, it would have to wait . . .

Taking hold of his halter, Beth guided Jinx to the gate, opened it and walked him through. "Let's get you out of the sun, old boy. I'll give you a good rubdown, and I could probably find you some grain, too. Would you like that?"

Beth did not look at Sam when she passed, but she felt his eyes following her. Inside the stable, she led Jinx into his stall, closed the gate and headed for the tack room. Everything inside the small room was as she remembered. Bridles and assorted tack rested on saddle trees, clean saddle blankets were neatly folded in half and stored on the shelf, and a bin with various grooming tools sat on a small wooden bench to the left of the door. Along the wall to the right, a small wooden desk held a telephone, and an ancient PC and printer. On the wall behind the desk, Miriam's show ribbons still hung, denying that anything had changed in the last five years. The room was warm and smelled of leather, Neatsfoot oil, and time. Beth rummaged through the grooming box, selected a soft brush and a clean rag, and turned to leave. Sam filled the doorway, watching her. Beth froze.

It had been five years since she'd gazed into those eyes. Sixty months . . . two-hundred and sixty weeks . . . eighteen hundred and twenty-five days. It really didn't matter how she measured it; it had been an eternity. In all that time, she had never stopped thinking about him; she had never ceased to wonder how he was doing; she had never been able to drive him out of her consciousness, her mind—and least of all—her heart. It had not been for lack of trying. She'd scolded herself repeatedly for entertaining the thought of him; she'd pushed him away with all the force she could muster. She'd thrown herself into her work at the Eagle Crest Resort—as Sam had thrown himself into the Copperhead. Had it worked for him? She couldn't say, but it hadn't worked for her. Her persistent love for him had been the backdrop for everything she thought, said, and did. If she had been given one choice at any random moment during those five long years, she would have chosen to be gazing into those eyes.

Now, as Sam stood before her, Beth noted a turmoil in those familiar, brown depths. Questions formed and struggled to rise to the surface only to be forced back down by new and more pressing questions. He hadn't bought the lie she'd told. He didn't believe that Bud had told her about Jinx's failing health. He was going to ask why she was really here, and she would say—what? She couldn't tell him the truth—simply because it was more unbelievable than the lie had been. *Well, you see—I was sound asleep and Miriam called . . .* No; that would certainly never do. Her hands were trembling, so she grasped the brush and rag more firmly. She had known this moment would come. After all, wasn't confronting Sam the real reason why she'd agreed to come? What was it Peter had said? She needed to save Sam, to make him believe that love was a real and tangible thing, and that life had a purpose. Did he really need to be told those things, or could both Peter and Miriam have been wrong? She decided that was a very real possibility. If that were the case, how could she fix what wasn't broken? In fact, she was certain that Sam wasn't the one in the tack room who needed saving; *she* was.

"Why did you leave, Beth?" Sam asked, his gaze holding her captive in the close room.

Well, Beth thought, *there it—wasn't!* She opened her mouth to reply, but closed it before any words could slip out. She hadn't even considered *that* question. Why did she *leave*? She thought he'd want to know why she came back, not why she'd left. But it made sense, didn't it? She was caught up in the moment—in what she needed to do. Sam was still struggling with that day when, five years ago, she had disappeared without a word.

"Lots of reasons," she finally said, and it sounded even more lame spoken than it had when it was simply spinning around in her head.

"Name two."

"There was nothing here for me anymore," she said, spewing out the first thing that came to mind.

"Nothing?" he asked, eyebrows raised.

"Nothing that would keep me here." Beth said. She regretted that they were alone in the room. Had someone been there to witness her performance, she might have been nominated for an Academy Award.

"And the second reason?" he pressed.

The second reason . . . Beth swallowed hard. She hadn't even faked the *first* reason well enough to be believable. She dropped her gaze and studied concrete floor. "Can we talk about this later?" she asked, sounding very small and defeated even to her own ears.

"That depends," Sam said. "Is there going to be a *later*?"

"Why wouldn't there be?" Confused enough by the question to forget her momentary uncertainty, Beth raised her eyes to meet Sam's again.

"Eagle River isn't that big," Sam explained. "Mark will run out of things to see and excuses to leave us alone. My guess is he probably won't want to listen to the explanation you'll give for deserting everything that mattered to you." Sam hesitated, and a look of understanding slowly washed over him. "Or, does he already know the reasons why you left here?"

"Meaning?" she demanded a bit more forcefully than she'd intended.

"Meaning you've already told him, or—"

"Or?"

"Or he was waiting for you wherever you ended up."

"What are you talking about?" Beth asked, anger creeping into her voice.

"No one leaves a job and their home without a reason, or without a destination in mind."

"Well, I did," Beth stammered, the color rising to her cheeks.

Sam nodded slowly and persisted. "So, where *did* you end up?"

"I don't see why that matters," Beth snapped.

Sam fell silent and studied her for a long moment. "I suppose it doesn't," he finally said. With that, he turned and stepped out of the doorway, allowing a rush of light and air into the room. "You can stay in the guest room at the far end of the hallway," he said over his shoulder as he strode toward the stable's large double door.

"Wait a minute," Beth said, hurrying after him. "That's fine for Mark, but—"

"But what?" Sam said, spinning toward her.

"But I need a room, too," she said. Sam simply raised his eyebrows in reply. "What?" she barked.

"You ride in here on the back of his motorcycle from God knows where and you want separate bedrooms?" The look on Sam's face reminded Beth of a teacher who had caught a student cheating on an exam and was enjoying watching the child squirm.

Suddenly, Beth understood. Sam had no way of knowing about the Bronco breaking down, or why she'd ended up on the back of Mark's motorcycle. Still, for some reason the assumption on Sam's part infuriated her. "You think that—" Beth couldn't finish the statement. Her cheeks went scarlet and her eyes flashed. "Where do you get off jumping to conclusions about me and a perfect stranger?"

"Is he—perfect? He doesn't strike me as being a stranger." Sam was enjoying the debate in which he clearly had the upper hand.

Beth gave him her best look of reproach and headed toward Jinx's stall. She threw the gate open and stormed through it as the old horse looked on, more amused than startled. Retrieving a lead rope from where it had been draped over the side of the stall, Beth attached the steel clasp to Jinx's halter and tied the other end of the lead to a post. Once the horse was secured, Beth began running the brush over his thinning coat, using more care than should have been possible considering her frame of mind. In a few moments, she sensed more than heard Sam leave. As her heart rate slowed and her trembling hands quieted, she played their exchange over and over again in her mind. It made no sense, no sense at all. It was almost as if—.

She froze, her arm poised over Jinx in mid-stroke. No, it couldn't be—could it? Was Sam jealous? But, that would mean . . . and Beth's heart began to hammer all over again.

Chapter Nineteen

Sam walked briskly to the machine/hay shed west of the house and loaded the pickup truck parked there with half a dozen bales of hay. The summer heat and sparse rain the previous month had taken their toll on the pasture. To supplement the grazing, Sam was now taking hay out to the horses that roamed over the bulk of the Thunder Ridge Ranch's fenced-in acreage. At last count, there were thirty-three head on the property—ten that were owned by Sam and the hired hands, and twenty-three that were being boarded.

With the hay loaded, Sam got in the truck and headed out to make the drop. Horses, like all herd animals, have an established pecking order. The more aggressive individuals dominate the herd. They insist on having first choice of any food or water that is available. With teeth bared and ears flattened against their skulls, they drive the smaller and weaker animals away from the hay until they've had their fill. For this reason, Sam spread the hay over a large area, ensuring that every horse got the chance to eat. Normally, he would talk to the horses as he opened the bales and tossed the square sections of dried timothy out. He knew each one by name, and had trained several of them to come when called.

Today, however, he offered no greetings to the horses that circled the pickup, waiting for the hay to be dispersed. Sam simply climbed into the bed of the truck, cut the taut strands of baler-twine with his pocket knife, and swung the sections of hay into the restless gathering of manes, glistening coats and thundering hooves. He repeated the process until only chaff remained in the bed of the truck. With the chore completed, he jumped over the side of the truck and crawled back into the driver's seat. Once there, he slammed the door shut, started the engine, and guided the pickup back to the yard.

Bud was waiting for him when Sam returned. The hired hand was standing outside the pasture, waiting to swing the gate open when the pickup reached it. Bud's work partner for the day, a young buckskin filly the Thunder Ridge Ranch was boarding and training for a doctor who lived in Green Bay, stood tied to the pasture fence, watching the approaching pickup with her head held high and her ears pricked forward. Once the truck cleared the opening, Bud closed and secured the gate as Sam returned the pickup to its spot in front of the machine shed. The older man retrieved his mount and led the animal over to where Sam was brushing the remnants of loose hay from the truck's bed.

"We have a visitor," Bud said when he was close enough for Sam to hear.

"That's 'visitors'," Sam said, correcting him, "as in two, not one."

"Two?" Bud asked.

"Yes, the man rode his bike into town to do some sightseeing," Sam explained. Seeing the look of confusion on Bud's face, Sam snorted. "Don't ask."

"How long is she staying?"

"You'd have to ask her." Sam slammed the tailgate into its closed position and brushed the hay from his jeans.

"You are angry," Bud said.

"Not at all," Sam replied. "It's always good to see an old friend—even one who disappears in the middle of the night without a word. In fact," Sam was almost sneering, "I understand that I have you to thank for her visit."

"Me, Boss?"

"Yes, she called and you told her that Jinx—"

"She never called, Boss. Or, if she did, I did not talk to her."

"Then, how did she know . . ." Sam's voice trailed off.

"Perhaps she talked to one of the other—"

"No, she specifically said it was you." Both men fell silent. In tandem, they turned to look at the stable as if expecting to be able to see Beth through the structure's walls. After a bit, Bud broke the silence.

"Is it not good to see her again?"

Sam ignored the question and motioned toward the horse that was patiently waiting at the end of the reins that rested in Bud's grasp. "You'd better get back to working that filly."

Bud nodded, coaxed the horse forward and mounted. Without a backward glance, he spun the horse around and trotted off. Sam watched him ride away, then he stared at the stable for a long moment before turning toward the house. He needed to get ready for work. As he passed the stable, the sound of voices drifted through the open door. He stepped close and peered inside, careful to remain out of view.

Beth was still in the stall with Jinx, but she had her back to the horse and was talking to Cassandra. The trainer stood in the isle. She held the mustang by the halter's side strap, keeping a tight grip on the horse's head. Sam was too far away to hear what they were saying, but their voices rose and fell like the chords of an unfamiliar melody. They were a mismatched pair if there had ever been one. Cassandra—

Cassie to those who knew her—was tall and slender. Her hair was long, and dark, and when not drawn back in what she called her 'riding bun', as it now was, it covered her shoulders in a shimmering cascade. Her face was narrow, with almond-shaped green eyes and high cheekbones. Her skin, bronzed by hours in the sun, shone softly in the stable's soft light. She had a confident air about her, a self-assured demeanor that intimidated most women and a lot of men.

Beth, on the other hand, was short and well-seasoned. She was not unattractive, but she was not—nor had she ever been—the eye-pleasing specter that Cassandra was. Beth's hair was short and going gray, something she had chosen to do nothing about. Her skin, a permanent component of its bartending host, was seldom exposed to the sun and remained pale even beyond the long days of summer. She was neither young nor lean, and although she had once been the former she had probably never been the latter. Did she have an air about her, as Cassie did? Sam thought about it. He pictured her at work behind the Copperhead's bar. The tile floor was her stage, and her movements, though not those of a temptress, were choreographed and carried out with both precision and grace. He could still see her rushing about, carrying a drink in one hand and some man's change in the other—and always with a ready smile. No, not an air, but a confident manner; that was what Beth possessed.

As he spied on them from his position beyond the double-door, Sam was struck by the feeling that he was seeing both women for the first time—Cassie in the isle, controlling a prairie mustang with one, unwavering hand, and Beth in the stall, grooming a dying horse with all of her heart. There was something here—something important, something he should make note of, but whatever it was it skirted his grasp and refused to be cornered. Sam backed away from the door and headed to the house. He'd think about it later. Right now, he needed to shower and head out. He had the feeling that it was going to be a very long night.

Chapter Twenty

Beth heard the sound of an approaching horse and turned to see if it was someone she knew. Surely some of the same hired hands still worked here; she hadn't been gone that long. A woman entered the stable leading a spirited pinto that tossed its head at every step, but stopped short of pulling away and bolting. The woman and horse came to a halt in the isle next to Jinx's stall.

"You're new here," the stranger said. To Beth, there seemed to be an unspoken challenge in that simple statement.

Beth studied the woman before answering, and a feeling of unease crept through her. She had the distinct feeling that she'd seen her somewhere before—but where? Here at the ranch? At the Copperhead? With all of the weddings she had worked for, it was impossible to say. Jinx nickered softly and backed away until his lead rope drew taut.

"Yes—I mean, no. I mean, I'm just visiting, that's all," Beth said, still searching her memory for the woman's identity.

The stranger motioned toward Jinx with a thrust of her chin. "If you're afraid of horses, we have several that are quiet. You don't have to spend time with that sorry thing. I could probably find one calm enough for you to ride if you'd like."

That sorry thing? Beth was infuriated at the woman's remark. How could someone be so calloused? She swallowed a caustic reply and offered, "I'm Beth." When she spoke, she didn't extend her hand or make a move toward the stall's gate. Instead, she watched the stranger for a reaction. Perhaps the woman had heard Beth's name mentioned at some point in time. If she had, she didn't let it show.

"I'm Cassandra; my friends call me Cassie. I'm the trainer here."

Beth's heart fell, though she wasn't certain why. The fact that this woman—such a blatantly calloused being—was employed at the Thunder Ridge Ranch disturbed her. One thing was for certain; Miriam would have never hired her.

"Is that so?" Beth asked. "And how do you like it here?"

"It's a good place to work. The setup is great and the horses are pretty doable. This one here," Cassie said, giving the pinto's halter a shake, "has given me a bit of a challenge, but he's just one horse. Actually, he's coming along fairly well, considering he was running wild on the range a few months ago."

"Mustang adoption program?" Beth asked.

"Yes," Cassie said. She cocked her head slightly to the left. "You're not one of those bleeding-heart activists that want all of the mustangs to remain free—and probably starve to death, are you?"

"Do you always presume the worst about people you've just met?" Beth asked.

"Of course not," Cassie laughed lightly. "But the very fact that you're wasting your time brushing that animal tells me all I need to know about you."

"Which is?"

"You've got a soft spot for lost causes. You're a 'bleeding heart'."

"Even if I am, what's wrong with that?" Beth said.

"Look at you. You're what—fifty years old?"

"No, and I don't see where my age has anything to do with this," Beth interjected, anger creeping into her voice.

"Of course you don't. You've been so busy trying to save the world and creatures like this," Cassie gestured toward Jinx with a flip of her hand, "that your entire life has passed you by. And what do you have to show for it?"

"How 'bout you answer a question." Beth's patience with this woman was spent. "Are you always such a big jerk or is this my lucky day?"

The smile disappeared from Cassie's face. Her eyes widened for a split second before narrowing into slits. "Watch yourself, Missy, I work here. The owner and I are close," she growled, "and I can have you thrown off this ranch. You'd do well to remember that."

"I doubt it," Beth countered, but secretly found herself wondering how close they could be. "Sam and I also go back a long way."

Cassandra gave Beth a quick once over with her piercing green eyes, then the woman smiled coolly. "Yeah, I bet you do—a long, long way back. But that was then, and this is now. Things are different around here now."

"You're right about that," Beth agreed and offered a cool smile of her own. "You'd have never landed a job as a trainer here if Miriam were still alive. That's a huge difference, and it's not for the better."

To Beth's surprise, Cassandra smiled, then broke into a soft laugh. "You've got spunk; I'll give you that. I hope you'll stay for the party. I think it would be so much more entertaining having you around for that."

"What party?" Beth asked.

"Our Labor Day bash. It's next Saturday. Do tell me that you're going to be here that long."

"I'm not sure, but it's none of your concern one way or the other," Beth said. She turned back to Jinx and began brushing him again, working from his ears down along his neck with long, gentle strokes. The horse trembled beneath the brush.

"I'm hoping Sam puts that horse down before the party," Cassie said. "No one wants to look at an animal in that condition. It's a downer, a real mood-wrecker, you know?"

"He might just surprise you and still be here next Labor Day," Beth said with stubborn defiance. "You never know."

Cassie laughed. "Oh, I know. That will never happen, Sweetie. I guarantee it—even if I have to shoot the thing myself."

Furious, Beth whirled, but before she could reply Cassie had pulled the pinto around and was leading the horse out the double door. Beth threw the brush into the isle and watched as it bounced harmlessly across the floor. Cursing, she leaned against the wall of Jinx's stall with outstretched hands and took several deep breaths. When she accepted that her anger was not going to abate any time soon, she unhooked Jinx from the lead strap and stepped out of the stall. She strode to the feed room, grabbed a small bucket of an oats, corn and molasses mixture, and took it back to Jinx's stall. She dumped it in his feed tub, and when the horse approached and began to eat, Beth stormed toward the house, wondering yet again why she had agreed to come back. Sam was certainly not happy to see her, it was painful to see Jinx failing, and now she had Cassandra to put up with. She hoped with all her heart that Peter would show up again. She had a thing or two she wanted to say to the man.

Chapter Twenty-One

When she reached the house, Beth did not bother to knock; no one did. The house was more a place of business—a gathering area for ranch hands and visitors—than it was a home for any one individual. True, Sam lived here, but he never treated the structure as a 'personal possession' and never even bothered to lock the doors. She simply opened the door and walked in. Once she stepped inside, Beth felt her anger begin to slip away. Everything was very much the way she remembered it. She took a deep breath and felt the tension slip away; there were too many good memories lacing these rooms for her to not feel comforted.

She passed through the enclosed porch that had been transformed into what Miriam lovingly called 'the mudroom' and into the kitchen beyond. It was as if she'd traveled back in time. The room was the same subtle shade of yellow. Beth remembered picking out the paint with Miriam; the color card at the hardware store had called it 'Honey'. The same bar stools sat at the island, the same table—surrounded by the same chairs—sat off to the left, the same stove and refrigerator sat in the same places, waiting to be used. The only thing missing was Miriam.

Beth set her purse on the counter and crossed to the sink for a glass of water. On the wall to the right of the sink, a small, black metal plaque hung. It read, "The hurrier I go, the behinder I get." To the left of the sink, a matching plaque read, "No matter where I serve my guests, they always like my kitchen best." Beth smiled when she read the phrases, and more memories came surging back through time. She had been with Miriam when the woman bought the plaques at a rummage sale in Rhinelander the summer before she died. Beth drank half of the water and carried the rest to the island. She sat for a moment, trying to process everything that had happened that day. It was a lot to process, and it was not yet noon.

The house had been remodeled at some point, creating an open-concept design. The light gray ceramic tiling giving way to the dark tones of a Berber carpet indicated where the kitchen/dining area officially ended and the living room began. An L-shaped sectional, upholstered in faux leather— Miriam would have never tolerated anything in her house that had been made at the expense of any animal's suffering—further demarcated the two rooms. There was a fieldstone fireplace on the north wall. Being August, it sat idle, yet its decorative stones and subtle colors still served as a focal point in the room.

The house was equipped with three bedrooms—the master bedroom and two smaller guest rooms. This was generally more than enough as the hired help all slept at their own homes, with the exception of Bud who slept above the stable. An arch at the far end of the living room led into a hallway; that hallway led to the bathroom and bedrooms beyond. The guest room Sam had offered to Beth was at the far end of the hallway on the right, just past the master bedroom. On the left side of the hallway, there were three doors. The first led to the bathroom; the next door opened into the second guest room, and a small office lay behind the last door on the left. Without leaving her spot at the island, or even looking in the direction of the hallway, Beth decided that she would take the guest room on the left—the one closest to the bathroom, and would leave the one at the far end of the hallway for Mark.

Relieved to have a tentative plan, Beth got up and carried her glass of water back to the sink. With a heavy sigh that she could contribute to no one thing in particular, she dumped the water out and started to wash the glass.

"It can't possibly be that bad."

Beth startled at the sound of Sam's voice. The glass slipped from her grasp and shattered in the sink.

"Damn!" Beth exclaimed, quickly crossing to the paper towel dispenser on the counter a few feet away. She tore off several sheets and turned back to the sink, but Sam was already carefully picking pieces of broken glass out of the sink.

"When you broke glasses at the Copperhead, they came out of your paycheck," Sam said.

"Only if you were there when it happened."

Sam stole a quick glance at Beth before asking, "Is that a confession?"

"That will never happen," Beth said, crowding him away from the sink. "And I can clean up my own mess, thank you."

Sam carried the pieces of glass to the garbage and carefully placed them inside an empty coffee can so they wouldn't cut through the plastic bag. He turned just as Beth was approaching with the last of the shards wrapped up in the paper toweling. She tossed them in the garbage as well and returned to rinse out the sink.

"Either way," Sam said, "this one is on me. I didn't mean to startle you."

"It was my own clumsiness. I should have known you'd be getting ready for work. I—I'm just jumpy, I guess."

"I'm probably a bit to blame for that as well." Sam joined her at the sink, and proceeded to rinse his hands. She handed him the towel when she was done with it. "When that motorcycle pulled up to the stable, I was a little put out—"

"A little?" The words slipped out before Beth could stop them, but there was no anger behind them. It was like the old days, when teasing one another was the easiest way to communicate.

"Okay, more than a little. A stable is no place for a motorcycle."

"We weren't *in* the stable!" Beth defended herself.

"Are you going to keep interrupting, or are you going to let me get this out?"

Sam had folded his arms across his chest, trying to appear irritated. He was dressed for work in khaki slacks and a burgundy-colored polo shirt that had the Copperhead logo embroidered on the upper right. His hair was still damp from the shower, but neatly combed. He was no George Clooney, no Clark Kent—but Beth thought he was still the best thing she'd ever seen. Not wanting to ruin the moment by making it awkward, she quickly looked away, hoping Sam could not be able to read what she was thinking.

"No more interruptions," Beth said. "I promise."

"As I was saying, the motorcycle was bad enough, but you were also the last person I would have expected to ride in on it."

"It's not like I planned it that way," Beth said.

"Come again? Were you kidnapped and tied to the seat? I must have missed that part."

"No," Beth exclaimed, feigning exasperation. "Mark was following me on the motorcycle when my Bronco broke down." Sam raised an eyebrow, so Beth pressed on. "The Bronco is at Steve Hanson's shop in Rhinelander. You can call him if you don't believe me. In fact, all of my stuff is still in the Bronco. I don't even have a change of clothes."

Sam thought for a moment. "You might be able to squeeze into some of Miriam's things."

"Excuse me?" Beth erupted, but there was no need to feign emotion this time.

"You know what I mean. Miriam was—taller."

Beth tried her best to glare at him, but the expression slid off her face far too quickly. "Are you telling me you kept that stuff?"

"You helped me pack it up, remember?" Sam explained. "We stuffed it all in totes and piled it out in the garage. It's still there. I just never had the time to haul it to Goodwill."

"No time, huh?" Beth asked, but it was a rhetorical question. "Thanks. I'll call Steve later. If it's going to be a day or two, I might just take a look at what's out there."

"What's wrong with the Bronco?" Sam asked, changing the subject.

"How would I know?" Beth said. "They thought it might be the timing strap."

"Timing strap?" Sam laughed. "You mean the timing *belt*."

"Belt—strap, what's the difference. Besides, you knew what I meant!"

A comfortable silence ensued, but all good things must end—or so Beth had been conditioned to believe.

"What brought you back, Beth?" Sam asked.

"A motorcycle?" Beth teased, but her heart wasn't in it. She really didn't want to string Sam along.

"That's not what I meant."

"I know." What answer could she give him? She couldn't tell him she came back because she loved him. Who does that—leaves without a word then returns five years later still carrying a torch for someone? No one sane, that's for sure. So, what would Sam think if she told him that she loved him? He'd think she was desperate—or crazy—or desperately crazy. Either way, she was relatively certain that it wasn't a good move. Could she tell him that Miriam had asked her to come back? No, probably not . . . that was just as crazy. Could she explain that Peter—a man she'd met in a snowstorm who most likely wasn't even human—had told her that she needed to save Sam? The possible options she was coming up with were getting worse, not better. So, she settled for a lie. "I don't know what brought me back, so I just threw that out there."

Sam frowned. "Let's see if I have this straight; first, you don't know why you left, and you also don't know why you came back."

"Yes," she said, not meeting his gaze. "That about sums it up."

Sam thought about that for a moment. "Well," he finally said, "can you at least tell me who Mark is?"

Beth started to answer, but stopped. As much as she wanted to, she truly couldn't tell Sam who Mark was. A friend? Sort of, but not really. A man she met in a bar and who later followed her home? No, that was definitely not the right answer to give Sam. A friend of Peter's? Did she really want to get into all of that right now? No, she didn't.

So, instead of answering, Beth did what women are so notorious for—she changed the topic.

"I met your new trainer," she said.

Sam hesitated, fully aware of what Beth had done, but ultimately he decided to let it go. "And?"

"Do you want the sugar-coated version or the truth?"

Sam sighed. "Listen, I don't pay her to be charming; I pay her to train horses."

"Well then," Beth said, "she must be one hell of a trainer."

Sam studied her for several seconds and shook his head. He looked away, but when he looked back there was just the hint of a smile on his face. "Are you coming down to the Copperhead later?"

"Yes, if that's alright."

Sam nodded. "I'll see you then." He crossed the kitchen and paused in the doorway to the mudroom. He turned back and his smile widened. "Try not to break anything until then, okay?" Before Beth could comment, he was gone.

Chapter Twenty-Two

It was nearly 3 P.M. when Beth looked at the clock yet again. She was still waiting for Mark to return, and listening for his motorcycle to pull in the drive. By then, she had called Steve Hanson's repair shop and learned that he would not even have time to look at the Bronco and offer a diagnosis until sometime the next day. With no other option, she had gone through two of the totes and found a denim top and a pair of jeans that she could squeeze into. Luckily, she and Sam had washed everything before packing it away, and the totes had kept the clothes relatively fresh.

At 3:14, Beth decided to call the Copperhead to let Sam know that she was no longer certain she would make it in. The screen on her phone read "1 New Message". She dialed voicemail, entered her password, and retrieved the message. It was Mark. They'd exchanged numbers before heading out on their trip, just in case they got separated due to a stray herd of cattle crossing the road, or a tornado that dropped out of a clear blue sky, or whatever. The message said that something had come up and he'd had to return to Baraboo. He'd try to head back up again in a few days. Either way, he'd be in touch.

Great, she thought, *just great*. Now she was without clothes and stranded. She flipped her phone closed and stuffed it back in her purse, wondering what—if any—course of action was available to her. Before she could begin formulating (and shooting down) any ideas, she heard the exterior door open and close, and Bud appeared in the doorway of the mudroom. Upon seeing Beth, he removed his hat and his eyes sparkled.

"I'd heard you were back. It is good to see you, old friend."

Not waiting for an invitation, Beth hurried over to Bud and embraced him warmly. When she'd finished hugging him, she stepped back and returned his smile. "You're a sight for sore eyes, Bud. It's been too long. Have you been well?"

"Yes. You?"

She hesitated; there was no sense in lying to this man. He would see right through her. "I've gotten by." There was another short pause before she added, "I still miss her."

Bud nodded, and Beth knew he understood. She shrugged and nodded toward the kitchen with a sad smile. "The place hasn't changed a bit."

"Not on the outside," Bud agreed, "but on the inside, I am not so sure."

"On the inside?" Beth asked.

Bud either didn't hear or chose to ignore the question. "You told Sam you would be at the Copperhead. He sent me to see what was keeping you."

"Are you saying he misses me?" Beth smiled again in spite of her best effort not to.

"No, those were not his words," Bud said.

"Then what *were* his words?" Beth asked.

"He is short a bartender, so he asked me to hurry you along. His words were 'She should not have forgotten how to mix a few simple drinks.'"

Beth laughed and shook her head. "Remind me to explain why it is sometimes important to *not* be so honest with a woman, okay?" Bud looked confused, but did not ask for clarification.

"We can go in my truck if you like," he offered.

"I'd like that very much," Beth said, and she grabbed her purse and followed him to the garage.

Bud's truck was a short-bed 1957 Chevy Pickup with step sides, a narrow bed, and external rear wheel wells. It had been painstakingly restored and painted robin-egg blue. The cab was upholstered in black mohair, with narrow-channeled seat skins and door panels. The only thing on the vehicle that didn't pass for original was a yellow bumper sticker with black lettering that was centered in the lower tailgate. It read "Teach Respect for the Earth and All Living Creatures." Beth smiled anew on seeing the truck. It, like so many other things, was exactly as she remembered.

She circled the truck, opened the door and crawled in as Bud started the engine. He reached up and hit the button on the remote garage door opener that was clipped to the sun visor. As the garage door labored upward with a mechanical chatter, Beth pulled the truck door closed with a resounding thud—the mating of solid American steel components—and Beth thought, '*They don't build them like this anymore.*'

Bud was a man of few words, so Beth expected the ten-minute ride to the Copperhead to be a quiet one. She gazed out at the countryside as they passed, taking in the fields and the forests with equal measures of disinterest. Her thoughts were on the Copperhead, and Sam, and what lie ahead. Bud surprised her by clearing his throat and saying, "The Boss said you came back because of Jinx."

"Yes, I did."

"You told him that you spoke to me, that I was the one who told you of the horse's illness." He paused and glanced over at her, then returned his eyes to the road. "We did not speak, Beth. I haven't heard your voice since you left, and that was years ago. So, I was wondering, who told you that Jinx was ill?"

Beth did not answer right away. It made no sense to lie, but the truth was too unbelievable to talk about, which left her—where? Would Bud buy the truth—would anyone? She clasped her hands in her lap and stared at them, as though they might hold the answer she was looking for. "I . . . I can't tell you that," she finally said, but her voice was low and soft, and lacked the conviction of a final answer.

"Miriam told you," Bud said. It was a statement of fact, not a question.

Beth stiffened, but refused to look at the old man. "Miriam is dead, Bud. We both know that."

"Yes," Bud quickly agreed. "But what is 'dead'?"

"Are you serious?" Beth asked, then offered her interpretation. "It means gone, cold, lifeless, six-feet-under. It means . . ." she hesitated, struggling to go on. "It means she's not here for us anymore." Beth turned to look out the passenger-side window, but she could feel Bud's gaze upon her.

"Yet, she *is* here, isn't she?" Beth didn't respond, so Bud persisted. "Do you deny that Miriam told you about Jinx?"

"No," she finally admitted, her voice little more than a whisper.

They travelled the remaining two miles in silence. When the Copperhead came into view, Bud spoke without taking his eyes from the road. "There are things you do not understand, but that does not make them less real. We exist on many levels, Beth. Our spirits are not of this world, and are not bound by the rules that govern the flesh. Miriam's body was broken and taken from us, yes, but her spirit—her essence—remains." Bud pulled into the parking lot and killed the engine. They sat in silence for a long moment, listening to the hot engine click and creak as it began to cool. Out of habit, Beth surveyed the parking lot. It was filled with row after row of parallel-parked motorcycles. There had to have been over a hundred bikes reflecting sunlight off chrome. Now she understood why Sam had needed her to come in. Just as she was about to open the door and step out, Bud turned to her. His eyes were solemn, yet filled with hope. "Have you seen a peacock at rest, Beth?

"What?"

"When a peacock is at rest, its tail extends behind it. Still, the bird is stunning; the plume on its head, the stark contrast of its speckled wings to the blue of its body. One looks at a peacock at rest and thinks they are seeing the entire bird—a magnificent bird whose beauty is beyond compare. But, then it fans its tail and we see the true beauty that is the peacock; we see what was hidden—yet right before us—all the while." Bud gazed out the windshield, his eyes bright. Without turning back, he said, "We are each as the feathers of a peacock's tail. We go through life closed, but the levels of beauty—of our essence—are all there." Glancing at Beth, he added, "As with the peacock's closed tail, just because we do not see something does not mean it doesn't exist—and, just because we do not see someone, does not mean that they are not there."

With that, Bud climbed out, closed the door and walked to the front of the truck. There, he waited for Beth to join him. When she did, he escorted her to the Copperhead's main entrance, her arm draped through his. As they walked, Beth thought about the analogy of the peacock's tail. What was it Bud had first said? *We exist on many levels.* She thought back to that night in the snowstorm. *Was that what Peter had been hinting at when he mentioned a dimensional theory? And why*, she thought, *had he even brought it up if he wasn't going to explain it to her?* She pushed the thoughts aside as Bud opened the door and she stepped inside the Copperhead. The sound of music and mingled voices—the smell of beer, and perfume, and aftershave—the sight of the well-polished bar, half-hidden behind patrons awaiting drinks—took her back in time more effectively than Orson Welles ever could. What was it people said, you can never go back? She absorbed the details of the scene around her, embraced the familiarity, and secretly prayed that those people were wrong.

Chapter Twenty-Three

Bud escorted Beth through the sea of leather vests and jackets that swarmed before them. Sam was hurriedly mixing a pair of whiskey-sours as Beth stepped behind the bar and back into the old routine. Julie, one of several bartenders Beth had hired and trained, slapped a customer's change down on the bar and turned. She was in her late twenties, with long, brown hair, soft brown eyes, and a round face full of freckles. She wore black suede pants and a white tank-top, and at five foot six in sandals, she towered over most of the female bartenders the Copperhead employed. When she saw Beth, she smiled and rushed to meet her. Laughing, she stooped and caught Beth up in a bear hug.

"Boy, am I glad to see you! This biker club just pulled in out of the blue, and Trish called in sick—"

"Just point me in the right direction," Beth said.

"Point you in the right direction?" Julie laughed. "How 'bout I just try to stay out of your way." The pair laughed as though five years and too many miles had not separated them for far too long, then they both got to work. Sam, upon seeing her behind the bar and mixing her first drink, gave her a smile and a nod. When it was apparent that the two women had the situation under control, he disappeared to play host and left them to their work.

Seven long hours later, the bikers began filing out, and the sound of motorcycle engines starting, revving, and heading out rose and fell as the Copperhead's doors opened and swung closed behind each departing biker. Sam claimed one of the now-vacated barstools and Julie brought him a drink. When Beth paused in front of him to add ice to the glass she was holding, he asked, "How are your feet holding up?"

Beth looked up to answer and the world stopped. Her hand froze, the metal scoop laden with ice halfway to the glass. Cassandra appeared, apparently from nowhere. Beth did not remember seeing the woman previously that night. She wore a form-fitting, strapless black dress, and Beth knew without looking that the dress was accentuated by black, fishnet stockings. Cassandra stopped when she reached Sam and kissed him lightly on the cheek. Sam turned to look and surprise registered on his face. He smiled, leaned toward her, and whispered something; her jet-black hair slipped to one side when she shook her head and laughed at his remark. Then she was leaning into him, whispering something in return, and Sam laughed aloud. The pieces fell into place with a sickening thud as Beth realized where she'd seen this woman before . . . it had been in her dream. Beth's heart fell and she tried to rationalize what was happening. So, she had seen this woman—or a similar woman—in her dream, so what? It didn't mean anything, did it? Dreams were nothing more than harmless images created by an unbridled subconscious mind. So, why was Beth's heart suddenly pummeling her ribs like the wings of a caged bird, and why was the hair standing up on the back of her neck?

"I'll take a glass of Chardonnay when you get time, barkeep," Cassandra said, her cool smile locked on Beth.

"Would you like that with or without arsenic," Beth countered. Sam's eyebrows shot up, but he remained silent. Cassandra laughed gaily and leaned in to speak to Sam.

"You really must keep this one. She's got spunk," she said, and although there was merriment in her voice, her eyes were frozen points of light trained on Beth.

"Funny," Beth said, "my advice to Sam would be just the opposite where you're concerned." There was an awkward pause.

"I'm still waiting for my Chardonnay," Cassandra said coolly.

"Well then," Beth replied, "I suggest you get off your butt and go get it." With that she turned and stalked her way to the farthest paying customer who was still inclined to order a drink. From the corner of her eye, Beth watched as Cassandra and Sam spoke for a minute or two, then the woman got up and left, never having received her drink. Sam watched her leave before turning his gaze toward Beth. When she would not look at him, he got up and slowly approached, then settled onto a barstool directly in front of her.

"Do I need to know what that was all about?" he asked.

"Nope," Beth replied.

"Are you sure?" he pressed.

"Yup." Beth snatched some half-empty glasses from the bar, dumped their, and placed them in the sink. When she returned, he said,

"Funny, I don't remember this side of you. I've never met a person you didn't get along with."

"That should tell you something," Beth said as she continued to tidy up, avoiding Sam's gaze.

"And what, exactly, should it tell me?" he asked.

"Maybe I'm a little older and wiser—or maybe I've just learned that there's no getting along with some people, and I'm not going to waste my time trying."

Sam studied her for a beat and then nodded. "Okay, point taken," he said. "Is it alright, though, if she keeps training the horses?"

For the first time since the discussion began, Beth met Sam's gaze. "Just keep her away from Jinx," she said, her voice firm and unwavering. Sam noted the conviction in her eyes and forced a smile.

"I don't think that will be an issue, do you? Jinx is about as trained as he'll ever be. Agreed?"

"I don't think 'training' is what she has in mind," Beth said.

Sam considered that remark and decided not to press Beth for an explanation. Whatever had transpired between the two women was a mystery to him, and he was content to leave it that way . . . at least for the time being.

"So, what happened to Mark?" Sam asked, changing the subject.

"Something came up; he had to head back to Baraboo."

Sam raised an eyebrow, but held his tongue on the matter. "Bud left a few hours ago; seeing your friend Mark seems to have abandoned you, can I give you a ride back when we lock up?"

"It's that or I walk," Beth remarked, and before he could reply she left to gather up the remaining abandoned glasses. Sam watched her march off and shook his head. He pushed away from the bar and headed to his office. He'd tidy up some paperwork while the last of the patrons drifted out, and Julie and Beth put things in order. He'd long ago given up on trying to understand women; he'd be happy just coexisting with them without too many problems.

Julie watched as Sam left. When he was out of sight, she hurried over to Beth and spoke in a hushed but excited voice. "I couldn't help but hear what you said to Cassandra. That was so cool! No one has ever stood up to her before."

"Why not?" Beth stated, her voice filled with disinterest. "What does the woman do, breathe fire when she's pissed?"

"No—at least, I don't think so," Julie giggled, sounding very much like a schoolgirl. "There's just been talk, you know?"

"Talk? What kind of talk?"

"Some people say she's going to buy into the Thunder Ridge Ranch, become a partner or something."

"Sam would never be that stupid," Beth declared, then—to herself—*Would he?*

"Other people say that she's planning to buy the ranch outright and Sam is going to just work the Copperhead." Julie frowned. "Either way, no one around here likes the woman very much—no one, that is, except Sam."

"And exactly how well does Sam like her?" Beth asked before she could think better of it.

Julie shrugged. "He's a man, she's a sleaze—at least, she looks like sleaze to me. *You* figure it out. Anyway, I'm outta here," Julie said with a smile. "It really was great working with you again, Beth. Kinda like old times." The younger woman hugged Beth warmly. "Listen, how long are you here for? I mean, Trish will probably be out for at least two or three days—she pulls this a lot. Her boyfriend is a trucker, and when he's in town Trish tends to get 'sick'." Julie made air quotation marks around the last word. "With you filling in, I won't have to train someone—or run my ass off."

"I'm not sure how long I'm staying," Beth replied. "Probably a week or so."

"Great, maybe we can catch up later then." Julie hugged her again and left to retrieve her purse and keys. Beth watched her go and smiled. *To hell with Cassandra,* she thought, *I'm not going to let that woman ruin what has essentially been a very nice evening.* With her new conviction solidly in place, she went to find Sam. It was time to lock up and head back to the ranch.

Chapter Twenty-Four

The clock on the corner of the desk read 2:14 A.M.
when Sam tore his eyes from his paperwork to check the
time. Beth and Julie would have escorted the last of the
diehard patrons to the door, and cleared the glasses and
bottles from the bar and the nearby tables by now. At any
moment, Beth would appear in the doorway, announcing that
it was time to lock the doors and call it a night.

Sam caught himself smiling and wasn't sure why. A
strange contentment came over him. It felt as if some unseen
pieces were falling back into place, putting things right
again. How easily Beth had stepped behind the bar and
slipped back into the rhythm that was her trademark back in
the day. *Back in the day*, he rebuked himself. It had only
been five years—not a lifetime. But it had felt like a
lifetime, hadn't it? In fact, until he'd seen her step behind
the bar, as though she'd never left, Sam hadn't realized the
extent of the emptiness she'd left behind when she
disappeared. And yes, it felt good to have her back, as much
as he hated to admit it.

Sam looked back at the last five years. He hadn't
thought of them as lonely; he hadn't spent too much time
wondering where she was. He rationalized that it had been
her choice to leave, and he had to accept—if not respect—
that. He'd run the ranch and the Copperhead, hired and
terminated personnel as was necessary, and generally lived
life and handled whatever came his way on a daily basis.
They had been good years . . . not outstanding, but
financially and objectively 'good'. But was that all there is
to life—finances and objectives? He had thought so, for
many years. It was a mindset that had mercifully rescued
him from feelings that were too painful to contemplate, let
alone deal with. Tonight, though, he was no longer sure.

Had he missed Beth? Yes, but as with all emotions that demanded more of his attention than he was willing—or able—to give, he had pushed it aside and denied it. But why, he wondered now, had missing her bothered him? Did he see it as a sign of weakness, a need he didn't want to admit to? Perhaps. Tonight, though, it no longer seemed to matter. He was going to be honest with himself for a change. He was glad she was back. How long she would stay was another matter, and something he needed to find out.

There was the sound of approaching footsteps and Beth appeared in the doorway, as predicted. "The place is secure, Boss, and awaiting your inspection," she said with a mock salute.

Sam laughed and pushed himself back from the desk. "I don't think that will be necessary. Is Julie gone?"

"Yup, and the front door is locked." A short pause, then, "But you can check it if you want. I won't be insulted."

"I think I can trust that you remembered how to turn a deadbolt."

"Then we're good."

Sam got up, came around from behind the desk, and strode toward Beth in the doorway. When he was two steps from her, he stopped. "Are you done in, or would you care for a nightcap? On the house, of course."

"You're buying? Can't refuse that kind of offer, especially on a bartender's salary." They exchanged a smile and the pair headed back to the bar.

"People drink too much in Wisconsin, did you know that?" Sam asked as Beth settled on a stool and he took up position behind the bar.

"Lucky for you," Beth agreed. "Present company excluded, of course."

"Of course." Sam filled two glasses with ice and reached for a bottle from the rack. He hesitated. "Are you still drinking that green Kool-Aid?" He asked, tossing her a grin.

"I'm surprised you remembered. But it's not Kool-Aid. Kool-Aid is sweet; I take mine with sour."

Sam nodded and extracted the lime vodka from the rack, along with his customary whiskey. When the drinks were mixed, he joined Beth on the opposite side of the bar and for a moment they sipped in silence.

"So, what's up, Boss?"

"For one thing, you can stop calling me 'Boss'. I'm not your boss anymore, remember?"

"You were tonight, sort of."

"I thought of it more as one friend doing another friend a favor."

"*That's* what this is about," Beth raised her voice slightly. "You don't want to pay me!"

Sam laughed out loud, got up, and circled back behind the bar. He punched a key and opened the cash register, extracted two fifties and laid them on the bar in front of Beth. "There," he said, "we're even."

"Your books are never going to balance if you pull cash out and don't get a receipt," Beth said as she picked up the bills, folded them and stuck them in her pocket.

"You can give me a receipt tomorrow," he assured her.

"Tomorrow, or today? It is technically 'today', you know."

"The only thing I know is that I'd forgotten what a smart ass you could be."

Beth cocked her head slightly to one side. "Is that a good thing or a bad thing?"

Mimicking her, Sam replied, "That I forgot or that you are one?"

"Touché," Beth smiled. She raised her glass and looked at Sam. "To old times," she said. Sam picked up his whiskey sweet and they touched the glasses together softly before drinking.

Sam did not return to his spot next to Beth. Instead, he pulled up a stool they kept behind the bar for slow periods and placed it across from her. There was a moment of comfortable silence before Sam said, "It's good seeing you again, Beth, but I can't help wondering why you came back."

"Earlier, you wanted to know why I left. Now, you are wondering why I came back. Which do you want to know?"

"I'm not sure," Sam confessed. "Maybe both, maybe neither. It depends on what the answers are, I suppose." He took another sip of his drink, then he set the glass down and clasped his hands on the bar. "I figure it this way. Why you left really shouldn't matter. If it was something I did, I'm sorry."

"Sam—"

He held up a hand to silence her and went on. "Which brings us to the second question, why you came back." Another sip of the whiskey-sweet. "Bud didn't tell you about Jinx, Beth. I know that. Yet, somehow you knew."

His eyes met her and a look of confusion covered his face. "Were you in touch with someone else from the ranch?"

Beth hesitated, then answered as honestly as she could. "Yes."

"Who?" Sam countered.

"I'll tell you, Sam, but not tonight—not here." It was Beth's turn to take a drink.

"Why all this 'cloak and dagger'?" he asked. "We've always been on the level."

"Have we?" she said and instantly regretted it. "I'm sorry; that wasn't called for."

Sam shook his head and looked away. "No, it was called for. You're right. There are things I never told you—never told anyone."

"Why?" Beth prompted, wondering where this conversation was headed.

"That's not the way I was raised. Even as a child I was told that men don't talk about things; we *fix* things."

"But . . . what if the thing can't be fixed? What then?"

Sam shook his head again. "That's where the theory sort of falls apart."

Beth considered this. "You're not a child anymore, Sam. What do you believe now?"

"That's the clincher," he said. "I don't know *what* to believe. My knee-jerk reaction is that, if something can't be fixed, then talking about it isn't going to do any good either."

"But," Beth argued, "you don't know if you don't try."

Sam stood up and took a long drink. "There's one thing I *do* know. It's late and we've both had a long day. I suggest we drink up, head back to the ranch and turn in for the night. We can continue this philosophical discussion later."

"Promise?" Beth asked.

There was a hesitation, than Sam agreed. "Promise." After another hesitation, he added, "How long are you here for?"

Beth took a sip of her drink before answering. "Three weeks, four at the most. Jake's expecting me back at the—" She stopped. Why was she reluctant to tell Sam where she now worked? It wasn't like he would stalk her, or show up there to try and talk her into coming back. And yet, it felt wrong somehow. Sam caught the hesitation and nodded.

"Three weeks then, four at the most." He finished his drink and dumped the remaining ice in the sink. "If you didn't mind filling in, I could probably use you over the next few days. Trish—"

"Yes, Julie told me. A trucker boyfriend, right?"

"Right." He grinned and added, "I don't think I'll be able to pay you $100 bucks every night though, just so we're clear about that."

"Fair enough—unless, of course, you decide to charge me room and board, seeing I'll be a temporary employee as opposed to an uninvited guest."

"Tell you what, we'll settle the bill when you leave. Fair enough?"

"Fair enough," Beth agreed.

They left the Copperhead via the rear entrance and Sam locked the door behind them. The short ride to the ranch was made in comfortable silence. Sam parked the truck in the garage and circled around to open Beth's door for her, but she was already getting out. Once inside the house, Sam putzed around in the kitchen to give Beth first dibs on the bathroom. When she was done, they said goodnight and she retired to the guestroom that would be her home for the next few weeks. A silence fell over the house, but it was not the same silence that Sam had grown so accustomed to. He had to admit it. It felt good to not be alone inside these familiar walls. Why, he wondered, was it comforting to know that someone else was there, snuggled beneath some covers in the spare room and drifting off to sleep? He didn't know. But that was alright; for the first time in a long time it was alright to not know the answer to a question. He turned out the lights and retired, contemplating what the next few weeks would bring.

Chapter Twenty-Five

Trish did indeed call in sick for the entire weekend, so Beth had the pleasure of working the main bar at the Copperhead four nights in a row. On Friday, the Copperhead's customary fish fry brought in a crowd of regulars, as well as a handful of strangers who were passing through the area and decided to stop in. Many of the regulars remembered Beth, and she visited with them when time allowed. Of those she talked to, the majority asked if she was back to stay. Not wanting to get into a long, drawn-out explanation, she simply replied that she was undecided at that point. Saturday and Sunday's crowds were considerably smaller, but steady enough so that Beth and Julie were not bored. Still, Sam decided to close early on Sunday and sent Julie home at 11 P.M. Beth served the few remaining patrons, and when the last one gave up his stool at 12:47 A.M., Sam locked the doors and helped Beth with the closing routine of gathering glasses and wiping off the bar and tables.

"I was thinking about our conversation the other night," Sam said. He pulled the plug on the bar sink, allowing the water to drain out, just as Beth brought two more glasses from a side table. "Those can wait till tomorrow," Sam decided, then he looked at Beth. "About that conversation—I'd like to finish it, if that's alright."

"We can try," Beth said.

Sam mixed them each a drink, pulled up the bartender's stool and sat. Beth climbed onto a stool on her side of the bar and they faced off in silence for a long moment.

"Who goes first?" Beth asked.

"Well, it *was* my idea, so I suppose I should start," Sam announced without any real enthusiasm.

"I'm in favor of that," Beth grinned at him, but it did little to relieve the tension.

Sam took a quick drink. He studied the ice in his glass as he set it down on the bar. "You know that I can't stand talking about something that can't be fixed."

"Yes," Beth said. "You always thought it was a waste of time."

"Still do, but I'll make an exception this once." He took another sip of his drink, set the glass down, and looked Beth in the eye. "I was married once," he announced, his tone not unlike that of a graveside preacher.

"Is that all?" Beth exclaimed, trying hard not to laugh. "I thought you were going to say you robbed a bank or murdered someone." She saw the pain in his eyes and reeled in her amusement. "Was it really that bad?" she asked, even though his expression had already given her the answer.

"Yes, it really was."

"But," Beth struggled to rationalize it, "people get divorced all the time." She stopped herself and her eyes opened wide. "You did get divorced, didn't you? I mean, she didn't die or something, did she?"

It was Sam's turn to chuckle, but it was a subdued one. "No, she didn't die—although sometimes I wished she had."

"That bad, huh?" Beth asked.

"That bad," Sam said and the silence dragged out for several long minutes. "You see," he finally continued, "she never gave us a chance to fix things. She never told me that she was unhappy, or that she was thinking about leaving. Oh sure, we fought. What married couple doesn't? But I just never thought it was to that point, you know? I didn't think she'd just throw it all away without a word."

"She didn't say anything?" Beth knew it pained Sam to talk about this, but she also felt they were things that he needed to say—needed to get off his chest, so she encouraged him to continue.

"Not a word. I just came home from work one day and she was gone. It was like one of those scenes from a bad movie where the husband walks into an empty house and calls out a woman's name—a woman he thought loved him and was going to spend the rest of her life with him—but no one answers." He took another drink and swallowed hard. "There is no silence like that silence," he said, his voice choked with emotion. "It's something that a man never forgets."

"I'm so sorry," Beth said. "That must have been so hard."

"It was, but I made it even worse. I blamed her, and the world, and destiny—everyone and everything but myself. Then, to make matters worse, I poured myself into a bottle and stayed there. Thankfully, I don't remember much about that time, but what little I do remember is enough."

Beth was silent. She didn't know what to say. It was hard to even imagine Sam like that; the image was so contrary to the man she knew, and yes—loved. Should she tell him that now; was this the right time? Should she confess that the reason she left was because it hurt too much to be close to him and yet so far away? She didn't think the time was right, or maybe she was just too afraid. Besides, he might think she was simply feeling sorry for him, and that wouldn't do. Whatever the reason, she swallowed the confession and went with the next thing that crossed her mind. "But you survived; you made it through. Isn't that what really matters?"

"Yes, I suppose so. But 'making it through' isn't the same as 'never been broken'. I'm not sure I could go through that again. There's nothing I can think of that would be worth the risk."

"Nothing?" Beth echoed.

"Nothing," Sam repeated. A sad smile crossed his face and he shook his head softly and took another sip of his drink. "It's funny," he said. His eyes were sparkling, but from her vantage point Beth couldn't tell if it was with merriment or tears. "Miriam wanted me to tell her about Cindy."

"Was that your wife's name, Cindy?"

Sam nodded. "Miriam asked about Cindy, but I shut her out. I told her that it was ancient history—that I'd put it all behind me." Sam took another sip, swallowed. "She knew better. Miriam could see through me the way a mother sees through a child's lies. Still, I never told her. I let her die thinking I didn't trust her enough to tell her the simple truth."

"Stop beating yourself up, Sam," Beth said firmly. "Miriam loved you beyond any doubt. You've got to know that."

"I suppose," Sam agreed, "but those are still the facts that I have to live with every day." He looked at her long and hard. "I have a track record of hurting the people I love. That's something I think you need to be aware of . . . and believe." Before Beth could argue, Sam changed the subject. "So, that's it. I told you what you needed to know. Your turn."

"My turn?" Beth feigned innocence.

"Yes, your turn. Who told you about Jinx?"

Beth's heart literally skipped a beat. Should she lie, and if so—what could she say that sounded even remotely true?

"I'm waiting," Sam said, but his tone was a patient one.

"If I tell you," Beth began.

"Yes?"

"You won't believe me. So, the question I'm struggling with is—do I tell you the truth anyway, or do I fabricate something that you'd be more likely to buy?"

"I'd like the truth, Beth. Whether I believe it or not is on me."

"Yes, I suppose it is." Beth took a sip of her drink and looked Sam in the eye. "Okay then, the truth. You want to know who told me Jinx was ill. It was Miriam."

Sam's eyes went wide. He got up and walked away. He stopped after four or five steps and turned around to study her. "You're joking, right?"

"Does it look like I'm joking? Or, better yet—you know me so well—is this the sort of thing I'd joke about?"

"But . . . how? Miriam's dead. How did she tell you?"

Beth shook her head and looked away. Confessing that Miriam had told her was one thing; coughing up the details—such as the deceased woman had telephoned her with the news—was quite another. "She called me," Beth finally managed to say.

"She *called* you?" Sam said incredulously. "Like—on your phone?"

"How else would you call someone?" Beth said, a bit too harshly.

"That's way out there, Beth. Dead people don't use telephones."

"Oh no?" Beth argued. "Then what do they do? Speak through weegie boards, wait to be summoned in a séance?"

"How the hell would I know?" Sam declared.

"Exactly!" Beth agreed. "So who are you to argue with me when I say that Miriam called?"

The two stood facing each other over the polished bar, their faces flushed, breathing through flared nostrils. When neither backed down, Beth said as calmly as was possible, "If you don't want to believe me, that's fine. But then, you tell me—how did I know about Jinx?"

Sam had no answer for that. There was no way she could have known. If neither he nor Bud had told her, then who? And what about Bud? Hadn't he claimed to have seen Miriam visit the horse? Had he been lying, too? He fought to wrap his mind around it, but the idea wouldn't fit the parameters assigned by his brain. "This is just great," he finally muttered. "First Bud, now you. What's gotten into you guys?"

"Bud?" Beth said. "What about Bud? Did he say something about Miriam? Did he talk to her?"

"Oh no," Sam chortled. "He's got you beat on that one. He *saw* her."

"He *saw* her? Where?"

Sam noted the excitement in Beth's voice where disbelief should have been, and he somehow found that more convincing than her entire confession had been. "She visited Jinx in the stable."

Beth considered this for a long moment. It made sense, didn't it? If Miriam was concerned, she would have visited the horse. It was perfectly logical. "And Bud was sure it was Miriam?"

"He'll swear to it," Sam assured her.

Then it was all true. Beth's mind was whirling. What did this mean? Miriam had called, of that she had no doubt—but what *exactly* had she said? Their conversation hadn't been about Jinx—not at first. It had been about— Sam. Miriam had wanted Beth to come back and Beth had refused. Miriam hadn't mentioned Jinx until Beth had said she wouldn't go back to the Copperhead. And even before Miriam, there had been Peter. Peter said that Beth had to do something. She had to save . . .

"Are you alright?" The concern in Sam's voice brought Beth back into the moment. She looked at him, her eyes wide with realization, concern, and fear. The three emotions joined hands and surrounded her, circling and taunting like some twisted childhood game. *Ashes, ashes, we all fall down.*

"Sam," she said, her eyes locked on him. "I think you're in danger."

The ride home that night had been devoid of any small-talk or useless banter. Beth was not sure whether or not Sam had believed her story about Miriam, but he had offhandedly denied any possibility of his being in danger. Beth had stopped short of telling him about Peter, or the snowstorm, or how Mark had also worked at convincing her to come, so she could think of no way to convey to Sam the extent of her concern.

Sitting in the silence, her thoughts wandered. Where would the threat come from? Did Sam have an enemy that Beth knew nothing about? Could it be Cassandra—was she a part of this? Was that why she had appeared in Beth's recurring dream? *Maybe,* Beth thought, *I'm going about this all wrong. Could the threat be from some random element— a bolt of lightning, a dump truck that crosses the centerline?* Beth didn't want to even consider that. How could she save Sam from something she couldn't predict, much less control?

When they got to the house, Beth used the bathroom first, as had become their routine over the last three nights. They said their goodnights quietly, neither one wanting to engage the other, or strike up the conversation for a second go-around. When both had retired, a stillness settled over the house like a warm and familiar blanket. It bore no hint of danger or foreboding, but gently anesthetized all it touched with its caress. Still, lying beneath their covers in separate rooms, it was hours before either Sam or Beth welcomed sleep, or allowed its stillness to carry them away.

Chapter Twenty-Six

The sun rose at precisely 6:24 A.M. the next day, and Beth was up to see it arrive in all its splendor. She had woken early and couldn't fall back to sleep. Not wanting to disturb Sam, she had quietly brewed a small pot of coffee and carried her cup out to the bench by the water garden. A slight breeze turned the windmill, and the slowly-turning water wheel quietly deposited its load into the pond, creating ripples that traveled outward across the dark surface of the water. Gradually, the dark sky lightened, and the grey then gave way to shades of lavender and pink. As the sun broke the edge of the sky, it brought with it oranges and yellows that paved its path as it made its climb.

At 6:45, Beth went to the stable to check on Jinx. He tossed his head and nickered to her when she drew near. After feeding him his morning mixture of grain and molasses, she rubbed his ears and took hold of his halter. The morning air was cool; it seemed like a good time to let him out in the pasture to stretch his legs. When they were in the paddock, she unsnapped the lead rope and set Jinx free. He tossed his head and trotted to the far end of the enclosure. Beth smiled as she watched him go; she was pleased that her old friend was doing so well.

Back at the house, she carried her empty coffee cup to the counter for a refill. She was surprised to see that there was only a small bit left in the bottom of the pot, but fresh coffee was slowly trickling in; its aroma filled the air.

"Sorry, I took the last cup," Sam said. He was seated at the island, but Beth had been too focused on the day ahead and the sight of Jinx trotting across the paddock to notice him.

"No problem. I can wait for the new batch." She hesitated, then added. "You *are* measuring the coffee when you put it in now, right?"

"You, too? That's the same question Bud had. All I can say is, 'Beggars can't be choosers.' There's several cafés in town that serve coffee this early if you don't want the stuff I make."

"What I don't want," Beth announced with one hand on her hip, "is hair on my chest, thank you very much."

Sam opened his mouth to comment, but thought better of it and said nothing. When the coffee was done, they each filled their cups and sat at the island. After a while, Sam asked, "Did you sleep well?"

"No, not really. You?"

He shook his head. "I thought that confessions were supposed to clear the conscience and help a person sleep better."

Beth shrugged. "Perhaps, in time." She took another sip of coffee then said, "I hear you're having some kind of doings here next weekend."

Sam slapped his forehead with the heel of his hand. "I totally forgot to mention it to you. My bad. It's a little doings we started two—no, three years ago. People who board horses here, and a few others from town, come out. We get a local band that's looking for a gig to get some exposure, and we set up a half-barrel of beer. Last year we set up an empty washtub and everyone that wanted to brought a bottle of booze with and added it to the mix. If I remember correctly—and that's questionable at best—it was a pretty deadly concoction. Luckily, few people chose to drive home that night. We had bodies sleeping on the lawn, in the stable, pretty much everywhere. It was a pretty informal party, but people seemed to have a good time."

"It sounds interesting, to say the least," Beth said.

"Oh, that it was. I think the Chief of Police from Eagle River ended up sleeping on the bench out by the water garden. Man, I'm just waiting to get pulled over for a traffic citation so I can put that little gem to use."

"Who covers at the Copperhead while all of this is going on?" Beth asked.

"That's the best part. The Copperhead is closed on that day. Everyone who's anyone ends up out here, anyway. It's a good way to show customer appreciation, and I write it off as a business expense."

"Pretty clever," Beth said. "And I assume—"

Beth never got to finish her sentence. The calm morning air was shattered by the sound of horses squealing and the solid impact of hooves striking something soft but unyielding. In unison, Sam and Beth pushed away from the island and raced outside. What they saw there stunned them and they froze. At the far side of the paddock, the mustang that Beth had seen Cassandra with had Jinx pinned against the fence. Savagely, the younger horse was kicking the trapped animal, again and again, and Jinx's screams filled the air.

Sam broke out of the reverie first and bolted for the stable door. Beth, acting on instinct, ran for the fence and pulled herself up and over it without stopping to consider what she was doing. She hit the ground on the other side running. As she approached the infuriated horse, she waved her hands over her head and hollered to get the mustang's attention. The horse whirled toward her, its ears pinned back, and charged. Beth was stunned. In all of her years helping out on this ranch, she had never been attacked by a horse. When it became apparent that the mustang was not bluffing, Beth dove to the right to escape. The horse squealed and struck out with its foreleg. The blow caught Beth in the calf as she went down, and the pain was excruciating.

Beth rolled when she hit the ground and caught sight of two figures racing toward her from the direction of the stable. One was Sam, the other was Cassandra. Sam carried a lead rope that he twirled over his head. He shouted at the horse as they closed in and the mustang spun toward the new adversaries, tossing his head and snorting loudly.

"Don't you dare hit him!" Cassandra warned.

"Shut up," was all Sam managed to get out before the mustang charged again. Sam continued to spin the lead rope; the metal clasp tied to the end of it whistled through the air. When the charging horse was close enough, Sam allowed the lead to snake out and meet the animal. The clasp struck the horse across the bridge of its nose with a resounding thud. The mustang dropped its head and spun to the right. It trotted a few paces away, shaking its head and snorting angrily. Assessing the situation, Cassandra raced back to the stable and disappeared inside. She reappeared less than a minute later with a feed bucket in her hand. She shook the bucket, rattling the oats inside and called to the mustang. It looked at her and tossed its head, but remained where it stood, positioned directly between Sam and Beth.

"Come on, Bucky," she called. "Good boy."

The horse looked from Cassandra to Sam, and back to Cassandra. At last, with a final toss of its head, it headed toward the stable, giving a wide birth to Sam who still stood with the lead rope at the ready. With the mustang heading for the feed, Sam hurried over to where Beth was struggling to get up. He wrapped his arm around her and helped her to her feet.

"Are you alright?" he asked, his voice tight with concern.

"I think so," Beth said, testing her leg. She took a half step and froze. "Oh my God," she whispered. Favoring her leg but forcing herself onward, Beth hobbled to the far side of the paddock. Confused, Sam looked in the direction she was headed and his stomach clenched, then fell.

Jinx lay by the fence, struggling to stand but unable to get to his feet. As Sam looked on, Beth reached the old horse and, dropping to her knees, took hold of the animal's head, effectively restraining him. Sam raced to the pair, did a quick appraisal of the animal and swallowed hard.

"That's it, Beth," he said gently. "Hold him. I'll be right back." Beth nodded, her arms wrapped tightly around the horse's neck, and Sam raced back to the stable. He hurried into the tack room and retrieved a .32 caliber pistol from the drawer of the small desk. With shaking hands, he pulled a box of hollow-point bullets from the still-open drawer and loaded the gun. With the task complete, he tucked the pistol under his belt at the small of his back and hurried back out to the paddock.

Torn, Sam approached Beth and the downed horse. A numbness was settling over him. It served to quiet the struggle Sam could neither avoid nor rationalize. He didn't want to do what he knew needed to be done—and he wanted it to all be over. The only way to get to that point of relief was to continue moving. Don't stop to think; don't make it harder than it has to be. For God's sake, just get it done.

He knelt next to Beth and pulled off his shirt. Gently, he tucked one end of the garment under the halter strap on one side of Jinx's head, then passed the shirt over the animal's forehead and tucked the other end under the halter strap on the opposite side, forming a crude but effective blindfold. Jinx struggled briefly against the blinding cover, then became still. Only his rasping breath bore testament to the life that still remained trapped in the broken and battered body.

Beth was crying, her tears flowing freely and washing the dirt from her cheeks in ragged streaks. "Is the vet coming?" she asked, sniffing loudly. "Did you tell him to hurry?"

Sam bit his lip and drew a deep and ragged breath. "No," he said and, knowing what needed to be done, he pulled the revolver from behind his back and held it where Beth could see. Her eyes grew wide and she shook her head violently.

"No—no! You can't! You can't just shoot him without giving him a chance," she pleaded.

"Beth," Sam's voice was gentle, but firm. "Beth, you're scaring him." Beth realized Sam was right. Her chest hitched as she tried to simply breathe, and she softly stroked the horse's neck. "Beth," Sam continued, "look at his back leg; it's broken."

Beth met Sam's eyes, her own still pleading, then she followed Sam's gaze along Jinx's familiar form. His coat was dirty, and a long gash over his ribs served as a channel for a thin stream of blood that meandered along the wound before dripping down and forming a pool in the dry dirt. There was another cut on the fetlock of his right front leg. But the worst wound, the one that sealed his fate, was the hind leg that jutted out at an unnatural angle from the hock. Beth squeezed her eyes shut as a fresh rush of tears threatened. She tried to catch her breath, tried to breathe, tried to be rational, but the truth was too hard to face.

"You can't shoot him, Sam. You just can't. Couldn't a vet put him to sleep? Wouldn't that be kinder?"

Sam looked at Beth, looked into the watering depths of those eyes that were threatening to become a part of him, and willed himself to be firm. "Yes, a vet could euthanize him, Beth. But the closest vet is at least twenty minutes away. Do you want Jinx to suffer that long?"

"But—"

"I know what I'm doing, Beth. It will be quick, and he won't suffer."

"How do you know?" Her chin was quivering, and she looked away, no longer able to face him.

"Trust me, Beth. Can you do that?" Beth didn't answer. "Beth?" he asked, more gently. Beth released her hold on the horse but didn't move. "You don't have to watch; it's up to you. But I need you to move, okay?"

Beth drew a long and ragged breath. Before struggling to her feet, she hugged the familiar head, hidden beneath the blindfold, and kissed him gently through the shirt. He smelled of horse, and sweat, and Sam through the faded cotton. She stroked his ears a final time and whispered something to him, then she rose up on her one good leg, turned and hobbled away. In a matter of seconds, there was the sound of a single shot. She shuddered and whirled around, even though she didn't want to. Jinx was stretched out and still, the tension and life gone from his body, and Sam was standing before him, his arms draped down by his side and the gun gripped loosely in his hand.

Beth went to Sam and stood by his side. He wrapped his left arm over her shoulders and pulled her close. Neither spoke; there was nothing to say. After several long moments, he let her go and tucked the gun back into his belt.

"Let me see your leg," he said. She pulled the fabric of her jeans up, revealing an angry bruised area in the shape of a hoof print on her calf. "Can you walk?" She rolled her pant leg back down and nodded, too overwhelmed by everything that had happened to even care. "Then do me a favor. Go to the house. There's some things I've got to take care of out here."

"Are you going to bury him?" she asked.

"Yes."

"Where?"

"We have a spot we use. I'll show you later if you like."

She nodded and limped to the stable. Inside, the building was quiet. Cassandra and the mustang were nowhere to be seen. Her stomach tightened and her pain turned to anger, then fury. Cassandra had said that she would make sure Jinx was dead before the party, but surely she couldn't have had this in mind. This type of savage attack couldn't have been orchestrated, could it?

She moved through the stable with her head lowered and her eyes downcast. She didn't want to see Jinx's empty stall. If only she hadn't put him out that morning. If anyone was to blame for this, it was her. This was her fault. The tears came anew, a fresh torrent that refused to be stopped. She hurried to the house as best she could and into her room. Slamming the door, she threw herself on the bed and used the pillow to muffle her sobs. Eventually, she drifted off, exhausted by lack of sleep the night before and the emotional nightmare of the past hour. Her last conscious thought was the realization of how much she had been dreading Jinx's death. A part of her was grateful that, as terrible as it had been, at least it was behind her. She drifted off with a sense of relief that at least the worst was over.

Chapter Twenty-Seven

It was early afternoon when Beth awoke and hobbled out of her room. Her leg hurt worse now than it had that morning, but she knew nothing was broken. It would be stiff and sore for a while, but using the leg would still be the best therapy. The tragedy of that morning was still fresh in her mind. It threw everything slightly out of focus, as though she were looking through a dream-induced haze. The house seemed unnaturally quiet. Outside the windows, the sun was shining and the sky was a brilliant, cloudless blue. But none of that seemed to matter. To Beth, the entire world seemed slightly askew.

There was half a pot of coffee on the counter. The warming plate was off and the coffee was only lukewarm, but Beth poured herself a cup, drank half of it, then refilled the mug before limping over to the island. She sat and gingerly lifted her sore leg to rest her foot on the lowest rung of the barstool. With that done, she took another sip of coffee and made a face. It was cold and bitter, but even that seemed fitting.

Somewhere outside, the sound of a truck caught Beth's attention. From the familiar clatter that accompanied it, she knew the vehicle was pulling a trailer. Sam's Toyota passed by the window with the two-horse trailer fastened to its hitch. It slowed at the end of the driveway before turning west and accelerating. A moment later, the mudroom door creaked and slammed, and familiar footfalls carried Sam into the room. Beth did not greet him; she didn't have it in her.

"I thought you were gone," she said, adding, "I saw your truck pull out."

"Bud is using it. I won't have a horse like that mustang on my ranch. Cassandra made a few calls and found someone that would board it. She's lucky."

"And Bud's hauling it for her?"

"Yes. I wanted it out of here today if at all possible."

Beth looked at Sam closely for the first time since he'd come in. His hair was disheveled and wet with sweat. The shirt he must have found in the tack room to replace the one he'd used to blindfold the stricken horse was wet with perspiration and streaked with dirt. Beth got up and limped to the refrigerator. She grabbed the ice tray out of the freezer and carried it to the sink. There, she retrieved a glass from the cupboard, added a liberal amount of ice and tap water, and carried it to him. He accepted it wordlessly and drank half of it down.

"Thanks," he said as he rubbed the glass across his forehead. He studied her, his face etched with concern. "Is the leg bothering you much? Maybe we should have it looked at."

Beth shook her head and returned to her spot at the island. She reclaimed her stool and sat down, trying to hide the wince of pain as she pushed herself squarely onto the seat. "It's not serious. It's just going to be sore for a while." She sipped her coffee before adding. "I suppose it's a good thing the weekend is over. Trish should be back so you won't have to worry about me hobbling around behind the bar."

"The Copperhead is the last thing I'm worried about right now. I don't like seeing you hurt." Sam refilled his glass of water at the sink before joining Beth at the island. "I am glad it's Monday, though, simply because we're closed.

I don't have to worry about going there and leaving you here alone."

Beth was going to argue that she wouldn't be alone, and that Bud would be back, but it didn't really seem to matter. Nothing seemed to matter at the moment; the haze was refusing to lift.

"So, what now?" Beth asked. When Sam looked at her, confused, she clarified the question. "I know this isn't how you normally spend your days off. Maybe what we both need is to make an effort to put this behind us."

"Just like that?" Sam asked.

"I didn't say it would be easy. Hell, I don't even know if it's *possible*, but sitting here like two whipped puppies isn't going to help." She fell silent for a moment, and when Sam had nothing to add, she pushed on. "What do you normally do on your days off?"

"Paperwork," was his confident reply.

"Now that sounds like fun," she replied, mustering a small measure of sarcasm. "Let's pretend the paperwork is all done. And, knowing how you are, let's also pretend that the stable is clean, the chores are all done, the lawn is mowed and every hayfield in the county has been baled. *Now* what do you do on your day off?"

Before Sam could answer, Beth's phone rang. She'd tucked it in her pocket earlier that morning in case Steve Hanson called with news about her Bronco. She dug it out now and flipped it open as Sam smiled at the sight of the old phone and shook his head.

"Hello?" Beth said. "Oh, hi Mark." Sam's smile faded. "No, the Bronco's not fixed yet; I'm hoping maybe tomorrow . . . No, I'll probably stay on for a bit, yet. At least through next weekend . . . Okay, I'll see you Thursday then. Bye." Beth flipped the phone closed and laid it on the island.

"So, you never did say," Sam studied Beth as he took another sip of water. "Who is this Mark fellow?"

"Just a friend," she replied, perhaps a little too quickly.

Sam continued to study her and Beth fought off the urge to squirm under his scrutiny. At last, he said, "Something about you is different, but I can't say exactly what it is."

"I'm older," she offered.

"We're both older," he agreed, "but that's not it—not entirely."

I saw a beautiful moth in the dead of winter, in the middle of a snowstorm, and a man who could summon it at will, she thought. *I've been told that this life is not as we see it—that we are en route to something wonderful and that we are not making the journey alone. Would that change someone—that and getting a phone call from someone you loved who'd been dead for five years?* Instead she said, "Then what?"

He continued studying her, but finally he simply shook his head. "I can't put my finger on it, but there's something."

"Is it a *good* something, or a *bad* something?" Beth asked.

"A good something," Sam said. "At least I *think* it's good; I'll let you know when I figure it out." Sam cleared his throat. "So, Mark will be back up here on Thursday?" He quickly added, "Sorry, I couldn't help but overhear."

Beth nodded, but offered no further information.

"I assume you'll both be staying for the party on Saturday."

"I know I will; I can't speak for Mark."

It was Sam's turn to nod and not comment. They sat in silence for a moment. Sam slid his finger down the side of the glass, wiping the condensation away. When he looked at Beth again, there was sadness and compassion in his eyes. "I'm really sorry about this morning."

Beth shook her head and tears welled up again. She blinked them away. "I'm the one who should be apologizing. He was your horse; I had no right to put him in the paddock this morning. I should have waited and checked—"

"Wait a minute," Sam interrupted. "If you're blaming yourself, stop it—right now. You had every right to let Jinx out. It was a gorgeous morning. Cassandra should have checked before turning the mustang loose in there." Beth frowned and turned away, hoping Sam had not seen. "What?" He had caught the look and was calling her on it. "What were you just thinking?"

Beth shook her head again. "Nothing. It was nothing."

"It must have been something," Sam pressed. When Beth didn't reply, he pressed a bit more forcefully. "Come on; out with it."

"It's just . . ." Beth gathered her courage. "It's something Cassandra said." She took a deep breath and tried to shrug nonchalantly. "She made the comment that Jinx would be gone before you held your Labor Day bash. She said he was a 'downer'—he made people sad." She hesitated, but she'd come this far; there was no reason to not finish what she had started. "She said he'd be gone . . . even if she had to shoot him herself."

Sam's eyes widened in surprise. "You're not suggesting she deliberately turned that mustang loose on Jinx?"

"I'm not suggesting anything," she replied coolly. "I'm just telling you what she said. She was right; Jinx is gone."

Sam was silent, his brow furrowed. After several seconds he shook his head. "It doesn't make sense."

"No, it doesn't," Beth agreed, "but there you have it."

"Do you want me to talk to her about it?" Sam offered.

"And say what?" Beth replied. "No, it's over and done. Let it be. Besides . . ." Beth hesitated and studied her coffee cup.

"Besides—" Sam prodded.

"I don't know. I guess everything happens for a reason." Beth finished the statement. She met Sam's questioning gaze and plunged on. "Have you ever really thought about life, Sam, and why we're here?" she asked.

Sam forced a chuckle and shook his head. "No, can't say I have. It never really came up, you know? I mean, we're here; isn't that enough?"

"No," Beth said.

"No?"

"No," Beth continued gently, "because it's such a small piece of the puzzle."

"There's a puzzle?"

"All of life is a puzzle, isn't it? I mean, think about it. Do you really believe that we're born, we grow up to train horses and mix drinks, then we die and that's it? There's got to be more than that, doesn't there?"

Sam considered her comment before shrugging. "Obviously you've given this a lot of thought. So, let me direct that question back to you. If we're not here to simply live—to train horses, mix drinks, or whatever it is a person may do—then why are we here?"

"To learn . . . and to love," Beth said matter-of-factly, but the comment sounded ridiculous and empty even to her ears.

"And that's it?"

"Yes, I think so."

Sam looked at her, his expression quizzical. "And what, exactly, is it that we're supposed to learn?"

Beth shrugged. "I can't tell you that. It's different for everyone. I suppose it depends on who you are, and what you already experienced."

"So," Sam considered Beth's statement out loud, "this is an ongoing process."

"Yes," Beth agreed.

"But why? I mean, can't we simply learn what we need to in one life? For example, if I needed to learn patience, couldn't that be done in the course of one lifetime?"

"Yes, I suppose it could," Beth agreed. "But what if you needed to learn how to be patient, how to be humble, how to be forgiving, and how to trust with all of your being—that would be a lot to cram into one life, don't you think?"

"Yes, I suppose it would be." Sam fell silent as he considered this. Finally, he said, "So, you feel that the solution to this is that we live more than one life."

"Yes," Beth said.

"How many?"

"I don't know," Beth's confession was genuine.

"Okay, so how do we know when we're successful— when we've learned what we needed to learn?"

"I don't know that either," Beth said. "I imagine we'll know because our journey will be over."

"And we won't return to live another life."

"Yes—at least, that's as close as I can figure."

"And . . . what happens then?" Sam asked. "I mean, if we no longer need to continue living and growing, where do we go?"

Beth considered this. "To heaven, I suppose. I guess we go home."

Sam studied Beth for a long moment. "Let me see if I have this straight," he finally said. "We are born, grow up, and live our lives working at some type of profession. But, the real reason we're here is to learn some type of valuable lesson, and everyone needs to learn something different— something unique to where they are in this 'so-called' journey. Then, when we've learned everything we need to know, we stop returning and get to go to heaven . . . whatever that is."

"Yes, that's pretty close."

"Pretty close?" Sam looked confused again. "What part did I miss?"

"You missed the 'love' part," Beth said.

Sam got up and carried his glass of water to the sink and dumped it out. Most of the ice had melted by this point, but a few small remaining bits struck the bottom of the sink with quiet clicks. He rinsed the glass and put it in the dish drainer. He turned around to face Beth, but remained where he was. He leaned back against the counter and crossed his legs at the ankle. "And the love part is—what?" he asked, making no attempt to hide his skepticism.

"The best part," Beth hurried to explain, hoping that Sam hadn't just lost all interest in the conversation and simply decided that she was crazy. "It's how we help one another, and it's what makes it all worthwhile."

"Really?" Sam asked, and the skepticism remained.

"It's a theory that some people call 'old souls'."

"Old souls?"

Beth could tell she was losing him, and she rushed to explain. "Yes. You see, when we live our lives, we don't do it all alone. There are others—people making journeys similar to ours—who travel with us. In essence, there are friends—people we love—who accompany us on our way." Sam raised one eyebrow questioningly, but didn't interrupt. Beth continued, "As we go through successive lives, our roles change, but our connection to one another doesn't. For example, in one life, two people may be brothers; in the next life, they may be a mother and child. In yet another life, they may be lovers. It really doesn't matter. What matters is that the connection is always there."

"Like a spiritual support network," Sam surmised.

"Yes," Beth quickly agreed.

To his credit, Sam seemed to consider this, but after a moment he frowned and asked, "What happens if one of the souls in your theory doesn't learn what it needs to learn? What if that soul lives several lives—a dozen—without making any progress? Would the other souls—the ones accompanying it—eventually leave it behind? Would they journey on to heaven without it?"

"I—I don't know," Beth confessed. "But maybe that's one of the reasons why we don't travel alone. Maybe we help one another with the lessons; maybe we ensure that those traveling with us learn what they need to learn—and they, in turn, make sure that we also learn what we need to. God *did* say that we are never alone."

"I don't think that's what he meant, Beth," Sam said, straightening up.

"Can you be sure? I mean, it works, doesn't it—at least, in theory?"

Instead of answering her question, Sam posed one of his own. "Where did you get this idea from—Mark?"

"No," Beth said. "Although he does believe it, at least in part."

"If not Mark, then who?"

Beth knew it was a logical question; she just didn't know how to answer it. She finally decided to tackle the easiest part first. "The part about old souls was something Miriam tried to explain to me. And believe me, I was just as skeptical as you are when I first heard it. Later, though, when I'd had some time to think about it, it started to make sense." Beth slid off the stool and limped to the sink. She also emptied her coffee cup, as Sam had done with his water glass, and rinsed it out. Standing next to him, she was aware of how her heart beat faster; she steadied herself, took a deep breath and turned to face him. "Later, when I met Peter, a lot of the missing pieces slipped into place. Then, when Miriam called about Jinx and asked me to come back—"

Sam held up his hands, cutting her off. "Peter—who's Peter?"

Beth shook her head. She wasn't going to even attempt covering Peter and the nor'easter—not today. She was physically and emotionally drained. "I can't tell you about Peter today, Sam; I'm not feeling up to it. But I will tell you . . . I promise."

Sam tipped his head slightly to one side. He was considering everything she'd just said and allowing the information to slip into some kind of ordered chaos in his mind. A subdued look of understanding came over him. "Peter is the one who first told you that I was in some kind of danger." Beth looked away and Sam knew he'd hit pay-dirt with his guess. "Who is he, Beth?"

"Not today," she reaffirmed and limped in the direction of her room. Halfway there, she turned back and forced a smile. "When Miriam called, I was stunned, and even though I talked to her—heard her voice and her familiar laugh—it was still hard for me to believe the call was real. Admit it, Sam, the only reason you believe my story about Miriam is because Bud told you that he *saw* her." Beth hesitated and looked away for a moment. When she looked back at Sam, her eyes were bright with what—excitement, fear, hope? Sam couldn't tell. She took a deep breath and said, "If you found it hard to believe that Miriam is still with us, Peter is going to blow you away." With that said, Beth turned and went to her room, closing the door softly behind her.

Sam remained at the sink, listening and watching, until the guestroom door had closed. It was then that he realized that he'd been holding his breath. He let it out, inhaled deeply, and released the latest breath in the form of a heavy sigh. This felt wrong—all of it. Beth's return, Mark's absence, Jinx's demise . . . it felt like a low-budget movie with a chopped script. And now there was yet another character—this Peter—waiting offstage to make his debut. It was all more than slightly insane. Still, he trusted Beth; that was the part that made this so weird. Was there really such a thing as old souls? Was there a lesson he needed to learn in this lifetime, or were there simply horses to train, spreadsheets to balance, and this persistent sense of emptiness that Beth's return had somehow resurrected? Beth seemed convinced that there was more; was that why she'd come back—to 'recruit' him? That, he decided, was even more insane than the idea of Miriam using a telephone and visiting Jinx. No one shows up out of the blue after five years to say, 'Hey, did you know that you get to live more than once—countless times—until you learn what you need to learn?' He shook his head and, following Beth's lead, he abruptly abandoned the topic and headed for the door. Whether he was on his first and only life, or his fiftieth life, the horse stalls were not going to muck themselves out, and he was relatively certain that this Peter character—whoever *he* was—was certainly not going to show up to do it anytime soon.

Chapter Twenty-Eight

Mark was sipping his third long island iced tea at the far left end of the Eagle Crest Resort's bar. Since meeting Beth here, the resort had become one of his favorite hangouts. On the whole, he really wasn't into the bar scene. He did his best work 'one on one', which didn't correlate well with sitting in a tavern. Oh, it was a good place to strike up a conversation; but, as had been the case with Beth, he and his target generally ended up someplace more private to chat.

Tonight, the bar had about ten people sitting along its length. Two of them were elderly gentlemen who came in almost every night to share a few drinks and complain about the women they had been married to for nearly fifty years. Three stools down from them was a young couple on a date. Mark found it interesting the way life worked; both ends of the dating spectrum sitting within a few feet of one another and totally oblivious to the irony of the situation. Mark, on the other hand, was anything but oblivious. He was fascinated by what humans considered to be love. It was at the root of all they cherished. There was love of money, love of freedom, self-love and brotherly love. People loved hobbies, exotic places, the thrill of exceeding at a sport or a personal challenge, and even the smell of popcorn at the local theater. Some people loved sunrises; others loved sunsets. Some loved thunderstorms and rainbows; others loved making snow angels in winter's first blanket of pristine white. So many applications for such a small—yet powerful—word. Mark found that fascinating.

As with most people, though, Mark found the love shared between a man and a woman the most fascinating of all. It was the most complicated form of love, and the most dangerous. No other human condition extracted such a heavy toll as did love. It awakened hearts, and shattered them. It was both a reason to live, and a reason to die. It drove some people to persevere—to strive for the impossible—and it was also the reason some people gave for folding and quitting the game. It was powerful, and dangerous, and fleeting—yet it was the most-desired thing on the face of the earth.

Oh sure, over the course of many years Mark had met several people who claimed that they were fine living alone. They had never really looked for, or found, that special someone that most people crave. Mark had likened them to alcoholics who had never taken a drink. You can't become addicted to or crave that which you know nothing about. Maybe those people were simply 'wired' differently. Whatever the case, if they'd experienced love, they would have re-examined how they had lived their entire lives up to that point. Love changes everything it touches—for the better or the worse; it leaves nothing the same.

Love was also humans at their most comical level. People did idiotic things in the name of love. They sold their homes, left their spouses, spent their life savings, quit their jobs, colored their hair, got tattoos, and abandoned both family and friends if the person they loved asked them to. And they did it gladly and without a second thought. It made them happy—at least for a while.

But that was the thing about love—it didn't last. Some saw this as a weakness, but it was actually this trait that gave love its greatest strength. It was how love crushed people and drove them into the depths of despair. It was how love turned lives upside down and extracted its greatest price. It was not love that was weak; people were weak, and ultimately they couldn't control the very thing that they wanted more than anything else in the world. Love, in Mark's opinion, was the most successful parasite that man would ever encounter. It found them, drew its existence from them, possessed them, ruled them, and finally moved on to countless other willing victims when it got bored with the current game. And, in its wake, it left shattered hearts and broken souls. Mark knew and understood this better than anyone else ever would.

He took another sip of his drink and thought about the week ahead. In a few days, he would head back up to Eagle River. By now, Beth and Sam may well have rekindled the smoldering flame, or Beth might have tried to and Sam shot her down. It didn't really matter which way it had played out; either scenario worked well for him.

"Leave them alone, Mark."

The voice was not threatening, but Mark knew it well enough to know that it was best not to ignore it, either. As he turned, Peter settled on the stool to his left, placing Mark between the newcomer and the rest of the patrons that had chosen this night to drink at the Eagle Crest Resort.

"Peter, I wasn't expecting to see you. How have you been?" Mark asked, amiably enough.

"I'll tell you once more. Leave them alone; you have no claim here."

"I beg to differ. I have as big a claim as you do. I'm sorry that you don't see it that way." He took a long sip, set the drink on the bar and gestured toward it. "Sometimes I wish I could get a buzz—like the old days. Do you remember the old days, my friend?"

"Well enough to know that you're not my friend, and never were," Peter replied.

Tim was tending bar that night. He was a stout, ex-high school jock with a rugged face and a five o'clock shadow. At twenty-four, his receding hairline made him look considerably older. "What'll you have?" he asked, setting a coaster in front of Peter.

"Bud Light," he said and Tim left to fetch it.

"Now, let's not be difficult," Mark said when Tim was out of earshot. "We both agreed to play by the rules a long time ago."

"Yes, we did," Peter agreed. "We just disagreed to what some of those rules were."

"Did we?" Mark asked. "I don't recall that."

Tim returned with the beer. Peter paid him with a five and told the bartender to keep the change. Tim thanked him and left.

"We can't interfere with their lives. You know that," Peter said when they were alone again.

"Really? And what do you call showing up in the middle of a snow storm and driving Beth home?"

"You know better, Mark. There's a difference between interacting and interfering."

"And that difference is?" Mark asked, taking another sip of his drink.

"Interacting is talking to them, explaining things. Interfering is changing the course of their life—or the lives of people around them—without their knowledge."

"Right," Mark agreed. "I remember now, but thanks for setting me straight on that again."

"You're heading back up to Eagle River, aren't you?" Peter asked even though he already knew.

"Yup, on Thursday. They're having this party on Saturday; I wouldn't want to miss it."

Peter sipped his beer and stared at his familiar adversary. As far as he knew, Mark had not done anything 'illegal' as far as Sam was concerned, but yet he wondered. Rules were often broken; perhaps that was the one human trait they could not successfully leave behind. "Sam is not yours; not yet," Peter said.

"Not yet, but I'm holding out hope. I sense a great disturbance in the force, Luke," Mark said, mimicking the old Jedi master from the original Star Wars movie.

"Very funny," Peter conceded, "but I don't find this to be a laughing matter."

"That's because you take yourself too seriously," Mark chuckled.

"Fate cannot be taken too seriously. The man's been through a lot—"

"Please," Mark interrupted. "That's what people do; they go through things. This one is no different." He took a quick sip before adding, "And what about the woman— Beth? I don't see where she's had it any easier. Are you rallying a few souls to save her, too?"

"You know the rules, Mark."

"Oh yes, as long as there's love, there's hope, right? Well, I disagree. In fact, I'm going to make a wager with you. I'm going to bet that it's her love that will be her downfall. And, just to make it interesting, let's make Sam the prize."

"We don't bet using souls; in fact, we don't bet at all. It's—"

"Against the rules. Oh yes; I forgot. Too bad, it would have made this all the more interesting." Mark picked up his glass and drained it. He raised the empty to signal the bartender. While he waited, he turned back to Peter. "So, are you heading up to Eagle River, too?"

"Should I?" Peter replied.

"Hey, I'm just trying to hold a casual conversation here, that's all. Where you go and what you do is your business."

Tim brought Mark his drink, collected the money and left. Through it all, Peter kept his eyes focused on Mark. "I've played my role in this, and so have you," Peter said. "It's out of our hands. Either Sam comes around and gets back on track, or he doesn't. It's up to him."

"And Beth," Mark added.

"The man either loves, or he doesn't. Beth can't change that any more than you or I could."

Mark considered this and took another sip of his drink before replying. "You've set the lady up for a world of hurt if this turns out the way I think it will."

"All I did was convince her to go back. What was in her heart was there all along. Even I don't have the power to change that."

"As well you shouldn't, my friend. But," Mark smiled, a surprisingly pure and simple expression that the man wore well, "she's going to regret going back to Eagle River. Mark my words, and she's going to regret loving that man. I guarantee it."

With that, Mark lifted his drink, raised the glass in Peter's direction, and then drained it. He gave Peter a mock salute and left the bar as sober as he had been when he came in four hours earlier. Peter watched him go and wondered, not for the first time, if Mark could be trusted. Even if he couldn't, it wasn't Peter's job to check up on him. That responsibility landed on someone a lot further up the chain of command than he was. Still, he couldn't shake the feeling that a trip to Eagle River might be in the very near future.

Chapter Twenty-Nine

Sam busied his hands with the task of cleaning out Jinx's stall, but his heart and mind were both somewhere else. Beth had been right; he needed to make an effort to put the events of that morning behind him, but the images of Beth's pleading eyes and the tears rolling down her cheeks as she knelt before the old horse were refusing to be pushed aside. What was it about that woman that stuck in his head like a familiar tune that refused to stop playing? Even when he wanted to, he couldn't turn it off. When he was busy at the Copperhead, or astride a new horse and putting it through its paces, his level of concentration was such that he was not aware of the persistent melody. But later, when the pace slowed and his mind was free to wander, it returned with clarity. It was not aggravating as much as it was haunting. It was, he supposed, now a part of him.

For the five years that Beth had been gone, he had thought of her often. Still, he had not tried to track her down. He supposed that it would have been an easy enough task. After all, he knew her social security number, and he could justify his search by actually mailing her the paycheck that she'd left behind . . . the one that was still sitting in his desk drawer. He lifted another forkful of soiled sawdust into the wheelbarrow and made a mental note to give Beth the check the next time they were at the Copperhead.

Using the fork, Sam leveled off the wheelbarrow's load and then added one more forkful for good measure. He leaned the fork against the wall, then hoisted the wheelbarrow by its handles and guided it out of the stall and toward the door at the back of the stable. He could walk the route blindfolded, so his mind settled on the melody once again. Why *had* she taken off without a word? That was, he knew, a rhetorical question, and he had posed it to Beth simply to see if she'd be honest. Instead, she'd side-stepped the question and refused to answer. The truth was, she'd left because of him; he'd been an ass and had given her no indication that he regretted it, or that he was going to change. Hence, she had left, and there you have it.

He pushed the wheelbarrow through the open door and over to a small pile of manure behind the stable. Tipping the wheelbarrow upward, he added its contents to the pile. On Saturday, Bud or one of the other hired hands would pick up the manure with the front end bucket on the John Deere tractor and load it into the manure spreader. Once the spreader was full, they would take it out to a field that would be plowed under come fall and spread the contents in even rows. But that wasn't what was going through Sam's mind. The familiar tune played on in his head; it had simply changed verses. The relevant—and true—question, he supposed, was why had she really come back? She had known about Jinx; that was true enough. But her explanation of Miriam calling was simply too far out there for Sam to wrap his mind around. Instead, he chose to disregard that point and move on. Beth *had* known about Jinx, and she *had* come back. She'd also said that he was in some kind of danger . . . this was far more complicated than it needed to be. Why couldn't she have simply pulled in the driveway, jumped out of her Bronco, and said, "Hey there, I missed you"?

For whatever reason, she hadn't. He let go of the empty wheelbarrow, turned around, and grabbed hold of the wooden handles again. He lifted up on the handles and, with the now-empty wheelbarrow in tow, headed back into the stable. Verse three. Would she be staying? No, she'd made it perfectly clear that this was only a visit. Could he change her mind and convince her to move back to Eagle River? Should he? Did he want her to come back? Reaching the stall he guided the wheelbarrow inside and set it down. Snatching the fork from its resting spot, he returned to the task of picking the manure out of the stall. Mentally, though, he'd arrived at a revelation. Why she had left was not important—not really. Neither was why she had returned. Those things were in the past. What mattered was, now that she *was* back, did he want her back for good? Could she have haunted his mind all these years because he loved her? He didn't believe that was the case; he didn't believe he was capable of loving anyone. It just wasn't worth the risk. Besides, his life was good just the way it was; a man simply wastes time fixing something that isn't broken.

The sound of his truck pulling in the driveway with an empty trailer rattling behind it pushed the song, and the annoying questions, to the back of his mind. He exited the stall and walked out of the stable just as Bud finished backing the trailer into its spot next to the machine shed. Together the men lowered the trailer's jack into place and cranked the tongue of the trailer skyward until the weight was off of the truck's bumper. After placing blocks of wood in front of and behind the trailer's wheels, Bud unhooked the trailer and Sam drove the truck to its customary spot in front of the garage, parked it and turned off the engine. Bud approached the parked vehicle and the two men rested their forearms on either side of the truck's bed and stood facing one another. Sam was the first to break the silence.

"Did you have any trouble at the Morley's?"

"No, Boss. The horse trailered and unloaded like he'd been doing it his entire life."

"You told Jim everything, right? I don't want that man to be blindsided."

"He knows," Bud said. "How's Beth taking it?"

"Like the Beth we've always known. She's a trooper; she told me that we need to put it behind us. Just like that."

"You are right; that is the Beth we've always known. She was never comfortable showing her pain, but that does not mean that it wasn't there."

Sam studied Bud for a long moment before asking, "Is there something you're trying to tell me?"

Bud shrugged. "No, Boss. You know as much as I do . . . probably more." He turned and began walking toward the stable.

Sam called after him, "And what, exactly, does that mean?"

Bud stopped walking, but he waited several long seconds before he turned around to answer. His brown eyes were filled with sadness, or was it pity? Either way, Sam was not pleased with what he saw there. When Bud finally answered, Sam was no less confused than he'd been when he'd asked for clarification.

"There are those in this world who suffer well for others," Sam finally said.

"Meaning?" Sam persisted.

"A wounded animal does not show its pain. To do so would imply weakness," Bud said. "You and Beth are both wounded animals."

"Really . . . wounded animals? And you base that on?"

"Watching you, listening to that which you do not say." Bud began to turn away, then stopped. He turned back, caught Sam's gaze, and held it. "What I don't understand is how you do not also hear it. Perhaps you listen too much with your ears, and not enough with your heart."

With that, the old man turned and disappeared into the stable. Sam leaned into the truck, rested his forehead on his forearms and let out a heavy breath. Could the day get much worse? *What do you do on your day off?* Beth had asked. The answer was suddenly very apparent; today he simply wished it wasn't his day off and that he was at work. Working *had* to be better—and easier—than dealing with all of this. The house door opened and closed behind him. He turned and saw Beth approaching. When she'd closed the gap between them, she said. "The garage called. My Bronco is ready. Could I possibly hitch a ride into town?"

Chapter Thirty

Sam took twenty minutes to shower and change before he and Beth walked out to his truck and headed for Steve Hanson's shop. The ride into Eagle River was a quiet one. Sam and Beth were each lost in their own thoughts until the repair garage came into view. Not wanting to seem unappreciative, Beth broke the silence.

"Thanks for the ride, Sam," she said. "I hope I didn't put you out."

"Not a problem. The timing was actually good. Truth be told, I needed to get away from the ranch for a bit," Sam replied.

Beth understood, but made no comment. Sam slowed and pulled into the parking lot of Hanson's shop. He parked the truck, killed the engine, and held up a finger toward Beth indicating that she should stay put. Without a word, he climbed out and circled around to her door. He opened it and offered his hand.

"And you thought chivalry was dead," he remarked as she took his hand and stepped down. From there they made their way to the shop entrance, where Sam also opened the door for Beth and escorted her inside. A small bell suspended above the door tingled merrily and a man's voice shouted from the back of the shop, "Be right with you."

A few minutes later, Steve stepped into the lobby through the door to the service bay. A heavy-set man in his late fifties, he was dressed in soiled brown coveralls and a dingy T-shirt. Nearly bald, a patch of unruly white hair curled over the tops of his ears, and his nose—apparently broken at least once—canted slightly to the left, giving him the appearance of a retired mobster, or boxer who had finally left the ring for a less violent path through life. Contrary to his gruff countenance, his blue eyes danced merrily when he saw Beth and Sam waiting at the counter.

"Well, just look at the two of you," Steve rounded the counter and held out his hand to Sam. The two men shook and Steve turned to Beth. "It's been too damn long," he said, then raised grease-stained pudgy fingers to his mouth as though he were a child caught swearing. "I beg your pardon, Beth. I've always been a little rough around the edges, but I reckon that's no excuse for swearing in front of a lady."

"I've heard worse; heck, I've *said* worse," Beth replied, "so forget it. I was pleasantly surprised—and grateful— when Rusty said your shop was still here."

"Why wouldn't it be? I'm too damn young and broke to retire," Steve said with a wink.

"Speaking of broke, what are the damages for the Bronco?" Beth asked. "I totally forgot to ask you for the total when you called. You *do* still take credit cards, right?" Beth was trying to sound nonchalant, but she wasn't sure she was pulling it off.

"Was it the timing belt?" Sam interrupted.

"Yup," Steve said. "But it also needed spark plugs and a set of wires. And, by the way, young lady, when was the last time you changed the oil in that poor thing?"

"I . . ." Beth tried to remember. "The oil light wasn't on, was it?"

Sam and Steve rolled their eyes in unison. "Idiot lights, my dear," Steve told Beth pompously, "are for idiots."

"Oh," was all Beth could think to say. "And the bill?" she asked again, more sheepishly.

"Put it on the Thunder Ridge account," Sam said. Steve raised his eyebrows just as Beth protested.

"No, I'll pay for it. It's my bill, Sam, not yours."

"The Bronco died on your way up here to check on Jinx," Sam stated matter-of-factly.

"But it would have died the next time I was on my way to *anywhere*," Beth countered.

"But it didn't, did it?" Sam said.

"So, you're not back to stay?" Steve interjected, his blue eyes no longer smiling. "I—I thought you were back."

Beth looked at Steve, uncertain what to say. Sam came to her rescue.

"She'd heard Jinx wasn't doing very well. She came up to see him . . . and to help if she could."

"Well. If that's what she's here for," Steve said, the smile returning to his face, "then I hope Jinx takes his sweet time getting better."

Sam and Beth exchanged a long look, and Beth said quietly, "Sam buried him this morning."

"Well, damn," Steve said. "I'm sorry, really. I didn't know he was that bad."

"It's alright," Sam tried to make light of it and ease Steve's discomfort. "You had no way of knowing. His passing took all of us by surprise."

Beth turned away and crossed the lobby to look out the dusty window that faced the parking lot. Cars hurried by on the street outside, heedless of the 30 MPH speed limit. She watched them pass and tried to collect herself. Behind her, she could hear the men talking and the jingle of keys changing hands. After a minute or so, she heard them behind her and she turned around.

"I'm sorry about Jinx," Steve said. "He was a great horse. He was Miriam's favorite, wasn't he?"

Beth nodded and forced a smile. "Yes, he was."

"Well then," Steve said with a slight shrug of his massive shoulders, "then he's in good hands, no?"

"Yes," Beth said and her smile brightened, "he is."

Sam shook his head, almost imperceptibly, and placed his hand on Beth's shoulder. "I think we should let this man get back to work, don't you?"

"You're right. I'm not getting any younger or richer standing around here visiting with the two of you." Steve turned to Beth and his expression grew serious. "But you, young lady, had better stop in before you head back to wherever it is you've been hiding for the last five years. Got that?"

"Got that," she agreed.

"Promise?" Steve pressed.

Beth grinned and the tension swept out of the room. "Promise."

The Bronco was waiting in the parking lot next to Sam's truck; one of Steve's helpers had pulled it around. Beth hurried to it, feeling like she'd been reunited with an old friend. She glanced in the back and saw her bags exactly as she'd left them—not that she'd had any doubt. Sam had the driver's door open by the time she reached it. She climbed in and started the engine. It purred like a kitten, and the gas gauge read 'full'. Steve had topped off the tank for her. She closed the door, fastened her seatbelt and opened the window. Sam leaned in.

"Do you mind following me to the Copperhead for a few minutes? There's something I need to pick up."

"Sure," Beth agreed, wondering only briefly why Sam did not want her to drive back to the ranch alone. As it turned out, it was not that he hadn't wanted her to return to the ranch; the something he had to pick up at the Copperhead was for her. She had followed him there, parked next to him, and accompanied him when he went inside. In his office, he withdrew an envelope from the center drawer and handed it across the desk to her. She glanced at it and realized that it was the paycheck she'd left behind when she'd fled that night five years ago.

"You actually kept this?" she said with disbelief.

"I guess I didn't really know what else to do with it. The amount was already entered into the payroll; I couldn't see upsetting the books, or reworking the balance sheet due to one check not getting cashed," he explained.

She considered that and handed the check back to him. "Use it to offset the bill for the Bronco repairs."

Sam refused to take it. "I already told you that I'm paying for that, but you can buy me a drink if you want to."

"You're not open. Won't that upset the books, too?"

He snapped his fingers. "You're right. Guess we'll just have to have one and not tell anyone. Would that work?"

"I think so, As long as nobody knows," Beth said with a smile.

They headed out to the bar and Sam mixed each of them a drink as Beth looked on. He set the glasses on the bar and came around to sit beside her. Before either drank, Sam lifted his glass to make a toast. "To old friends and good memories," he said. Beth nodded and they clinked glasses before taking a sip.

"Can I ask you a personal question?" Sam said.

"I suppose," Beth replied hesitantly, though she wasn't sure why.

"You've never been married, right?" he asked. After Beth nodded, he said, "Why not?"

She shrugged. "It just didn't happen."

"So you've never been in love?"

"I didn't say that. Being in love and being married aren't exactly the same thing."

"No, I suppose they aren't," he agreed. "So, if you loved someone, why didn't you marry him?"

"It's not that simple. Everyone seems to think that two people just look at each other and they know. They fall in love and live happily ever after."

"Well, *I* sure don't think that," Sam scoffed and took a long drink.

"No, I don't suppose that you do. More likely than not, you belong to the next largest group of people—those who believe that love is just a term used for raging hormones and romantic encounters that were never really meant to last."

Sam considered this. "Is there a third group—one that isn't either naïve or jaded?"

Beth smiled and took a sip of her drink. "There are many groups, I suppose. Those two are just the biggest ones."

"And what group do you belong to?" he asked. "I'm guessing the 'hopeless romantic' group."

"Nope," she disagreed. "More like the realist group."

"I see. And what, exactly, is the difference?"

"Realists understand the truth about love."

"Which is?" Sam asked with a twinkle in his eye. Beth thought that he was enjoying this just a bit too much. She shook her head and frowned.

"It's not that simple," she explained. "It's not like there's one great truth about love and, when you know it, life becomes easier. Love has many truths."

"Okay," Sam said, playing along. "Name two."

"First, it doesn't allow us to choose who we love. We don't meet someone and say to our self, 'I'm going to love this person someday.' You either do or you don't; it's not a conscious decision you make."

"Agreed," Sam said. "But you *can* fall in love with someone over time."

"Yes." It was Beth's turn to agree. "And you can also fall out of love with the passing of time."

"True enough," Sam said. He took another sip of his drink. "And the second truth about love is?"

Beth thought for a moment, then said, "It changes everything it touches."

"For the better or the worse?" Sam said, and the question held more than a hint of sarcasm.

"That depends on the person, not on love," Beth said.

"Let's go back to the original question. You don't deny being in love at some point in your life, but you've never been married. If he'd asked, and if you loved him as you claimed you did, you would have probably said 'yes'."

"Probably."

"So, one can safely assume that he didn't ask," Sam surmised.

"With the given information, that would seem like a fairly safe bet," Beth agreed. To his credit, Sam did not continue his analysis of the situation out loud, but Beth felt the need to explain. She took a deep breath. "The third truth about love is that it's not a 'couple' thing. Love doesn't care how the other person feels toward you. Love just "is". Sure, it's great—magical even—when both people feel the same way toward each other. And it's even more magical if they not only fall in love but find that way to make it last. But that's up to them; it's *their* challenge. Love doesn't care one way or the other."

"That sounds a little harsh."

"There's no guarantees. You should know that, Sam."

He took a sip and nodded. "Aren't we a sorry couple . . . love lost and love unrequited." He waited a beat before adding. "Do you have any regrets, Beth?"

She shook her head. "No, I don't. I've had a lot of time to think about it." She took another sip before turning the question back on him. "How about you, do you have any regrets?"

He considered that and chuckled, but the sound came out more sad than merry. "I think I would have made a good dad."

Beth laughed. "That's not a regret," she said. "It's just a postponed event. You're still young; you've still got plenty of time to have kids."

"It's a little hard to do on my own, in case you don't know exactly how it works," he said, and his voice held a teasing quality.

"What, has the entire female population been wiped from the face of the earth and I missed it? What are you waiting for?"

"The right one, I guess," Sam said.

"Well, good luck with that. What do you think, she's going to have 'The Right One' branded on her forehead when she walks in here some night? You've got to put a little effort into finding her, you know."

"I suppose. And what about you?"

"What about me?" she countered.

"Would you do it all differently if you had the chance?"

"No, not really."

He looked at her with his head cocked a little to one side, reminding her of a cocker spaniel she had as a child, and she loved him all the more for it. He rephrased the question. "There's nothing you'd change—nothing you'd do differently if you had it to do all over again?"

Beth thought about it and took another sip of her drink. Finally, she looked Sam in the eye and said, "I would have kept Miriam at the bar a little longer that night—just ten or fifteen minutes. Not long at all, really, but it might have changed everything."

Sam placed his arm around her and pulled her close to him. They sat there on their bar stools, side by side, and Beth laid her head on his shoulder. He felt strong and warm, and she leaned in closer, allowing the scent of him to envelope her. She could have sat like that forever, heedless of time or the world outside the Copperhead. No, she had no regrets where love was concerned. As long as Sam was safe and near, all was right with the world. In her heart, it felt right . . . even if she couldn't tell him, even if he didn't love her back, even if he didn't know.

"Is this a private party, or can anyone join in?"

The question startled both of them. Sam lifted his arm off of Beth's shoulders and both of them twirled around to face the intruder. Mark stood several paces away, wearing a leather jacket, his motorcycle helmet dangling from his left hand. He smiled at their surprised expressions and an unexplainable chill washed over Beth. *What other surprises,* she wondered, *did this day hold in store?*

Chapter Thirty-One

"I didn't mean to startle you. I saw the Bronco in the parking lot, and the back door was unlocked. I hope I'm not intruding." He walked past them and circled around to the business side of the bar. He pulled a twenty dollar bill out of his pocket and laid it next to the till. "I'm buying a round; what's everyone having?"

"I'd better pass," Beth said. "I've got to drive back to the ranch yet; one's my limit."

"Come on. I'm sure Sam could give you a lift—or you can catch a ride with me," Mark argued. "Your choice."

"We've both had a long day—" Sam began, but Mark cut him off.

"All the more reason to unwind. What do you say—one more for the road? You can drink it while you ask all of those questions you've got tumbling around in your head."

"Such as?" Sam prompted.

"Such as, 'What am I doing here?', 'What was the real reason why Beth came back?', and, oh yes, 'Is there really such a thing as an 'old soul?' How's that for starters?"

"Pretty good," Sam admitted after a slight hesitation. "And you can tell me those things?" Sam asked.

"Those and plenty of others. So, what's your pleasure?" Mark met Sam's gaze and held it.

"Whisky sweet, and the lady's having—"

"No," Beth cut him off. "Nothing for me. I'm still nursing this one," and she held up her half-full glass for the men to see.

"Alright," Mark said, "I guess it's just us men for this round." He set about to mix their drinks, moving about behind the bar with an ease that denied that he had never been in the Copperhead before. He seemed to intuitively know the exact location of the whiskey bottle in the rack, and which button on the gun would supply the proper mixer. Sam looked on in amazement, but said nothing. After Mark had placed Sam's drink on the bar, he mixed his own with equal ease and took a sip. Abruptly, he looked at Beth and said, "It's too bad about the Eagle Crest. I can't imagine how surprised you must have been when you heard."

Beth's eyes went wide and she set her drink down with a solid thud. "Heard what?" There was a distinct sense of urgency in Beth's question.

"You mean Jake didn't call you? I just assumed—"

"Why would Jake call—what happened?" Beth sat up straighter, bracing herself for the worst.

Mark slowly looked from Beth, to Sam, and back to Beth again before answering. "There was a fire. The resort was a total loss."

"Oh no," Beth said softly. "When?"

"Last night. That's one of the reasons I came up early; I assumed you'd heard."

"No, not a word. How . . . how did it happen?"

Mark shrugged and took a quick drink. "It's anybody's guess at this point. When I left Baraboo this morning, it was still smoldering pretty good. But, there was talk; there always is when that sort of thing happens."

Sam joined the inquiry. "Are they thinking arson?"

"Probably. The fire started sometime between three and four A.M. The place was locked up, and—with the 'no smoking' law—there's little chance that it was due to a smoldering butt that got dropped somewhere by accident. The kitchen closed at ten, so everything in there was cooled down long before they locked the place up."

"Wiring?" Sam asked.

"Nope," Mark replied, shaking his head. "All new; they upgraded in 2012. And, before you ask, there wasn't a single lightning strike in the entire state last night."

"That does seem to narrow down the possibilities," Sam agreed, taking a sip of his whiskey sweet.

Beth slid off her stool, wincing a bit as she settled her weight on her injured leg. "I've got to call Jake." She looked at Sam and added. "I locked my phone in the Bronco. The car charger is the only one I brought with, so I don't know how much juice is left in the thing. I might have to plug my phone in and make the call from out there."

"Do what you need to do, Beth. If your drink gets warm, I'll mix you a fresh one."

Beth managed a slight smile and, without even thinking, she kissed Sam lightly on the cheek before leaving to call her boss. Sam and Mark watched as she limped out of the bar, and they heard the back door open and close behind her. Something about that bothered Sam, but he couldn't quite put his finger on what it was. When he looked over at Mark, the man had turned toward Sam and was watching him intently. For several seconds, neither spoke.

"What's your story with her?" Mark finally asked, his tone of voice and his face equally unreadable.

"I fail to see where that's any of your business," Sam replied without thinking about it.

"Touchy subject?" Mark pressed, but there was neither sarcasm nor ire in his voice.

"Truth is," Sam explained, "I don't like you very much. I can't say why, but I don't."

"Let me guess, you also pride yourself on your ability to tell a person's character from your first impression of the individual." When Sam only nodded and continued to study him, Mark pressed on. "I can respect that. So tell me, what was your first impression of Beth, then?"

"As I said before," Sam began.

"That's really none of my business," Mark finished the sentence for Sam, took a sip of the long island iced tea he'd mixed for himself, and sighed contentedly. "I'm not the enemy here, Sam."

"And you're not what I consider to be a friend."

"Fair enough—I'm a friend of a friend. That's not the worst thing in the world to be. Still," Mark took another sip of his drink, "if Beth trusts me, I don't see why you should find it so difficult."

"Does she—trust you?" Sam asked, his hands resting on the bar, fingers interlocked. The moment was all about control, and who held it, and both men knew.

"She brought me up here, didn't she?" Mark stated matter-of-factly.

Sam nodded slowly. "Yes, yes she did. I'm just not sure why."

"Would you believe that I am the one who convinced her to come?" Mark asked, meeting Sam's gaze.

"She mentioned you," Sam gave Mark that much, but little more. "She credited you for your belief in old souls— you and someone named Peter." There was a brief spark of emotion in Mark's eyes, but it passed too quickly for Sam to read it with any certainty. Had it been anger, surprise? Sam couldn't be sure, but there had been a reaction; of that, there was no doubt. It was Sam's turn to press on. "Do you know Peter?"

"I've talked to him a time or two," Mark confessed, and the lack of hesitancy added a measure of credence to his answer.

"So, who is this Peter character?" Sam asked.

Mark ignored the question and countered with one of his own. "Did she tell you that she came back just to save you?" Sam stiffened involuntarily and instantly regretted the tell. Mark noted the reaction and a slight smile transformed his features. He did not look like he posed any threat to either Sam or Beth, so why did Sam distrust this man so? For the life of him, Sam couldn't say. "*I* know that you don't trust me, Sam. That's fine. But there's something that *you* need to know." Mark hesitated and Sam wondered if it was done simply for a dramatic effect. "There's more going on here than even Beth realizes. She came back here because she loves you, Sam." A look of disbelief bloomed and was instantly extinguished in Sam's eyes, but not before Mark read it. "So, she hasn't told you. That's immaterial, I suppose. Ask her; I don't think she'll deny it. The woman doesn't have it in her to lie. But there is so much that she doesn't know—so much that Peter hasn't told her." Another hesitation, and Sam rode it out without comment. When Mark finally spoke again, his voice was quiet—nearly ominous. "I know men, Sam—I know them very well. If you tell a man he's in danger, he will begin to circle, looking tirelessly for the threat in every person, every place, every item that he sees. But usually, man's greatest danger doesn't come from the outside world—it comes from within.

The sound of the back door opening and closing ended the exchange. Beth rounded the corner and limped back to the bar. She gingerly stepped onto the rung of her stool and settled herself back into her spot at the bar. Without looking at either man, she took a drink of her lime vodka sour and wiped the condensation from the sides of the glass with her thumb. "Well, it's official," she said. "The Eagle Crest is gone, and so are all of the jobs that the resort maintained—including mine."

"I'm sorry," Sam said.

"Don't be. And don't even think about offering me my old job back here—at least, not tonight. The only thing I want right now is to crawl into bed and bring an official end to this day before anything else can go wrong."

"Drink up." Sam said. "I'll take you home; we'll come back for the Bronco tomorrow."

"Normally I'd argue with a suggestion like that," Beth said. "But tonight, you've got yourself a deal." She guzzled her drink and set the glass down forcefully on the bar. As an afterthought, she asked, "Mark, are you coming out to the ranch?"

The man shook his head. "No, I think I'll get a room in town. I'll head out there late morning. That is," he added, looking at Sam, "if that's alright."

"Of course it's alright," Beth said, oblivious to the tension that resonated between the two men. "If Sam doesn't have any objections, I'll make lunch. How does 11:30 sound?" she asked, looking from one man to the other.

"Sounds good to me," Mark agreed.

Sam was not so quick to agree. "You're going to cook?"

"Very funny. If you don't like it, you don't have to eat," she reprimanded him gently.

"That's true. I could always have Trish throw a pizza in here when I come down," Sam agreed.

"Very funny. I hope you choke on it." With that, Beth limped toward the back door. Sam waited for Mark to come out from behind the bar. The man retrieved his helmet from the side table where he'd left it, and then Sam followed Beth and Mark out of the supper club. Once they were all outside, he locked the deadbolt and the doorknob before heading to his truck. He opened the door for Beth as Mark fired up his motorcycle, put the kickstand up, and headed out of the parking lot. Both Sam and Beth watched him go.

"What is it?" Beth asked, suddenly sensing Sam's uneasiness.

"Probably nothing," Sam replied. "It's just that, I could have sworn that I locked the door when we got here and went inside to get your check. It's a habit I have; I don't like people coming in the back way—especially when we're closed."

"So," Beth said, "then you probably locked it. What of it?"

"If I locked it," Sam said, watching the tail light of Mark's motorcycle grow smaller as it disappeared down the road, "then how did he get in?"

Chapter Thirty-Two

"I don't mind saying, that man gives me the creeps." They were halfway back to the ranch when Sam spoke, breaking the silence. Beth had been miles away, thinking about Jake and picturing the Eagle Crest burning to the ground. The sound of Sam's voice brought her back to the moment.

"What?" she said.

"Your friend Mark. I don't like him."

"Why? What did he do?" she asked, but only half-interested.

"That's just it. He didn't do anything—at least nothing I can put my finger on. There's just something about him." Sam rubbed his chin thoughtfully with his right hand and held the steering wheel with his left.

"Maybe you're imagining it. He's never been anything but a perfect gentleman to me. He's never been rude, or sarcastic—"

"The model citizen, right?" Sam interrupted.

"I didn't say that. He's just always been nice, that's all."

The silence returned and the cab of the truck pressed in around them. When they were only a mile or two from the ranch, Sam said, "I'm sorry about that resort where you worked. How's your boss taking it?"

"Hard," Beth said. He's sixty-three; he would have retired in a few more years anyway, but if they prove it was arson . . . I don't know. It's just a real crappy way to have your life's work end, you know?"

Sam turned the truck into the drive and parked in front of the garage. Not bothering to open the garage door, he simply killed the engine and lean back in the seat. Taking a deep breath, he shook his head sadly. "If someone torched the Copperhead," he began, "I couldn't help but take it personally. It's not just a building they destroy when they strike that match. It's a business; it's jobs for the people who work there. It's a sense of security—a sense of accomplishment for the owner, and whoever built the business up before him."

Beth listened and nodded. "The Eagle Crest has been in Baraboo for more than sixty years."

"Even worse," Sam said. "It's part of that town's history." He waited a beat before adding. "It's also part of your history." He turned his head toward her, his brown eyes questioning. "What are you going to do now that your job is gone—are you still going back to Baraboo after the harvest fest?"

"I have to go back. I live there."

"You might have to go back to square things away, but you don't have to stay."

An expectant hush filled the truck cab, broken only by the soft ticking sound of the cooling engine.

"And if I didn't stay there—if I came back here, then what?" Beth asked.

Sam turned slightly in his seat and leaned against the truck's door, angling his body toward her as he spoke. "You know that your job at the Copperhead is still there. All you have to do is say the word."

"Whether or not I have a job here is not the issue," Beth said. "We are."

Sam cocked his head slightly to the right, as he often did when Beth gave him food for thought. "Care to explain?"

"Do I have to?" Beth replied, and the slight edge that crept into her voice was harsher than she intended. She took a cleansing breath and looked out the window. She mentally arranged, discarded, and rearranged what she wanted to say, but nothing sounded right. Finally, she gave up wrestling with the details. At last she said, "It's my problem, not yours."

"I think it's *our* problem." Sam countered. When Beth did not question or object to his remark, he said, "Look me in the eye and tell me I'm wrong." Beth's gaze dropped to where her hands were folded in her lap, and she shook her head. Sam waited, but Beth remained silent. Softly, he said, "Beth, hurting you is the last thing I wanted to do—"

"Don't," Beth turned to face him, tears welling up in her eyes. "Don't defend what happened after Miriam's funeral. My God, we're consenting adults, Sam. It's not like we killed someone, or robbed a bank. We didn't break any laws, we weren't cheating on our spouses—why did you feel like you had to apologize? Was it that wrong?"

"Of course not," he said, his voice still gentle.

"But?" she prodded.

"But—something must have happened that day. You left."

"Not because of that. It took almost a year for me to leave. I could have gone for a multitude of reasons."

"But you didn't; you left for one reason—and I have the feeling that it was something I did."

Beth shook her head again, but she didn't look away. "No, it wasn't something *you* did. It was something *I* did. I fell in love with you, Sam. I didn't *plan* for it to happen; I didn't *mean* for it to happen, but it happened never the less." Sam opened his mouth to reply but Beth raised her hand, silencing him. "Don't you see? It wasn't you, Sam. It was *me*—and it's still me. You mean more to me than you'll ever know, and I'd trust you with my very life if it came down to that, but I can't trust myself when I'm with you. Everything in my life—as God-forsaken and trivial as it may be—makes sense. Everything is comfortable, and safe, and predictable . . . everything except the way I feel for you." She took a deep breath and used the heels of her hands to wipe the tears from her eyes. "I'll stay for the harvest fest," she said as she opened the truck door and slid out of the cab. "But after that—I just don't know, Sam. I've had a lot of time to think about it—a lot of time to get over you, but only one thing is clear to me. It's a whole lot easier missing you from somewhere far away."

With that, Beth closed the truck door and headed for the house. Sam watched her, a vague silhouette retreating in the moonlight, until she'd made her way inside the house, disappearing from view. Why hadn't he gone after her? He'd wanted to, but he'd stayed where he was, frozen in place. A single light came on beyond the kitchen window, and Sam felt drawn to it—like a moth to a flame—yet still he didn't move. Twenty minutes later, when the light winked out and darkness returned to the house, Sam was still sitting in the truck, considering what Beth had said.

Chapter Thirty-Three

The next day, Beth was up with the sun. She dressed quietly so as not to wake Sam and headed out to the stable. Somewhere close by, a farmer had recently cut a field of alfalfa and the still, morning air was sweet with the smell of drying windrows of hay. An assortment of birds were singing, but their songs were muted by the familiar honking of a Canadian goose that passed overhead. Beth looked up and tracked its flight, wondering why it was traveling all alone. She had read somewhere that Canadian geese mate for life. Was this solitary wanderer too young; had it yet to find a companion? She chose to believe that scenario; it was more kind than the explanation that its mate had been shot down by hunters last fall, leaving it to fly alone.

She opened the stable door and stepped inside. It took a moment for her eyes to adjust from the bright, sunlit sky to the stable's shadowy interior. When her surroundings came into focus, she was surprised by what she saw. Two horses were standing in the isle, fully saddled and tied to the side of a nearby stall. Sam was tightening the cinch on the nearest horse, a tall, chestnut thoroughbred named Ginger. In addition to riding Jinx, Beth had often ridden this mare when she and Miriam spent their days off from work galloping around the ranch and simply enjoying life. The other horse that was saddled was a black Morgan-Arabian mix named Blaze. He was a spirited gelding that Beth also knew well, but had made a point to never ride. He was a beautiful animal to behold, but once the saddle was in place, Blaze viewed all of his immediate surroundings as a position somewhere behind enemy lines. Every leaf that blew across his path, every car horn that sounded in the distance, every bird or rabbit that passed close by was a mortal threat to be avoided at all cost. If his rider was not constantly alert to these numerous threats—both seen and unseen—then a rapid, unplanned dismount was often the result. At last count, Blaze had thrown more riders than any other horse in the Thunder Ridge's history. Though he was five years older now, his lifted head, pricked ears, and pawing front hoof told Beth that he was still a force to be reckoned with, which suited Sam just fine.

"Good morning," Sam said as he finished tightening the cinch and lowered the saddle's fender over the knot. He patted Ginger's neck and stepped to the railing to untie her. "I was beginning to think that I was going to end up riding alone this morning."

"But, I never said anything about wanting to go riding. How did you even know I'd be here?" Beth asked.

"Lucky guess, I suppose. But then, people are creatures of habit. I remembered that you used to go out riding most mornings back when . . ." He hesitated and the unspoken words hung over them.

"Yes, I did," Beth said, and added. "I'm surprised you remembered."

"I'm full of surprises; you should know that."

Beth smiled at the mare. She approached and ran her hand over the animal's familiar flank, feeling the warm, soft coat pass beneath her fingers. "Yes, you are, and yes I should," she said, turning her smile toward Sam.

They walked the horses out of the stable and through the gate that led to the large western pasture before mounting up. Beth rode several paces ahead at first. Battling with Sam for the right to take the lead, Blaze side-stepped for several yards, tossing his head in an effort to slacken Sam's hold on the reins, but Sam sat deep in the saddle and held him in check. When the horse gave signs that it accepted who was in charge—at least for the time being—Sam moved up alongside Beth, coaxed the gelding into a slow gallop, and the pair of riders headed toward the ranch's far western boundary.

The majority of the pasture was open field, but it was flanked on both the north and the south by wooded areas several hundred feet long and equally as deep. Here and there, smaller groups of trees dotted the face of the pasture, providing shade in the summer and wind-breaks during the winter months. As they cantered along, horses that were currently using the pasture fell in with the riders, raced beside them for a spell, then abandoned the chase and returned to leisurely grazing the morning away. When they reached the far end of the pasture, Sam reined Blaze in and Beth guided Ginger in alongside him. He pointed to a group of six horses that were grazing at the edge of the northern woods.

"See that white mare in the middle?" he asked Beth.

"Yes," Beth replied, patting Ginger's neck affectionately.

"Her name is Ghost. She belongs to a gentleman in Sister Bay named Robert Quentin," Sam continued. "She's three-quarter Arabian and one quarter Morgan—a real pistol. She makes Blaze here look like an old man."

"I don't see the attraction in owning a horse like that," Beth frowned. "Even if you overlook the fact that they're downright dangerous, they're no fun to ride—so what good are they?"

"They're flashy," Sam explained. "And, when it comes to horses, flashy means money." Blaze whinnied to the nearby horses and tossed his head, but Sam maintained a firm hand on the reins. "She's due to foal in a month. Her owner paid a $5000 stud fee to have her serviced by Duke

Gavin, a purebred Arabian that's all the rage right now in the world of 'hot blooded' horses."

"Hot blooded?" Beth asked. "I thought all horses were 'warm blooded'."

"Hot blooded is just a term for certain horse breeds— such as Arabians and thoroughbreds. It generally applies to high-spirited breeds. 'Warm-blooded' horses are middle-weight horses that aren't as flashy. A good example of that would be the quarter-horse. And 'cold-blooded' is a term they use to designate work horses and draft animals."

"I see," Beth said, but she really wasn't sure she did.

"Anyway, her owner sent her up here because she has a habit of rejecting her foals. She's given birth twice; she'd have nothing to do with either foal and both died within days."

"It sounds like a bad investment to have her bred," Beth remarked.

"It has been so far," Sam agreed.

"Is that common—for a mare to reject her foal?" Beth asked.

"No, it's actually rare. It's more common for a mare that gives birth for the first-time, but even that doesn't happen often."

"Well, what are you supposed to do? I mean, how do you make a horse want her foal?"

"I'm not sure," Sam admitted. "Bud will be taking her off pasture and bringing her into the stable on Friday. We'll keep her confined, and Bud will keep a close eye on her. Hopefully, if we're there to work with her when the foaling takes place, we'll have both a mare and a foal to send back to Sister Bay in October."

"And what if that isn't enough—what if she still won't have anything to do with it?"

"We're prepared—I hope. There's a lot of good info to be found online, and we've talked with some other ranchers who have had good luck raising orphaned foals. But, let's just think positive thoughts for now, shall we?"

"You're the boss," she said.

They sat quietly in the warm morning sun and watched the small group of horses graze for a few minutes longer. Finally, Sam slowly turned Blaze around to face Beth. "Would you like to see where we buried Jinx?" He asked, hesitantly. Beth nodded, and Sam headed Blaze back toward the stable, holding him at first to a fast trot, then a slow gallop. When they were halfway there, Sam guided them in closer to the woods that ran along the northern edge of the pasture. At one point, a small clearing jutted into the trees, creating a secluded area that was sheltered from the wind and any onlookers—human or otherwise.

Sam reined Blaze to the left, and they entered the clearing and came to a stop. Before them, at the northern edge of the opening, was a patch of freshly turned ground, devoid of grass and weeds, and Beth knew it for what it was—a grave. She stared at it, and her heart ached for what lie beneath the dark soil. When she could bear to look no longer, she glanced about and noticed five white crosses randomly placed about the clearing. Four feet high and nearly as wide, they jutted out of the fertile soil, and each was inscribed with the name of the horse that rested beneath its stoic watch.

"Bud is making a cross for Jinx," Sam told her, his voice little more than a whisper. Sensing the emotion of his rider, even Blaze seemed subdued. He held his head lower than Beth had ever seen and nickered softly.

"Thank you for bringing me here," Beth said, looking at the grave once more.

"It seems to me," Sam thought it was time to change the subject, so he forced a more jovial tone, "that you offered to make lunch today. Should we get you back so you can get started?"

Beth emerged from her daze, and although she'd only half-heard, she agreed. "Yes, I suppose."

"I'd race you there," Sam remarked, "but—"

"But it's never a good idea to race horses toward the stable. It makes them barn sour," Beth said, finishing the statement for him. Sam and Blaze were already out of the clearing and moving back in the pasture. Beth turned the mare around and started to join them, but a subtle movement from the direction of Jinx's grave caught her eye. Reining Ginger hard to the right, she spun the large horse around to get a better look. A large, black moth, iridescent in the morning sunlight, flitted over the freshly-turned ground— dark wings against the dark soil. Beth blinked to clear her vision and looked again, but the moth was gone.

"Are you coming?" Sam's voice seemed to echo from the pasture beyond.

"Yes," Beth hollered back. After a final glance, she gave the thoroughbred her head and Ginger carried her to where Sam and Blaze were waiting in several quick strides.

Sam sensed the change in Beth, and his voice took on a note of concern. "Are you okay? Maybe bringing you here wasn't such a good idea."

"No, I'm fine . . . really. I'm glad you brought me. It's comforting to know where he is."

Sam considered her comment, coupled with her pale complexion, and decided to let it go. If—and when—she wanted to talk about it, she would. Until then, he decided, it was best to just leave it be. He turned the gelding into the morning sun. The ranch buildings waited beyond, engulfed in the sun's brilliant light. Beth brought Ginger up alongside Blaze, and she and Sam exchanged a smile. Sam's heart gave a lurch—just a small one, but undeniably a lurch. He'd enjoyed their morning ride, in spite of the somber note on which it had ended. Four days until the harvest fest, and then—what? He didn't want to think about it, not yet. Throwing caution to the wind, he released his tight hold on the reins and gave the gelding his head. After a small cluck of encouragement, Blaze bolted toward home. The thoroughbred, with her racing lineage and long legs, effortlessly remained alongside him as Sam bent low over his horse's neck and the wind glided over and around them. With reckless abandon, they raced for the stable at breakneck speed and, if he'd only had the ability, Sam would have willed the race and the moment to last for all eternity.

Chapter Thirty-Four

With the challenge now before her, Beth found herself regretting that she'd offered to make lunch. It had seemed like a good idea at the time, though, and she wasn't the type of person who went back on her word. While Sam put away the horses following their morning ride, she'd raided the pantry, the freezer, the refrigerator, and even the small garden that Bud tended behind the house. The fruits of her labor were now spread out on the table before her, such as they were. Lunch would consist of a tuna-pasta salad, fresh corn on the cob, a tossed green salad with vinaigrette dressing, baking powder biscuits, and carrot cake with cream cheese frosting for dessert. It seemed to be missing something, but Beth couldn't put her finger on what it was. Moments later, when Sam came in from the stable and passed through the dining room on his way to the bathroom to wash up, he glanced at the table and frowned.

"Where's the meat?" he asked, winked, and smiled his warmest smile.

Beth crossed to the refrigerator, found a package of Oscar Meyer bologna, and held it up for him to see. "Right here," she replied with a 'how's that for you' smile spread across her face.

Sam shook his head and rolled his eyes. "*Now* I know why you never got married," he said. Beth made a motion to throw the bologna at him and he ducked into the bathroom to clean up.

In a few minutes, the sound of a motorcycle announced that Mark had arrived. Beth listened as the bike pulled into the drive and parked by the garage. Mark killed the engine and moments later there was the sound of a knock at the door. Beth went to answer it, and Mark entered wearing jeans and a gray polo shirt. He carried a bottle of Sangria wine with a Door County winery label.

"I wasn't sure what we were having," he said, gesturing to the wine. "I hope this is appropriate."

"Even if you *had* known what we were having, you would have had a hard time deciding what was appropriate," Beth said, smiling. "And, I'll let you open it. The corkscrew is in the top drawer left of the sink."

While Mark worked the cork out of the bottle, Beth retrieved four glasses from the cupboard. Sam came out of the hallway and approached the table, drying his hands on a towel which he then draped over the back of one of the dining room chairs. The two men nodded at each other in lieu of a greeting. There was the sound of the door opening and closing and Bud appeared in the mudroom doorway. He nodded at Sam and studied Mark.

"This is my friend, Mark," Beth explained in way of an introduction. "He's up from Baraboo, visiting. Bud," she spoke to Mark now, and pointed toward the elderly man, "is employed here at the ranch. You might say that he's Sam's 'right hand' man." Mark set the open bottle of wine on the counter and crossed to Bud with his hand extended. The two men shook briefly, and Beth motioned for everyone to be seated.

The meal began in relative silence, broken only by an occasional 'Pass the salad,' or 'Please pass the corn.' No one asked for the bologna, which made Beth smile to herself. So much for the popularity of meat. Midway through the meal, Sam initiated a somewhat substantial conversation.

"So tell me, Mark, if you don't mind my asking," he began. "Where did you and Beth meet?" Sam had no intentions of making friends with the man; he still didn't like him. But it wouldn't hurt to learn more about him. How did that old saying go—'Keep your friends close and your enemies even closer'?

Mark swallowed the pasta he'd been chewing and said, "I happened to stop in at the Eagle Crest for a drink and she was tending bar."

"It must have been a slow night if you struck up a conversation with her," Sam chuckled. "I had to practically twist her arm to get her to be nice and visit with the clientele at the Copperhead when she worked there."

"When was that?" Beth protested.

"When did you work there? You mean you don't remember?" Sam winked and grabbed another ear of corn from the tray in the center of the table. Avoiding eye contact with Beth, he spread a lavish helping of butter on the cob and took a bite.

"Don't be a smart ass," she said. "You know exactly what I mean. When was I ever stuck up and refused to talk to the customers?"

"I didn't say that you were stuck up; I said that you were antisocial. There's a difference."

"No I wasn't!" Beth protested more loudly.

"If you say so," Sam said, shrugging and turning the cob to prepare for another bite. "All I know is that no one ever simply came in for the banter when you were on duty."

"You paid me to tend bar, not to 'hob nob' with the patrons."

"Perhaps, if you would have 'hob nobbed' a little more, you might have gotten better tips."

Beth opened her mouth to comment, changed her mind, then began again. "How do you know what kind of tips I got?"

"I was your boss; it was my job to know." Sam polished off the cob of corn and reached for another. As he buttered it, he thought it wise to change the topic. "Beth tells me that you believe in this whole 'old soul' theory," he said to Mark. "Is that true?"

"Yes, I do—parts of it at least. I don't know how much she's told you about it, but it makes a lot of sense."

"What is this 'old soul' theory?" Bud asked, opting to join in on a conversation.

"It is a belief that our souls—or 'spirits' if you prefer that term—come back for multiple lives," Sam explained. "Do I have that right?" he asked Beth and Mark collectively.

"That's a bit over-simplified, but yes—you have the right idea. The main concept is that there are lessons we must learn, and those lessons cannot be covered in a single lifetime. Because of that, we need to experience life more than once," Mark explained.

Sam watched Bud closely as the older man listened to Mark's explanation. He expected Bud to roll his eyes, or look to Sam for input as to whether Mark was sane or pulling everyone's leg, but Bud seemed to be paying very close attention to what was being said.

"And, if we fail to learn these 'lessons'?" Bud asked.

"We simply repeat living until we do," Mark said. "But that's not the entire theory. There's another part—the best part; we don't have to do it alone. Other souls—companion souls, if you want to call them that—accompany us on our journeys. They help us understand what we need to learn, and they travel with us through each successive life."

Bud's brow furrowed and he frowned. "So, we live many lives, and we do not live those lives alone. Others travel with us and guide us along the way."

"Yes, that's it in a nutshell," Mark agreed.

"But," Bud asked, "what of those who do not wish to help?"

"Excuse me?" Mark said.

"There are people in the world who do not wish to help others; they exist only to challenge our beliefs and stand in the way of our true path. Are they then what you might call evil souls?"

"Evil souls?" It was Beth who posed the question.

"Life does not exist without balance," Bud explained. "There is peace and turmoil, love and hate, good and evil . . . each cannot exist without the other. Therefore, if there are 'good' souls, there must also be 'evil' ones."

"You mean like angels and demons?" Beth asked.

"No, I am not even sure that angels and demons even exist. But we each possess a soul," Bud explained, "and, if there are souls with good intentions, than there must also be souls with evil intent."

"That sounds logical enough," Mark agreed. "I guess I never really considered it."

"But, what would evil souls do—tempt us, try to trip us up?" Beth asked, confused by the very concept.

"They would torment the good souls," Bud said. "They would not want others to have that which they themselves had been denied."

"Which is?" Sam re-entered the conversation, more amused than enthralled by the exchange.

"Peace," Bud said matter-of-factly.

"Peace?" Beth's confusion was apparent in her tone, and her voice went up an octave.

"It is the one thing that we each seek, but it is illusive. Also, it has many faces. For one person, peace comes from having enough money, or enough friends. For another, peace is only attained by finding that one special person with whom to share one's life. A truly wise man knows that there is no one set path to peace."

"And these evil souls?" Sam asked.

"They exist to block one's path. Because they can never have peace, they would want no one else to have it."

A silence fell over the lunch table as each considered this. A full minute passed before Beth asked, "So, if there is such a thing as an evil soul, could a good soul be converted?"

"What do you mean by 'converted'?" Sam inquired. He was apparently done eating, and he pushed his plate aside and leaned back in his chair as he waited for an answer.

"If a good soul comes back, time and again, and if each time they come back—despite the help from other old souls—the peace they are seeking is denied them, could the mounting frustration make them evil?"

Everyone considered this, but an answer was not immediately forthcoming. After a long silence, Bud said, "Even the strongest spirit can be broken. And yes, a broken spirit would be very vulnerable to an evil influence."

"Okay," Beth was thinking out loud. "So, if a soul is basically good but overwhelmed, and an evil soul decides to try and convert it, what could save it?" Beth asked.

"Love," Bud's reply came without hesitation.

Mark shook his head. "I never understood that line in the bible," he said. "There are three things that last: faith, hope and love, and the greatest of these is love."

"1st Corinthians, 13:13," Beth said, remembering a snow-filled night months past and the words that Peter spoke.

"Yes," Mark agreed. "But I don't get it; what makes love better than faith and hope?"

"Without love, the other two will not last," Bud explained.

"How so?" Beth asked.

"You can hope that your child grows up to be brave and true," he explained. "But, if you do not love that child well enough to help him or her to learn the right way, then your hope will not be rewarded."

Beth considered this for a bit. "And, you can have faith in a marriage—you can believe that it will last forever—but, if the love is not there, then faith will not be enough to hold two people together."

"Mark, I think we've learned something here today," Sam said as he rose and stretched. "Door County Sangria wine does not mix well with Vilas county, homegrown sweet corn." He snatched the towel from where he'd left it earlier and headed for the bathroom. "You guys go right ahead and continue trying to figure this mystery out. I'm going to shower and head to work," he announced.

"And this mess?" Beth asked, indicating the table and the remains of their lunch.

"Sorry, should have been at the Copperhead by now. But I'll take the cleanup detail next time; I promise," Sam replied, disappearing down the hallway. Beth turned to the others.

"I need to ride out and check on Ghost," Bud announced as he got up and headed for the door.

"Have you got an extra horse? I haven't ridden in years," Mark added, also rising and stretching.

"You men are impossible!" Beth exclaimed, but they'd bailed out of the room so quickly that she wasn't even sure they'd heard.

Beth set about clearing the table. She packaged the leftovers in tinfoil, saran wrap, and whatever appropriately-sized Tupperware containers she could dig out of the cupboard. As she worked, she listened to the sound of the shower turn on, run, and eventually turn off as she cleared the last of the plates from the table and carried them to the sink. Never a fan of dishwashers, she ran a sink full of hot, sudsy water and washed the dishes by hand, drying them as necessary when the dish drainer became full. It was a mundane task to be sure—washing dishes—but a sense of peace came over her as she worked. This was where she wanted to be, at least for the moment; it was someplace she felt she belonged. She didn't know what tomorrow would bring; no one did. But one thing was for certain. If there *was* an evil soul out there that wanted to deny her this newfound feeling of peace, it would be wise to not bother her right now. Not only were her supplies of faith, hope, and love all currently intact, she was also a damn good aim when cracking a damp dishtowel.

Part Four: Revelation

Chapter Thirty-Five

Cassie was born Cassandra Lynn Fredericks in Fort Campbell, Kentucky in 1984, and was a true Army brat in every sense of the word. Like most military families, hers moved often, making relationships with children her own age all but impossible. To compensate for her daughter's lack of close friends, her over-indulgent mother bought her whatever Cassie's heart desired, much to the chagrin of the young girl's disciplinarian father. An only child, Cassie attended the best schools in whatever area her family currently called home, owned the latest brand-name clothing as soon as it came out, wore makeup in public at the age of nine, and was never responsible for a single household chore of any kind. Cassie had the world by the tail, and she was smart enough to know it.

Like most young girls, Cassie loved horses; she just didn't love them for the same reasons. To Cassie, it wasn't about spending time riding and brushing the magnificent animals; it wasn't about the sense of freedom one got when galloping a horse across a meadow or around a show ring; it wasn't an appreciation for the bond one developed with an animal when working with it on a regular basis. For Cassie, it was all about power—not only the power she had over the animal itself, but also the power that she and a well-trained horse had over anyone who watched them cantering around any arena or paddock, moving as one. Cassie attended endless riding camps, learned dressage, and often hung out at any stable that would allow her to, not because she loved horses—but because she loved the fact that working with horses enabled her to get whatever she wanted, whenever she wanted it. Case in point, the Thunder Ridge Ranch.

Cassie was working at a small stable in Kaukauna, training snot-nosed kids and their horses, in 2008. The Thunder Ridge Ranch was viewed as an 'up and coming' facility that year, and the news of Miriam's fatal car accident spread through the equine community like a wildfire. Months later, when rumor had it that Miriam had willed the ranch to a single man in his late thirties, Cassie had developed a sudden interest in the Eagle River facility. Not one to rush into anything, Cassie took the time to do her homework. She researched the ranch—how many people did it employ, what was the average number of horses boarded there at any given time, what type of training facilities did it offer, and who really ran the show? Based on the answers she uncovered, she prepared to make her move. The Thunder Ridge Ranch—and more specifically, Sam Phillips—was about to have the best trainer available fall into his lap . . . quite literally, if Cassie had her way, and she usually did.

The plan was this: Cassie would secure a job as a trainer at the Thunder Ridge Ranch. Over time, she would win the trust of everyone there, both man and horse. With more time, she would—to be blunt about it—seduce Sam, convince him to marry her (without a prenuptial agreement, of course), and take over legal control of the ranch. But training horses there was not her vision. The ranch covered over three hundred acres. Due to the popularity of Wisconsin Dells among tourists, a development firm from Chicago was tentatively searching for a site to build a water park attraction in far northern Wisconsin. The acreage that the ranch occupied would be perfect. She would bait the hook by inviting representatives of the development firm to visit, and the rest—as they say—would be history. And if Sam was opposed to selling? That wasn't a roadblock she had even considered. She could be very convincing, and even if Sam found it within his power to deny her, she had some extremely convincing friends that would be more than eager to help her out. They were thugs, actually—ex-military men with less than honorable discharges—but they served their purpose very nicely.

It was just over a year after Miriam's death when Cassie decided that it was finally time to make her move. She had thought it best to give Sam sufficient time to adjust to the loss of his friend and running the ranch before she set foot on the scene. In November of 2009, she drove over three hours—and one hundred and fifty miles—in order to 'happen to drop in' at the Copperhead and introduce herself to Sam. Her timing, however, had left a little to be desired. It had been busy that night at the supper club. Sam and one other employee were tending bar, and it was all she could do to simply get an occasional drink, let alone strike up a conversation. Eventually though, as the hours passed, Sam must have realized that she wasn't in any hurry to leave, because he began to initiate brief bursts of conversation with her as he bustled about mixing drinks and making change. Much to her surprise, Cassie had actually liked the man, which served to make her long-term plans for him all the more interesting.

"I don't suppose you know how to make a Tom Collins?" he asked when several patrons were tapping their empty glasses on the bar, apparently in an excessive hurry to all get their next drink at the same time.

"Marry someone with the last name of Collins and have a son," she'd replied with a perfectly straight face.

Sam had rolled his eyes. "Can't blame a man for asking," he had said, and hurried off to mix the drink.

Sometime around midnight, the crowd had finally started to thin. Sam mixed a few more drinks before releasing himself from duty and turning the bartending duties over to his employee—some lady named Trish. He'd wiped down Cassie's end of the bar a final time before straightening the bar rag and draping it over the edge of the sink. He'd then fetched a barstool from where it had been resting in the corner behind the bar and had dragged it over to a spot directly in front of her. He'd sat on it with an audible sigh and extended his hand.

"I'm Sam," he said in way of an introduction.

"Cassandra, but my friends all call me Cassie," she'd replied, shaking his hand.

"You're not a fugitive of the law or anything, are you?" he asked. When a confused look was her only response, he added. "I can't imagine another reason for someone hiding out here alone for an entire evening. You must be bored out of your mind."

"Not at all. In fact, I've rather enjoyed watching you race around fetching drinks and making change. It struck me as a Yooper's version of ballet—if there is such a thing."

Sam had laughed at that. "Well, I am so glad that I have managed to entertain you." There was a brief pause before he'd asked, "What brings you to the Copperhead, Cassie?"

"I understand that, in addition to being such a first-rate bartender, you operate a ranch in these parts—the Thunder Ridge Ranch. Is that correct?" Sam had stiffened just a little. Cassie recognized the tell for what it was and made a mental note that the man did not like strangers prying into his business. It was a good fact to be aware of—the first of many she would uncover, she was sure. "I'm not a stalker," she had rushed to reassure him, giving him her most convincing smile and leaning forward slightly over the bar, which exposed a little more cleavage—the exact intent she'd wanted. "I work for the 5-Star Riding Academy down in Kaukauna; your ranch has been mentioned by more than one person I've worked with."

"Really," Sam had said. "Like who?"

Cassie had done her homework; she had anticipated this question and was ready with an answer. "A Glen Stonebridge said you trained a mare for him in 2005. I believe he said the horse's name was Shooting Star."

Sam visibly relaxed a bit and allowed a slight smile to ease the tight lines of his set jaw. "That was a good horse," he'd said. "Does Glen still have her?"

"Oh yes. He shows her every chance he gets, and he always tells everyone who worked with her. You should be pleased; he's a walking-talking advertisement for you and your ranch."

Sam had taken some time to consider this, and had tilted his head slightly to the left. "So, I take it you didn't just wander in here to see if you could balance on that stool for five hours without a break."

"No," she laughed softly, "not exactly. I was hoping to meet you and get a chance to talk. I never knew the place would be this busy, though. It would seem that training horses is not your only talent."

There had been another hesitation while Sam studied her. Cassie knew it for what it was. Sam was deciding whether or not he could trust her. He was balanced on some invisible line from which he could choose to land on either side. Ultimately, her top rate performance and winning smile had won him over.

"So, exactly what did you want to talk to me about?" he'd asked.

"Straight and to the point; I admire that in an individual," she'd replied. "I'm looking for a job, and was wondering if you were hiring."

"We've got a phone at the ranch. You could have called and saved yourself a trip."

"Yes, I suppose, but that wouldn't have been nearly as effective as talking to you, now would it?"

"No, I suppose not," he'd agreed.

"People aren't that much different from horses," Cassie smiled. "You need to physically meet them; you need to go 'one on one' with them, and watch for cues in the way they move and the way they hold their bodies. You can't do that over a phone."

"All right. Suppose I go along with your theory. What has your trip taught you thus far?" Sam had asked.

Cassie had taken a sip of her drink and paused to tuck a strand of hair behind her ear before answering, establishing hesitancy on her part to reply. In truth, she was anything but. She had this nailed, and she knew it. "For starters, you're a man who doesn't like surprises." His eyebrows shot up a fraction of an inch, but she pretended to not notice. "Also, you don't like being in the spotlight; it makes you uneasy when someone you haven't met—myself, for example— knows things about you and you aren't sure why. Also, you're a man who applies himself to the task at hand. You work quickly and efficiently, and you probably expect the same from your employees. Am I close?" she'd asked, repeating the smile, but turning up the intensity just a bit.

Sam had simply nodded. "You're right," he'd finally agreed. "A phone call wouldn't have worked."

"So, can you use a trainer?" Cassie had pressed.

"Do you have references?"

Cassie's smile was brilliant. "I can have my portfolio on your desk in a week."

"And I'll look it over; we'll go from there." They shook hands again and Sam had gotten up and put the stool away. As an afterthought, he'd turned to her and said, "I hope you're planning on staying in town tonight. It's a long way back to Kaukauna; I'd rest easier knowing you waited and made your return trip in the morning."

'Good looking and sweet' she had thought at the time. She was almost going to regret using this man. Almost.

"Yes, I've got a room in town. Thank you for your concern."

"Great," Sam had said. "Then I'll look forward to getting your portfolio. Goodnight." With that, he'd left her sitting there and had returned to playing host to the few remaining guests.

It *had* been a long drive back to Kaukauna that night, but the trip had gone so splendidly that Cassie had hardly even noticed. She'd sent her portfolio out the next day via certified mail, and she was hired on as a trainer in January of 2010. As they say, though, that was water under the bridge. Since then, her well-laid plan had been set into motion. When she looked back, Cassie chose to not dwell on the speed-bumps that had developed along the way. First, Bud had not liked her. That was a minor detail, at worst, but the man had a long history with the Thunder Ridge Ranch. It was going to take some doing to get rid of him. Then some lady named Beth had arrived. Cassie had not seen that coming and, just as she had previously noted about Sam in November 2009, Cassie was someone who did not like surprises. Well-researched and well-executed plans were not supposed to have surprises, so Beth's arrival was more than a little disturbing. Then, of course, there'd been their confrontation in the stable upon meeting, and the incident with the mustang and that worthless old plug that Beth had so favored. There was something more, too—something Cassie couldn't quite put her finger on. It was almost as if Sam were more than fond of Beth, which made no sense at all. She decided that she needed an adaptation to her plan, and soon.

Cassie picked up the cellphone that rested on the table of her small apartment in Eagle River—a place she managed to tolerate only because she forced herself to remember that it was only a temporary resting place on her way to bigger and better things. The ranch was what she had her sights set on, and she could be a very patient person when she had to be. She punched a number that she had stored in speed-dial and waited for the man to pick up.

"Hello?" A deep, emotionless voice answered on the third ring.

"I need you to do something for me. Find out everything you can about a woman named Beth Simons. She's probably in her late forties, and she lived in Eagle River around 2007 to 2008. Put it on my tab."

The call disconnected without either person saying goodbye. Cassie placed the phone back on the table and headed to the bathroom to shower. Tomorrow was another day, and she was confident that it would bring her the ammo she needed to deal with this Beth character once and for all.

Chapter Thirty-Six

Sam punched the calculator keys, frowned at the display, and entered the figure on the spreadsheet before him. It was 2 P.M. on Thursday, two days before the harvest fest, and the Copperhead was quiet. It would be two hours before they opened, and only the prep cooks were currently clocked in. Luckily, whatever pots and pans they were rattling in the kitchen in preparation for tonight's featured entrée were too far away from his office to bother him. Sam totaled another set of figures, added that sum to the earlier one, and then entered that amount in yet another column. He subtracted this latest column from a previous one and frowned again.

Setting the pencil down, he leaned back in his chair and laced his fingers behind his head. The numbers looked great. The Copperhead's account receivables had increased each week for the six weeks, while expenses had remained stable. He understood accounting only too well; this was a *good* thing, wasn't it? Yes, it was; he was certain of it. So why on earth was he frowning? It made no sense.

Was it the upcoming party? He didn't think so. Preparations were all but taken care of. The entertainment, beverages, food, ice, tents, tables and chairs had all been ordered, and on-time deliveries had been confirmed. The invitations had gone out six weeks prior, and posters had been hung in every storefront and on every bulletin board in Eagle River. Julie and Beth had spent yesterday morning in town, shopping for decorations, only to turn around and repeat the trip this morning for some additional items. With those two women in charge, the ranch was going to be decorated to the teeth.

So, what was it that was troubling him? His mood reminded him of the 1994 Blackhawk song that stated "I can't see a single storm cloud in the sky, but I sure can smell the rain." That was one of the funny things about growing older, not funny 'ha ha', but funny in that 'I can't explain it' sort of way. Your inner voice gets stronger with time. It warns you about impending danger, or suggests that there may be a better way of doing whatever it is that you're trying to do. Of course, a man's free will also grows stronger with time; he cares less about what other people think and more about himself. These two developments—the inner voice and free will—often collide, with free will winning and the man coming out the loser . . . at least a good part of the time.

If that was the case, and he often thought that it was, then what was his inner voice trying to tell him now? Whatever it was, he couldn't help but feel that it was connected to Beth in some way. Was the voice warning him to not get involved, to ignore the feelings that seemed to be creeping back from the past? Or, was the opposite true— was it telling him that this was his best—and last—chance at finding happiness? Then again, wouldn't that imply that he wasn't already happy? No wonder he was frowning; you don't mess with a good thing, and his life was good right now. Screw the inner voice. Maybe he'd follow its advice when it came time to file his income taxes next year, but he wasn't going to allow it to influence him between now and then.

"Hard at it, Sam?" Cassie stood in the doorway to his office, waiting to be asked in. Sam did so with a wave of his hand. "I hope I'm not interrupting; someone in the kitchen said that I'd find you in here."

"No, I was just crunching some numbers. What can I do for you, Cassie?" Sam said, sitting forward and resting his forearms on the desk.

"I wanted to stop by and apologize again for that incident on Monday; I know how much that old horse meant to you, and I feel terrible and totally responsible."

"It was a fluke accident . . . leave it at that," Sam closed the ledger and slid it to the side.

"But it's not right. At the very least, please let me pay you what you think the animal was worth—"

Sam shook his head and got up. Sitting felt like a position of weakness in this conversation. He circled around from behind the desk and leaned against it, arms crossed in front of him. "We both know the horse was in poor health. From a strictly monetary standpoint, he wasn't worth anything."

Cassie hesitated and glanced away. "Is this going to go on my record? I mean, when I try to get another job as a trainer—"

"Are you thinking about leaving—is that what this is about?"

"No," she quickly said, not able to look Sam in the eye. "It's just, if I was responsible, I want to set it right, that's all."

Sam studied her for a moment, weighing the truth of her statement. Finally, he said, "There's nothing to set right. Forget it."

Cassie took a deep breath, faced Sam, and forced a smile. "Thank you. That means a lot to me." She hesitated and an awkward silence ensued. "So, business here is good?" she asked in way of making conversation.

"Yes," Sam nodded, not certain he liked the change in topic.

"I don't know how you do it all—run this place *and* the ranch. How do you keep up?"

"I hire good help," he said, then added, "and try to stay out of their way."

"Like me, I hope?" she asked.

Sam stepped on his inner voice, pinning it to the floor of his conscience and out of the way. "Yes, Cassandra, like you. Is that all you wanted, to apologize for Monday?"

"Actually, no," she confessed. "There was one other thing."

"Oh?" Sam raised his eyebrows and waited for her response.

"I feel really stupid, but I figure the worst thing you can do is say 'no'." Cassie took a small step forward, just one.

"And what, exactly, am I going to say 'no' to?"

"Well, when you hired me, you told me that you'd take me out to dinner sometime, and you never did."

"You're right; I do remember something about that." Sam's tone was even and unremarkable. It gave no indication of the struggle between Sam and the small voice that lay pinned beneath his mental boot.

"You have a reputation of being a man who keeps his word, so . . ."

"Can I check my calendar and get back to you?" he asked.

"Actually, I had something else in mind," Cassie said and looked away, suddenly bashful.

"Oh?"

"I was just thinking. We're both going to be at the harvest fest; I'd love it if you could just let me tag along with you. I mean, I know the ranch hands, but I really don't know too many people from town, and I'm really bad at striking up conversations with strangers."

Sam laughed. "You drove over a hundred and fifty miles to hunt me down. I don't recall you having any trouble striking up a conversation that night."

"That was different. I was job-hunting; I had a *reason* for meeting you. I'd heard about you and the ranch." She faced him and forced a nervous smile. "It didn't feel like you were a stranger. Do you know what I mean?"

Sam briefly considered her proposition. In reality, what harm could it do? They were both already attending the event; what harm could come from spending a few hours introducing Cassie to some of the local people? And, as much as he hated to admit it, there *was* the fact that she was young, and beautiful . . . and single. A man would have to be crazy to say 'no' to escorting her anywhere when there was no logical reason for not doing so. He nodded, slowly at first and then with more conviction. "Sure, why not? I have no idea who all will be attending, but I can introduce you to the ones I know—which will probably be most of them."

Cassie rushed forward and threw her arms around Sam's neck. He stood up, uncertain what was happening, and she quickly kissed him—an act of gratitude, really, nothing more—then she released him and stepped back. "I'll bring clothes and change at the ranch when I'm done with my last horse of the day—if that's alright with you."

"No, take the day off. Everyone at the ranch is going to be getting ready for the party; you won't be able to train a horse very well with all that commotion going on. Just drive out when you're ready—unless, of course, you wanted me to pick you up. That's the least I could do seeing the original agreement was for a dinner out somewhere." Sam found himself saying all of the appropriate things, but he was still wondering what exactly had taken place in the last ten minutes.

"No, I don't need a ride, but thank you. You were sweet to offer. It's going to be fun, you'll see," Cassie was already heading for the door and she paused when she reached it. "I'm really looking forward to this, Sam. You won't regret it—promise!" And then she was gone.

An acute silence blanketed the room after she left. And yet, it wasn't a true silence, was it? There was a distant mumbling, a little voice that refused to be shut out. Trampled and ignored, it whispered to Sam, fighting to be heard. Sam did his very best to shut it out, and he had some help. The mental rain he'd smelled earlier had closed in, and the accompanying thunder was loud enough to drown out even the most persistent inner voice.

Chapter Thirty-Seven

With the harvest fest only two days away, Thursday morning arrived with a cloudless sky and warm, late-August temps. Sam awoke to the smell of a nearby field of newly-mown hay drifting in on a breeze through an open window, and the aroma of freshly-brewed coffee wafting from the kitchen beyond his closed bedroom door. He stretched, crawled out of bed, and stepped into a pair of jeans he'd left draped over a chair near the door. He needed a shower, but a cup of coffee—or two—was far more appealing at the moment.

Sam wandered into the kitchen, still half-asleep. Beth sat alone at the island, embracing a steaming mug of coffee with both hands. She looked up and smiled when he approached.

"I tried to be quiet; I hope I didn't wake you," she said.

"Never heard a peep," he said. "It was the smell of coffee. Does it every time."

"I'll have to remember that—you know, just in case."

"In case of what?" he asked as he grabbed a cup from the mug tree and poured his first dose of caffeine for the day.

"In case you oversleep or something."

"Not likely," he said as he sipped his coffee and sat at the island across from her.

She shrugged teasingly, "There's a first time for everything."

"Yes, I suppose there is . . . like that crowd last night. I've never seen that many people at the Copperhead on a Wednesday. You and Julie did an awesome job keeping up."

"And Trish—don't forget her."

"I wish I could. It's this younger generation, I suppose. I gave her a third and final warning for using her phone when she was on duty last night."

"She just misses her boyfriend; you can't fault her for that."

"No, but she's got to learn to miss him on her own time. When she's behind that bar, all of her attention needs to be on the clientele and what she's doing. You know that better than anyone, Beth." He took another sip of his coffee. "What has you up so early?"

"My phone was beeping. I had a missed call."

"Anything important?" he asked.

"Just Mark. He left a message. Seems he had to road-trip to Baraboo for something. He's planning on being back for the party, though."

"I think Trish should dump her trucker boyfriend and take up with Mark. They both seem to enjoy the art of taking off at the drop of a hat."

Beth smiled and gestured at his mug. "Drink up; you're crabby before you get your caffeine fix."

Sam took another swig and returned Beth's smile. "If I'm so crabby, why don't you cheer me up?"

"And how, exactly, would I do that?"

"By telling me that you've thought it over and decided to stay on in Eagle River. You can keep the room you're currently sleeping in—until you find a place, I mean. And you know your job at the Copperhead is yours for the asking."

Beth nodded, but her smile dimmed a little. "I'm still thinking it over, Sam. I told you how I felt, and I just don't know what to do about it."

"Yes you told me, but I don't get it. What do you mean by, 'You don't trust yourself when you're with me'?"

"I'm not sure that I can explain it, Sam." Beth got up and crossed to the coffee pot. She set her mug on the counter and poured herself a fresh cup before carrying the pot over to the island and topping off Sam's. When she returned the pot to the brewer's warming plate, she remained at the counter with her back to him. "Some spiritual experts claim that we can control our destiny simply by concentrating on something and wanting it badly enough. They have this crazy theory that they call 'manifesting our destiny'. It's based on all of life being nothing more than pure energy—our bodies, our surroundings—everything is comprised of molecules and energy. They claim that thinking positive thoughts and believing in something creates a change in the energy flow and brings whatever we desire into our lives, no matter what it is."

There was a moment of silence before Sam spoke. "Did we change topics or something? Because I'm not seeing what this has to do with trusting yourself."

Beth laughed softly and shook her head. She picked up her coffee and turned around to face him. Leaning back against the counter, she looked into his eyes for as long as she dared, then she dropped her gaze and watched as the steam rose from her cup. "There's a lot that you don't know about me, Sam. Things have happened in my life that forced me to become a survivor. I won't bore you with the details."

"Who said I'd be bored? Isn't that for me to decide?"

Beth looked up at him, then looked away again. "Perhaps another time. The point is, I survived because I trusted myself. I learned to recognize what I needed to do, and I did it." She turned the mug around in her hands, as though seeing it from all sides was far more important than what she had to say. "It's like having an inner voice that speaks to me—a voice that has never lied—but I can't trust it when it comes to you."

"Why?"

"Because," Beth drew a deep breath, "when it comes to you, the voice has nothing to say. It leaves me to make up my own mind and find my own way. And I'm just not sure I can do that."

Sam considered this before asking, "And what does this have to do with that 'manifesting our destiny' stuff?"

"Not much, I guess," Beth replied. "It's just something I stumbled on and spent time contemplating over the last few years. It gives a person hope, you know? The thought that believing in something hard enough can make it come true."

"And," Sam began, waiting for Beth's eyes to meet his before he finished his question. "Can it?"

Beth stared into Sam's familiar brown eyes; she felt herself growing weightless and being pulled into their depths. She shuddered, broke free, and turned away. "No, I don't think so. Because, if it could, I—"

The mudroom door burst open and Bud rushed into the room. Despite the early hour, the man was bathed in sweat and short of breath. He removed his hat out of habit at the sight of Beth, but he offered no greeting.

"Boss, Ghost came in from pasture this morning with the rest of the herd. It is obvious that she has given birth, but there was no foal with her."

"Damn!" Sam rose, slamming his mug down hard on the island's laminated surface. "I should have brought her in earlier. She wasn't due for two weeks!" He ran his hands through his short hair before turning and hurrying off toward his room. He spoke as he moved. "Saddle up Blaze, and a horse for every man on the property. I want every available hand helping with the search; everything else can wait."

"Do you want me to come?" Beth asked.

Sam paused outside the bedroom door just long enough to consider the request. Finally, he said, "No, call Doc Peterson. Ask him to get out here right away. Bud will put the mare in the stable. Explain everything to the vet when he gets here and take him to the mare. He'll know what to do." With that, Sam stepped into his room and the door slammed behind him.

Beth and Bud looked at one another, both caught up in the uncertainty of the moment.

"Is it me?" Beth finally asked, her eyes filled with tears. "Did I bring all of this bad luck with me when I came back?"

"No, it is not you," Bud said, gently. "My forefathers would have said that the spirits are restless, and that they bring chaos and destruction with them. Few men today believe in such things as spirits, but of this much I am certain—you are not to blame," Bud reassured her.

"And you—do you still believe in these spirits?"

Bud nodded slowly. "I believe there is much that we cannot see. Now," he turned and hurried back to the door. "I must go saddle the horses."

"But," Beth shouted after him. "How can we defeat something we can't even see?"

"By believing we already have," Bud replied and was gone.

Chapter Thirty-Eight

As the hot late-August sun burned its way higher into the sky, Sam, Bud, and three hired hands scoured the pasture looking for the missing foal. The search party's mood was anything but optimistic. Even if the foal had been live at birth, the first few hours are critical for the newborn's survival. Without the mare present to provide colostrum—the first milk, rich with nutrients and anti-bodies—the foal would quickly grow weak and begin to fail. To make matters even worse, the ranch was known to be frequented by coyotes, and even an occasional wolf or bobcat. Sam chose to not think about what might have happened to this valuable foal if such a predator had wandered through the area overnight.

The grazing portion of the pasture was easy enough to scour on horseback. The prone form of a foal—whether dead or alive—could be spotted from a good distance. What made the search difficult were the numerous wooded areas that lined the edges of the pasture. Searching those was a slow and tedious process. Many times, the riders were forced to dismount and tether their horses to sturdy tree branches as they continued the search on foot. While it was cooler out of the sun, the woods harbored swarms of biting deerflies that left painful welts on exposed areas of flesh. The men periodically slapped at the biting insects, and fallen branches snapped underfoot. Crows, disturbed by the presence of humans in their woods, circled overhead, cawing loudly, and blue jays screamed as they flew from branch to branch, tracking the passage of the two-legged intruders. All of this provided for less than ideal search conditions. Sam reasoned that, if the foal *was* in the woods, instinct would have told it to lie low, to hide. If that were the case, they might never find it—at least, not in time to save it . . . and that was assuming it was even alive. If Sam was wrong, and the foal was fleeing before them, then they were equally screwed; they'd never hear it with all of the noises accompanying them in their search.

At noon, the men climbed into their saddles yet again and headed back for the ranch house. They would grab a quick bite to eat and water their mounts before heading back out. When they returned to the pasture, they would continue the search until the daylight gave out and darkness forced them back in.

Sam had phoned ahead and Beth had sandwiches and freshly-made ice tea waiting for them. She brought the food to the table as the men took turns washing up in both the bathroom and the kitchen sink. Sam hurriedly dried his hands on the kitchen towel and asked, "Was Doc Peterson here?"

"Yes. He came right away. I told him about the missing foal, and that you'd said he'd know what to do."

"And?" Sam prompted as he grabbed an egg salad sandwich from the tray and took a bite without bothering to sit down.

"He gave her a couple of shots; one was an antibiotic, I think, the other one made her pretty loopy. Then he snub-tied her so she couldn't move and milked her—just like she was a cow. He didn't get very much, but he got some. He made me put it in the frig," Beth said, then added. "He left a syringe and said we should probably repeat the process tonight, unless you don't find . . ." Beth allowed the unfinished sentence to float between them.

"We'll find it; we've got to." Sam finished his sandwich in two large bites and poured himself a glass of tea.

"Do you want me to cover for you at work tonight?"

"Damn," Sam wiped his mouth with the back of his hand and sighed. "Wow, I hadn't even thought about work. Yes, if you could oversee things there, that would be great."

"Of course. I'm sure Julie, Trish and I can handle it okay. You'll call me if—when you find it, right?"

Sam nodded and grabbed another sandwich before heading for the door. He called back to the men who had actually bothered to sit before eating. "I'll water the horses; be out in ten minutes." The door slammed behind him as the men ate in silence.

Sam finished tending to the horses, tightening cinches and tethering them to the long railing along the water trough. While they drank, he went into the stable. From the old desk drawer, he extracted the .32 caliber pistol and loaded it. He then tucked it safely under his belt at the small of his back. He also retrieved a flashlight, which he switched on to test the battery strength. If they were going to be out until dark—and if some predatory animal *had* found the foal—he was going to be ready. That done, he left the stable and returned to the horses just as Bud and the others were filing out of the house.

* * *

Beth paused from clearing the table and crossed to the window. She watched as the men rode off toward the pasture, their horses' hooves kicking up tiny clouds of dust that hung suspended in the hot August air. Her heart went out to the little, lost foal—hungry and all alone—in a strange world that it had never asked to be brought into. She prayed it was still alive; it had to be, for Sam's sake as well as the foal's. She remembered Bud's comment about restless spirits bringing destruction and chaos to the ranch—to their lives. The thought angered her. Didn't they already have enough to deal with simply trying to figure their own lives out? Her mind was currently reeling with questions of whether she should stay or leave, and how she would deal with the perpetual aching in her heart for Sam—no matter where she chose to call home. Wasn't all of that enough without the added task of dealing with a lost foal and an angry mare? Obviously not, for the task had been dealt to them, ready or not.

She returned to the job of clearing the table. She wrapped the leftover sandwiches in foil, and put them and the ice tea in the refrigerator. While the dishes soaked in the kitchen sink filled with hot, soapy water, she went out to the stable to check on Ghost. The mare was in Jinx's old stall. It was appropriate, she supposed. Life had a way of marching on, whether or not you embraced its journey. It was obvious that the mare was not happy to see her. It pinned its ears back, tossed its head and snorted loudly.

"So, you don't want to be a mother. We get that," Beth scolded the animal, but her tone was still soft. "You don't have to be, but you could have cared for him long enough to bring him in." The mare shook her head until her mane fell in a wild disarray and she whirled toward the far side of the stall, putting as much space as possible between herself and Beth. Beth's sadness deepened. As she watched the mare, she realized that all of the issues she was facing boiled down to love—or the lack thereof. Or was the real issue trust? The mare did not trust them enough to have the foal in their presence; Beth did not trust her heart to be strong enough to handle whatever decision Sam made about how he felt toward her; Sam did not trust himself enough to take another chance at caring for someone. No, that wasn't it; that wasn't it at all. The issue wasn't either love *or* trust; it was fear— the mare's fear of humans in general, her own fear of pain, and Sam's fear of failing if he dared to take yet another chance. This revelation did little to comfort her, though; in fact, it pissed her off. Life was too damn short to allow fear to dictate their fates.

    With this revelation came an unbidden anger—anger at
the mare, at Sam, and at herself. The mare couldn't be
blamed, of course, but she and Sam could. Yes, she had to
decide whether or not she would stay on in Eagle River, but
mostly she needed to be willing to face the fear that Sam did
not—possibly could not—love her, that he would always be
a friend, but nothing more. So, her decision to stay or go
was on hold. Sam would need to make his decision first.
Either they were worth a chance or they weren't; either he
loved her now or he never would. It was really that simple.
She would stay or go based on his decision. With a renewed
sense of conviction and a courage that she feared wouldn't
last, she left the stable and headed back to the house. She
needed to finish the dishes and get ready to go to work. At
the Copperhead, she would temporarily lose herself in
serving the clientele and making small talk with the
customers. She would await word from Sam on the search
and the foal's fate. Then, when this present hurdle of the
mare and the missing foal had been dealt with, she would
press Sam for a decision. How did that old saying go? 'Not
everything that is faced can be changed, but nothing can be
changed until it is faced.' It was time, at last, to simply face
it.

Chapter Thirty-Nine

At 7:20 P.M., the sun had slipped low in the sky but the temperature still hovered near 80 degrees. Hot, exhausted, and discouraged, both the men and the horses that made up the small search team wanted nothing more than to give up the search and head in. Sam had pressed them hard all day, but there seemed to be little reason to continue. The odds of finding the foal alive were slim at best. Even if, by some miracle, they did find it and managed to get it back to the ranch, its odds of survival would not be good. Too much time had passed. A newborn foal, alone in this heat without its mother, would have quickly become weakened and dehydrated. As many as twenty hours may have passed since the foal was born; those kinds of odds were not good. Perhaps it was best to give up and let nature take its course.

The riders sat motionless in an open area of pasture, waiting for Sam to give the word. He leaned forward on the saddle horn and took in the pasture with a slow, searching turn of his head. He felt defeated; his body ached from hours in the saddle, and mounting and dismounting countless times to search on foot. To add to his misery, the pistol tucked in his belt had carved a niche into the small of his back; he had brought it along like a good boy scout in an effort to 'Be prepared!', but that action—like the entire search—had been for nothing. His gaze finally dropped to the reins resting in his hands. Even Blaze had had enough; the reins hung slack.

"You guys head in. There's one more section of woods I want to check. It shouldn't take long," he told the men.

"Over by the cemetery," Bud remarked.

Sam nodded. "It's probably a waste of time, but I won't be able to sleep if I don't at least take a look."

Bud nodded slowly. "Would you like me to come with?"

"No, that's not necessary. You and the boys head on in. Rub those horses down good and give them some extra rations. They've earned it. I'll join you in a little bit." With that, Sam turned Blaze toward the last unsearched strip of woods and coaxed him into a gallop. Daylight was waning. The sooner they got the search over with, the sooner they could call it a day.

Sam reined the gelding in when they reached the edge of the trees and the opening into the clearing that served as the equine cemetery. Five horses now rested there; five horses that had served too well or been loved too well for the ranch owners to allow their carcasses to be carted off to the mink farm or the rendering facility. Hell, every horse on the ranch was above such a fate, but you could only bury so many fourteen-hundred pound carcasses before the DNR eventually stepped in. To Sam's surprise, the wind—which had been absent all day—was making an appearance. A light breeze stirred the treetops and whispered through the surrounding branches. Even Blaze pricked his ears forward, listening, but he was too tired to show much more interest than that.

Sam dismounted and wrapped the reins around a sturdy pine branch at the edge of the clearing. Blaze snorted loudly and dropped his head, apparently contemplating if it was worth the effort to lie down with the saddle cinched firmly in place. Sam patted the gelding's withers in empathy, retrieved the flashlight from the saddlebag, and headed into the clearing.

Waning sunlight, like its counterpart the dawn, was kind to the visual world. Colors that are washed away by the intense light of midday will seep into the world as the sun treks downward—daring you to see them. Wisconsin was weeks away from its first frost, but the foliage, and Mother Earth in general, were already showing signs of tiring. The grass in the clearing had grown tall and fallen over to rejoin the earth, like inland waves on a calm terra sea. The leaves on the poplars, now quaking in the gentle breeze, already bore hints of yellow along their edges, and the tips of the spruce trees' branches had traded their new, vibrant green to a shade indiscernible from last year's growth. Time was, as always, marching on.

The clearing had only begun to recover from the assault of Jinx's burial. The grass was still flattened along the path the front-end loader had followed, and the soil that now covered the old horse had not yet begun to heal. It would most likely be June or July of next year before the mound of fresh soil would settle and grass would completely cover the wound. If only hearts could heal so quickly.

Sam pushed these thoughts from his mind, forcing himself to concentrate on the task at hand. He walked the perimeter of the clearing, looking for evidence that a living horse had been there in the last twenty-four hours. He was three fourths of the way around when a movement caught his eye. Thirty feet ahead, at the edge of the trees, a stillborn foal lay on a bed of matted grass. Blow-flies, better equipped by nature for just such a search, had beat him to the tiny carcass; a cloud of them hovered over the still form. Sam approached, his feet moving of their own accord. This was not how he had wanted the search to end. A growl, low and intense, stopped him dead in his tracks. The movement that had caught his eyes had not been the winged scavengers; a young wolf, undoubtable a member of one of the packs that were re-establishing themselves in the area, stood directly beyond the dead foal, its eyes locked on Sam.

Instinctively, Sam took one step back, then another. With a slow, fluid motion he reached behind and withdrew the gun from beneath his belt. The warm metal stuck to his flesh before releasing and sliding free. Too young to recognize a gun, the wolf watched Sam with a keen interest, but showed no signs that it was willing to abandon its treasure. Sam raised the gun, took careful aim, and fired one shot directly over the wolf's head. In an instant, the animal leapt from view and was swallowed by the forest beyond.

* * *

Back at the stable, the men had pulled the saddles from their horses' backs and were just beginning to put the tack away when the distant sound of a single gunshot echoed through the stable. They froze, some with saddles still clutched in their hands, others with a bridles hanging from their grasp. Steve, the youngest man who had been part of the search, turned questioning eyes to Bud.

"Should we go back out?" he asked.

Bud drew a deep breath. There was little chance of Sam being in trouble. There hadn't been a bear sighting in these parts for years, and the pistol was more than a match for any coyote or wolf that might have crossed Sam's path. There was, of course, another explanation for the single gunshot. Sam had found the foal and put it out of its misery. After a long moment, he shook his head. "The boss has done what he needed to do. He will come in when he's ready."

Chapter Forty

Sam approached the dead foal, his heart heavy and rocks where his stomach should have been. The still form, its coat covered with dried amniotic fluid and traces of blood, was pure white, and miniscule, and perfect. Sam studied the tiny hooves and thought how they would never race across a meadow, or carry a rider with a confident grace. It was such a waste, plain and simple, and anger arose to replace his sorrow. He took a deep breath, contemplating a course of action. Daylight was quickly fading. Should he ride back to the ranch for a shovel and add this tiny body to the list of the other horses that would remain in this clearing for all time? It seemed fitting; it also seemed like a lot of work and fuss for something that had never drawn a single breath. Still—

"Even in death, it is beautiful."

Sam whirled toward the voice, the gun still in his hand. There had been no sound of footsteps, no echo of hoof beats of an approaching rider. No one should have been here, but someone was. The stranger stood before him, dressed in an old Wisconsin Badgers sweatshirt and faded jeans. He had shoulder-length brown hair and was clean-shaven. There were no visible tattoos, no earrings, nothing that appeared sinister or threatening in any way. The only truly remarkable trait was the stranger's sapphire-blue eyes, which studied Sam with an amused interest. But Sam was not concerned with the stranger's eyes. The man's clothing was slightly over-sized, and hung loose on the man's frame. Sam wondered if a weapon was concealed under the roomy sweatshirt—perhaps at the small of the man's back. If there was, the man made no move to retrieve it. Sam was torn. Half of his brain, the half that had prompted him to raise the gun, was telling him to beware. The other half, the screaming, logical side, argued that—if the man *was* armed and if he *had* wanted to hurt Sam—he could have done so without ever speaking and drawing attention to himself. He took a deep breath.

"Who the hell are you and what are you doing here?" he asked, struggling to hold his voice steady.

"Did you find what you were looking for?"

"I don't see where that's any of your business."

The stranger smiled and cocked his head slightly to one side—a habit that Sam himself often did. "I have startled you, and for that I apologize. You've had a long day searching for this one." He looked at the small dead foal and a sadness seemed to pass over him, only to fade as quickly as it had come.

"What were you doing, watching us?"

"Yes, I suppose I was."

"And you knew the foal was here all along?" Sam's voice rose a notch and anger flashed in his eyes.

"Yes," the stranger said, then the smile returned to his face. "Could you put the gun away? It's not necessary."

"I'll decide what's necessary. At the very least, you're trespassing. Aside from that, I have no clue what you're up to. Until I do, the gun stays."

"You misunderstand. The gun does not bother me, but you're scaring her," the stranger said.

As if on cue, an albino doe appeared at the edge of the forest close to where the foal lay. It took one tentative step, then two, before stopping. In the spreading shadows, its white form appeared to shimmer, as though it were not a solid mass but only the image of one.

Sam was dumbfounded. First a man had appeared in the clearing, apparently out of thin air, and now an albino deer—rare enough to be seldom seen—was standing before him, studying him with watchful eyes.

"I assure you, she won't attack," the stranger said with a crooked grin. "The gun is not necessary. Besides, you don't like killing. If you did, the wolf would be dead."

Sam looked from the deer, to the stranger, and back to the deer. Complying, he lowered the gun slowly, then tucked it back into its familiar—if not comfortable—resting spot. "I think I deserve an explanation," he said.

"That you do. We've come to help."

"Help?" Sam's voice was bitter again. "How can you possibly help? I've found the foal; it's dead. It was probably born dead. I've wasted my whole day looking for fifty pounds of rotting horse flesh."

"Yes, I would say you're right. It looks like it might weigh fifty pounds, at the most. So small."

"That's what happens when a foal comes early. It doesn't get the chance to gain weight and strength."

"Yes, I suppose. And yet . . ."

The stranger looked at the doe and gave an almost imperceptible nod. The deer approached the tiny, lifeless form and lowered its head as though taking a closer look—or registering its scent. *But that's crazy*, Sam thought. *Why would the doe want the dead foal's scent? Deer aren't dogs; they don't track by scent. They don't track at all. And, even if they did, what was there to track? The foal was right before them—and dead. End of story.*

By now, dusk had fully arrived in the clearing. The lengthening shadows had consumed the open area, and darkness was beginning to erase the distinctive outlines of surrounding objects and blend them into one. Light-colored objects—the crosses marking the graves and the albino deer—seemed to glow in the gathering gloom. The doe raised its head and looked back into the forest. Its ears pointed forward, then back, then forward again. Finally, the deer shook itself and turned to face the man in the Badger sweatshirt. The stranger smiled at the deer and turned to Sam.

"It's hard to find something when we are not even sure what we are looking for."

"Excuse me?" Sam interrupted. He was tired, and discouraged, and in no mood to be philosophical. Yes, he had to admit that there was no explanation for what was happening here, but he could see no use for it, either. It was pointless.

"There is much you don't see, my friend—"

"I'm not your friend," Sam cut him off, but the stranger continued.

"—and even more that you don't understand. Do you think that this forest, this world that surrounds you, is all that there is? You are wrong—and yes, you are my friend, Sam; you just don't know it yet. It is one of many things that you don't know."

"How do you know my name—who told you?"

The stranger laughed softly. "No one had to tell me; I know your name and the names of many others. We are not strangers. Just because you don't remember, that does not mean that the past didn't happen. I assure you, it did. There have been many pasts, and there will be many more, God willing."

"Listen, buddy," Sam's anger had mounted again and his tone was short. "This is all very fascinating, but it's been a long day and I'm heading in."

"Without the foal?"

Sam looked at the tiny still form a final time. "Let the wolves have it. At least it will have served some purpose."

"This one, yes . . . perhaps that would be the best thing for it, poor soul. But what of its brother?"

Sam had been turning away and he froze. He looked at the stranger with disbelief in his eyes. "Brother?"

"Its twin," the stranger explained.

Sam quickly looked around the nearly dark clearing, half expecting to see a tiny foal stumble out of the woods. None did. He looked down, then back at the man. "Even if there is a second one, I'd never find it out here . . . not before morning. And that would be too late, far too late."

"We could help," the man said.

Sam scoffed, "How?"

The hint of sadness returned to the stranger's face, but it disappeared as the familiar smile resurfaced. "Is your faith so very weak, my friend?"

Sam opened his mouth to argue, but changed his mind. "Fine," he said abruptly. "Show me how you intend to find a tiny, lost foal in this darkness."

"Okay," the stranger agreed. "We shall."

The man crossed to where the doe waited at the edge of the forest. When he reached her, the stranger took the doe's head gently between his hands and placed his forehead against the animals. They stood that way, two figures joined as one, for several seconds before the man released the deer and stepped back. Although Sam saw what happened next, he did not believe it.

The doe, its white coat already luminescent in the fading light, appeared to glow from within. In a matter of seconds, the shape of the deer softened, reasserted itself, and softened again. As Sam watched in awe, the edges of the doe trembled, shifted, and broke apart. Tiny flecks of light—thousands of fireflies—drifted away from what had clearly been a living, breathing deer only seconds before. The insects spiraled upward like a shifting, glittering column of smoke rising from an unseen fire. Twenty feet overhead, the column erupted into multiple fingers of light that spread outward in all directions, resembling spokes of a suspended wagon wheel adorned with twinkling, white Christmas lights. In the blink of an eye, it was over; the fireflies were gone, and only darkness remained where the doe had been.

The stranger continued to stare at the sky, his eyes closed. He appeared to be listening, but Sam could hear nothing except the breeze stirring in the trees all around. After nearly a minute, the man turned to Sam. "This way, hurry," he said and sprinted toward the far edge of the clearing. Sam followed, struggling to keep up. They ran as a pair, but the stranger stopped short where the clearing ended and the trees began, and Sam slid to a halt beside him.

"See?" the stranger remarked and pointed into the woods. A dim procession of tiny twinkling lights—a living trail of fireflies—marked a path through the darkness beyond. Sam blinked in disbelief and turned to the other man. The stranger smiled, shrugged, and extended his hand. "By the way," he said, "I'm Peter."

Chapter Forty-One

Moving quickly, the men followed the firefly-marked trail through the woods. Unable to see the terrain before him, Sam extracted the flashlight from his back pocket and aimed its beam on the ground. The bouncing circle of light revealed branches and exposed roots that threatened to trip him as he ran. Up ahead, Peter raced along the same path with no light to guide him, as sure-footed as the deer that had dissolved before their very eyes. Luckily, they didn't have far to go.

Peter stopped running as suddenly as he had begun. Stepping up next to him, Sam shined the flashlight over the area directly in front of them, and there was the foal—identical to its sibling—but this one was alive. It lay in a hollow at the base of a large tree, its white coat matted and stretched over its tiny frame, its delicate neck curved back over its shoulder, and its tiny head resting on its hind hooves. In the flashlight's beam, it resembled a porcelain statue of a miniature horse at rest.

"I'll be damned," Sam whispered.

"Almost a miracle, wouldn't you say?"

Sam shook his head. "If it's still alive in a week, then yes. We've got our work cut out for us."

"Do you always have such little faith?" Peter asked.

"What I have," Sam replied, "is a solid dose of reality. This little guy's mother has foaled three times, and abandoned all of the foals."

"Perhaps it will be different this time," Peter said, studying the small, still form.

"All I know is I've got to get this guy back to the ranch. Once I get there, I can see how the mare reacts. But I'd lay 'two to one' odds that she'll kill it if I try to put it in with her."

"And you base this judgment on?" Peter asked.

"The mare's history and temperament."

"Has this night taught you nothing?" Even as the question was posed, the albino doe stepped out of the darkness and into the flashlight's beam. "You see so little of what can be seen," Peter said. "It's not your fault; it's the way humans have learned to survive. There are advantages to only trusting what you see in a 'kill or be killed' world. But it doesn't have to be that way." Peter went to where the foal was lying, bent down, and effortlessly scooped it up. "Let's get this little guy back to your horse. We can drape him over the saddle and he can ride back with you."

"Blaze is tired, but—"

"The gelding will not put up a fuss; trust me."

Sam shook his head and trained the flashlight's beam back in the direction from which they had come. "Do you want me to lead the way?"

"That won't be necessary," Peter replied, and he and the foal disappeared into the darkness.

By the time Sam reached the clearing, Peter had already placed the foal over the saddle and was waiting for him. The gelding stood with his head lowered, and his eyes half-shut. *He must be more tired than I had thought*, Sam reasoned. He untied the reins from the branch and climbed into the saddle, placing one hand over the foal to hold it in place. The doe had followed them out of the woods. It stood several yards away, watching.

"Where will you go?" Sam asked, which made more sense at this point than asking Peter where he had come from.

"Someplace close by, but that's not important," Peter replied. "But I want you to do something for me."

"And that is?"

"When you get back to the stable, give the foal to its mother."

"Listen, Peter. I appreciate what you did here tonight. Hell, I don't even know *what* you did, but I would have never found this foal without your help. But to put it in with its mother . . . The man who owns that mare will skin me alive if I let her kill this foal."

"She won't kill it; trust me."

Sam wanted to argue, but he didn't know what to say. "And if you're wrong?"

"I'm not wrong." Peter looked up at the night sky. Darkness was now complete, and it seemed like a million stars were suspended over them, watching. "If you tell anyone what happened out here tonight, they won't believe you—with the exception of Beth; she would understand. The point is, just because people refuse to believe in something doesn't mean that it isn't so. Even more important, things that people *do* believe in are often far from the truth." Peter looked at Sam, and his blue eyes appeared to be lit from within. "Be careful, my friend. Some things in your life right now are not what they appear to be." He hesitated a long moment before adding. "You've built a wall around your heart to keep out the pain. You are not the first person to have done this, and I doubt you'll be the last. But realize, my friend, that the wall you've built also holds out the joy and the one thing that makes living worthwhile; it holds out love. Think about it . . . please."

The foal shifted its weight, distracting Sam for an instant. When he looked up again, both Peter and the deer were gone. He searched for them, craning around in the saddle, first right then left, but they were nowhere to be seen. Knowing that a search for them would be pointless, Sam reined Blaze around and headed for home.

Back at the ranch, Sam slid to the ground and carefully lifted the tiny foal from where it had been draped over the saddle. Bud appeared in the stable doorway and watched, a look of disbelief on his normally unreadable face. Sam pushed past him and entered the stable, still carrying the foal, as Bud fell in behind them. When the older man saw where Sam was heading, he reached up and grabbed Sam by the arm.

"It won't work," he said.

"Let's see. We won't know if we don't try."

"The foal isn't yours to gamble with, Boss."

"We can't help but gamble, Bud. If I don't try to reunite it with the mare, I'll have to get it to eat somehow. You know as well as I do that the odds are stacked against an orphaned foal. Those odds become almost astronomical when the foal comes early—and is a twin."

"A twin?" The surprise registered in Bud's voice as well as on his face.

"Yes. The other one was stillborn."

"And the shot we heard?"

"I frightened off a wolf that had found the carcass."

Bud nodded. "What do you want me to do, Boss?"

"Open the gate to her stall," Sam said, "and pray."

The mare tossed her head and snorted as they approached. When they reached the gate, she began racing to and fro, her hooves thundering on the packed dirt floor.

"Are you sure you want to do this?" Bud realized that it wasn't his decision to make, but he couldn't help but ask.

"No, not at all," Sam said, "but we're going to do it anyway."

Bud swung the gate open and Sam carried the foal inside. He bent down and waited as the foal got its legs beneath it, then he stepped back. The newborn wobbled precariously and almost toppled over. The mare had backed herself into a far corner of the stall. She remained there, frozen, watching the foal. With a giant knot where his stomach should have been, Sam slowly backed away. The mare snorted and tossed her head—once, twice—then a strange thing happened. The snort became more of a nicker. The foal, fully in command of neither its body nor its voice, squeaked more than whinnied and took one staggering step forward. The mare approached in turn, cautiously at first, then more eagerly. Sam and Bud looked on, but neither believed what they were seeing. The mare reached the foal and nuzzled it, as though realizing—for the first time in her life—that these tiny creatures that caused her such excruciating pain with their arrival—really meant her no harm. Within minutes, the foal was nursing and the crisis was apparently past. Leaning with their forearms resting on the top board of the stall, Bud and Sam watched as their bone-deep weariness faded away.

"How did you ever find that thing in the dark?" Bud asked. "We'd all given up."

Sam hesitated, then said, "I had some help."

Bud considered this for a long moment. "Anyone I know?" he finally asked.

"Nope," Sam assured him, "of that I'm sure. And you don't know what you're missing, my friend."

Chapter Forty-Two

Sam was sitting at the island, waiting, when Beth pulled in the drive at 2:45 A.M. He had called her at the Copperhead at 9:38 P.M. after the foal had been found, brought in, introduced to the mare, and bedded down for the night. Beth had insisted that things were under control at work and that he stay put at the ranch. Thinking that it would be a good idea to periodically check on the mare and foal, Sam had acquiesced. He'd also grabbed a bite to eat and a shower, in that order. Now, as Beth pulled in the drive and the Bronco's headlights swept through the silent house, Sam suddenly found himself wondering how much he should tell Beth about what had transpired in the clearing. Beth, of course, was the one person he could tell the entire story to and not appear to be crazy. What was it she had said about Peter—that he would blow Sam away? She had been so very right.

"Can I see it?" Beth burst through the door, beaming. Apparently, she had known Sam would be waiting up for her. Anxious to see the rescued foal, she quickly crossed to the island, took Sam by the arm, and pulled him to his feet. "Come on," she said, tugging gently, "show me!"

Sam pulled free and crossed his arms over his chest. Forcing a scowl that was anything but convincing, he said, "You certainly don't look like a forty—"

"Tut tut, careful," Beth cut him off by crossing her arms and faking her own scowl.

"Okay, you don't look like someone who has been on her feet tending bar for the last nine hours. Where did you get this burst of energy from?"

Beth shrugged. "Relief over finding the foal, I suppose. Can I see it?"

"Of course." Sam placed his hands on Beth's shoulders, spun her around, and gently shoved her toward the door. Once outside, Beth ran her arm between Sam's arm and his body and rested it in the crook of his elbow as they walked.

"Is it cute?" she asked.

"It's tiny," he replied.

"Tiny and cute, right?"

Sam recalled when he first saw the foal. "It looks like a porcelain doll."

"That would be a cool name," Beth said.

"Porcelain?"

"Yes, Porcelain . . . or, China would be nice."

"Yes . . . yes it would. I'll be sure to mention it to Mr. Quentin."

"Mr. Quentin?"

"The mare's owner."

"Oh yes, him."

Sam had left the lights on inside the stable. The building's electrical had not yet been upgraded, and the old incandescent bulbs cast a soft, yellow glow on everything they touched. Sam and Beth crossed to the stall and peered over the side. The mare was standing, but at rest, her left back leg bent at the hock. She turned a watchful eye toward them, but didn't move. The foal was stretched out on the sawdust floor, sound asleep. Its sides rose and fell in the soft light, peaceful and still.

"It's absolutely beautiful," Beth said, "and so tiny!"

"Its twin was identical to it."

"Its twin?" Beth looked at Sam, confused.

"Yes, I found the twin first. It was still born." He hesitated, then pushed on. "It was nearly dark by then; I was ready to head in. I would have never considered the possibility of twins. I would have stopped looking and this little thing would still be out there. God knows how long it would have survived, waiting to be found."

Beth covered Sam's hand with her own. "But you did find it; that's all that matters." When Sam didn't offer any comment, she asked. "So, what changed your mind—why did you keep searching?"

Sam slipped his hand out from under Beth's and laced his fingers together. He stood there, studying his hands, still uncertain how much to say. "Peter was there," he said, his voice soft and small in the surrounding stable.

Beth's eyes grew wide. "Peter—are you sure?"

"Oh yeah, from what I've seen, there's little chance of mistaking him."

Beth was silent for a long moment and Sam wondered what she was thinking. She looked away and her eyes focused on the foal again. "So, Peter saved him."

"In a way, yes."

"Why?" Beth voiced the same question Sam had been pondering. "And why would he show up to save the foal, but not Jinx?" Beth quickly shook her head, as though she regretted the words as soon as they were spoken. "I didn't mean that. I mean . . ."

Sam placed his arm around her shoulders and pulled her close. "It's alright. I know what you mean." He hesitated once again, and took a deep breath. "I don't think it was really about the foal."

"What do you mean?" Beth asked.

"I think . . . I think he wanted me to meet him—to know who he is." Beth was quiet and Sam wasn't certain exactly how to take this. He slipped his arm from her shoulder and turned her to face him. "How did you feel when you first met him?" Sam asked.

A thin smile formed on Beth's lips as she remembered. "I was terrified. He just appeared out of nowhere; I couldn't understand who he was or where he had come from, let alone why he was there."

"Yes," Sam agreed, "that was exactly it. Hell, it's a good thing I didn't shoot him."

"I—I don't know if you could have, you know what I mean?"

"Yes, I think I do," Sam agreed.

"Anyway," Beth continued, "Peter could do things, you know? He seemed to have these powers or something. I don't know . . . it was all very surreal, and very confusing."

"So, what finally convinced you that he was for real?" Sam asked.

Beth shook her head slightly, as though settling the memory back in place. "He knew things about me that no one could have known. That, and the moth, made it impossible to believe that the whole experience was just a dream."

"The moth?"

"Oh, that's right . . . I never gave you any details about when Peter and I met." She smiled and went on. "It was last January. I was driving home in a snowstorm and I'd pulled over to the side of the road. I'd wanted to," she hesitated, then fudged the story a little, "check to see exactly how much snow had actually fallen. Anyway, I got locked out of the Bronco. Peter just sort of showed up, from nowhere. And while he was there . . ." Beth's voice trailed off. How could she possibly explain how the snow and wind had stopped, but only where she was parked? How could she make Sam believe that Peter had somehow created an invisible dome that covered them, holding the weather at bay? She finally decided that she couldn't, and she moved on, and her eyes had a faraway look in them as she took that step back in time. "There was this moth. I mean, I'm in the middle of this crazy nor'easter—a real doozie—and there's this moth. It was beautiful—unlike anything I'd ever seen before, and Peter asked it to land on my hand." She shook her head, "It was crazy. Talking about it now just makes me realize *how* crazy it was. And yet, it happened." She looked at the foal for a beat, then turned her gaze back to Sam, curiosity dancing in her eyes. "What about you—what made it real for you?"

Sam considered this for a bit and motioned toward the foal with a nod of his head. "Ultimately, that did, I guess."

"Who is Peter, Sam—I mean, really?"

Sam shrugged. "I don't know, but I'm glad for one thing. He seems to be on our side."

"Yes," Beth agreed. "But . . ." She hesitated, struggling to find the right words, "Why? I mean, is it just us, or have a lot of people seen him?"

Sam considered the question, but an answer eluded him. "We have no way of knowing. And chances are, if you start asking people, men in white coats will probably lock you away—so I don't advise it." A frown appeared on Beth's face, and Sam asked, "What is it?"

"Peter said that he wanted me to come back here . . . he wanted me to help you, but obviously he could have simply done that himself. I thought that he didn't want you to know about him. It made sense at the time. The whole thing seemed to be steeped in mystery."

"And now?"

"Now you've met him—he introduced himself to you—so that explanation doesn't fit."

"So, you need a new explanation," Sam deduced.

"No, *we* need a new explanation. You said it yourself; it really didn't seem to be about finding the foal—it was more about meeting you."

Sam nodded, "Yes, it seemed that way."

"But why?" Beth pressed. "Why did you need to meet him? What is it—exactly—that Peter is here to do?"

Sam shrugged. "I have no idea, but he didn't strike me as being dangerous. If he *is* here for one specific reason, I'm sure we'll find out when the time is right."

"Yes, I suppose you're right," Beth said softly, locking eyes with Sam. "But why does that scare me so?"

Chapter Forty-Three

"So, have you made up your mind yet?" Julie leaned into Beth and practically had to shout to be heard. It was a busier than usual Friday night. The kitchen was struggling to keep up with the demand for plates of deep-fried perch, and there was standing room only at the bar. Once again, Trish had been a no-show, and both Beth and Julie were scrambling to serve the requested drinks as quickly as possible. All in all, Beth had the distinct feeling that Trish's days as a bartender at the Copperhead were over.

"About what?" Beth leaned in Julie's direction to answer.

"Don't give me that crap, girl. You know exactly what I'm talking about! Are you staying on after tomorrow's bash?"

Beth shrugged, skewered two cherries for the old fashion she'd just mixed, and said, "I guess I'm still mulling it over."

Julie nodded, grabbed two bottles of Corona from the upright cooler, and headed back to the waiting customer.

At 9:30, Sam arrived. He'd been detained at the ranch waiting for Mr. Quentin to arrive and inspect his new $5000 foal. The supper club's owner walked in with a smile on his face and Cassie at his side. At the sight of the two of them, Beth's heart gave a lurch before settling into the pit of her stomach. Sam came around to the business side of the bar and mixed himself and Cassie each a drink; he had not needed to ask the woman what she wanted. He smiled at Beth and nodded toward the crowd, which had thinned considerably. "Looks like you've been busy here."

"Yes," Beth offered only a one-word answer.

Sam took a second to look around before handing the drink across the bar to where Cassie was waiting. "No Trish?"

"No Trish," Beth said as she scooped ice into a glass and reached for a bottle of brandy that rested in the tray.

Sam studied her for a beat. "Something wrong?"

"What could be wrong?" Beth finished mixing the drink and delivered it to the far end of the bar without waiting for Sam's reply. Once there, she forced herself to make small talk with a patron to avoid returning to where Sam still stood, watching her. She hated feeling this way, but feel it she did. The question was, what should she do about it?

Using only her peripheral vision, she watched until Sam rejoined Cassie on the other side of the bar. They lingered there for only a few minutes before Sam headed toward his office with Cassie in tow just two steps behind. Beth waited until they were out of sight before snatching up two empty beer bottles from the bar. She crossed to the metal tub that was reserved for glass and tossed them in a bit too forcefully. They shattered on impact, but their destruction did little to abate Beth's anger.

"Hey, you okay?" Her smoking break over, Julie had stepped back in position behind the bar just as the bottles shattered. There was genuine concern on her face as she studied Beth. "I don't think I've ever seen you upset, let alone angry." The woman took a quick look around the bar. "What did I miss?"

"Nothing."

Like Sam, Julie knew she was being blown off; unlike Sam, she wasn't going to let it go that easily. "Come on, what's going on?"

"Nothing, really. I just need a few minutes, that's all. I'll be fine."

"Maybe you should clock out; it's been one hell of a night. I saw Sam pull in when I was out having a smoke. Do you want me to ask if he'll fill in for you so you can head out?"

"Don't you dare!" The words slipped out before Beth could stop them. Julie's head snapped back a bit, as though she'd been struck.

"Are you mad at Sam—is that it?" Julie knew she'd hit pay dirt by the reaction on Beth's face and she whistled softly. "That *is* it. Is it because he's taking Cassie to the doings tomorrow, is that why?"

"He's what?" Beth spun toward Julie.

"He's escorting Cassie to the harvest fest—although I'm not sure that *escorting* is the right word, seeing Sam lives there and Cassie works there on a daily basis, but you know what I mean."

"No," Beth said coolly, "I don't think I do. Why don't you explain it to me?"

"Um, maybe not," Julie said, and she backed away. She turned to the first person she could find who was looking to have his glass refilled and she set about refilling it. Beth watched her, her hands hanging limp at her side, trembling. She'd had it; she'd had enough.

"Tell Sam I left," she said as she brushed past Julie on her way out. She didn't wait for Julie's reply; she didn't even consider disturbing Sam in his office to see if it was okay to leave. She left . . . period. The time for indecision was over.

Chapter Forty-Four

" . . . that was the plan anyway," Cassie hesitated. She sat across the desk from Sam in his office, studying him as he tapped the eraser end of a pencil on his desk—over and over again. "Earth calling Sam," she finally said. "Hey, are you in there?"

The pencil stopped mid-tap and Sam looked up. "What?" He shook his head. "I'm sorry. What were you saying?"

"Is something troubling you?" she asked.

"No, not at all. It's just been a very long week, that's all," he assured her.

"Are you sure?" she pressed.

No, he wasn't sure . . . not at all. Something—some unnamed detail—was rattling around in the back of his mind. It was loud enough and determined enough to make it impossible to ignore, but it wasn't clear enough for him to make out exactly what it was trying to say. The meeting with Mr. Quentin had gone exceptionally well. The man was thrilled by the sight of Ghost nursing her foal, and had insisted in keeping the mare at Thunder Ridge Ranch even though his initial plan had been to take her back to Door County once the foal was born. He had even asked Sam to begin working with the young horse immediately, so Sam had called Cassie in to meet both Mr. Quentin and China. The man had liked the suggested name and agreed that the foal should be addressed as such.

The meeting with Ghost's owner had run late, and it was after nine when he and Cassie had finally arrived at the Copperhead. Cassie had hinted at a business proposition when Mr. Quentin had finally left, and she'd asked if they could discuss it upon their arrival at the supper club. She'd joked that she was nervous to even bring it up, and that it might take a good, strong drink to give her enough courage to discuss the matter—preferably a Seven and Seven. Sam had set to work and mixed the drink without hesitation when they arrived. He saw no harm in giving Cassie what she wanted if it expedited the discussion. It had been a very long week; he was all talked out, and the sooner he got this over with, the sooner he could call it a day.

So here they were, but he had no clue what Cassie had been saying over the last several minutes. His mind was— where? He recalled Beth's attitude upon his arrival. She'd been upset; that was obvious, but he could think of nothing he had done to upset her. Maybe she was simply overwhelmed. Obviously, it had been a very busy night, and with Trish's absence it may have been too much for the two ladies to handle. Sam made a mental note to place an ad in the local papers for yet another bartender. He felt better having reached that decision, but he was still not convinced that the large number of patrons at the Copperhead that night had been the real issue. So, what was?

"Would it help to talk about it?" Cassie's voice broke through his reverie yet again.

"I was just . . . I don't know." Sam leaned forward and ran his fingers through his short hair. It was something he did as of late whenever he was frustrated; he was lucky that he had not rubbed his head bald. "Please, just start again. I promise to stay focused this time . . . honest."

Cassie studied him for a beat. "Would you prefer the abridged version?"

"Yes, to be honest; I would. You have to admit, it's late for a business discussion."

"Of course," Cassie agreed. She took a sip of her drink and a deep breath, and plunged ahead. "I'd like to buy into the Thunder Ridge Ranch. I think there's a lot of untapped potential in what you have going on there. I'm not looking for a handout. I've got some money squirreled away from when my grandparents died—about a quarter of a million. If I bought into the operation, you could take that money and invest it back into the operation. Imagine what you could do with that kind of capital."

"Cassie, I'm not looking for a business partner. When Miriam left me the ranch—"

"Please, Sam. I mean no disrespect, but Miriam is gone. You can't run a ranch to fit a dead person's dreams."

"Why not, if they were good dreams?"

"Because the world goes on. New things become possible every day—new training practices, new investment opportunities—as a business person, you have to see the truth in that. Being stuck in the past is one sure way to fail."

"No, I guess I don't see that," Sam said. He was not happy with Cassie's proposal or the direction the conversation had taken, but she definitely had gained his undivided attention. "The ranch is operating in the black. It's holding its own and supporting several employees— yourself included. It's a waste of time and energy trying to fix something that isn't broken."

"But the ranch could be so much more!" Cassie argued. "You're focusing on peanuts and missing the bigger picture."

"Which is?" Sam asked. He was anxious to see where she was heading, if for no other reason than to head her off at the pass and bring this discussion to its end.

"There are more ways to turn a profit on the acreage of the ranch than simply growing hay, oats and corn."

"Really?" Sam said. "Even if that's true, those are the things that we need to grow if the horses are going to be fed properly."

"Please, Sam. I'm a trainer; I have been for years. I know what a horse needs to eat."

"Of course you do," Sam agreed. "So I don't see where this is going."

"What if you could get a bigger return on your land than you currently get growing crops?" Sam opened his mouth to argue and Cassie raised a hand to quiet him. "What if you could make enough money using the same acreage to simply buy all the feed necessary to keep the ranch operating at its current level and still triple your income per year?"

"Cassie, it's late." Sam was struggling to be patient, but he was losing the fight. "I don't think—"

"Please don't say no until you've heard me out," Cassie interrupted him. "And even if you *don't* want to change the way you currently operate the ranch, you have to admit that having an investment partner makes good sense—logically *and* financially." She took a breath and studied Sam, who remained quiet. "Promise me that you'll at least think it over."

"Cassie, I—"

There was an abrupt knock at the door. It opened and Julie stuck her head inside. "Sorry to interrupt, Boss," she said, "but Beth left and I could use an extra pair of hands behind the bar."

"Damn." Sam rose and came out from behind the desk, speaking as he moved. "We'll finish this discussion at another time, Cassie. It would seem that the Copperhead is suffering from a chronic shortage of bartenders tonight."

"Sam, it's really none of my business," Cassie said, "but be careful where Beth is concerned."

Sam froze, coming to an abrupt halt directly in front of Cassandra. "Meaning?"

"Meaning exactly that—be careful. After all, what do you really know about her? For instance, where did she grow up, what's her story, what did she do before you hired her seven years ago?"

Sam frowned and his eyes narrowed. "You're right, Cassie; it's none of your business. Now, if you'll excuse me." Sam pushed past the trainer without as much as a backward glance. Their conversation would be all but forgotten as soon as he left the room; his attention was focused on Beth's disappearance.

"We'll talk later . . . count on it," Cassie called after him as he slipped through the door, but Sam ignored her and continued on.

Why had Beth left? He wondered. *Was she ill?* She hadn't looked ill, but then, something had been up with her—something he'd chosen to ignore. She'd been short with him—angry—and he'd simply decided that he'd deal with it later. But wasn't that exactly what had happened five years ago? Wasn't that the reason why Beth had originally left without a word—because he'd chosen to avoid dealing with it—with her? He sighed as he made his way to the bar. There was no sense in beating himself up about it now; he would help Julie tend bar until closing and see what Beth was like in the morning. They could talk then . . . or after the harvest fest if the preparations got too hectic for them to speak before hand. Either way, he would make a point of addressing the issue—whatever it was—and hearing her out. He owed her that much.

Chapter Forty-Five

As fate would have it, Beth was sitting at the island, waiting, when Sam got home. He hadn't expected to find her still up, but neither was he shocked. A part of him was relieved; he hoped to be able to remedy whatever it was that had upset her.

He noted the glass of wine in her hand, so he crossed to the refrigerator for a beer before joining her. Her eyes were red and slightly swollen, a sure sign that she had been crying, but she offered him a faint smile as he sat down next to her. She spared him the dilemma of wondering what to say.

"I've made my decision, Sam. I'm leaving." The words were spoken with a calm conviction that was every bit as real as the silence they shattered.

Sam was genuinely stunned; he hadn't seen that coming. "Why?" he said, studying her.

"Because it's what I need to do," she explained.

He shook his head. "I don't understand. Is it something I did?"

"No." Beth tried to laugh, but it fell flat. "Let's face it, Sam. I don't even know what I'm doing here, and if I stay on I'll only make us both miserable."

"But—"

Beth shook her head, cutting him off. "I did the right thing when I left five years ago, Sam. It hurt like hell—it still does—but it was the right thing to do." She set her glass down and grasped his hand. "I love you with all my heart, Sam," she said. "I always have and I always will. I believe in what Mark and Peter said about old souls, and that life is more than just what we see all around us." She squeezed his hand and looked into his eyes. "In this life, we're friends; I've got to learn to be okay with that. It's just . . . it's just so hard, because deep down inside of me my heart remembers being so much more." She released his hand, picked up her glass and downed the last few swallows.

Sam set down his beer and turned to face her. "Beth, I don't want you to go."

"Because you love me?" she asked, without hesitation.

"I . . ." Sam struggled for the right words.

"Don't you see it, my friend, can't you understand? It's okay . . . we don't control our hearts. They do and feel whatever they want to, with or without our approval. You mustn't feel bad because you don't love me; it's not your fault."

"But, I *do* love you," he said.

Beth leaned into him—slowly, deliberately—and kissed him. Her heart skipped a beat, then surged onward, and she was filled with a longing so intense that it took her breath away. It was everything she imagined it would be, and everything she longed for, and she prayed that the memory of this moment would last forever, because she would need to cling to that memory to stay strong. She pulled back, her eyes locked on his. She saw his confusion, and remnants of a buried pain that he would not let go. Tears filled her eyes, but she forced another smile.

"Tell me *now* that you love me," she said, her voice little more than a whisper.

"I . . ." Words failed him.

She reached up and placed her hand on his cheek, stroking the stubble of his beard with her thumb, and he felt—what? "It's okay, really it is," she said. "But, feeling as I do, I can't stay. You understand that, don't you?"

Sam was torn. Conflicting emotions surged through him. He did not want Beth to leave; of that, he was certain. But was it love, or was it simply that she was a connecting point to a good period in his life—to a time he'd return to in the blink of an eye if it were within his power to do so? He couldn't say; he honestly couldn't say . . . which meant, of course, that he had no right to ask her to stay. He knew that she loved him; he could see it in her eyes—there was a gentleness there, a passion, that he'd have to be blind to not see. But as tempting as that look was, it was equally terrifying. *What's wrong with me?*, he chastised himself for feeling—nothing.

"Where will you go?" he asked. "The Eagle Crest Resort is gone."

She laughed, but it was neither a joyful nor a carefree sound. "There's always work to be found if you're an experienced bartender; you should know that." She shrugged. "Maybe I'll head out to the Rockies, or Oregon would be nice."

"Your Bronco will never get you that far," he argued.

"Sure it will, on a wing and a prayer." She shrugged. "Maybe I can convince Peter to ride shotgun, or Mark can follow me on his bike. There are endless possibilities."

Sam stared at her, and there was a touch of sorrow in his brown eyes. "Will you be back?" he finally asked.

"You betcha," she said. "Just try to keep me away." She got up and headed toward her room. Once there, she paused in the doorway. Turning back to him, she said, "I'll leave Sunday morning."

Sam just nodded; words eluded him.

Beth hesitated; she appeared to be studying something on the floor at her feet. When she looked over at him, her eyes glistened with fresh tears. "You will miss me, Sam, won't you?" she asked with no trace of a smile.

Sam swallowed hard. "You know I will," he said, forcing a smile. Beth met his gaze for the briefest moment, then she went into her room and closed the door.

Sam took a deep breath and downed his beer. He crushed the can, and the stark sound of crumpling aluminum tortured the resident silence, forcing it to retreat into the far corners of the house. But it did not stay at bay for very long. On silent cat paws, it stole back into the rooms and dared Sam to disturb it yet again. He did not rise to the challenge. Let the silence take over his home; he didn't care. As far as Sam was concerned, there was nothing left for anyone to say.

Chapter Forty-Six

The first harvest fest had been a simple picnic for Thunder Ridge ranch hands and a few guests. It had featured a simple metal wash tub filled with chunks of ice and various canned beverages. For entertainment, a boombox blasted tunes courtesy of a local country station. Slow-cookers covered the surface of a six-foot folding table, along with paper plates, plastic cutlery, napkins and an assortment of home-made desserts. No one left hungry, and everyone had a good time.

From its simple beginnings, the Thunder Ridge Ranch's harvest fest had grown into the 'must attend' annual event of Vilas county. A refrigerated Bud Lite beer wagon eventually replaced the metal wash tub. A local 'up and coming' band offered their services and played well past midnight, until the last of the die-hard dancers had claimed their shoes from the nearby lawn and finally went home. Two portable pig roasters were brought in, along with people who knew how to use them, and a local bakery supplied rolls and a variety of desserts. Only two things remained virtually unchanged; no one left hungry and everyone still had a good time.

Julie arrived at the ranch mid-morning, and she and Beth set about decorating and getting the place ready for the flood of visitors that would begin trickling in by mid-afternoon. If Julie noticed that Beth was quieter than usual, she didn't mention it. Ranch hands set bales of straw at strategic points around the yard and along the driveway, and Beth and Julie adorned them with the silk flowers and autumnal plant arrangements they'd purchased that week. Rented tables and folding chairs were unloaded from the delivery trucks, along with canopies and umbrellas complete with wrought iron stands. A flatbed hay wagon, which would serve as the stage for the band, was positioned between the water garden and the road, enabling the would-be dancers to utilize the paved driveway to kick up their heels. Sam and the others in charge of the festivities had thought of everything.

At 1:45 P.M., the sound of an approaching motorcycle caught their attention. Both Beth and Julie looked up as Mark slowed his bike and pulled in the drive. He gave a quick wave to the ladies who were setting the last of the flower arrangements along the edge of the hay wagon band stage, then he proceeded down the drive to park his bike in front of the garage.

"Friend of yours?" Julie asked.

"Yes, that's Mark. He followed me up here from Baraboo."

"Oh?" Julie said, her eyebrows raised with interest.

"It's not what you think," Beth assured her.

"Then what is it?" Julie persisted.

Beth did not have a ready response for that. *What, indeed, was it?* She had no solid answer for that question. "I don't know. It sounds lame to simply say 'It's complicated', but that's what it is. I really don't have a clue what he wants."

"Come on," Julie rolled her eyes. "Nobody's that naïve. Men are SO predictable; they all want the same thing."

Beth laughed softly even as she shook her head. "Not this one. He's . . . different."

"Gay?" Julie's eyebrows shot up further than they had before.

It was Beth's turn to roll her eyes. "No, he's not gay."

"Then I don't get it. When's the last time you took a good, long look in a mirror? It's not like you're not pretty, Beth. Why wouldn't he be after the customary 'roll in the hay'?"

"Because he isn't." Beth hesitated, wondering how much she should say. But then, she was leaving the next day anyway, right? So, what did it matter? "He's really just a friend. In fact, he's one of three people who talked me into coming back."

Julie considered that. "So, why *did* you come back—for real?"

"I . . .' Beth struggled for words.

"I know; don't tell me. It's complicated," Julie said as she stuck the last of the silk asters in the pot at her feet and straightened up.

"Yes, it is—more than you could know. But I guess it doesn't matter anymore. I'm leaving in the morning."

"Oh no!" Julie exclaimed. "Why? Does it have anything to do with Sam spending time with Cassie?" She winced. "I'm sorry, I guess I'll never learn to keep my big mouth shut."

"Don't be silly, Julie. Yes, I was upset when I left work last night, but I've thought about it and I had no right to be. I think I was upset with myself more than anything."

"But you're not angry anymore?"

"No. There's really nothing to be angry about."

"Then, why are you leaving?" Julie asked, frowning.

That was a legitimate question, and it deserved an honest answer. "Sam is very special to me, Julie," Beth said, forcing a slight smile for her friend's sake. "I think the world of him. I know he cares about me, too, but not in the same way." She paused, then pushed on. "I've simply come to realize that it would be best for all concerned if I left."

"Does Sam know you're leaving?" Julie asked.

"Yes, I told him."

"What did he say?"

"What *could* he say? Besides, he knows me too well to try and change my mind once it's made up."

There was a long moment of silence, then the women saw Mark approaching. Before he was within earshot, Julie said, "I wish you'd stay. I like having you around here, you know? You're alright." Beth quickly hugged the woman as Mark strode over to them. He was wearing a black leather jacket over a white T-shirt, faded jeans, and cowboy boots with scuffed toes.

"Can I help?" he asked, smiling at the two women.

"Typical man," Julie said, placing balled fists on her hips. "They always show up *after* the work is all done."

"Come now, surely there's something I can do," Mark protested, trying his best to look wounded.

"Actually, there is," Beth said. "If you look in the back office in the stable you'll find a large cardboard box. It came in by UPS yesterday, and I don't think anyone has even opened it yet. It should have fifty tiki torches in it. We want to set them up all over the yard. Do you think you can handle that?"

"It doesn't sound too difficult," Mark replied.

"If you want to, you can also fill them. There are several gallon containers of citronella torch fuel just inside the stable door. You can't miss them."

"Will do. Anything else?" Mark added with a smile.

"Not that I can think of at this moment."

"Well, if something comes up I should be very easy to find; just look for the man carrying the torches." He bowed slightly, turned, and headed for the stable.

Julie giggled. "I like him; he's cute."

"Yes," Beth agreed, "and very charismatic."

Julie continued to study him as he moved away. She cocked her head slightly to one side. "Are you sure he doesn't want to—you know?"

"Yes, I'm sure."

"Too bad; such a waste."

Beth rolled her eyes and shook her head. "So, do you think we're done here?"

Julie looked around. "Except for the missing torches, I think we're good."

By 2 P.M., everything for the 2014 harvest fest was in place; by 3:45, nearly forty guests had arrived, and more were streaming in by the minute. It was well on its way to becoming the best celebration in the ranch's history.

Chapter Forty-Seven

Even as Julie had helped her decorate for the festival, Beth could not help notice Sam as he made his way around the ranch, orchestrating all of the various tasks that needed to be completed. With the exception of Ghost and China, all of the horses had been removed from the stable and the east paddock, and had been placed in the far pasture where they were less likely to be spooked by the festivities. Sam had tossed baled straw from the haymow as men down below piled it neatly on the wagon. When enough straw had been tossed down, he had jumped down and followed the loaded wagon as it circled around the yard, helping the men strategically place the bales in appropriate spots. When it had made a complete loop around the yard and back to the stable, there were still a half dozen bales waiting on the wagon. To free up the wagon for other tasks, Sam had effortlessly unloaded the bales and piled them just inside the stable door. In the east paddock, he had helped to set up two volleyball nets, using spray paint to mark the boundaries of the courts. At times, he seemed to be everywhere at once, but maybe that was just because Beth was trying to get him out of her mind.

At 4:45, Cassie arrived in her 1974 Mustang convertible. The vehicle was pristine—white with a red interior—and Cassie was dressed to blend in with her ride. She wore a red halter top and matching, skin-tight leather pants. Her high-heel sandals were white, as was the open, fishnet cardigan that completed the look. Beth watched as the woman parked the car in a spot by the garage that had been reserved for her, and her heart fell. Instantly, she began to scold herself. *What difference does it make if she's beautiful? What difference does it make if Sam likes her—or not? It's none of your business, and none of your concern!* Beth whirled and quickly made her way toward where the first of the two roasted pigs was being carved into manageable-sized chunks. Food was the last thing she wanted, but helping to serve it up would keep her mind engaged and off of other things. *Wishful thinking*, she told herself, but she continued on her way.

Cassie entered the house without knocking. Sam, who had gone inside twenty minutes earlier to cleanup and change for the festivities, walked out of his room still buttoning his shirt. He saw Cassie standing there and momentarily froze.

She smiled as she took him in with large, engaging eyes. "You don't have to button that on my account."

Sam chuckled and broke free from his momentary paralysis. "I should have known you'd be early," he said. He'd opened a can of beer before hitting the shower and he now crossed to where he'd left it sitting on the counter next to the frig.

"The early bird catches the worm, remember?" Cassie said.

"Yes," Sam agreed, "but I don't recall seeing any worms on the party itinerary."

She laughed lightly. "No, I suppose you're right."

Sam glanced down at the jeans and the button-down gray shirt that he was wearing, then back at Cassie. "I feel like I'm underdressed."

"You look great, really," she assured him.

He finished his beer and crossed to the sink to rinse out the can, which he left upside down in the sink to drain. "Ready to go meet some people?"

Cassie didn't answer right away. There was a hesitation that suggested that there were, perhaps, other things they could do, but she finally nodded. "Sure, let's go see who's here." With that, she turned and walked out the door without waiting for Sam. He watched her move away from him, taking in the total package—tight pants, heels, her tiny waist and swaying hips—and he wondered, not for the first time, what he was getting himself into.

True to his word, for the next four hours Sam escorted Cassie among the guests, introducing her to some people who were prominent in the surrounding communities, and to some who were simply fun to be around. Their presence together caused heads to turn and tongues to wag. Cassie absorbed the attention like a dry sponge; Sam didn't seem to either notice or care. By nine o'clock, they had visited with practically all of the guests when they bumped into Mark who was carrying several unopened cans of beer. He'd taken on the role of waiter, and was now heading toward a group of people sitting a short distance from where the band was doing a reasonably good rendition of 'Friends in Low Places'.

"Mark," Sam shouted to be heard above the three foot tall Peavey speakers that surrounded the band. "This is Cassie."

Mark balanced the beers and held up a finger, indicating 'wait'. He delivered the beers, patted one of the men on the shoulder, and came back grinning. He motioned toward the stable with his chin and said, "Let's head that way; it's too noisy here to even hear yourself think, let alone talk."

Once they were a fair distance from the water garden and the band, Mark turned and extended his hand. "Cassie, is that right?"

"Yes," she smiled and accepted his extended hand. "It's good to meet you."

"The pleasure is all mine," he said with a smile.

"Listen," Sam said to Cassie. "There's some things I need to do. Would you mind hanging out with Mark for a bit?"

"Sure," Cassie agreed, though her smile dimmed considerably.

"Mark?" Sam repeated the request.

"Not a problem; I'd love to get to know this lady better—if she can carry cans of beer wearing those heels, that is."

"I'll run circles around you," Cassie assured him, "with or without the heels."

"Then we're set," Mark said with his customary grin. Sam nodded and walked away.

"So," Cassie began. "Have you lived in the area long?"

"Never," Mark replied. "I came up from Baraboo with Beth."

Cassie's expression changed, and genuine interest crept into her eyes. "Really, are you and she an item?"

"Beth and I? No, just friends."

"I see," there was a trace of disappointment in Cassie's voice. "Have you known her long?"

Mark tilted his head a little further than he normally did and studied the woman before him. "This is beginning to feel a little like an inquisition. Is there something I should know?"

"I'm sorry," Cassie said. "Truth be told, I have a very strong interest in this ranch—"

"And its owner?" Mark speculated.

Cassie looked closely at Mark and noted the confident conviction in the man's eyes. "Yes, well—there's that. Let's just say that Beth's arrival has complicated things a bit."

"In what way?"

Cassie hesitated, then said, "Perhaps we could talk about something else."

"Such as?" Mark asked, apparently unaffected by the requested change of topic.

"I don't know," Cassie began. "You said you've never been up this way before. Perhaps there's something I could tell you about the area, something you'd like to know."

Mark looked around and shrugged. "It's very nice up here. The people are friendly; the scenery is beautiful . . . I can't imagine what else I would need to know."

"Are you interested in horses?" Cassie asked. "I'm a trainer; have been for years."

"Horses are nice," Mark agreed. "They just haven't played a role in my life, I guess. Did you know that lots of people go through their entire lives without ever seeing a horse in person, let alone ride one?"

"That's sad," Cassie frowned, then brightened. "We have a new foal in the stable. Would you like to see it?"

"Why not," Mark agreed, then he added with a frown. "It doesn't bite, does it?"

Cassie laughed lightly before taking Mark's hand and leading him to the stable. It was nearly 9 P.M. and the daylight had long since passed its reign over to the gathering darkness. The yard was well-lit by overhead vapor lights, and tiki torches dotted the outlying areas with a soft, inviting glow. Once inside the stable, the pair crossed to Ghost's stall. The foal was sleeping on a pile of clean straw—a still white form on a golden bed—and Ghost was standing nearby, watching. She turned her ears back as the two approached, and she watched them with a keen interest.

Mark and Cassie stood outside Ghost's stall, leaning against the rails as they studied the mare and her foal. Neither had spoken since entering the stable, so Mark decided to strike up a new conversation. "Sam has quite the setup here. Has he owned the place long?"

"No, only about five years. He was friends with the previous owner, and when Miriam died, she left the entire ranch to him."

Mark recognized the name; he remembered his conversation with Beth during their trip up. What was it she had said, something about it being his and Miriam's idea to come back here? Apparently, Cassie had also known the woman, or at least known of her. "Who was this Miriam?" Mark asked, maintaining his 'matter of fact' tone of voice.

Cassie shrugged. "I'm not sure. I think she was a bartender at the Copperhead."

"And she owned this ranch?"

"Yes. She and Sam were quite close, obviously, or she wouldn't have willed this ranch to him. I think she and Beth were also close, or so I've heard. All I know is I heard both she and Sam took it hard when she died."

"Was she ill?"

"No. She died in a car accident, just a few miles from here. She was coming home after closing up the Copperhead and some drunk hit her head-on."

"Ouch," Mark said, still maintaining a controlled level of interest.

"It's not such a bad way to go—if your time is up, I mean. Fast and painless."

"It sounds like this Miriam was pretty popular in the area. I'll bet the local judge came down hard on the other driver."

Cassie's brow furrowed as she searched her memory. "I don't remember reading anything about the trial. In fact, I don't think there was a trial; I don't believe they ever caught the other driver."

"You mean, he wasn't at the scene?"

"Nope . . . I guess he walked away, as hard as that is to believe."

"That's pretty remarkable," Mark said, but his tone was nonchalant in spite of his racing heart. This was the missing piece; it was the one thing he'd needed to learn to ensure his success. He faked a very convincing yawn, and shook his head as though trying to clear out some cobwebs that had suddenly taken up residence there. "Wow, I'm all in but my shoestrings. It must be all of this fresh air."

"Probably," Cassie backed away from the stall. "It was nice meeting you, Mark. I enjoyed our visit."

"As did I, more than you know." He smiled warmly. "If you're looking for Sam, I'd try over by the band. I thought I saw him heading that way a short while ago."

"Thanks," Cassie said, smiling at Mark. "I'll look there first." She left then, with as much spring in her high-heeled step now as there had been when she arrived. Mark watched her go, and he smiled. The harvest fest festivities would be winding down soon, but the real party had just begun.

Chapter Forty-Eight

"I don't suppose you'd dance with a friend."

Beth turned and smiled, though she knew she really shouldn't. Sam's voice, so gentle, so wonderfully familiar, was a balm for her aching heart even as it was the source for the pain. She'd been standing on the sidelines, watching, as the band returned from a break. They'd slung their guitar straps over their shoulders and strummed a few chords as the drummer got seated and picked up his sticks. Bands typically played a fast number upon returning to the stage. They want to get the audience engaged and moving as quickly as possible. But that was not the case this time. The drummer counted out the beat and they began playing Willie Nelson's hit. "Always on My Mind". She stood now, with the familiar strains of music in the background, looking up into Sam's eyes.

"I asked the band for a favor and requested this song; I thought it fit somehow," he said. Without waiting for an answer, Sam took Beth's hand and pulled her away from the sidelines. He wrapped his arm around the small of her back and held her close as they began to dance. Beth closed her eyes, rested her head on his chest, and breathed deeply. The smell of him—faint traces of fabric softener, cologne, and a hint of sweat—mingled together and swept her away. The rhythm of his heart, only inches from where her head rested on his chest, beat strong and true; it measured out the steps she and Sam took as they moved over the blacktopped dance floor. She clung to him, wishing with all of her heart that time would stand still . . . but it never does.

When the last strains of the song ended and the band started playing the first song of their normal set, Sam and Beth remained where they were, frozen in place, for just a little bit longer. At last, he released her and they returned to where he had found her when the song began. Cassie was there, waiting, her thin lips stretched into a tight smile.

"Thank you, Sam," Beth said and gave him a hesitant smile. "If you'll excuse me, there's something I need to do." She walked away then, leaving Sam and Cassie to whatever it was that the woman surely wanted to discuss.

Beth wandered around the yard, her arms crossed in front of her, holding her broken heart in place. She studied the details of the ranch—the buildings, the white-board fences, the manicured lawns. They stood silent, muted somehow by the darkness, and Beth had the confused feeling that she was seeing them all for the first time instead of the last. People passed on either side of her, some in silence and some greeting her as they moved, but no one stopped her to visit at length. Eventually, she found herself in the stable, watching China who'd recently decided that it was time for her next meal. She stood at the mare's side, nursing eagerly, and Beth found herself watching this still-fresh miracle and smiling through her tears.

"The boss tells me that you are leaving in the morning." Bud's voice, like Sam's, was warm and familiar, and Beth cherished the sound of it. She did not turn around, but continued to watch the foal.

"Yes," she said, her voice little more than a whisper.

"I am sorry to hear that. Your presence here has been a good thing, for the ranch and for Sam."

Beth shook her head. "Am I being selfish, Bud? Am I trying to cut my own losses and hurting everyone else in the process?"

Bud moved up alongside her and joined her in watching the foal. Instead of answering her, he posed a question of his own. "Why did Miriam bring you back here?"

"I . . . I don't know, and that's the truth," Beth replied.

He weighed the sincerity of her response, then said, "Would she want you to leave?"

Beth turned to Bud and started to answer, but ultimately she just stood there facing him with her mouth slightly open and no sound coming out.

"Miriam is still here; you and I both know that. She still cares about what happens to this ranch—and to you. She knows what you are going through; she will help you if you let her."

"Can she change Sam's heart—can she heal it and make it feel again?" Beth said, still facing Bud, but her chin began to quiver so she turned away.

"Time heals all."

"Yes, well," Beth said, wiping the tears from her cheeks, "we're human. We don't have forever."

"Maybe not forever, but longer than this life. Miriam has given us proof of that. If you search your heart, you will know it to be true."

"I'm tired of searching, Bud . . . and waiting. I've come to realize that there are things in this life that I need, too, and I'm running out of time to find them."

"Well, life can be cruel, can't it?"

Both Bud and Beth turned to watch as Cassandra strode into the stable. Without hesitating, she crossed to Ghost's stall and stood next to Beth.

"Will you excuse us, old man? There's some things I need to discuss with Miss Simons." It was not a request, but a command, and Cassie delivered it as such.

"I prefer to stay," Bud replied.

"It's okay," Beth placed a hand on his arm. "Why don't you go and see if the party is winding down enough to start putting some of the food away."

Bud gave Cassie a long, hard look, then he nodded at Beth. "Very well. We will say our goodbyes in the morning." With that, Bud left the stable, closing the door softly behind him.

"Goodbyes? Is one of you leaving?" Cassie asked, her face expressionless.

"I don't see where that's any of your business," Beth said.

"Well then, I'm making it my business," Cassie said, her lips curled into the likeness of a smile. "Let's see, Bud has been employed here since time began, so I don't think he's going anywhere in the morning. So," her smile became more genuine, "that leaves you."

"As I said before, it's none of your business."

"There's no need for you to be so defensive." Cassie laughed lightly. "I applaud what you're doing. To be honest, I didn't think you were smart enough to see that leaving here is the absolute best thing you could do, given the circumstances."

"Which are?" Beth asked, turning to face the woman head on.

"Come now," Cassie gave Beth her most patronizing smile. "Everyone knows how you feel about Sam. It's as plain as the nose on your face, but it's never going to amount to anything. My guess is, you've come to your senses and you're leaving to spare him any more humiliation."

"Humiliation?!" Beth stepped in closer to Cassie, who made no move to back down.

"So, he gave you a dance out of pity. What's that worth? Nothing. Think about it, Beth. Everyone here sees Sam and I together the entire evening, and then he has one dance with you. They all suspect he misses his mother, I suppose. What else could it be?"

Beth glared at Cassie, too angry to speak, and the woman smiled at her coolly.

"I have plans for this ranch, Beth—and for Sam."

"He would never have anything to do with you," Beth replied, struggling to keep from spitting the words in Cassie's face.

The cool smile warmed a little. "Look at me, old woman. Do you think he doesn't want me? Even you aren't that stupid. Eventually, I'll win the man over; I always do."

Beth regained control and managed a taunting smile of her own. "You won't live long enough to win that man's heart; of that, I'm certain."

Cassie laughed aloud, and the sound echoed through the nearly empty stable. Ghost snorted and whirled, looking for a way out of the stall. When none could be found, she

positioned her body between the two women and her foal
and nervously pawed the floor beneath her.

"His *heart*? What the hell would I want with that? I
want this ranch, and what it is capable of providing me with.
If I have to pretend to care for some man and do the dirty
work that goes with that, I have no problem paying that
price. Think about it—several months, or years, making
Sam happy in exchange for becoming the wealthiest woman
in the state—perhaps in several states. I'd say that's worth
it, wouldn't you?"

"That's all you want him for—to *use* him?" Beth was
seething.

"What *else* would I want him for? He's nearly old
enough to be my father; where's the attraction in that?"

"How could you be so cruel?" Beth asked, shaking her
head in disbelief.

"That's not cruel, sweetie, that's life. Get used to it. At
your age, I would think you'd have learned that a long time
ago." Cassie studied Beth for a beat before offering the
older woman her best smile. "Do you want to know what I
learned a long time ago?"

"I couldn't care less," Beth said, but she refused to look
away. She was not about to back down from this woman—
tonight or ever.

"I learned that things often outlive their usefulness. It's
such a pity. They just hang on and suck in oxygen that the
rest of the world could use."

"I—" Beth started to reply, but Cassie cut her off.

"Now Miriam, from what I understand, did everyone a
favor. She was what, fifty-five or fifty-six when she died?

She'd had her chances and lived her life, then she bowed out gracefully, leaving more behind for the rest of us."

"How dare you!" Beth clenched her fists at her side and stepped closer.

"What, am I wrong?" Cassie asked with a mock shrug. "And then there was Jinx. The best thing that Sam did this summer was to put a bullet through that horse's skull. Do you have any idea how long I waited for the perfect opportunity to arrange that confrontation between him and the mustang?" The smile returned to Cassie's face, brighter and more genuine than before. "I'm sorry; I guess I never got around to thanking you for putting Jinx in the paddock that morning."

Beth was too stunned to move. Her mind was reeling. Just as she'd suspected, Jinx's death hadn't been an accident after all. What kind of person was this woman who stood before her? She'd killed Jinx, and now she was willing to use Sam to get whatever twisted profit she thought this ranch could provide. Was Cassie the reason Peter, and Miriam, and Mark had wanted Beth to come back? Was this woman the reason why Sam needed to be saved?

"I pity you, Beth; I really do," Cassie pressed on. "Would you like to know why? It's not because you can't have the man you love; it's because you're getting old and your chances are all gone. Hell, you're not even a 'has been'; you're a 'never was'."

Beth lunged at Cassie, pure rage driving her forward, but the younger woman was ready for her. Cassie had read Beth perfectly; she had seen the hatred mounting in the older woman's eyes and had anticipated the attack. When Beth made her move, Cassie snatched a lead rope that had been draped over the top stall board and swung the end with the snap at Beth's head. The metal struck Beth on the side of her face, stopping her in her tracks. She spun away and raised a hand to her cheek. A welt was already forming where the lead had struck, and droplets of blood beaded its edges.

Beth turned back toward Cassie. She removed her hand from her cheek and raised her eyes to meet the younger woman's. She took a step toward her assailant, then froze. Something had caught her eye; something that drew her attention even more than this woman whom she despised with all her being. Sam was standing just inside the stable door, watching.

Cassie instinctively sensed the change in the other woman, and she turned to see what had so completely captured Beth's attention. When she saw Sam, she dropped the swinging lead rope and froze.

"Get off this ranch, Cassandra, and don't ever come back."

"What?" Cassie asked, bewildered.

"You're fired. Collect your shit and leave. I'll figure out whatever wages you have coming and mail them to you," Sam's voice was low and threatening.

"But . . . you can't fire me," she quickly recovered. "We have a contract—there's two years left on it!"

"Consider it cancelled," Sam said, his anger mounting. He had crossed to where Beth was standing and was examining her cheek.

"Then I'll sue!" Cassie declared, her fists planted firmly on her hips.

"Then I'll press charges for assault and battery. Get your shit and leave!"

Cassie was fuming; she glared at Sam and Beth, her eyes livid with hatred for both of them. "So, I'm fired, am I? Why, because I'm not who you thought I was? Well, there seems to be a lot of that going on in your life, Sam." She spit out his name as though she had a bad taste in her mouth, but then she raised her chin and smiled—an expression her eyes didn't share. "Take Beth here, for example. Do you think you know who she is? Do you, Sam?" Cassie's smile widened. "Well, did you know she killed someone? That's right, your sweet, little Beth is a murderess." Sam turned to look at her and Cassie laughed at the shocked expression on his face. "Tell me, Sam, do you still want her tending bar for you? Oh, that's right—she's leaving in the morning; I forgot. Well, good riddance. Go back to Cleveland; I'm sure there'd be someone there who remembers you."

With her words still hanging in the air, Cassie stormed out of the stable. Sam turned back to Beth, but her head was bowed. He placed a finger under her chin and tried to raise her face, but she wouldn't look at him.

"I'd like to be alone," she whispered.

"Beth, whatever Cassie was talking about—"

"Please," she pleaded. "Just leave me be."

Sam stepped back, his shoulders slumped. He didn't know what to say, or what he should do. He reached for Beth. "Please, let me help . . ."

Beth turned and ran to the office, slamming the door behind her, and Sam simply watched her go.

Chapter Forty-Nine

"Was that Cassie who just ran out of here?"

Sam was still contemplating what Cassie had said concerning Beth's past when the sound of Mark's voice broke his concentration and brought him back to the moment. Reality was not everything it was cracked up to be; it was still late, he was still confused, and Beth was still in the office, hiding behind the closed door.

"Yes," Sam said, a faraway tone to his voice. "I fired her."

Surprised, Mark seemed to momentarily be at a loss for words. He quickly recovered. "What did she do?"

"She attacked Beth," Sam said, the anger returning at the mere memory of what he had just seen.

"So you fired her?"

"What is this," Sam exploded, "twenty questions?"

Mark raised both of his hands, palms out, as though showing he was unarmed. "Hey, I was just wondering, that's all."

"Well, maybe it's none of your business," Sam said, but a good portion of the anger had ebbed from his voice.

"You're probably right." Mark looked around the stable, as though seeing it for the first time. "Cute foal," he said.

Sam looked hard at the man, but offered no reply. The office door creaked open and Beth stepped out. She would not meet Sam's gaze. Instead, she crossed to Ghost's stall and stood there, watching the mare and foal in silence.

"I understand you had a hard time finding the foal," Mark said. "I heard you had some help."

Sam glanced at Beth, but she stood with her back to him. Had she told Mark about Peter and the foal? He didn't think so, and yet . . . what other explanation could there be for Mark knowing what had happened?

"Old souls, remember?" Mark asked, his eyes meeting Sam's confused gaze. "Other souls—companion souls, if you want to call them that—accompany us on our journeys, and sometimes they help us find what is lost."

"Listen, Buddy, it's way too late for this tonight—" Sam began, but Mark cut him off.

"Too late? Maybe, maybe not." Mark studied Sam for a beat, then said, "There are lessons you must learn in life; do you remember that part, Sam? And, until you learn those lessons, you can't move on." Mark fell silent for a moment, waiting for Sam's response. None came, so Mark shrugged. "What the heck, perhaps this will jog your memory." Mark pulled Sam's revolver from its hiding place at the small of his back. He smiled when Sam's eyes grew wide at the sight of the gun. "There was a part about those lessons expanding beyond a single lifetime, remember? So, in order to learn all we need to know, we must live again, and again, and again."

Sam watched as Mark turned the gun over in his hand, studying it intently. He struggled to understand what Mark was doing with the weapon, and when they had once again slipped into the twilight zone. More importantly, he wondered when they would leave it and find their way back.

"What are you doing with that?" Sam asked, his eyes riveted on Mark's.

Beth turned to see what Sam was talking about, and her breath caught in her throat when she saw the gun in Mark's hand.

Mark ignored the question and pressed on. "Bud was right; did you know that? Your friend's whole spiel about there being people in the world who do not wish to help others, who exist only to challenge our beliefs and stand in the way of our true path. Except, they're not people; not exactly."

"Get to the point, or get out of here," Sam warned.

"How exactly did Bud put it again?" Mark said. "Oh yes, 'There is peace and turmoil, love and hate, good and evil . . . each cannot exist without the other. Therefore, if there are 'good' souls, there must also be 'evil' ones'."

"Do you expect me to believe that you're an evil soul? Sorry, I don't buy that crap. You're a psycho, I'll give you that much—but you're human; I'd stake my life on that," Sam said, his eyes still following the gun.

"Would you? Is that really a safe bet? I suppose Miriam thought so, too, for a little while at least."

Sam raised his eyes to meet Mark's; he didn't even breathe. The only signs that he'd heard the comment were his clenched jaw and icy, cold stare.

"She was of no consequence to me, really. It was you I wanted. The way seemed clear; kill her to get to you."

Beth turned away from the stall and crossed to Sam. She tried to stand beside him, but he pushed her away.

"*You* killed Miriam?" Sam's voice brought goose bumps to Beth's arms and down her back.

"You were faltering, Sam, so close to the edge. You'd given up on the one thing that really mattered—love. Miriam saw that, too, and she was going to help you. She was going to try to convince you that it was alright to *feel* again. I saw my chance, so I took it."

"You're insane. Miriam died in an automobile accident," Sam growled.

"Yes, she did," Mark agreed. "And tell me, what ever became of the other driver—the one who hit her head-on that night and walked away?"

A silence, brief and heavy, fell over them. "You lie," Sam said.

"Do I? What would it take to convince you, Sam? Should I describe what she was wearing, or the exact second the accident took place? I know, you want to hear about the terror in her eyes when she realized that her life was over— that she was going to die alone." Sam took a step toward Mark, who raised the gun and smiled, halting Sam's approach.

"What good did it do to kill *her*?" Sam's voice, dark and low, carried throughout the quiet stable. "What did she ever do to you?"

"Nothing, that's the beauty of it. She was simply in the right place at the right time. No hard feelings, right?" Mark stepped over to Ghost's stall, and with a smile, leaned against the nearest post. "Tell me, Sam, how did you feel when you heard she was dead?"

"Peace," Beth whispered, her voice quivering.

"Very good!" Mark complimented her. "You remembered."

"Peace is the one thing that the evil souls don't have . . ." Beth went on.

"What the hell are you talking about?!" Sam snapped, and Beth knew, without a doubt, the extent of his rage.

"Bud said that evil souls exist because they cannot find peace. He . . . Mark knew you were weak, vulnerable. He killed Miriam to torment you, to hurt you, to drag you down."

"And now," Mark said, his smile still intact, "it's payback time." Then he did something very strange; he rested the gun on top of the post he'd been leaning against and stepped away. When he had gone several paces, he turned to face Sam. "Did they say she died instantly? That's not true. I manipulated time, just a little. I froze the seconds before impact so she could fully realize what was happening. I actually expected her to beg for her life, but she disappointed me. She didn't even seem scared; she just seemed—sad, I suppose. She wasn't quite ready for it to end; but then, few are." He met Sam's gaze. "But I assure you, Sam, I am ready. I am *so* ready. What is it the Bible says, 'an eye for an eye'? There's the gun. Go ahead; get it. Blow my brains out; you know you want to. Do it for Miriam; you owe her that much. Let's see how much you really loved that old bitch."

Sam crossed to the gun in three quick strides and picked it up. He turned and stared at Mark with hatred in his eyes.

"That's it," Mark said. "Now point and shoot, unless you haven't got the nerve. Perhaps Miriam didn't mean as much to you as I thought. It would be such a pity if I killed her for nothing."

Sam brought the barrel of the gun up until it was even with Mark's chest. Beth's breath caught in her throat and she hurried to Sam. She grabbed his free arm, but again he pushed her away.

"Don't do it, Sam," she pleaded. "Can't you see what he's doing? He's goading you into shooting him! If you do that, he wins! Can't you see that? God, Sam; he's probably not even human—"

"There's one way to find out," he said and he pulled the hammer of the revolver back until it clicked.

"No!" Beth screamed and stepped in front of the gun. The pistol wavered in Sam's hand, and she watched as tears started to spill down his cheeks. "No," she said more gently. "Miriam wouldn't want this, can't you see? You can't let him win—you just can't!"

"Get out of the way, Beth," Sam whispered through clenched teeth.

"No!" she replied, her voice suddenly quiet, but firm. Her heart hammered and her knees threatened to give way, but she stood her ground. "If you ever felt anything for me, Sam, please—for the love of God—put the gun down."

"Boss," Bud joined them, seemingly from nowhere, and his voice—calm and familiar—descended over the group. "Shooting this man will not ease your pain. The old souls you travel with are waiting down another path; if you choose this one, they—and Miriam—will be lost to you forever. Beth is right; Miriam would not want this."

"Come on!" Mark chided and his smile intensified. "This is the moment, Sam; it's all up to you now. Are you going to allow Miriam's death to count for nothing? What kind of man would that make you? Or maybe—maybe you just didn't love her that much . . . maybe you're not a man at all."

Beth stepped in closer to the gun's muzzle and met Sam's eyes. She caught them and held them in hers. "I know how much you loved her, Sam. I saw how you wept for her; I held you in my arms and prayed I could ease your pain." She inhaled and her chest hitched. "Mark wasn't there, Sam. I was—I was there. Which one of us are you going to believe; who are you going to listen to?"

Fresh tears welled up in Sam's eyes and rolled down his cheeks. His shoulders shook as sobs racked his body. Beth reached for the gun, but Sam shook his head and steadied the gun with renewed determination. "Who did you kill, Beth?" he asked.

Beth's eyes grew wide and her breath caught in her throat.

"Was Cassie lying? Tell me!" Sam demanded. He studied her face as he waited for an answer, trying to see if she would be honest with him. The blood had already dried on her cheek where Cassie had struck her, and a dark bruise was spreading over the area.

"I . . ." Beth's voice failed her.

"Tell me!" he found her eyes and held them, demanding an answer.

Beth shook her head slowly, struggling with the admission. "No, Sam," she finally whispered and dropped her eyes. "Cassie wasn't lying."

"Then how dare you tell me what to do now—what gives you the right? Did the person you killed deserve to die more than this man?"

Beth lowered her face and started to cry. She backed away from the gun and from Sam, slowly at first, then more quickly. Finally she turned and fled past Bud and out of the stable. Bud watched her go, then he turned back to Sam. Without hesitation, he walked over and assumed the position Beth had left, placing himself between the gun and Mark.

"I will not tell you what to do, Boss. It is your choice. You are filled with hatred for this man; I can see it in your eyes. It has overtaken everything within you. This is your test, your lesson for this lifetime—hatred for this man, or love for Miriam and the other old souls who have shared your countless journeys. You must choose which to embrace; there can be no turning back."

The two men faced off for several long seconds. The gun trembled in Sam's outstretched hands. Eventually, his gaze softened and the anger ebbed away as tears filled his eyes. Finally, Sam shook his head and lowered the gun. Bud stepped forward and held out his hand. Sam placed the gun in it and looked away, his shoulders slumped. Bud turned to confront Mark, but he never got the chance. The man was nowhere to be seen.

"What the hell just happened here?" Sam asked, his voice barely more than a whisper.

"A test, Boss. You chose well; that is all that matters," Bud said.

"Did he really kill Miriam, Bud? I don't trust him, yet—would someone lie about something like that?"

"It does not matter. Even if he did, you could not prove it, and the law could not touch him."

Sam looked toward the heavens, but the roof of the stable was all he could see, so he dropped his gaze to the stable floor. "And we can't bring Miriam back," he concluded, his voice heavy with sorrow.

"No," Bud agreed. "We cannot bring her back; what is done is done. It is time to move on from all of this—from Miriam's death, from the broken heart you have carried with you for too many years. Peace will come, Boss, but only if you let it."

Still dazed, Sam raised his head and looked around the stable. His look of confusion faded as understanding, then fear washed over his face. "Beth . . . Jesus, where'd she go? I've got to find her, talk to her. Cassie said . . ." Sam stopped midsentence, unable to repeat the words.

Bud's expression did not change. "Whatever Cassie told you, it doesn't change Beth. She is the same woman you have always known. We each have demons to wrestle, Boss. She was here to help you face yours. Go now; it is your turn to be there for her."

Sam hesitated and ran the fingers of his right hand through his short hair. "What will I say?"

"You will know," Bud said, then the man did something that he had never done before. In all of the years that the two men had worked together, Bud had never touched Sam. He had never patted the man on the back, or even shook his hand. He now placed a hand on Sam's shoulder and squeezed it gently. "This test is over, Boss, you have put it behind you. Let the past be," Bud said. "Go and find Beth. Talk to her; tell her. It is time to move on."

Chapter Fifty

Sam searched for Beth for the better part of an hour. Her Bronco was still parked by the garage, so he knew she hadn't left. He checked the house, the yard, the water garden—everywhere that she could have possibly gone. With each minute that passed, the urgency to find her grew more intense. Now, he was frantic. It was 10:52 P.M. and full into night; the last remnants of sunlight had slipped away hours earlier. With a new moon just past, the heavens offered nothing in the way of light. The yard lights and tiki candles helped, but shadows and darkness prevailed. To complicate matters, the band was scheduled to play until midnight, and there was still plenty of cold beer and warm pork to keep the crowd fed, content, and present. Because of this, many of the guests remained, and people were walking, sitting, and taking up space wherever he looked. Sam asked everyone he met about Beth; most knew her and would have recognized her if she passed their way. No one had seen her.

Eventually, Bud appeared at his side and asked, "Nothing?"

"Nothing, and I've looked everywhere."

Steve Hanson, the mechanic who had fixed Beth's Bronco, approached them. He held a sweating plastic cup filled with beer in one hand and a cigarette in the other. "I heard you were looking for Beth."

"Have you seen her?" Sam asked, fighting to keep the urgency out of his voice, but not entirely succeeding.

"No, not really," Steve replied and took a drag on his cigarette. "But someone said they heard a rider race off through the pasture about an hour ago. It might have been her."

A rider? Could it have been Beth? All of the horses were in the far pasture and the tack was in the stable; he did not see anyone even go into the stable, let alone see a horse and rider leave. Still, most of the horses were wearing halters, and there were lead ropes draped over practically every pasture gate. Beth was an experienced rider, so riding a bareback horse and guiding it with a lead rope fastened around its muzzle—bosal style—was not out of the question. But, if it *had* been her, where would she have gone? Sam did not have to wonder long; somehow, he knew.

"I'm going out with the truck; keep an eye open for her here," he told Bud. "If I'm wrong, you may still find her before I do." The older man nodded and Sam went to fetch his keys.

Minutes later, when Sam drove up to the pasture gate, Bud was there, waiting to swing the wooden structure aside and let the truck pass. A myriad of insects flitted about in the headlights' beams as Bud opened the gate and Sam drove the truck forward. Halfway through, he stepped on the brakes and stopped.

Bud leaned in through the open passenger window and said, "You think she's at the cemetery."

"Yes. I'm going to check there first."

Bud nodded and stepped back. He slapped the truck's fender, as though it were a horse that he was urging on through. Sam took his cue, put the truck in gear and stepped on the accelerator. In the soft red glow of the taillights, he watched in the rearview mirror as Bud closed the gate behind him. *Now is not the time to be looking backwards*, Sam reprimanded himself. If Beth was out here somewhere, he needed to find her.

It did not take long to reach the clearing. The wooden crosses appeared to glow in the swath illuminated by the truck's headlights. Sam put the vehicle in park, left the motor running, and got out. He strode partway into the clearing, walking in the center of the lit path, and turned around in a tight circle.

"Beth?" No answer. He called again, louder. "Beth?"

A slight breeze stirred the surrounding trees, and crickets chirped in the tall grass all around him. The air smelled of decaying wood and damp earth. There was a soft rustling in the grass to his left . . . something small, not human. Perhaps a rabbit, or a raccoon that had stopped to see what all the ruckus was about before continuing on its way.

Sam sighed. He had been so certain that this is where she would have gone—if, in fact, it had even been her who had ridden off. Hands on hips, he studied the ground before him. Dozens of horses could have passed through this clearing over the last day or two. Now, frozen in the truck's headlight beams, it was impossible for Sam to tell how old any of the hoofprints were, or exactly when they had been made. As much as he hated to admit it, he'd been wrong. Beth was not here, and his search would have to continue on somewhere else.

He returned to the truck and climbed in. He stepped on the brake, reached for the shifter, and froze. Beth *was* here; he saw her clearly. She was standing at the far edge of Jinx's grave, looking at him. He threw the truck door open and jumped out, slamming it closed behind him.

"Beth, didn't you hear me calling? Why didn't you answer? You had me worried sick." He glanced around as he approached her.

Beth smiled at him, but it was a sad smile. Her eyes were moist, and Sam wondered if she'd been crying, or was about to. "I didn't mean to worry you," she said.

"Well, you did," he said firmly. "It's not safe riding in the dark, Beth. You know that. Your horse could have stepped in a hole and broken both of your necks," he was trying his best to scold her, but his voice lacked the necessary sternness to be taken seriously. "What horse did you ride out here, and where is it?"

"So many questions," Beth said.

"And I expect some answers, too, so start talking, little lady. And exactly which horse did you ride out here on, and without any saddle, and why did you take off without telling me?" Sam didn't really mean to interrogate Beth. He was so relieved to have found her that the adrenaline was causing him to spew out questions in rapid succession.

"You didn't shoot him," she said, studying his eyes. "You let Mark go."

"No, I didn't shoot him. I . . ."

She nodded and her smile brightened, but she wiped at a tear that was sliding down her cheek. "Bud stopped you," she said. "He's a good man."

"Don't change the subject, Beth. What are you doing out here?"

"I just needed some time alone; this seemed like the perfect place," Beth said. Sam opened his mouth to reply, but Beth cut him off. "My turn to ask a question," she said. "What did Bud say that stopped you from pulling the trigger?"

Sam hesitated before answering, "Does it matter?"

"Yes," she said quietly, still studying his eyes as they spoke.

Sam looked away, studying whatever lay in the darkness beyond the headlight beams. Finally, he turned back to Beth and said, "Bud said to let the past be; he told me to find you and tell you that it's time to move on."

"Bud is a wise man," she said.

"Beth," Sam tried again, "please tell me why you ran off."

Beth shook her head. "That's not important . . . that's not what you really want to know?"

"Which is?" he prompted.

"You want to know who I killed."

Beth's eyes remained locked on Sam's; she did not turn aside or look away. To Sam, it felt as if she was trying to read his mind, and his heart skipped a beat.

"Maybe I *don't* want to know; it's none of my business," he said. "You'll tell me someday, if you want to. If you don't, that's okay, too."

"His name was James Kordack," she said without hesitation and Sam was taken aback by the abruptness of the statement. "We were living in Janesville. I was nine years old; he was fifty-two."

"Beth, I—" Sam tried to protest, to assure her that he didn't need to know, not now—maybe not ever—but she pushed on.

"He was probably the seventh or eighth foster father I'd had." She laughed softly, but there was sorrow at its core.

"You see them everywhere—the billboards and the commercials endorsing foster families, telling of how they give orphaned and abandoned children a place to call home—a place to feel safe. For some kids, that may be true, but it was never that way for me." Beth shuddered and went on.

"I was four when a fire killed both of my parents. Somehow, the fire fighters managed to get me out of the house, but not my mom and dad. I hated firemen for years. I guess I blamed them for failing to get to my parents in time, or maybe I just hated them for saving me." She forced a smile; it lacked sincerity. "But then, we can't choose our fate, can we?" she asked Sam, and waited for his answer.

"No," he said. "No, we can't." A moment of silence followed, and Sam asked, "Would you like to sit in the truck and talk?"

Beth shook her head. "No, I like it out here. Don't you?"

"It's peaceful," Sam agreed, uncertain what more to say. That feeling of being in the twilight zone had returned. The edges of the clearing seemed further away than they had been just moments ago. The crickets were silent, and even the wind had paused. Only Beth and the ground beneath his feet seemed to be real, but he was certain that could change at any moment.

Beth approached until she was only four or five feet away. There, she paced—back and forth—speaking as she moved. "Mr. Kordack was a terrible man, and I hated him. You can't possibly understand how strongly a child can hate someone, not unless you've lived that child's life and seen what they've seen, or felt what they've felt. And no, he didn't rape me—or physically assault me. I suppose when someone imagines the worst-case scenarios between a fifty-two year old man and a nine-year-old girl, those are the first things to come to mind. But there are other, perhaps even more terrible, ways to hurt a child—to create scars that will never show, no matter how closely someone looks."

Sam's phone chirped. He checked the caller ID and saw that it was Bud. He looked at Beth, who had stopped pacing. She gave a quick nod and looked away, so he answered it.

"Hello?" He listened for a beat before saying, "We'll talk when I get back," and he disconnected the call.

"That was Bud," Beth said, half-smiling.

"He's worried. I should have told him that I found you, and that you're safe."

"He'll know soon enough where I am," she said.

Sam considered this and nodded.

Beth resumed pacing and Sam studied her, confused. Something was off—out of place, but he couldn't put his finger on exactly what it was. It was that whole twilight zone thing, he supposed, but it bothered him none the less. What was it that that had the hair standing up on the nap of his neck, and that voice in the back of his mind screaming to be heard? Beth was certainly here; they both were. And she was definitely real; he was sure of that. If he reached out to touch her, he'd feel the warmth of her skin and the texture of her clothing. So what was it that was gnawing at his consciousness—demanding to be noticed, but refusing to be seen? For the love of him, he couldn't say.

"Listen, Beth . . . you don't have to do this."

"But I do. I don't know why, but I have to tell you. I *need* to tell you." She stopped pacing long enough to gaze into his eyes. "I need you to understand, okay?"

"Okay," Sam nodded, and Beth resumed pacing.

"The Kordacks lived in a run-down house on three acres of land in the middle of nowhere. They had three kids of their own, and two foster children in addition to me—at least, not while I was there. They also had a female collie. She was the sweetest dog, and the only living thing in that household that ever showed me any affection. She was like a shadow and followed me everywhere. At night, she'd sleep at the foot of my bed and keep watch. She made me feel special and safe, and I loved her for that.

That spring, she had a litter of puppies. They were so adorable . . . just little balls of fur with their eyes closed tight. They squeaked, and grunted, and crawled around on the old blanket that she'd had them on in my closet. You should have seen her, Sam. She was the greatest mother to those pups, and she was so proud." There was a faraway look in Beth's eyes, and the trace of a real smile appeared, only to vanish.

"Beth—"

"No, don't stop me . . . please."

Sam closed his mouth and simply listened.

"Mr. Kordack learned about the puppies when he was seven cans into his daily twelve-pack. He was furious. He went on and on about being broke and having too many mouths to feed. He stormed out of the house and returned with a burlap bag. He went to my room where the puppies were. He grabbed one and tossed it in the sack. The mother dog went nuts; she growled and lunged at Mr. Kordack and grabbed him by the wrist. He dropped the sack and kicked her, and beat her, and wailed on her. When she wouldn't let go, he reached in with his free hand and pulled down the metal bar from the closet where the clothes had been hung.

He used it to bash her head in. Even then," Beth drew a ragged breath, "even then he had to pry her dead jaws from his arm. I'd never seen him so furious," Beth continued. "He was still holding his injured wrist with his good hand, so he made me put the rest of the puppies in the sack. They were so terrified; they seemed to know that something was terribly wrong. I begged him, I pleaded with him, but it was no use.

There was a small lake a few miles down the road. It belonged to some friend of the Kordacks, and they kept a small rowboat tethered to a makeshift dock there. Mr. Kordack dragged me out to the car and tossed both me and the bag of puppies into the back seat; the front seat was reserved for him and what remained of his beer. By then, he had tied the sack shut with a shoelace, so I couldn't see the puppies anymore. But I could hear them whimpering, and I could see them moving about beneath the cloth. When we got to the lake, he parked the car and took us down to the dock. He ordered me to get in the boat, and he tossed the puppies in. I can still hear the muffled thud their bodies made when they landed on the hard metal floor, and their squeals of pain and terror." Beth hesitated, then continued the tale.

"There was only one lifejacket in the boat, and he made me put it on. I don't know how much money they got each month for keeping me, but he certainly didn't want to do anything that would jeopardize that. My falling overboard and drowning would have been too difficult to explain to the case worker and the county. Once I had the jacket on, he rowed out to the center of the lake. I knew what he was planning to do." Tears streamed down Beth's face, but she didn't stop. "I begged him, pleaded with him. He just grinned at me and stopped rowing long enough to pop open a can of beer and down it, then he began rowing again. Eventually, we reached a spot that pleased him. He pointed at the sack and told me to drop it over the side. I couldn't do it; I couldn't even bear to watch. So he grabbed me and forced me to stand up beside him in the boat. He picked up the sack and I could hear the puppies crying, and I started screaming. He held it over the side, three feet up from the surface of the lake, and he just let go. It hit the water with a muffled splash and sank.

I was furious. I tried to grab for the puppies—tried to save them. Mr. Kordack pushed me down hard and I fell into the boat's hull. I guess he must have lost his balance, because there was a loud splash and suddenly the boat was rocking from side to side and I was all alone. I heard him hollering and I peered over the side. The boat had drifted several feet away from him by then. I didn't know he couldn't swim, and I guess I didn't care. He told me to take off my lifejacket and throw it to him, but I didn't. I couldn't move; I couldn't deal with it. I remember closing my eyes, and all I could see was the sack of puppies disappearing beneath the water, and all I could hear were their cries, and I couldn't move." Beth looked up at the stars, seemed to contemplate something, then she told the end of her tale.

"It was seven o'clock the next morning before they found me. It was so cold that night; I'd curled up on the floor of the boat, but the metal was chilled from the water and I was freezing. They took me to a hospital, then to yet another foster home when I was finally released." She shuddered, and added, "It took them a week to find Mr. Kordack's body. I'd hoped they would never find it. I wanted him to stay at the bottom of that lake, his sightless eyes staring at that silent burlap bag. I wanted him to be there forever."

Sam swallowed hard, but the lump in his throat would not be dislodged. "I am so sorry, Beth." His heart was breaking for her. She had stopped pacing when her story ended and he went to her. He stepped in front of her, wrapped his arms around her and pulled her close. He had been right; she was very real. The warmth of her body felt right within his arms. "Aren't we the pair when it comes to love? It seems like all we've ever known was pain, and I am so sorry for that."

"Was I wrong, Sam, to not save him? He asked for the lifejacket, but I didn't give it to him. I really did kill him, didn't I?"

"You didn't kill anyone. It was his choice to get in that boat when he'd been drinking. My God, Beth, you were nine years old. You can't possibly blame yourself."

"All I ever wanted, then or now, was to be loved. Was that too much to ask?" Beth pushed against Sam's chest and backed away. Slowly, she turned and walked back to Jinx's grave. "After my parents died, I was passed from one home to another. In the beginning, I believed what the social workers told me; I believed that I'd be part of a family again. I soon learned that wasn't true. Still, a part of me hoped for love; a part of me hoped I'd be good enough, eventually, for some family to take me in—really take me in—but that didn't happen. Love became something that existed for everyone else, but not for me." She turned back to Sam, and smiled. He stared at her, mesmerized; her expression seemed so out of place, and yet so right.

"Then I fell in love with you, Sam. It was funny; Miriam knew it before I even did," Beth's eyes shone brightly in the headlight beams. "She teased me about getting up the nerve to ask you out and ' the first move' Back then, I thought that love was all about being together; that to love someone you had to become a part of their life and spend forever at their side." There was a brief pause, then Beth said, "I know better now. Love simply is; it doesn't matter if you're physically with that person or not. It's a tie that binds two souls together for all eternity. I can love you no matter where I am, whether we're together or not. I can love you if I'm standing by your side, or several hundred miles away. Love knows nothing about distance or time. Love simply is."

Sam's phone chirped, but he ignored it.

"You should answer that," Beth said. "Bud needs you."

Sam reached in his pocket for the phone, and froze. Suddenly, he knew what it was about Beth that was out of place. His heart raced and his mind struggled for an explanation for what he now saw so plainly.

"Answer the phone, Sam. It's okay," Beth assured him. Like a theater spotlight, the truck headlights continued to illuminate Beth and the forest behind her. Yes, she was beautiful, in that 'country girl' sort of way. Sam had seen her hundreds of times; she looked the same now as she had a week ago when she rode up to the stable on the back of Mark's motorcycle. In fact, there wasn't a mark on her face; the welt where Cassie had struck her was gone.

Moving as though in a dream, Sam looked away from Beth. He pulled the phone out of his pocket, pressed the talk button, and lifted it to his ear.

"Get back here, Sam, now!" Bud said. "The stable's on fire!"

Sam looked up, ready to yell at Beth to get in the truck—and quickly! They had to get back, but only trees and brush and grass remained where she'd stood only seconds before. Beth, like the angry welt on her face, had simply disappeared.

Chapter Fifty-One

Beth hugged the shadows on the east side of the stable and waited for the dreaded sound of a gunshot. Seconds stretched into minutes, and the sound did not come. Perhaps Sam had come to his senses, or perhaps Bud had talked him down. The details didn't matter; all that mattered was that Sam had not given in. Somehow, he had found the strength to let his anger go.

Beth considered that. Did it mean that she'd succeeded in doing what she had come back to do? Did it mean that Sam was ready to forgive and move on? She knew he would never forget—neither of them would. They would always carry the scars of Miriam's death and so many other wounds with them. But, *carrying* them meant moving forward, didn't it? And if Sam could move forward, then maybe— just maybe—things would be alright now for him. She hoped so, with all of her heart.

She huddled in the stable's shadow, alone, for several minutes. When she was certain that Sam was not going to pull the trigger, Beth felt an undeniable urge to get away. She slipped between the boards of the paddock's fence and headed toward the road. Darkness surrounded her. A hundred feet to her right, the band was halfway through their rendition of Marty Robbins's hit "El Paso". Bodies swayed in the semi-darkness, and for some of them—the ones who were truly in love—she knew that time would be standing still.

When she reached the eastern end of the paddock, she slipped between the boards yet again and scrambled through the ditch to the road. Once there, she simply started walking. For nearly thirty minutes, she strode into the darkness, heading south. She had no destination in mind; she was not going anywhere in particular. She simply wanted some time alone to clear her head. Several times, tears threatened, and each time she forced them back. She was through crying over Sam, or her past, or anything else for that matter.

Still, she couldn't stop her mind from whirling around and around. How had Cassandra found out about Mr. Kordack and Beth's past? More importantly, what did Sam think of Beth now that he knew what she had done—now that he knew that she'd killed someone? Should she tell him the truth—the whole truth?

Anger welled up inside her. This wasn't about her—why couldn't she get that through her head? Yes, she'd come back because of Sam, but not because she loved him—she'd come back to help him see that love was all that really mattered—even if he didn't, couldn't, love her. That was the reality that *she* had to face. How could she be so stupid, over and over again, to hope for something more? Why did she even care what Sam thought about her? It clearly didn't matter. *It's over. Can't you get that through your thick head?* She scolded herself sharply for the millionth time. Why, she suddenly wondered, was she waiting until morning to leave? She didn't have to, did she? Hadn't she done what she'd needed to do? Wasn't now as good a time as any? *Yes*, she thought, *it was*. Her mind made up, she turned around and began walking briskly back the way she had come.

When she was still fifty yards away from where the Thunder Ridge Ranch's driveway met the road, Beth heard the sound of squealing tires and looked up. Cassie's white Mustang sped out of the driveway and turned in her direction, its rear end fishtailing the first thirty feet down the road. It was moving quickly and gaining speed, so Beth slipped into the ditch and watched it race past. Why was Cassandra first leaving now—had it simply taken her this long to gather her things? That was a possibility, and—if she was still angry—that would account for the way she had left in such a hurry. Still, it seemed odd. Cassie was the type of woman that generally preferred a slow burn, not an outright explosion. A tantrum this late after the fact would not have been her style. Then Beth turned back toward the ranch and saw the orange glow in the sky above the stable. Her stomach fell and her heart skipped a beat. Ghost and China were in that stable. Without even realizing it, Beth's was suddenly racing toward the burning building, and gaining speed.

She turned into the driveway and was met with instant chaos. People milled about, pointing and shouting, and blocking her way. She pushed them aside, time and again, without bothering to apologize. When she finally reached the stable, flames were traveling up the outside corners of the building and licking the eaves, and smoke crept out through the spaces between the boards. From inside the stable, Ghost's screams rose and fell like horrid waves that spread outward through the night. People standing nearby stopped talking and listened in horror to the trapped animal's pleas for help. The small stable door hung open, and slightly askew on its hinges. A ranch hand, uncertain what to do, raced back and forth in front of the stable, but each time he approached the open door, the escaping heat forced him back. Beth barreled past him and shot through the doorway, intent on only one thing—reaching Ghost and China in time.

Beth had never been in a burning building before. The intense heat and acrid smoke made breathing nearly impossible. Light cast by the flames mingled with the smoke, creating macabre images that crept and danced along the stable's walls. She pulled her shirt out of her waistband and raised it to cover her nose and mouth. Coughing, she made her way to Ghost's stall and opened the gate.

In the movies, the horse would realize that the open gate was an escape route. As the audience cheered, it would gallop out of its stall and sprint for the nearest door, then beyond to safety. In real life, however, Beth knew that it never worked that way. Cows, horses, goats—any animal raised and housed in a stable or barn for the majority of its life—learn to associate their stalls and the familiar surroundings with safety. Time and again, she'd heard stories of animals that, once freed from a burning building, turned around and rushed back inside, only to perish in the flames. So it was now with Ghost. Terrified by the flames, she refused to leave the implied safety of her stall. Beth rushed at the mare, waving her arms and shouting, but the animal backed itself into the farthest corner of the stall and reared back, frantically pawing at the air.

"Easy girl," Beth said, attempting to now soothe the mare instead of chase her out. "Easy, it's okay." A timber from the overhead mow crashed down behind them, and Ghost reared up again. "Easy girl, I'm going to get you out of here, okay?" Slowly, Beth approached the frightened animal, speaking loud enough to be heard over the roaring fire. At last, Beth was close enough to grab the mare's halter. She got a firm grip on the leather and began to lead the mare toward the gate. Ghost balked at first, then took several hesitant steps. In a matter of seconds, they were through the gate and headed toward the door, but Beth looked back and stopped.

China was still at the far end of the stall, too terrified to move. Beth had three options. She could lead the mare to safety without the foal; she could release the mare and go back for China—which would probably result in Ghost rushing back to the stall and all three of them perishing in the fire; or she could forget about both Ghost and China, accept that she had tried, and simply save herself.

There was no time for contemplation; she had to decide. She looked back at the tiny white foal huddled against the far end of the stall. Had Peter saved it—had he led Sam to the foal only to let it perish now, in this burning hell? She couldn't believe that, wouldn't believe that. Another timber fell, crashing in a shower of smoke and scattered sparks. Ghost reared and pulled away, and Beth felt a searing pain in her shoulder. Free, the mare looked confused, hesitant as to which way to go. Beth turned away from her, leaving the mare's fate to whatever decision the horse would ultimately make.

Back inside the stall, Beth stooped, positioned her arms under the foal's stomach and lifted—in much the same fashion that a toddler might pick up the family cat. The foal struggled, kicking wildly, and the searing pain in Beth's shoulder intensified. She cried out, but refused to let go. Either both she and China were going to make it out of the stable, or neither would. The decision made, Beth turned and rushed for the door.

The smoke was thicker now; it swirled around them, engulfed them, and Beth was no longer sure which way led out of the stable. She stumbled once, then again, jarring the foal that had settled itself in her arms. She had to find the way out, and it had to be now.

Then, the strangest thing happened—again. In a twinkling, the sound of the roaring fire was stilled. The heat and smoke, which had grown so oppressive that she could no longer breathe, were simply gone. It was like a dream that crouches on the edge of one's memory—just out of reach but hauntingly familiar. Then Beth *did* remember, but it hadn't been a dream, and it hadn't been a fire. It had been a snowstorm on a cold, late-December drive home.

Beth raised her eyes to the stable area above her. The fire still raged—she could see its flames angrily feeding on the overhead timbers. It would not be long now before the entire structure collapsed, but she was no longer afraid. While previously the dome had held out the cold and the wind-driven snow, it now held the fire at bay. She bent down and propped the foal up on its own legs. It shook itself and took a few tentative steps before looking around, its eyes bright and wondering.

"She is beautiful," Peter said.

Beth simply smiled. She recalled how startled—how frightened she had been the first time he appeared from nowhere. It seemed funny now, and oh so long ago.

"Yes, she is."

"But," he asked, "was she worth dying for, Beth?" His voice was neither judgmental, nor condescending.

Beth's heart hitched. She thought of Sam and everything she had hoped for with him. She remembered the dance they'd shared that evening . . . and the one night they'd shared years earlier. Her smile faltered. What was it Bud had told Sam? It was time to move on. "I think so," Beth said, fighting to keep the conviction in her voice, "if she gets to grow up and live out her years. Is that how it will be?"

Peter walked over to Beth, and the foal followed. It stretched out its slender neck and nuzzled Peter's hand. Beth stroked its back and side; its coat felt like satin beneath her hand.

"You did a good job here, Beth. I'm proud of you."

"So the foal will live?" she asked again.

"Yes," Peter said.

"And Ghost?" Beth wondered aloud.

"She is already outside; Bud has her in the paddock. She is waiting there for China."

"Good," Beth swallowed hard and turned to look at Peter with uncertainty in her eyes. "So, what happens now?" she asked.

"When I said that you did a good job here, I wasn't just talking about rescuing Ghost and China. I was talking about Sam as well."

"But, I . . . did I help Sam, really? I mean, in so many ways, he's the same man he was when I left here five years ago."

"Is he?"

Beth turned away, and her voice dropped to a whisper. "He's still strong, independent—and alone," she said, then added. "And he still doesn't love me."

"Sure he does; he just doesn't realize it."

"What good is that?" Beth scoffed. "And, if I die . . ."

Peter turned Beth around to face him and smiled at her. "There is no death . . . not really; don't you see that now? You are not defined by this flesh and blood body that will cease to function and return to the earth. You will go on. Sam will also go on—in this life, for a while, then on to whatever lies ahead. You see, the energy—the essence that is at your very core—knows nothing of death. It only knows love, and that is eternal."

"So," Beth ventured, "someday—"

"You want to know if you'll be with him again," Peter said.

Beth's chin quivered and she bit her lip. "Maybe, someday . . ."

"Not someday," Peter said. "Now—now and always. You still believe that, by dying, you are leaving him behind. But, if there is no death, then there is no distance between you and Sam. You will journey on together, until you find your way home one final time." Peter used his finger to wipe away a tear from Beth's cheek. "You've done well," he reassured her a final time. "Sam overcame his anger; he chose to move on and leave all of the pain and heartache behind. You played a part in that, Beth."

"Maybe I did, but even if that's true—what happens now?" she asked again.

Peter gently placed his hand on her shoulder. "What is meant to be."

Beth tried for nonchalance, but failed. "That's a little cryptic, isn't it?"

"Yes, I suppose it is." Peter removed his hand from Beth's shoulder and stroked China's upraised head for a long moment. At last, he said, "What happens now is directly connected to everything that has happened up until this moment." He held up his forefinger, cutting off the remark that he knew was forming in Beth's mind. "Yes, that's still too cryptic, but being cryptic doesn't make it any less true." He hesitated and began again. "Tell me, Beth, what have you learned since we first met?

"What have I learned?" Beth repeated the question as she rolled it around in her mind. "I've learned that life is not set in stone, and that things are not always what they appear to be."

"And?" Peter prodded her to continue.

"I've learned that we've got to leave the past in the past. Whatever terrible things may have happened, we've got to simply accept them and move on."

"And?" Peter said, a bit more forcefully.

"I've learned that love, no matter how much it hurts or how hard it is to believe in, is still worth more than anything else that life has to offer. I loved Miriam, and discovered that she never really left me. I loved Jinx, and even though I couldn't save him, loving him was the right thing to do—it made his life, and mine, count for something. I love this little foal," she said, resting her hand on China's withers, "and she'll have a chance at life now because you cared enough to help to find her, and because I came back for her."

"And Sam?" Peter said, gently.

Beth wavered. Once again, tears welled up in her eyes and spilled down her cheeks. She neither blinked them back nor wiped them away. "Sam," she said softly. "What a pair of misfits we are. I've learned that . . ." she hesitated, trying to find words that would fit. "I think we're like the little concrete Dutch boy and girl statues you see in so many yards. They are leaning forward with their hands clasped behind their backs and their lips puckered, waiting to kiss. The problem is, most people set the statues three or four feet apart, so their lips never meet. The statues spend forever in that pose, waiting and hoping for that kiss, but they never seem to get the chance."

"Never is a long time," Peter said.

"Yes . . . yes it is," Beth agreed.

"You had many chances—over many lifetimes—and you always found a way to make it work. The bond between you and Sam is something very special. You believe that, don't you?"

"Is that why it hurts so much now?" she asked. "I get the feeling that," she hesitated, then pushed on. "I get the feeling that my heart remembers, even though I don't. Is that possible?"

Peter nodded. "Yes, it's possible—and very likely. The mind forgets from one life to the next. It cannot recall the faces, the events, and all of the details that it experienced, but the heart remembers and holds on fast."

Beth considered that. "I'm glad," she said and managed a smile.

"There is much that both of you still need to learn," Peter said. "There will be many more lifetimes, many more trials, and many more heartaches. You've accomplished much in this lifetime, Beth; but as I said, you won't recall most of it. You won't remember me, or the names and faces of those who have journeyed with you until now, but your heart and your soul—your spirit—will remember, and those elements will draw you and Sam together again."

"Because of the love we share," Beth ventured.

"Yes—that, and your faith, and your commitment to one another."

Beth furrowed her brow, trying to remember the verse, and it came to her. "These three things remain: faith, hope, and love. But the greatest of these is love."

Peter stroked the foal one last time before meeting Beth's gaze and holding it. "I think it's time to get this little one back to its mother."

"What—what will happen to me?" Beth asked. Her chin quivered and tears threatened anew, but unlike when they had been discussing Sam, this time she tried to hold them back.

"There's nothing to fear, Beth. You're going home—for a little while—until it's time for you to begin your journey again." Peter reached out and offered her his hand. His smile was filled with unspoken understanding and his eyes were filled with hope. "It's okay, Beth; I'll stay with you if you like." She hesitated, for just a second, then she placed her hand in his.

The dome above them disintegrated. The sound of the roaring fire filled her ears, but it was not charred wood and billowing smoke that descended upon them. A myriad of iridescent black moths—glittering in the light of the surrounding flames—engulfed her and Peter, lifting them skyward and carrying them away. From some distant vantage point that was both within the burning stable and somewhere far away, Beth watched as China fled unharmed through the open stable door, and Beth saw the ranch hand catch the foal on the other side of the burning wall. She floated, carefree and weightless, through the scorching fire and swirling smoke. Looking down, she saw a familiar figure stumbling through the inferno, searching for the door. The figure almost made it, and she was surprised to recognize herself in the fire. The figure that was her—yet couldn't be—was almost clear of the burning stable. It was mere steps from the opening—from having yet another chance at this life—when a beam, weakened by the fire and no longer able to support the load it was designed to bear, came crashing down. There was an abrupt cloud of fire and smoke, then Beth succumbed to silence and a welcome peace.

Chapter Fifty-Two

Sam hesitated outside of the door and drew a deep breath. Despite the dedication of hospital staff, the corridor smelled of antiseptics, soiled laundry, and stale sweat, but he didn't notice. His heart racing, he stood frozen in place on the polished tile floor, his trembling hands thrust deep in his pockets. It was not too late. He could leave; he didn't have to do this. He'd gotten here as quickly as he could, but the doctor had told him that it was just a matter of time. He'd said Beth would probably never regain consciousness. Sam could leave the same way he had come and no one would ever know, or care. And yet, she *would* know, wouldn't she. He squeezed his eyes shut, hesitating—waiting—for what? Humans wait their entire lives—for a split-second of time . . . a moment that seems just right. But the truth was, time had callously run out; if it hadn't, he wouldn't be here . . . frozen in place in the third-floor corridor of Our Lady of Mercy Hospital, knowing with all of his heart that this was where he needed to be, and wishing with all of his might to be anywhere else.

Standing in the well-lit hallway, Sam was acutely aware of nurses, and doctors, and visitors, and all manner of hospital personnel bustling about. The mingled scents of his surroundings filled his nostrils, and the low tones of hushed conversations filled his ears. Still, surreality was as much a part of this moment as it had been in the forest clearing only hours earlier. How was he to ever again know what was real? Ever since Peter had assisted him in finding the foal, he had found himself questioning everything around him. How could Beth have been in the clearing, and been trapped in the stable at the same time—how could she have been standing before him and caught beneath a burning timber a mile away? His mind reeled and he closed his eyes tightly. In the clearing, there had been no wound where Cassie had struck her, but it had been Beth; he was sure of that. Beth had been there, yet she had also been in the stable—if not, she wouldn't be lying on the other side of this hospital door, barely hanging on. *What was real?* he wondered, and the answer slammed into him, crushing him beneath its imminence. The fire had been real, the hospital was real, and the aching in his chest was very, very real . . . as were all mortal goodbyes.

He leaned against the door and it swung inward on well-worn hinges that dared not groan in protest. Stepping from the brightly-lit corridor into the dimly-lit room, Sam hesitated just inside the doorway, waiting for his eyes to adjust. Slowly, the bed at the center of the room came into focus. Upon it, an unimposing form rested, covered in white sheets that cascaded down on either side of the mattress, partially covering the necessary tangle of tubes that were a very temporary part of her existence. He stepped toward her and the door closed quietly behind him, cutting off the bustle of the hospital beyond and sealing him in this silent room where even time was holding its breath, waiting.

Moving to her side, he gazed down at her. Pale hands, their skin translucent, rested on the sheet to either side of her. Surgical tape crisscrossed the top of the left hand, securing the intravenous needle and the transparent tube that delivered a trickle of fluid into a protruding vein. Under the thin veil of the hospital gown, her chest rose and fell, not calmly and in perfect measure, but in uneven and labored breaths, as though—even in this state of unconsciousness—she was searching for something, something she couldn't find. Color-coded wires led from her chest to the heart monitor, which recorded the frantic, irregular rhythm, and callously announced it to the empty room. The monitor's mechanical beeps assaulted the silence, denying its power, even as the quiet struggled to reassert itself in the dimly-lit space. Fighting the urge to leave, Sam turned his face upward in search of heaven, but there was no angelic realm to be seen—or, if there was, a ceiling composed of aging suspended tiles blocked it from view.

Uncertain of what was expected of them, his hands awkwardly slipped back into his pockets, as though awaiting some instructions or task. However, in a quiet disturbed only by the mechanical report of the heart-monitor, no task came. Sam had read somewhere about the human "fight or flight" response, but he had never understood it better than he did at this moment. Why the hell had he come? What had he hoped to accomplish here? Beth was dying; there was nothing for him to do here, no way that he could help. A feeling of helplessness welled up inside of him, twisting his guts and forcing his hands into balled fists that strained against the pockets of his jeans. He was a man of action; he prided himself on his ability to tackle a challenge—to divide it into manageable tasks and conquer them, one by one. But there was nothing to conquer here. It was this inability to do anything at all that fueled his desire to flee. If one can't fight, then the next best thing is to escape—to cut one's losses and move on. He understood this well. Still, his feet remained frozen in place, ignoring his racing heart and his jumbled thoughts. This was, he understood, where he needed to be.

"Beth?" He had not meant to speak, but her name slipped from his lips without thought or intent. It floated through the stillness for a brief moment before fading away into the corners of the room without a trace. He withdrew his hand from his pocket and gently covered hers where it rested at her side; her skin felt sterile and cold. "Beth?"

* * *

There was no pain; there was no fear; there was no uncertainty. There was only the feeling of a space, warm and familiar . . . not unlike what she imagined the womb must have been like when the concept of her life was just beginning. She was overwhelmed by contentment, and the sensation of moving—of being absorbed into some unfathomable, yet familiar, place where physical limitations and mortal questions ceased to exist. She welcomed the release, the sense of letting it all go for the sake of—what? She had no clue, and it didn't matter. She knew this was where she needed to be; this was where all of her mortal struggles had brought her. This was where the end and the beginning met, where the strange and the familiar blended and became one, where the questions ceased and the answers came effortlessly from nowhere and everywhere. She absorbed it, and it her, and it was right, so very right.

Then something changed. In an instant, the contentment pulled away—withdrew from her—to wait just out of reach. Her chest tightened, and fear—human yet feral—returned to her, unbidden and undesired. With it came an unbidden resentment, overwhelmingly strong. It wasn't fair! Something was pulling her backward, away from the long-awaited journey's end, and she resented it, fought it, hated it for finding her . . . She was tired, couldn't it see? She didn't want the burden of living anymore; she didn't want to be chained to the earth by the need to draw a breath—again and again—when it was so much easier to just let it all go. She wanted to scream, but she was too weak—too far gone. She wasn't strong enough to return, of that she seemed certain, and yet return she did. And as mortality coursed through her—pouring into her and weighing her down into the hospital bed, she finally understood. It was okay. The resentment subsided, and she drew a welcomed breath, deep and empowering. There was one more thing she needed to do.

She opened her eyes and the room swam into focus. There was a ceiling, and a light fixture, and a suspended IV bottle . . . and there was Sam. She drew a shallow breath and smiled. The pain was intense; it coursed through her, and drained her, and tried to force her back into the darkness, but she wasn't ready to go. Not yet.

"I'm so sorry, Beth," Sam said.

She tried to shake her head, failed, tried again, and managed a few weak movements.

"It's okay," she whispered. Was that really her voice? It sounded so old, so strange to her ears. She found that funny in an odd sort of way. "How's China?" she formed the words and spoke them, but the effort drained her and her eyes slowly closed.

"She's fine—as beautiful as ever." He hesitated, searching for something—anything—to say, and the lie slipped out before he could stop it. "You're going to be okay . . ."

She opened her eyes again and met Sam's gaze. There was a sadness in her stare, but somehow Sam knew the sadness had nothing to do with self-pity. The sadness was for him, and he swallowed hard.

"I . . . I don't know if I can believe in your theory of old souls—or that we've lived before," he said. "I mean, I believe that we have a soul, and I believe in eternity, so that's a start, right?"

Beth smiled weakly, and closed her eyes again.

"Maybe," he began again, hoping to draw just one more smile from Beth's tired face. ". . . maybe it's more that we're angels that once dwelled in the grace of God, but somehow fell away. We did stupid, human things and lost our way. Now . . . now we're just trying to somehow find our way back. Does that make any sense?"

"Fallen angels," Beth smiled and nodded. "I like that . . . we're fallen angels." A stifling silence ensued that was only seconds long, but felt like an eternity.

"I'm so sorry," he said a second and final time. His voice cracked and he found himself closing his eyes against the pain. He squeezed her hand, holding on tight.

"Don't be." She whispered, took a shallow breath, and began again. "It's alright, Sam; everything's alright." There was a long pause; he was afraid she'd slipped away, but she rallied and came back. In a voice that was barely audible, but filled with an undeniable peace, she said, "I love you, Sam. I have for a long time, and I always will."

The heart monitor beeped—once, twice, three more times—then its rhythmic pulse was replaced by a steady tone, solid, frightening, and stoically final. A nurse came into the room to check on Beth. Her eyes met Sam's with an unspoken apology, then she gently asked him to leave.

He drifted out of the hospital room and moved through the corridor, placing one foot in front of the other with no thought of where he was going or why. By some miracle, he made his way back to the parking lot where he'd left his truck. He unlocked the door and climbed in, but he didn't start the engine. The tears came from nowhere and refused to stop. He cried selfishly for a life without Beth—without everything that might have been if he would have just tried. He cried for Miriam, for the familiar pain of losing a friend and for the senseless way she had died. He cried, dreading the quiet, empty house that was waiting for him, and he feared always would be. After twenty minutes—or maybe it had been an hour, he didn't really care—he finally slipped the key into the ignition, started the engine, and headed for home.

It was nearly 8 P.M. The days were growing shorter, and his truck's headlights cut a path through the semi-darkness, guiding him back to the ranch. Ten minutes from his destination, Sam would drive past the spot in the road where Miriam had died. He passed it every day, and every day he would tighten his grip on the steering wheel and try to not think about it. Today was no different, except today Sam was trying to not think about *anything*. He was numb, and tired to the core. All he wanted was to get home, crawl into bed, and wish the world would go away—if not for forever, at least for a very long time.

A movement in the road up ahead caught his eye and he took his foot off of the gas pedal, watching. He stepped on the brake, slowing the truck even further, as he searched the road and the ditch on either side for movement. A second later, he slammed on the brakes, bringing the Tundra to a sudden, rocking halt.

An albino doe stepped onto the road and turned to look at him. When it determined that the truck was not a threat, it dropped its head and sniffed the blacktop, then it turned its head from side to side, apparently searching for something. It approached the truck, one tentative step, two, three, then it stopped, waiting. A second doe, also an albino, joined the first one. Sam startled, wondering what the odds were of seeing two albino deer in the same place and at the same time. But then, sometimes things were not what they appeared to be. His mind returned to the recent search for a missing foal, and the deer that had really not been a deer at all. Surely the appearance of these two does was just a coincidence, wasn't it?

As if he'd spoken the question out loud, the does raised their heads and looked at him. They remained frozen in that position, waiting. Sam opened the truck door. Moving slowly, he got out, closed the door, and strode to the front of the truck. The deer were fifteen feet away, and in clear view.

As he watched, the first deer began to shimmer and change, then the second one followed suit. Sam was expecting a swarm of fireflies, as he had witnessed before, but the masses that had been deer only seconds earlier now resembled swirling clouds of smoke, not insects. The smoke shifted, rolled, and eventually settled into human shapes, each a woman. In what had been the first doe, Sam saw traits resembling Miriam; in the second, he saw Beth. When the images had finished solidifying, his two friends stood before him, smiling in the same way that they always had.

Wordlessly, they came to him. Miriam rested her hand on his cheek, and her palm felt solid and warm. The older woman smiled at Sam, a million emotions racing through her eyes. Then, without speaking, she stepped back, turned, and winked at Beth. Beth, whom Sam had just left at the hospital, broken and still, came to him and wrapped her arms around him. She pulled him close and held onto him for dear life. And she was real—so very real. She kissed him on the cheek before pulling away, and Sam felt a sensation race through him—a peace he'd sworn he would never know— and then, in an instant, they were gone.

Sam stared at the area illuminated by the Tundra's headlights. This empty stretch of blacktop had haunted him for years. It had been a tragic place—a place where he'd lost a dear friend. That loss, when added to his already-wounded heart, had torn his world apart and tormented him for years. No more; from now on, this would be the place where he'd witnessed a miracle. Beth and Bud had both been right all along—it was time to move on.

Sam would never tell a soul what he saw on the road that night. He would arrange Beth's funeral, rebuild the stable, hire a new trainer, and generally get on with his life. He would find love in a great many aspects of his life—in his friends, and his job, and his ranch—but he would not marry again. Sam would never find that one special soul that made his heart soar . . . at least, not in this lifetime. To fill the void, he would take in foster children. He would give them a stable home at the ranch, and would teach them to ride, and to laugh, and to love. He would live to the ripe old age of eighty-seven, and would one day leave the Thunder Ridge Ranch to a nonprofit organization whose mission was to better the lives of foster children throughout the state. When he finally passed away, the residents of Eagle River would arrange for his funeral to be held at the high school, for too many people would attend the service for any single local church to accommodate them. Sam would be buried in Eagle River's Evergreen Cemetery, where the setting sun would shine on his headstone, illuminating these words:

Samuel D. Longstein

Sept. 3, 1969—Feb. 4th, 2056

"These three things remain: faith, hope, and love. But the greatest of these is love."

Author's Note:

Thank you for reading *Fallen Angel*. This book was written over a six-month period in my life when I was dealing with several personal challenges. Writing has always been the salve in my life that has helped me to keep it all together— and saved me a small fortune in counseling expenses. While several aspects about Beth could certainly be viewed as autobiographical (who doesn't love riding on the 'Tilt 'o Whirl'?), rest assured that all of the characters in this book are fictional. And, while Eagle River, Baraboo, and the other towns mentioned throughout the story really do exist in Wisconsin (please, come visit us!), the supper clubs, the ranch, and Steve's Garage are all figments of my imagination. Thank you for joining me on this journey! If you've enjoyed reading *Fallen Angel*, please take the time to post a review on Amazon.

Sincerely,

K. C. Berg

Other Books by K.C. Berg Available at Amazon.com:

In the Light of the Passing: Book 1, Infinity Publishing, 2005

Find it at: http://goo.gl/MIqgQc

Brinda's Promise: Book II, Infinity Publishing, 2006

Find it at: http://goo.gl/syXjhO

Visit my website at www.writetoplay.com

Visit my Facebook page at https://www.facebook.com/KathyCampshureAuthor

85855951R00217